DARK WHISPERS

IVY KING

HEARTLEAF PUBLISHING LLC

 Formatted with Vellum

CONTENTS

TROPES & CONTENT WARNINGS

TROPES: why choose, suspense, workplace romance, age gap, morally gray characters, single mom, new in town, revenge

CONTENT WARNINGS:
Abuse & Child abuse
Assault
Attempted Suicide
Bullying (not by the main characters)
Light CNC
Death
Disturbing imagery
Homophobia (not by the main characters)
Mention of human trafficking (off page)
Parental manipulation and gaslighting (not by the main characters)
Psychological and supernatural horror
Sexual assault

Torture
Violence

PLAYLIST

Grrrls by AViVA

Woman by Doja Cat

Nightmare by Besomorph & RIELL

No Man's Land (feat. Grimes) by Bella Porch

WONDERLAND by Neoni

End It by RIELL

My Oh My (feat DaBaby) by Camila Cabello

Paint it Black (feat. Rånya) by Hidden Citizens

Slow Hands by Niall Horan

Freak by UNDREAM, Silent Child & Hannabelle

Skeletons & Ghosts by UNDREAM & Brad Arthur

Cradles by Sub Urban

Itty Bitty by Henri Werner & EHLE

Call Out My Name by The Weeknd

Back from the Dead by Besomorph, AViVA & Neoni

Say It (feat. Tove Lo) [Stwo Remix] by Flume

PROLOGUE

RAVEN

The calluses on my hands help me keep my grip on the shiny silver pole as I slide down to the floor of the main stage, gliding into the splits.

Euphoria is busy, just like any other night. My usuals surround the stage, eager for any amount of attention I'll give them. Mr. Calloway waves a twenty in my direction, beckoning me closer. Knowing I have to comply, I drop down onto all fours and crawl over to him.

His bourbon breath fans my face. "I paid for us to use the Red Room later."

My stomach rolls, but I don't let it show on my face. "Sounds good, honey."

"I expect some quality screams tonight, pet." Calloway slips the twenty into my bra, right between my boobs, and winks.

The smile on my face is forced, but men like Calloway don't know the difference.

Dipping my head down, I whip up, giving my hair that flipped look as I lean back onto my knees. I gracefully get to my feet in a twirl, successfully getting myself away from Calloway. I don't want to spend any more time with him than I have to.

Discreetly, I check on Mya. She's dancing on one of the two smaller stages. She always attracts a sizeable crowd. Her red hair is easy to find. As she spins around the pole, she looks at me as well. We exchange a slight head nod, something we do regularly to check in on each other, and go back to our routines.

One of the men in front of me is new. And as hard as he tries, I know he's not paying attention to me. He glances over his shoulder again, and I follow his line of sight to the girl I met earlier, Carmen. She's handcuffed to the pole on the other small stage. Anthony and Pierce are her only audience.

"Raven, my love," another regular calls to me. Mr. Seymour.

In my five-inch heels, I sashay to him next. He stands, sticking his money in my thong at my hip. He motions with his index finger for me to get closer. I go along with his request. I don't want to think about what the consequences would be if I refused.

Swirling my hips, I dip lower and lower until we're face to face.

"Don't let Calloway wear you out too much. I'm next." Seymour enjoys my pain even more than Calloway. I usually have to be carried out after time with him.

I'm able to hold back the gag in my throat, but Seymour doesn't miss how my eyes widen momentarily.

His hand whips out, grabbing my face in one hand and squeezing my cheeks. "I expect you to be a good whore for me."

A bouncer steps forward. "Hey! No touching the dancers!"

Seymour releases his grip, wearing an easy smile. "We're

good." He fixes the sleeves of his suit and looks at me out of the corner of his eye. "I paid for this one."

Pop! Pop! Pop!

I drop to my stomach on the stage as screams echo off the high ceilings. My hands shake as I push my hair out of my face.

The customers shout in alarm, running for the exits. Pierce has a gun to Carmen's temple as the man who was seated in front of me and two others close in on him. Anthony stalks backward toward the stairs leading to his office, firing off more bullets from his handgun as he goes.

Glimpsing Mya's stage, I find it empty. I scan the room for her. As I spot one of the bouncers ushering her into the dressing room, she finds me at the same time. Her eyes widen but are no longer fixed on me. Twisting, I find the cause of her alarm as I'm yanked off the stage.

"You're coming with me." Seymour holds my upper arm and stares into my face with crazed eyes.

"No! Let go of me!" The pounding in my chest pushes me to fight. Survival takes over the closer we get to the side emergency exit. I shove his shoulder and yell for help repeatedly, but it's to no avail. If he gets me in his car, I won't be able to get away. He'll get me to his home where he'll chain me to his bed until he kills me.

Not happening.

I use my nails to claw the side of his face, leaving five red streaks. He flinches, and I aim for his neck. More broken skin.

Seymour turns to me, fuming. "Stop fighting me! Whores don't get a say in where they go! They—"

Cutting him off, I use my heel to bash him in the side of the head. I hit him again and again until he falls to the ground.

"What do you think you're doing?" The bouncer from

earlier wraps his arms around my stomach, lifting me and carrying me to the dressing room.

"I wasn't going to run!"

"Whatever. Tell that to the bosses later."

He doesn't understand. I can't leave. Not without Noah.

"You're healthy as a horse, sweetheart." The kind nurse looks like she auditioned for Barbie before coming to work as she flips through my medical chart.

Sitting on the hospital bed, I nod my head instead of giving her a verbal reply.

What am I supposed to say? Yeah, the man who kidnapped me kept me up to date on my vaccines because that meant he could get more use out of me. Even while I was pregnant, he found "customers" who had a pregnancy kink.

The nurse's slight smile gives away her sympathy. "Is there anyone I can call for you?"

"No, thank you, ma'am." My southern drawl slips out.

She chuckles. "Oh, please, honey. Ma'am is for old people. Just call me Nurse Amy."

I don't feel the small curve of my lips, but I know it's there. It's my "I'm going through the motions" smile. I've been going through the motions for the last eight years. It's been longer than that, if I'm being honest with myself.

Shivering in my donated scrubs, my toes curl. My desperation to escape this place makes an itch spread across my skin. I don't like hospitals. I'm a cliché, but with my history, no one can blame me. And there's more than just my dislike of hospitals that has me yearning to get out of here.

The door bangs open, and in rushes my little mini me. "Mom!"

Gawking in disbelief, my mouth falls open, and my thoughts of discomfort are gone. Pure joy sparks in my chest, and I leap off the bed, meeting my son halfway. "Noah!" I catch him when he jumps, and we wrap our arms around each other.

Looking up, I find Nurse Amy and a beautiful brunette woman exiting the room, shutting the door behind them to give Noah and me some privacy.

Noah buries his face in my neck, and silent tears roll down my cheeks as I rest my chin on top of his head. I silently curse the assholes at the club who used to mock me when I'd beg for a glimpse of Noah.

Fortunately, those men got what they deserved.

My little boy may only be six years old, but he's big for his age. His weight becomes too much to hold, so I sit back down on the rock-hard bed, situating Noah in my lap.

Leaning back, I look him over, taking in all the small changes that have transformed his little features since I saw him a month ago. He's taller, and his hair is longer. The scar running along the side of his face has faded a bit. Nausea churns in my stomach as I recall the day he got it, but I don't let the guilt show on my face. He doesn't need a complex about his appearance.

Brushing off the remorse, I allow myself to clutch onto this time with him. "How did you get here, Little King?"

"Mrs. Dahlia and some of her friends got us out of the house. They killed all the shitbags—"

"Language," I chide. I can't let myself think too much about all the horrible things he's heard while growing up in that damned house, or else I'll fall apart, and I won't be able to put myself back together.

"Sorry, Mama," he concedes even though he doesn't look

contrite. It's like I have a sixteen-year-old rather than a small child. "Mrs. Dahlia's friends shot all the *men* in the house, and then we walked out the front door. They were really nice and got us ice cream. Then Mrs. Dahlia's boyfriend took us to his house in Bosh-ton. There were guards everywhere with guns, but they weren't mean, and I was allowed to play outside with August and Margaret."

A hole opens in my chest, and I struggle to keep a smile on my face as Noah tells me all about his adventures. I hate that something as simple as going outside is a big deal to him. With Anthony and all his men dead, I'm going to start a new life for us. Noah deserves a home where he can play in the yard whenever he wants.

The guilt fades as gratitude overwhelms me. I will forever be in Dahlia's debt. She and her friends have given me an opportunity to have what I never thought was possible—a real life.

CHAPTER ONE

RAVEN, TWO MONTHS LATER

"Mom! Hurry! I'm going to be late!" Noah stands at the front door with his backpack slung across his back and one hand on the door handle.

"I'm coming, I'm coming!" Hopping on the stairs on one foot, I slide my shoe onto my other foot. I got up early to get ready, but everything that could go wrong has gone wrong. My coffee spilled on my nice shirt, I burned my wrist on my hair straightener, and I messed up my eyeliner when my "just in case I didn't wake up on time" alarm went off. I jumped at the sudden noise, and when I looked back in the mirror, there was a black streak going from the corner of my eye all the way to my hairline. With the way I'm scrambling to get my shit together, it would seem like this is my first time hunting for a job.

Oh, right! Because it is!

Sarcasm isn't helping my nerves, but coping is coping. I'm calling it a win.

We got lucky with this house, especially since I bought it without seeing it first. But when we arrived a few weeks ago, we loved it right away. It's an open concept, modest home, and it's absolutely perfect for us. The living room is in the front of the house with a large window on the first floor. The newly remodeled kitchen and half bathroom are also on the first floor, along with the laundry room of every mother's dreams. Upstairs is Noah's room, a rec room, and my bedroom. What solidified my love of this home was the master bathroom and walk-in closet. That jetted tub has hosted many bubble bath parties for me.

"Mom!"

"I'm right here!" I call out.

I juggle my folder of resumes, purse, coffee, and keys as Noah opens the door for me. This house may be nice, but damn that front door. It makes the most ungodly loud creak when we open and close it. The sound is like nails on a chalkboard, but worse.

Rushing out into the dry heat, sweat instantly gathers in every crevice of my body. I swear, Texas only has two seasons. Summer and warm winter. Right now, at the end of August, it's like the devil himself turned up the thermostat in Mystic River.

With this heat, I should've purchased a house with a pool.

I brush Noah's hair out of his eyes. "Thanks, little king."

"Mom," he grumbles. "I'm not a little king."

"Right." I nod my head once, feeling sufficiently chastised by my six-year-old.

Six going on sixteen. Just what every mother dreams of.

Realizing his backpack is unzipped, I move to close it. He jumps back before I can even touch the zipper, but he's not fast enough for me not to have seen that his backpack is filled to the top with snacks. He turns from me, pink tinging the pale color of his cheeks.

"Noah, what's all that doing in your backpack?"

"Nothing."

"Are you planning on feeding an army with that feast?" I tease, hoping to lighten the mood.

"It's nothing, Mom. Just let it go." He doesn't give me a chance to respond and stomps off to the car.

Blowing out a breath, I gather my strength and follow behind him.

My white Ford Escape beeps when I press the unlock button, and Noah runs off to get into the back seat. I admire the brand-new car I was able to afford when Rio Flores let me know that he and his friends were distributing Anthony's and Pierce's money amongst all of us rescued women. The lump sum was enough to buy the car, drive to Texas, purchase our new home, and still have some left over so I could be at home for a bit and help Noah transition into public school.

"Mom! I can't be late," Noah complains as I slide in, dumping my armful of essentials on the passenger seat and setting my travel mug in the cup holder.

My eyes wander to the house next door and the empty driveway. We've been here for about a month, and I still have no idea who our neighbors are. I don't think they have any kids for Noah to play with, or else I would've done the brave thing by now and introduced myself. The only glimpse I've seen of them is a truck and a couple of motorcycles driving to and from the house at all hours of the night. And the streetlights here are basically nonexistent, so I can't even tell what color the truck is. Once or twice, I've heard giggling women coming and going, so I'm guessing it's a couple of single men.

Securing my seat belt, I adjust my mirrors. "Buckled?"

"Yes, Mom," Noah sighs as he points to the strap across his chest.

Should I still have him in a car seat? Maybe. One website says yes, while another says no. And the information in parenting books is just as conflicting as it is condemning.

Don't get mad at your kids. You'll give them extreme depression and anxiety.

Don't feed your kids any sugar. Sugar is addictive and can lead to other addictions.

Don't let your kids watch TV for more than thirty minutes each day. Screentime lowers their intelligence.

Holy hell. I knew that going from being a captive to a full-time mom would be hard, but I was not prepared for this.

At least in New York, I had people I could lean on. We had to in order to survive. But here, it's just me. I only have me.

The only real road map I have is of what *not* to do. Walter and Georgia Kelly. Now, they knew how to fuck up a child. My parents were experts. I was supposed to be their prima ballerina. What a disappointment I turned out to be. Thankfully, they can't do any more damage since they're six feet under. I'm determined to be nothing like them. I won't even claim their last name as my own. Rio Flores helped me legally change it to Henry.

Besides my *healthy* upbringing, there's social media, which shows these picturesque moms who read all the parenting books, make the perfect nursery, prepare organic homemade meals, and keep the house perfectly clean. But that life isn't in the cards for me or Noah.

I was kidnapped and knocked up within a couple of months of being forced to turn tricks for Anthony and Pierce.

Noah lived with evil men all these years. Men who didn't care if the woman begged them to stop. Thankfully, Noah knows it was wrong. He hated those men, every single one. In our long road trip to Texas, he talked to me the whole way about living in the prep house. I listened to every horrid detail and made sure he understood our lives would never be like that again. We talked about our expectations and dreams for our new life.

"Remember, I'll pick you up after school in the library parking lot," I remind Noah. It's easier to pick him up there because it's right next to Mystic River Elementary, and it's easier to get out of that parking lot than it is to get out of the school parking lot. Almost every parent picks up their kid from school.

"Yeah, yeah, Mom. I know."

Maybe I really am doing this whole parenting thing wrong.

We pull into the school parking lot five minutes before the bell is supposed to ring. Our car is sandwiched between slick luxury brand cars.

Mystic River may be small by New York City standards, but the people here are almost richer than God himself. It's one of those towns where everyone knows everyone, and all the businesses have the town name in the title. "Mystic River Grill, Mystic Beans, Mystic River Market, Mystic River Hardware, Mystic Scoops." It's all very original.

There's even the Mystic River Psychiatric Hospital, where I will definitely not be applying. No way in hell. I have other plans for that place.

Pulling up to the drop-off point, Noah has his seatbelt off and the door open before I can even put the car in park.

"Noah!" I shout in surprise. It makes my heart stop every time.

"Sorry," he says remorsefully. Instead of bolting away, he pops his head into the front seat and kisses my cheek. "Good luck today, Mom. Love you!" Then he's out of the car and running into the school before I can return the sentiment.

Okay. Maybe I am doing something right with this parenting thing.

My heart jumps into my throat as short inky black hair

flashes in my rearview mirror. I squint my eyes, focusing on the mirror, and a figure sits up in the back seat. His face is covered in shadow, and he lifts his hand, waving me to come to him.

My hands suddenly feel slick, and when I look down, they're covered in red. My heart lodges itself in my throat.

It isn't real. It isn't real.

With a deep breath, I face forward and lean back into the headrest. Squeezing the steering wheel, I close my eyes and give myself a sad excuse for a pep talk. "Keep it together, Raven. You can't go down that road. He's not here anymore, and you're no longer in that house. Don't let your mind play tricks on you."

When I open my eyes again, the blood is gone from my hands, and no one is in the back seat.

Fuck. That hasn't happened since I was a teenager.

It's this town. It's bringing all my monsters back to life.

Resume in hand and my game face on, I walk into Mystic Beans with the confidence of a middle-aged privileged man. The rich aroma of coffee and baked goods soothes my nerves as I approach the counter.

Mystic Beans is a cute little shop. It's simple, with five tables, wood and matte black metal accents, indoor plants, and large windows to let in ample amounts of light. The menu is a big black chalkboard that hangs on the wall behind the counter and bakery display to the right.

There is one woman about my height with long black curly hair and a light olive complexion. She's wearing a green apron and simple clothing that somehow looks more than simple on her. Her back is to me as she wipes down the countertop in between the espresso machines.

A young man with freckles and copper blonde hair enters through the door that I assume leads to the kitchen. He's wearing a similar uniform and is carrying a tray of fresh chocolate croissants. My mouth waters just looking at them.

"Put those out then head on over to school. I don't want you to be late, and then your parents show up here to yell at me," the woman says to the young man. He nods and gets to work.

Keeping my faux confidence wrapped around me like armor, I approach the counter.

"Hi! Welcome to Mystic Beans. What can I get for you?" The woman senses my presence and sets her rag in a sanitation bucket.

"Hi," I reply with a friendly smile. "I'm looking for the owner."

"That's me. Kat Deveraux." She smiles brightly back. "What can I do for you?"

"My son and I just moved here. He just started at the elementary school. I'm hoping you have a job opening." I hand her my resume, some of which may be made up, but not completely untrue. I did manage employees. I just left out that they were strippers and that I comforted them after a particularly bad encounter with a John.

"This looks great. But I'm sorry. I'm not looking for anyone right now." Kat seems truly apologetic.

My chest deflates. Rejection isn't fun, and I expect to be rejected at many more places, but that doesn't mean it doesn't suck.

"Okay, no worries. Thanks, anyway!" I turn to head for the door.

"Wait!" Kat stops me, and I turn back. "Try the library a couple of doors down and across the street. Florence is a bit surly, but she won't hold it against you that you're new to town."

"That's a thing here?" I ask as my eyebrows shoot up.

Kat gives me a look of sympathy. "You're in small town Texas. Yes, it's a thing."

"Geeze," I whisper.

Nothing says, "Welcome to Mystic River," quite like not being able to get a job because I wasn't born and raised here. I shouldn't be surprised. I grew up in a different town in Texas. It was larger than Mystic River, but the people there still had a small-town mentality.

Small town. Small minded.

"Not everyone is like that, present company included," Kat is quick to explain. "Only some. Like, don't bother trying Mystic River Hardware across the street. Old Man Hicks is a sweet man, but ignorantly sexist."

"Noted." I nod.

I should be writing all of this down.

Kat continues, "Mystic River Market is all right, but the hours are hell. With a son, that job may not be the best option. Susan owns the grill, and your experience as a waitress should help you there. She might be willing to give you lunch shifts."

"Lunch shifts. Got it."

Kat looks around as if she's making sure no one else can hear, so I take a step closer. Lowering her voice, she continues, "I don't recommend the hospital."

"Hospital?" I question, feigning ignorance.

"Mystic River Psychiatric Hospital," she confirms.

Like I'd ever go back to that hellhole. I mean, I know I will at some point. Can't take down a piece of shit hospital unless I actually step foot in there…again.

"Don't worry. Wasn't even on my radar," I inform her with a slight shake of my head.

Kat stops talking and hesitates, rolling her lips in.

I widen my eyes, pleading. "Please don't stop now. You're a wealth of information on this town."

"It's just…Do you mind working in a not-so-nice place?"

The hair on the back of my neck stands up. "What do you mean?"

"There's a small bar just off Highway 35. It's a bit run down."

Quirking a brow, I question further. "Is the owner a creep or something?" A bar would be a great spot to get the people of Mystic River talking.

"Oh! No, not at all." Kat shakes her head. "There are two of them, and they're actually nice, despite what you might hear other people say."

My shoulders relax. I don't need a fancy workplace. If the people aren't trying to stick their dick in me without consent because they think their wad of cash is enough, then I'm good.

"Why aren't people nice to the owners of the bar?"

Motioning me to come closer, Kat lowers her voice. "When they were in high school, their girlfriend Scarlett went missing. Their father was convicted of her murder and is currently serving a life sentence in Texas State Penitentiary."

"What!" I exclaim too loudly.

"Shhhhhh." Kat waves her hands, glancing around to make sure no one else heard. "People don't generally talk about it anymore. Scarlett was your typical small-town sweetheart, nice to your face and a bitch behind your back. She collected boyfriends like trophies, and those two were just a notch in her bedpost." Kat sighs, looking up at the ceiling then back at me. "Lord, forgive me. I shouldn't speak ill of the dead, but she was a mean girl, and I was one of her targets. The fact that I'm almost a decade younger than her didn't matter. If you were breathing, you had the potential to have Scarlett make your life hell."

"Wow. Nothing like small town living." I shake my head, trying to comprehend how all of that can happen. Blowing out a breath, I say, "You had me worried there for a second." I nervously chuckle. "With the 'not-so-nice place' comment. No, I don't mind 'run down.' You should see the last place—" I stop myself and wince.

Not supposed to mention that. On my resume, it says I last worked at Abstract Dreams. Spencer told me to put it down.

"Was it—" Kat begins to ask.

"Thank you so much for everything! You've been a huge help," I interrupt, avoiding her question.

"Here." Kat quickly grabs one of the fresh chocolate croissants from the tray her employee is still unloading and puts it in a small brown bag. She hands the bag to me and smiles. "Good luck today and come back to tell me how it all goes." Her offer feels genuine.

I nod and take the bag from her hand.

As I go to exit, two huge, scary-looking men hold the door open for me. They're both covered in tattoos and wear black leather vests. Their skin looks dirty and weathered by the sun, like they just had a ton of sand thrown in their faces.

"Good mornin', sweetheart," one says to me as he looks me up and down. He has a toothpick in his mouth and one hand on the door. His wind-whipped golden brown hair shines in the light, and the tattoo of a skeleton wearing a cloak gleams on his right bicep.

The other man winks at me and greets me. "Haven't seen you 'round here before, beautiful." His hair is deep ebony, and he has a matching skeleton with a cloak on the same arm.

They'd terrify me if I hadn't already faced a different kind of monster. But I still keep my guard up.

"Atlas! Bas! Leave her alone," Kat barks.

The one with golden brown hair turns his head to Kat, and I get a look at a tattoo of the world on the side of his throat.

"Aww, don't be like that, honey."

"We had a long ride here and are in need of some caffeine."

Narrowing my eyes at them, I call over my shoulder, "You okay, Kat?"

"Yeah, I'm good." Her voice is firm.

I walk to my car with surety in my step and lock the doors as soon as I'm inside. I don't know what I thought I could do at that moment. I'm a twig compared to those two.

Peering into the coffee shop window, I see an irritated Kat begin making two coffees without asking what they want. They eye her appreciatively, and she acts as if she doesn't notice. But every woman notices. It's instinct.

Kat said she's okay. So, I'll go but check back later.

Time to meet more business owners of Mystic River.

CHAPTER TWO

GRIFFIN

Leaning against the rustic wall, I sift through the wallet in my hands and tsk. "This would go a lot easier for you if you would just tell us what we want to know." I come across the driver's license and pull it out. "Chet Turner of Boston."

The man tied to the dingy chair lets his head hang forward. His flannel shirt is ripped around the collar, and his jeans have droplets of red all over the thighs. Chet found himself here in the barn over an hour ago.

We should probably replace the chair, but there's something about being strapped to a rusty chair that usually gets people talking. The dirt floors, lack of windows, and general stench of pain probably contribute to people's loose lips as well. It helps that it's still so early in the morning that the sun hasn't even begun to peek its head out over the horizon.

"Did you hit him too hard?" I ask, folding my arms.

Knox, my twin brother, scoffs at the insinuation. "No way. I was pulling my punches. We need answers, not a corpse."

He folds his arms, analyzing the motionless heap of a man in front of us.

Knox is my mirror in every physical way except for our eyes and the scars that cross his upper lip and left eyebrow. Where my eyes are a russet brown, his are a green hue.

"Maybe pull a little more," I suggest with a shrug.

Knox rolls his eyes, drops his arms, and approaches Chet with heavy footsteps. He crouches down so he can look Chet in the face. "You're a little far from home, Chet, and we don't take too kindly to out-of-towners 'round here. And encroaching on claimed territory isn't the smartest move. So, how about you answer our questions so we can all move on with our days. Who do you work for?"

Chet groans, swinging his head to the side and righting himself so he can return my stare. "The tooth fairy."

Digging into my pocket, I pull out a small plastic bag filled with little blood-red pills. "Where did you get these?" I question, giving the bag a shake.

"Easter Bunny gave them to me."

Knox stands to his full height of six feet four inches and shakes his head. Then, without warning, he draws his fist back and lands the punch in Chet's gut. Coughing, Chet hunches forward as far as he can with his wrists and ankles tied to the arms and legs of the chair.

Stepping forward from my spot, I bend down to get Chet to look at me again. "We can do this all day, but I'd prefer if we didn't."

"Fuck you," Chet spits out.

In perfect synchrony, I stand up as Knox strikes Chet across the face with an open hand. Chet's head whips to the side, and he spits out bits of blood over the side of the chair.

Knox rests his hands on his hips. "Should we——"

"It's probably about that time," I interrupt.

"Knees or——"

A malicious smile lights up my face. "Let's start with his fingers."

Knox mirrors my expression, probably giddier than I am. He reaches into the maroon toolbox resting against the wall and pulls out a hammer. Chet's eyes widen, and he starts rocking back and forth with a hop, trying to scoot the chair away from Knox.

"No, no, no, no, no," Chet begins to beg.

I grab the small rickety table that also needs replacing and set it in front of Chet's spastic form. Knox stops Chet's movement of the chair and gives me a nod. Having done this before, we go through our next movements easily. Knox pulls out a pocketknife and cuts the tape wrapped around one of Chet's wrists. I grip Chet's freed arm and slam it down on the table, holding him steady.

My voice gets deeper and darker. "Hand flat, Chet, unless you want my brother here to start by breaking your radius."

Chet whimpers but complies.

Knox skims the cold metal of the hammer down each of Chet's fingers. Each time Knox lifts the hammer and starts again, Chet twitches.

"Man, this hammer is getting heavy," Knox fibs as he acts like he's going to drop the tool on Chet's pinky. Chet cringes, tensing his body. "You might want to start answering our questions before it just slips out of my hand."

Chet flattens his lips into a thin line and shakes his head in denial.

Knox's face darkens. "Wrong choice." He lifts the hammer in the air and brings it down on Chet's little finger with a disturbing crunch. Chet wails, his cries bouncing around the room, but no one will hear him. And anyone who can, won't come to his rescue.

The barn is located on the same land as our childhood home. Acres and acres of land. We've since torn down the house we called home, and live elsewhere now, but the land is still good for some things. Like questioning people undisturbed. We usually only use it when someone owes us money, but putting the beatdown on a rival deal is a good excuse too. Plus, it's just a short drive to the other end of our property to our place of business.

"Does your boss pay you to keep your mouth shut?" Knox taunts.

Chet's rapid breathing shakes his body. "I'm not a fuckin' rat!"

Knox frowns. "Are you sure? I could swear I saw a little tail earlier. Shit, you even have whiskers." Knox mockingly pats Chet's scruff-covered cheek. "What do you think, Griff? Rat?"

"Definitely a rat," I agree, continuing to hold Chet's arm in place.

Chet's face flushes. "I'm not a rat!"

"Agree to disagree," Knox replies sarcastically and slams the flat hammer on the table right in front of Chet's ring finger. But Knox doesn't show the aggression he's feeling. "Does your boss give you hazard pay? How much do you think he'll pay for each finger? A thousand?"

"Doubt it," I comment.

Again, Knox raises the hammer and smashes it on Chet's hand, but this time, breaking Chet's fourth finger. Chet screams again, reaching a pitch I didn't know was possible for a grown man.

Knox repeats his process with each of Chet's fingers. Ask questions, threaten and tease a bit, then break bones when answers aren't received.

"The other one," Knox instructs me, and I get right to it.

"Wait! No!" Chet pleads, but Knox and I ignore him.

I sigh. "You should've given us a name."

After we work together, taping his broken hand back to

the chair and releasing the other, Knox doesn't even start with a question. He aims for Chet's thumb.

"WAIT!" Chet screeches.

Knox pauses. "You got something to say, tough guy?"

Knox and I both pause as Chet gives us the name of the last person we expected. His voice is scratchy. "Alienist."

"Say that again," I grit out through clenched teeth, losing my patience.

"The Alienist," Chet repeats.

I roll my eyes. "His real name, dip shit."

"I-I don't know."

Blowing out a sigh through loose lips, I stare at the ceiling and rest my hands on the back of my neck.

Chet truly doesn't know anything, or he's not willing to turn into a rat. Either way, he's useless to us now.

Knox is the first to fragment the silence. "Say, Griff, how many hands does a man need to rub one out?"

"One."

Knox's eyes fill with an ice that I can only describe as spine-chilling. When he speaks, the room fills with a terror so thick that even the hair on my arms raises in alarm.

"I don't think he even deserves that." Knox uses the hammer to shatter all the bones in Chet's hand.

Screams, once again, decorate the desolate room.

SLOW COUNTRY SWAYS AROUND THE ROOM, FLOWING FROM THE jukebox against the far wall. The lighting in here is dismal, but that's by design. If people can't tell what time of day it is, they stay longer, like Benny here. But then again, Benny is always here. He doesn't care what time it is. Besides, he has his uses.

The Wandering Raven is a town staple. People don't like to admit they come here, but everyone does. We're the only place in Mystic River with dart boards and pool tables. The neon beer signs, license plates, and band posters on the walls add to the aesthetic. We have a few booths, some high-top tables, and stools along the bar. The wood floor is scuffed from years of use, and the bartop probably needs a polish. But I'm proud of it.

This bar has been in my family for generations. I've helped reupholster the booths more than a few times and grew up sweeping and mopping the floors. When Knox and I took over, we replaced the billiards and purchased new stools. We couldn't change the place too much because then it wouldn't feel the same. We didn't want to get rid of Pops's mark on the place.

Pops, our grandfather, treated us well and raised us right. Despite the town motto of "the sins of the father are visited upon the children," we turned out okay. All our business dealings may not exactly be legal, but it is what it is.

Our mom left when we were young, and our father, Amos, never got over it. After she packed up, he spiraled his drunk ass all the way to prison. Right before Amos was sentenced, our older brother, Trey, turned eighteen, joined the military, and never looked back. We haven't heard from him since.

Knox and I were left without a home because the bank seized it, and we were placed in the foster care system. Pops fought like hell to get custody. When we got to go home with him, I slept like a baby. And thankfully, he's not a drunk or an ass.

Well…

He was an ass to some. He died of lung cancer over a decade ago.

But Amos left his own special mark here. It's ugly and no one will ever forget it. When your father is convicted of killing the daughter of the local psychiatric hospital administrator, people tend to hold onto that and deem you a murderer as well.

I guess they'd be right about that now. They weren't back then, though.

I sling a rag over my shoulder and rest my elbows on the dinged wood of the bartop. "What'll it be, partner?" I ask in my best cheesy southern accent like I'm a bartender in an old western movie.

"I'm drinking whiskey, you dumb shit. Always whiskey." Benny's head remains low and keeps his hand on his old-fashioned glass as he answers my question. He's always cantankerous. I can't blame him. I'm about five seconds away from joining him.

After the excitement of this morning, everything seems dull.

The sound of Knox's heavy boots meets my ears before he comes into view. When he enters the space from the hallway at the back of the bar, he's rifling through a stack of mail.

Knox doesn't look up as he weaves through the high-top tables and walks up to the bar. "Hey, Benny," Knox greets.

"Hello to you, too, Mr. Montgomery," Benny returns. His use of our last name is supposed to be mocking, but we know he doesn't have any real ill will behind it. Benny is just a grumpy drunk.

Knox turns to me. "Is Camden here?"

"When is Camden not here?"

Knox just gives me a blank look. My brother is a no-

nonsense type of person, which gives me all the more reason to throw my nonsense at him.

"He's in the kitchen, as always," I reply, giving up on my jab.

Camden is a nice kid. I say "kid," but he's in his twenties. To me and Knox, though, he's a kid. He's worked for us since he graduated from high school. His dad kicked him out for his "lifestyle choices." That's just code for, "I'm a bigoted asshole and want to save my reputation." Camden came to us scared and alone. We gave him a job, and Pops rented him the guesthouse.

Thankfully, the kid knows how to cook and is a master at it. He's only gotten better over the years. We probably should have interviewed him before hiring.

Oh well.

Knox walks through the kitchen door behind the bar, probably to ask Camden to make him a sandwich.

I return to making myself look busy by wiping the counter with my rag and rearranging the glasses for the hundredth time. Before I can mop the floor again, Knox comes storming back from the kitchen without any food in his hands. Instead, there's a single envelope in his fist. His face is contorted with rage.

"With me. Now," he demands. His jaw is tense, and his hands are shaking, letting me know that he isn't joking. Not that he ever does.

I follow him through the back hall and into the office. We only have one desk in here and only need one desk. This room is for show, so it's bare. Even the filing cabinet only holds the minimum. We only come in here when we don't want to be heard. Our real office is downstairs.

"Look." Knox shoves the wrinkled envelope into my hands.

I squint and notice it's addressed to both of us. In the top right corner, I find who and where it came from.

Amos Montgomery
815 12th St
Huntsville, TX 77348

My vision blurs and is tinged with red. "What kind of sick joke is this?"

"I don't think it's a joke," Knox answers coldly.

I toss the unopened letter on the desk and cross my arms. "What could he possibly have to say? He killed Scarlett. It was him. There's no convincing me otherwise."

Knox's fists clench at his sides. "I know. I feel the same way."

"Then why does it feel like you want to open it?" I accuse him.

"Because they never found her body. Hasn't that always bothered you? He had her clothes in the bed of his pickup, and there was blood in the cab, but the police didn't find her body." His stare is piercing.

I glance away, unable to look him in the eye. He knows it bothers me. We lost Scarlett over twenty years ago. We've mourned and moved on, but there's always been that little voice in the back of my mind that reminds me that Scarlett's body is still out there somewhere.

Police found a bloody shovel that had traces of dirt in the bed of his truck as well, but Amos never admitted to her murder.

"If you want to open it, that's on you. I don't want to know what he has to say all this time later." I stomp out of the office, leaving my brother behind. I know his curiosity will get the best of him. Amos's words might crush Knox, and I'll be there for him when that happens. I'll always be there for him, just like he will be for me. But that doesn't mean I'll let Amos's words eat away at me.

As I return to my post, light pours into the bar from the front door, upsetting the damp atmosphere. An alluring figure is illuminated in the doorway. Even though I'm squinting, I'm able to make out rounded hips, flowing hair, and long legs.

The door swings shut behind her, and my eyes readjust to the room. A woman in a white button-up blouse, flats, and dark slacks stands with her shoulders back and a solemn expression.

Scratch that. Not just a woman. A goddamn knockout.

She's captivated me, and she hasn't even noticed me yet. Her eyes are as blue as the endless sky, and her hair is as black as my damned soul. I don't get attached to women. But I can easily see myself becoming obsessed with this one.

Her gaze finds me easily, and I'm pulled into her shattered sapphire eyes. I now know why they say that the eyes are a window to the soul. I see her passion, her determination, and her fortitude. This little vixen is the definition of strength wrapped in beauty.

I finally realize that she's making the same face I am. She has to be some kind of curse from the devil himself. It's like he reached into my head, created the perfect woman, and sent her here to punish me.

She blinks rapidly, breaking our connection, like she didn't mean to give me that glimpse inside her soul.

Too late, Sunshine.

CHAPTER THREE

RAVEN

*W**here the hell is this place?*

I'm starting to think Kat is a lying jerk. For the last twenty minutes, I've been driving up and down this road on the skirts of town, looking for any sign of life. But all I see is dead grass, trees, more grass, and more trees. Nothing else. Not even a telephone pole!

This is how I die. Months from now, they'll find my body, and the locals will have a good laugh at my expense. All because I couldn't find a simple dive bar.

I'll give it one more trip down the road, then I'm calling it quits.

Slowing down to twenty miles an hour, well under the speed limit, I give it my best shot.

Grass. Grass. Tree. Tree. More grass. Another tree. Tire tracks.

Slamming on the brakes, my body jerks forward. My eyes survey the imprints closely. Those are definitely tire tracks, and I think that's a sign hidden behind some foliage.

Taking a chance on this sketchy dirt road, I make the

sharp turn. After being jolted around my seat on what is the bumpiest ride of my life, I pull up to a clearing.

No.

A gravel parking lot.

I park my car a good twenty yards or so from the only other car in the lot and take in the front. It's a lone standing building with a wooden porch and a neon sign that says, "Bar & Billiards." There are a couple of blacked-out windows, and next to the door is another sign with the bar's name.

The Wandering Raven.

I'll forgive Kat for not giving me better directions, but she's back to being a jerk for not giving me a heads up on the name of this place. I'm not sure if Kat thought it would be funny or what. But Raven working at The Wandering Raven seems a little too cliché for my taste. However, beggars can't be choosers.

A job is a job. If I don't have to take off my clothes, then I'm good. No shame to those who choose to. Live your life. But that's not my choice, and I shouldn't be forced into it ever again.

I'm sure to some, the place looks unfriendly, but I've learned that the exterior doesn't usually reflect what's on the inside.

Grabbing my small purse and resume, I exit my car and stroll right through the entrance. It takes my eyes a moment or two to adjust to the low lighting. Looking around, I'm not surprised to find that The Wandering Raven is indeed a dive bar. There are some booths along the front wall, the bar is off to the left, and the pool tables and dart boards are at the back. There's a hall past the pool tables, and some tall tables are scattered here and there. The place has probably seen better days, but at least it's not falling apart.

There's an older man sitting at the bar with his focus fixed on the drink in front of him. During my time at

Euphoria in New York, I came across many men like him. They're a bit jaded from what life has thrown at them, and they just come for the company. They could have cared less whether or not I was clothed. They only wanted someone to talk to. Those customers were my favorite, and they always tipped the best.

The bartender stands in front of the patron on the other side of the bar with a towel on his shoulder and a shocked look on his face. He's much taller and wider than me. His shoulders are defined and broad. His white shirt doesn't look to be a muscle tee, but it shows off his muscles, nonetheless. The damage from the sun on his sand-colored skin makes him look older than my twenty-five years, but the light in his amber eyes echoes a playfulness. His hair is shorter on the sides and longer on the top. It sits in a way that makes me want to run my fingers through his cool brown waves.

But it's his amber brown eyes that have me feeling like a deer caught in the headlights. He pierces me with an enchanting fire, and I can see his desire—his lust. But more than that, I feel the scars that have marked his soul. I've never had a man look at me like this.

I don't believe in love at first sight. That's for fairytales, and my life has been anything but fantastical. It's more like the Brothers Grimm type of story.

However, I do believe in compatibility, and I get the feeling this man could take me for a wild ride.

The pressure on my chest becomes too much to bear, and I blink, severing the invisible string that connected us in the moment. The surprise falls from his face, and a small, confident smirk takes its place.

Holy shit on a cracker. That smile needs to come with a warning label.

A flutter ripples through my stomach and shoots straight

to my core. I'm no stranger to sex, but when these feelings are my choice, I feel empowered.

Adding a subtle sway to my hips, I strut straight to the end of the bar, where he meets me. His eyes track my approach with predator-like precision, and a satisfied smile graces my lips.

"Well, hello. What's your name, Sunshine?" He has a southern twang in his voice that tells me he grew up here.

As I stride closer, the heady scent of sea salt entwined with bergamot makes me feel like I'm in need of a sunny beach day.

"Raven," I answer. "I'm looking for one of the owners."

His eyebrows raise in amusement. "No shit? Raven walks into The Wandering Raven. Sounds like the start of a joke."

"Trust me, I'm well aware." I chuckle.

"Your flirting needs some work," the man nursing his drink comments.

My cheeks turn pink, thinking his remark is meant for me.

"Oh, shut up, Benny. You're just jealous that she wants to talk to me and not you," the bartender shoots back in good fun.

"Are you the owner?" I question.

He folds his arms across his chest in a self-satisfied manner. "One of them, yes. I'm Griffin. What can I do for you, Sunshine?"

Handing over my resume, he releases one arm to take hold of the paper. "I'm looking for a job," I inform him.

Griffin takes a quick glance over the paper, not seeming to read it at all, and earnestly says, "You're hired."

"Are you sure?" I sputter. I had this cool persona going until he threw me off with this immediate hire. "Don't you want to ask me some questions first?"

"Right. Sure." He frowns and thinks it over. "Nah. I'm

good." Griffin winks, causing my panties to flood. His looks were enough to make me want, but his charm is a whole different game.

"Um. Well, at the moment, I can work days. Give me a week, and I'll be able to work nights. I have some experience waitressing at another club called Euphoria. You're more than welcome to call the manager there." I don't disclose that the "manager" who will answer the phone is actually going to be Dahlia.

"Perfect. So, like I said before, you're hired." His sexy smirk seems to be permanently etched into his face. Not that I'm complaining. However, I don't think it'd be a good idea to have a one-night stand with my boss. Plus, as soon as I accomplish what I came here to do, Noah and I might have to move somewhere else.

"You're only hiring her because you think she's pretty," Benny chimes in crossly.

Griffin ignores him.

"Don't you need more information from me?" I question.

"Nope," he responds. "You start next week. Stop by tomorrow or the next day to fill out some paperwork, and you'll be good to go."

I nod my head. "Well, okay. I'll do that then. Thanks!"

As I walk out, I hear Benny say, "You're just doing this because you want to get in her pants."

"So?"

I squirm as the door shuts behind me.

Maybe I'll have time to play while I'm here…

CHAPTER FOUR

RAVEN

Sitting in the library parking lot with my car facing the elementary school, I wait to hear the bell ring, indicating the end of the school day. Instead, my phone vibrates in the cupholder.

> Dahlia: How did job hunting go?

> Me: I got hired at a bar.

> Dahlia: Did you flash your tits or something?

I can't help but laugh at her crude humor. Dahlia has always been the one ready with a joke to lighten the mood, and we needed all the lightheartedness we could get at that time.

> Me: No. He thought I was cute. Are you still able to answer the phone if someone calls?

Dahlia: Duh. I got your back, babe.

Me: Thanks. Be safe. Love you!

Dahlia: You too.

My rear passenger door pops open, and I jump, dropping my phone on the floor. Glancing in my rearview mirror, I find Noah buckling his seat belt. I didn't even hear the school bell. Leaning down to retrieve my phone, I try not to sound like I'm out of breath.

"How was school?"

"Did you get a job today?" Noah is purposely ignoring my question.

"What happened? You were excited to go to school this morning. You practically shoved me out the door."

Noah stares out his window. "Nothing that hasn't happened before," he mumbles.

"What do you mean?"

He sighs. "Nothing. Can we just go home?"

I know he's purposely avoiding my question. He usually answers in his own time, but I can't help but worry.

"Okay. Sure. But we have to stop at the store first." Shifting the car into drive, I turn onto Main Street. The grocery store isn't that far from the library.

"You didn't answer my question," Noah accuses innocently. He used to be quieter and more reserved, but ever since we left New York, he's more talkative. His filter is basically gone. It has put me in some awkward situations, but it's good to see him opening up.

"And you didn't answer mine," I rib back, hoping to get at least a hint of a smile. When he doesn't return the joke, I answer, "Yes, I got a job. I actually got two. One at the library and one at a place called The Wandering Raven."

He doesn't respond. His eyes are absently staring out the window.

When I pull into a spot in the grocery store parking lot, I unbuckle and reach for Noah, placing my hand on his knee. "Talk to me, little king. What happened?"

He doesn't acknowledge my plea and keeps his focus fixed on the tinted glass.

"Noah. Look at me, please." He concedes, and I'm gifted with the view of his ebony irises. "I'm here. I'm always going to be here. I wasn't before, and I know you understand why." The ache in my chest threatens to drag me under as my eyes look over the healed cut on his face. "But I'm not going anywhere anymore. All those men are dead or in prison. And I will spend every day for the rest of my life making up for all the times I couldn't be there before."

Tears line his lower lashes, but he doesn't let them spill over. Noah swallows a few times before he finally lets the truth free. "A boy in my class got everyone to call me Freddy Kruger."

Fucking cruel kids.

I hold my body perfectly still as I keep my ire in check. "Did you talk to your teacher about it?"

He shakes his head.

"Why not?"

"I don't want to be a tattletale," he admits.

"Has this happened before?"

He answers with a nod.

"Is that why you took all the snacks this morning?"

Another nod.

I let my shoulders drop, not realizing that I had them so tensed. "I'll talk to your teacher about it, but I need you to do the same, okay?"

"I guess," he agrees.

"Noah, what those kids are doing is not okay. It's bullying.

If we don't stop them, it'll just continue, and they'll do it to other kids too. Talking with your teacher can only help."

He twists his lips from side to side, thinking through what I've said. "Okay. I'll try."

"That's my little king." This time, he gives me a smile at the use of his nickname. "Do you want to call Margaret and August when we get home? I know you miss them."

Noah brightens at the idea. "Yes, please." We get out of the car together and walk hand in hand toward the store. "What are we getting?"

"Well, someone stole all the goodies from our pantry, so we need to replace them," I tease.

Noah tries hiding his smile by scrunching his face. But when I tickle his stomach, he lets his laugh ring free. It's a sound I'll never tire of. It means he's happy. It means he's safe. And I will do whatever is necessary to keep him laughing.

We snag a shopping cart as I inform him, "I was thinking we could try making spaghetti tonight."

Noah gives me a skeptical look. "What if it turns out like the hamburgers?"

I groan.

Being a full-time mom means I'm learning how to cook for the first time in my life. Growing up, I didn't have to cook for myself, and I spent the last few years relying on protein bars. So, I've been trying to learn from Pinterest and the cooking channel. Unfortunately, I need a lot of help.

"We agreed never to speak about what happened with the hamburgers," I remind him playfully.

We meander up and down the aisles as I check the recipe on my phone over and over, making sure we get all the right ingredients. As I reach for a second can of tomato sauce, a man in a three-piece pretentious suit catches my eye. The glimpse is enough for me to lose my grip and fumble with the can.

The man shows signs of aging since the last time I saw him seven years ago. He has more white in his hair, but he still walks with an air of self-importance that makes my pulse elevate. He stands at the end of the aisle with another man, who's also wearing a suit. They wear fake smiles as they discuss what I'm sure is a menial subject. I'm too far away to know for sure. But I don't miss the little bag with crimson pills in his hand as he tries to hide it in a handshake. As quickly as the exchange began, it ended. The customer walks out of the store without purchasing any groceries.

Placing the can in the cart, I keep my eyes fixed on the monster who used to torment me for fun. I remember the first time I sat in his office…

"Why don't we talk about why you're here, Raven?" He crosses his legs and rests his black leather notepad in his lap.

I grind my teeth, locking my jaw to keep the rage-filled words from coming out. When I was forced here, I learned quickly that if I keep my mouth shut, then the orderlies leave me alone…for the most part. Flexing my fingers, I attempt one more time to get free of the restraints keeping me in the cold metal chair.

He removes his glasses and leans forward, resting his elbows on his knees. "I won't know how to help you if you won't talk to me."

Still refusing to speak, I roll my lips inward.

He sighs and motions to the large man wearing blue scrubs in the corner. The man steps forward, pulling my hair so I'm forced to look up at the ceiling.

"You leave me no choice, my beautiful Blackbird," the psychiatrist says as if this whole situation is my fault. He pulls a syringe from the tray next to him and walks toward me.

"Mom?"

I blink away the red fog clouding my vision and look down at Noah, who is tapping on my leg. "Hmm?"

"Are you okay?" His brows scrunch together.

Running my hand over his hair and bringing my attention back to our grocery list, I reassure him, "Yeah. Yeah, little king. I'm fine. We only have a few more things to get."

"Mom," Noah grumbles.

I jokingly roll my eyes. "I know, I know."

Satisfied that I've been fully admonished, Noah asks, "What else do we need?"

Pulling out my list, I scan it. "Looks like we just need to get spaghetti noodles and then we're done."

"I know where those are!" Noah exclaims. He bounds down the aisle before I can tell him to slow down.

"Noah!" I race after him, trailing behind him to the next aisle over. "You can't just run away from—Oh!" My face pales as Noah accidentally runs into someone. As I realize who it is, my teeth grind together—Dr. Lewis Whitlock.

My stomach bottoms out, and I freeze in place. It's as if I'm being confronted by a coiled rattlesnake, ready to strike. Sudden movements will make him lash out, but he might do that anyway. That's the way of the snake. I'm out of options.

"Sorry, sir," Noah expresses with remorse reflecting in his eyes.

"Well, hello there, buddy. I think I'm in your way." Dr. Whitlock bends down with his hands on his knees to get his face level with Noah's.

Don't you dare, you sick monster.

"Come here, Noah," I demand in my mom voice. Noah scrambles over to me, and I put my arm around him, securing him in my embrace.

Screw the snake. This mama will step on him and break his neck.

Dr. Whitlock stands up straight. "He's a beautiful boy," he remarks, and I hold my breath, keeping a mask over my fury.

I've imagined this moment for so many years. I've imagined what I would say and do. I want to let every dark secret, every depraved act out into the light. I want everyone to know what kind of man Dr. Lewis Whitlock truly is.

But this isn't the time or the place. That time will come, and I will end him.

Permanently.

"Excuse us," I assert curtly. Placing Noah's hands on the cart with mine, we turn and head for the checkout line.

"But Mom, we still—"

"Not now," I cut off Noah with a harsher tone than I mean to, but it doesn't deter him.

"We need the noodles," he persists.

"We'll order pizza instead," I negotiate, and he seems satisfied with my answer.

Noah helps me push the cart all the way to the checkout line. As we load our items onto the conveyor belt, a prickling sensation travels up my spine. The doctor's gaze has always made me feel like I need to shower to wash away the grimy fantasies I can see swirling in his brain.

I need to be careful. If he recognizes me, my plan is blown. But even if he does, I'll still make sure Mystic River Psychiatric Hospital closes for good.

CHAPTER FIVE

KNOX

Amos's letter burns a hole in my pocket as I take my turn behind the bar during lunch. The itch to open it has been nagging at me all week. The fact that I haven't is a testament to my willpower, but I'm close to cracking under the pressure.

Griff made it clear that he doesn't want to know what dear old Amos has to say, and I can't blame him. When Amos went away for killing our girlfriend, we felt that betrayal deeply. Then, the way the whole town treated us afterward was as if we had killed Scarlett ourselves, only added to our grief. Everyone seemed like they were ready to gather their pitchforks and lynch us. I know they wanted to.

"Knox, I want another," Benny demands.

"That's his fifth, Montgomery. You should have cut him off by now," Sheriff Jackson comments from a few stools down from Benny.

"Mind your own damn business, Sheriff," Benny bites back.

Lunchtime at The Wandering Raven is busy. When

there's only one other restaurant in town, people are bound to find somewhere else to go. It's a big reason why Griff and I extended operating hours when we took over. That, and Camden was asking for more shifts.

So now, during lunch, about half of our tables are full. Music drifts from the jukebox as Griff and I take turns waiting tables and bartending while Camden cooks in the kitchen. I don't know how he does it all on his own back there, but he does, and he likes it.

Kaitlyn LeBlanc, Nicole Harlow, and Heather Davis all sit together at the four-top closest to the bar. They're in here almost every day, tugging their low-cut shirts down and pushing their elbows together. Griff and I made a pact back in high school that we would never go there with any of them. And the fact that they're all married now makes them a big "no go" zone.

Most of the hoity toity townsfolk who deem my brother and me murderers by association don't bother to come here. Unfortunately, we don't have a screening process for everyone else. My vote is still to kick out anyone who has ever looked down their nose at us, but Griff makes a good argument when he reminds me that would mean we won't get much business. So, no matter how badly I want to punch Sheriff Clayton Jackson, he gets to stay…for now.

Filling Benny's glass, I answer, "Actually, it's his third. Are you volunteering to drive him home, Sheriff?"

Sheriff Jackson stammers, "What? I—Uhh—"

"Heaven forbid you do your damn job for once," I murmur under my breath.

Sheriff Jackson pounds his fist on the bar. "Excuse me? What was that, boy?"

Griffin is by my side, stepping in between us before I can respond. "Hey, Sheriff. I'm sure my brother didn't mean anything by it."

Griffin has always been the one to try and keep me out of trouble. We've gotten into our fair share of fights since Amos was locked up. Griffin grew tired of always having to defend himself, so I've taken up that mantle. But he always steps in to diffuse the situation before shit can go down.

"Yeah, I'll bet," Sheriff replies with little conviction. "You tell Knox he needs to get his head on straight and remember who it was who stopped that group all those years ago from burning your house down."

Sheriff Jackson goes back to his burger and fries while Griffin pushes me through the kitchen door. Camden ignores us as Griff gives me what he thinks is a stern talking to.

Griffin rests his hands on his hips. "Seriously, Knox? What the hell?"

"I don't care. Acting like he was our savior when Frank and his buddies dragged us out of bed in the middle of the night, it's bullshit. Jackson showed up after they had beaten us bloody. I still have the scars," I bluster and point to my face.

That night wasn't a pretty one. Before we were put in foster care, Frank decided he wanted to take the law into his own hands.

"He's an ass. I know. But you can't start a fight with the goddamn sheriff." Griffin sighs, shaking his head. "Ignore him. He's just pissy because we don't let him go downstairs."

Griff is right. We may not be selective about who comes into the bar, but we are very exclusive when it comes to downstairs. And although Sheriff Jackson can't prove that our basement even exists, he's always trying to get himself an invite.

"Fine," I agree reluctantly.

Before I can get back to bartending, Griff stops me. "Oh, and I hired someone. She starts tonight."

I whirl on him quickly. "What? And you didn't tell me about it?"

"Relax, I vetted her." Griffin makes a pacifying gesture with his hands.

Narrowing my eyes, I inquire further. "Vetted how?"

Griffin makes an annoyed face. "Not like that!" Then he smirks. "Yet."

"No. No, no, no. We do not need a sexual harassment charge brought up against you. That'll give Sheriff Jackson exactly what he wants."

"I make no promises," Griffin singsongs.

Sighing, I pinch the bridge of my nose. "Did you at least check her references or employment history?"

"Yeah, they're there," he says matter-of-factly.

"I mean, did you call them?"

"Why would I do that?"

If it wouldn't hurt, I'd facepalm myself right now. "To make sure she's not a criminal and going to rob us or something."

"But *we're* criminals. If she has a record, then we're all in good company." He shrugs a shoulder.

"Oh my God…" Blinking, I shake my head.

I swear if we didn't share a womb…

"After the rush, we're calling," I demand. "Do you have her application or resume?"

"In the office."

I nod in parting and return to the bar. Many of the patrons have cleared out, leaving money on the tables to cover their bills, including the sheriff.

Good riddance.

Benny picks at the basket of fries I brought him earlier. "Ya gotta be careful, kid. He ain't gonna tolerate that disrespect for long."

Ignoring his warning, I begin bussing the empty dishes. After dropping off my second load in the kitchen, Kaitlyn waves me down.

"Hey, Knox! We're ready for our check." She gives her shoulders an extra shimmy. I know she thinks she's tempting me, but it's the opposite. Twenty-two years ago, in high school, Kaitlyn was one of the people leading the charge on the "Hate the Montgomery Twins" campaign, which is part of the reason Griff and I won't touch her or her friends. And she doesn't know that we know.

Instead of replying, I go to the register and print out their receipt. When I hand her the scrap of paper, she purposefully runs her fingers down my wrist and palm. I keep my face blank, letting her know she has no effect on me, but I know it won't deter her. She'll be back tomorrow with her little posse and do the same thing all over again.

When the bar is finally clear except for Benny, I meet Griffin in our office. He has the woman's resume in his hand and begins dialing the phone number for a place called Abstract Dreams.

There are only two rings before someone picks up on the other end. "Abstract Dreams. This is Dahlia. How can I help you?"

"Hi, Dahlia. This is Griffin Montgomery. I'm calling because Raven Henry put Abstract Dreams down as her last place of employment. I was wondering if you could tell me a bit about her as an employee."

"Oh, yeah. Raven. Love that woman," Dahlia dramatically replies. "She was a star employee. It was tough losing her, but she wanted a fresh start. She's great with customer service and a hard worker."

Griffin shoots me a smug smile.

I roll my eyes and butt into the conversation. "Is there anything we should be aware of when it comes to Raven?"

"Oh, hi, second person. Umm…No. Raven is a good person with a good heart. She's just wanting to start over."

"Okay, thank you."

"No problem! Bye!"

I press the end call button without returning her sentiments.

"See?" Griffin puffs up his chest.

"Not so fast. One good reference doesn't mean shit. Call the next one on the list," I instruct.

Griffin punches in the phone number for the next place. Somewhere called Sal's Pizzeria.

"Sal's Pizza. This is Alma. How may I take your order?" The female voice has a Hispanic accent.

"Hi, Alma. This is Griffin Montgomery. We're calling about Raven Henry," Griffin greets, annoyed that I'm making him go through this again.

"Ah, *sí, sí*. We love Raven. Miss her so much. She was a fantastic worker," Alma responds.

"Do you know why she left your employment?" I butt in.

"Oh, *sí*. She was offered more money at another job," Alma answers mournfully.

"That doesn't show loyalty," I whisper to Griffin.

"So what?" he whispers back. Turning back to the phone, he thanks Alma for her time, and they say their goodbyes. "See? She checks out."

I fold my arms and grumble, "We'll see."

"Oh, yes, we will," Griffin comments slyly.

"You better not," I warn him.

Griffin exits our office but turns to remark, "Whatever you say."

GRIFFIN'S ILL-TIMED SURPRISE HAD ME FEELING LIKE I WANTED to crawl out of my skin, so I hopped on my motorcycle and went for a short ride. But instead of heading back to The Wandering Raven, I went home for a brief round with the punching bag.

Our house is located just outside of town. It's on a street where there are only a few houses, and the space between each house is enough so it doesn't feel like I'm living on top of my neighbors. It's the second house on the right. The left side of the street is a field owned by a local farmer.

After Griffin and I tore down the house we grew up in, we bought this one. It's two stories with two spacious bedrooms and two and a half bathrooms. I don't mind sharing things with Griffin, but we both need our own space. The first floor is simple in my opinion. It has everything we need. Kitchen, half bathroom, living room, and an attached garage. The second floor has both of our bedrooms and individual bathrooms.

Once I'm showered and ready to head back to the bar, I head into the garage where I parked my bike and put my helmet on. I want to get there before our new employee does.

Griffin would say that I'm hiding. He could shout it from the rooftops, but that doesn't make it true.

Walking my motorcycle out to the driveway before I start it, I'm caught by surprise when a football hits the side of my helmet.

What the…

I set my bike on the kickstand and remove my helmet, bending down to pick up the football. It doesn't take me long to find out where it came from. A kid stands on the grass between my house and the next. I can't tell how old he is, but he stands around four and a half feet tall. His big brown eyes are bulging, and his mouth hangs open.

But it's the thin line of healed skin running down his cheek that has my attention. I catch myself reaching for the scars on my own face, but I stop myself. A heaviness weighs down on my shoulders as I have difficulty swallowing.

Lifting the football in my hand, I ask, "This yours?"

He doesn't blink as he bobs his head.

"Here ya go." Keeping the laces on top, I pull the ball back behind my head. As I step forward with one foot, I send the ball flying forward with just enough force for the ball to reach the kid.

The boy holds his hands out awkwardly, trying to catch the ball. But it falls to the ground next to him. He looks down at it with sagging shoulders.

"What's your name, Bud?"

He purses his lips as he studies me closely. I know the moment he finds my own scars because his eyes widen again, but it's brief. "My mom says I shouldn't talk to strangers."

"Your mom is right, but I think we're neighbors. This is my house." I use my thumb to point over my shoulder, then point to the first house on the street. "And I'm guessing that one is yours."

He nods, confirming my conjecture.

"That makes us neighbors. I'm Knox." I relax my posture to seem less intimidating.

"Noah," he replies.

"It's nice to meet you, Noah. Do you know how to throw a football?"

He winces and answers in a weak voice. "No."

"Maybe your dad or brother could teach you," I suggest.

"I don't have a dad or a brother. It's just me and my mom." He hangs his head.

Swallowing down the wave of emotion that builds in my throat, words come flying out of my mouth. "I could teach you if you want."

"Really?" Noah bounces on his tiptoes.

"Absolutely," I confirm.

Hells bells. What am I doing? I don't know the first thing about kids. This might even be the first time I've ever talked to one. But there's something about Noah that hits me in the gut, and it's not just the scar.

"Thanks, Mr. Knox!" He picks up the ball and runs straight to me.

"Just call me Knox. The mister part isn't necessary."

"Okay…Knox," he responds, trying out my name without the title.

I hold my hand out for the football, and he eagerly hands it over. I show him how to hold the football and explain throwing and catching. He moves a few yards away, and we practice throwing the ball back and forth. On Noah's first throw, the football wobbles and he doesn't put enough strength behind it, causing the ball to fall short. Then he doesn't catch it when I throw the football back. I encourage him to keep trying and give him more pointers, and after a few minutes, he's already showing signs of improvement.

Noah adjusts the ball in his hands, getting ready to throw it again. "How do you know so much about football?" He launches it into the air; this time, the ball actually makes it all the way to me.

I catch it in my hands and only spend a moment readying myself to throw. "You're in Texas, Bud. If nothing else, we know two things: barbecue and football." I throw the ball back, and it bounces a couple of times in Noah's arms before he finally catches it.

When Noah realizes he caught the ball, he holds the ball over his head and jumps up and down. "Did you see that? I did it! I caught it!"

Celebrating with him, I clap my hands. "I saw! Good job, Bud! You'll give CJ Stroud a run for his money in no time."

He stops jumping and tilts his head. "Who's that?"

"He's a quarterback."

Noah frowns. "What's that?"

That same emotion from earlier tries to come back tenfold, but I hold it back. Another swallow and I have myself under control again. I glance at my phone, checking the time. "We can go over all that stuff next time. I have to head to work."

Noah's smile is huge. "We're gonna do this again?"

"Of course," I promise. Grabbing my helmet off the seat, I swing my leg over my motorcycle. "Keep practicing." My helmet slides on my head, and I start up the engine.

"I will!" he shouts over the noise.

I give him a salute and set off down the road.

Memories flood my consciousness, sending a pang through my chest. They flash through my mind like the world's worst movie.

I don't want to remember. But my desire is just wishful thinking.

CHAPTER SIX

RAVEN

After dropping Noah off at school, I went straight to my job at the library, just like I have for the last few days. Kat was right in that Florence Baker is surly. She walks around with a small scowl on her face. It's a wonder that anyone comes to the library at all.

The library has large windows all over and a beautiful skylight in the center. Nylon blue carpet covers the floor and comfortable seating is spread throughout the building, tucked amongst the shelves. The circulation desk is right next to the entrance and covers most of the front wall. Behind the circulation desk is Florence's office.

Searching for Florence, I find her shelving some romance novels that were returned earlier today. Florence has long gray hair that is always tied back in a low bun, and she wears black thick-rimmed glasses. I swear she keeps the air conditioning below sixty degrees so she can wear a cardigan every day. I feel like I need to start wearing a snow coat.

"Hey, Florence! I'm taking my break in five."

"Yeah, yeah," she mutters to herself.

Always the charmer…

Behind the circulation desk, I finish sorting some returns we just received. When five minutes have come and gone, I grab my purse and head out for lunch at Mystic Beans. My phone vibrates in my pocket.

> Dahlia: I got a couple of calls from Griffin Montgomery today.

> Me: What did you say?

> Dahlia: What do you think? He called Abstract Dreams first, so I was myself. Then he called Sal's, and I couldn't be Dahlia again, so I was Alma.

> Me: Who's Alma?

> Dahlia: Don't worry about it. But as far as you're concerned, Alma is a middle-aged Hispanic woman and was your coworker at Sal's.

> Me: Good to know. Thanks lol.

Stowing my phone in my purse, I open the glass door to the coffee shop and walk in. Pastries may not be a suitable lunch, but I'd give Kat my left kidney if it meant I could have a lifetime supply of those chocolate croissants.

Kat beams at me from behind the counter. "Hey, Annabelle! I'm taking a lunch break!"

Annabelle pokes her head out from the kitchen. "I got this. Take your break, Kat." Annabelle is an older woman who bakes all the delicious treats at Mystic Beans. She's a little shorter than me with bronze cropped hair.

Kat rushes to make me what has become my favorite drink. A light iced white chocolate mocha with Irish cream and hazelnut. Then she grabs a chocolate croissant, a brown paper bag, and a water bottle. I sit at our usual table by the front window and wait for her.

She sets down the coffee and croissant in front of me and sits in her seat. "I don't know how you eat like you eat and still have a waist like that."

Glancing down at my size ten hips, I swallow the mouthful of croissant and answer, "With the shit I've had thrown my way, life has to bless me with something. But at my last job, I wasn't exactly deemed 'skinny.'"

She reaches into the brown paper bag and pulls out two sandwiches. "You need to eat *something* healthy." Then she sets the second sandwich next to my treat.

"Yes, *Mom*," I joke. It's weird having someone look out for me. I'm used to the situation being the other way around.

Kat has quickly become a close friend. She's like my platonic soulmate. I miss Dahlia and Mya dearly, but meeting Kat has lessened that pain.

"So, how's dear old Mrs. Baker doing today?" Kat asks sarcastically as she digs into her sandwich.

"Just peachy," I respond with an eye roll. After another swallow, I ask, "Are you sure about watching Noah tonight?"

"I wouldn't have offered if I didn't mean it. I got you, Raven," Kat responds without hesitation.

"Okay, but I promise I'll find someone more permanent soon."

She waves off my concern and continues eating her sand-wich. "Accept my help and move on, love. Besides, I may have found someone who can help."

That makes me perk up. "Oh? Who?"

"Her name is Lucy. She's one of my employees. She asked for more hours, but I can't give them to her. She's responsible, loves kids, has lots of experience…all the things."

"I don't know…"

"Look, just meet her and see what you think. I promise you'll love her."

"Okay. Why not? Thank you," I respond genuinely.

"Sweet! I'll get you her number so you can contact her. You'll be so grateful that you'll be giving me praises for the rest of your life."

Chuckling at her dramatic statement, I let it pass. "So…" I sip from my delicious coffee and sigh. "Tell me about those two guys from the other day."

Kat chokes on her bite and coughs.

"I think that means there's something to tell," I tease.

She clears her throat and takes a sip from her water bottle. "Definitely not."

All I do is raise my brow, conveying that I don't believe her for one second.

"They come in once a week…maybe more sometimes," Kat confesses, refusing to look me in the eye as she takes another sip of water.

"Oh, really? Is that all?"

"I'm not sure what you're looking for…" Her words say one thing, but her voice says another. She's being evasive.

I tilt my head to the side. "Hey, is everything okay? Are they bothering you?"

She shakes her head. "No, they're harmless. It's just…" She looks to the side and purses her lips.

Placing my hand on hers, I offer what I can. "Hey, I know they may not look like upstanding citizens, but in my experience, looks can be deceiving. Nice suits are just nice suits. They have nothing to do with the person's character."

"I agree. I just…" Kat trails off with her thought train.

"No judgment here, I promise," I reassure her with a squeeze of her hand. She returns my gesture with a half-smile. "Enough of the heavy. What tea do you have for me today?"

Kat lights up with the subject change and gives me all the details on someone named Kaitlyn LeBlanc and how she pitched a fit at a recent pie contest because someone else made the same pie as her. Apparently, people treat their barista like they do a hairdresser, meaning they have no filter and spill all the gossip. So, Kat always has a new story for me.

What else would we do when living in such a small town?

After listening to a story with characters I haven't met yet, I take a chance. "So, what's up with the Mystic River Hospital?"

Kat sips her water. "You mean the asylum?"

"So, it's a psychiatric hospital?" There's a pinch in my gut.

"Yeah, but many of the people here pretend it doesn't exist. To them, it's a stain on this town, but it brings in money and provides jobs, so it stays." Kat shrugs.

Pretending to be ignorant again, I question, "If it helps the local economy, why do they hate it so much? Has the hospital been part of a scandal or something?"

Another pinch.

Kat tilts her head back and forth. "There have been rumors."

"Oh? Like what?"

A loud bang comes from the kitchen. "Aw, shit. Annabelle, are you okay?" Kat shouts.

Annabelle pokes her head out of the door. "I'm fine. Finish your lunch, hon." Then she ducks right back in, and the sound of another item crashing to the floor meets our ears.

Perfect timing…

"I should see what's going on," Kat states as she gathers her trash and stands from the table.

Not wanting to seem too interested, I let our topic of

conversation drop. "Yeah, of course." I stand with her, and we embrace before she darts away.

I clean up my mess, gathering my purse, and start my short walk back to job number one.

As I reach the street corner to turn toward the library, the revving of engines grates on my eardrums. I watch as the two bikers I met the other day come down the road and park side by side in front of the coffee shop. They're perfectly in sync as they stand from their seats and remove their helmets. It's like they rehearsed this or something. They leave their helmets on the handlebars and stroll right up to the glass doors with an intimidating confidence.

"Seriously? What the hell are you two doing here?" I hear Kat shout as she comes back from the kitchen.

Grins spread across their faces, and they walk straight into the mess they've made.

Pressing the crosswalk button, I wait for the signal to cross the street. A steady flow of traffic proceeds through the intersection. As a large red SUV passes, I get a glimpse of a little boy standing on the opposite side of the street.

Is he alone?

Another few cars pass, and between each one, I get quick glances of hair the color of a dreary empty sky, sickly pale skin, and eyes the exact same hue as my own.

There's a break in traffic, and I find him standing there staring in my direction. He's wearing the same thing I last saw him in—gray sweats and a Kingdom Hearts tee. I bought him that shirt our last Christmas together. In his hand, he holds a single stalk of belladonna.

"This isn't real. This isn't real," I chant to myself. But then I get another look at him, and my hand covers my mouth as a whimper escapes me.

His eyes shift from their intense blue to an empty black,

then turn into deep holes in his skull. The ink spreads, creating deep pits in his face.

More cars rush by.

He needed my help, and I wasn't there to save him. I didn't do enough. But I'm here now. I can help him.

An arm wraps around my middle, and I'm carried backward. "Woah, there! Are you okay?"

Was I just…

Across the street, the sidewalk is empty. He's gone. The frown on my face becomes so deep it dimples my chin.

"Hey, hey. Are you okay?"

Craning my neck so I can face the voice of the person holding me, my heart jumps ten feet into the air. I find a man with sunset blonde hair hidden beneath a cowboy hat and familiar brown eyes. He has perfect posture and muscular arms. His dark wash jeans hug his thighs, and his heathered gray tee stretches across his chest. The freckles dotting his cheekbones are endearing and speak to long hours working in the sun.

"Ma'am?" he interrupts my gawking.

I close my gaping mouth and sputter, "Oh. Umm. Sorry. Yes." He sets me down, and I brush out my shirt, smoothing out the wrinkles.

"Sorry, ma'am. I didn't mean to startle you. But it's not safe to walk yet." He points to the red pedestrian light in the shape of a hand.

"Right," I admit embarrassingly.

He smirks and fingers the brim of his beige cowboy hat. "May I?" He holds out his arm in question.

Have I been transported back to the 1800s?

"That's okay. Thank you, though," I answer and move to step off the curb. His thick hand grabs my upper arm and pulls me back onto the sidewalk. "Excuse—"

"The pedestrian light is red," he points out as a lifted pickup truck zooms by.

My cheeks pinken when I realize I didn't even bother looking both ways before attempting to cross the street, again, apparently. A lesson every child learns. "Oh. Thanks." He releases his hold, and I tuck a lock of hair behind my ear.

"You must be new," he surmises.

"What makes you say that?"

"I haven't seen you around before."

The light changes, indicating we can safely cross. The man offers me his arm again, and this time, I decide to take it. His solid body warms me even more on this dry, hot day. I have to bend my neck at an odd angle to be able to look at his face. He has an appealing strong jaw with a full beard.

"So, are you?" he asks as we step onto the opposite sidewalk.

Caught staring again. "Am I what?" I let go of his arm, and he steps in front of me, blocking my path.

"New in town?"

I fake skepticism. "Mmm. I don't think I should give that information to a stranger."

"I'm Jed." He holds his hand out, and I accept, shaking his hand. It's rough and calloused, and I imagine him running his hands over my skin.

"Nice to meet you, Jed."

"And you are?" he prompts.

"New," I reply with a wink and step around him, heading for the library entrance on the other side.

"Hold on, now," Jed calls as he races to catch up to me. "You didn't tell me your name."

"Why does it matter what my name is? And don't give me a creepy answer, please," I demand with an eye roll.

"Wouldn't dream of it." He stops with me outside the Mystic River Library doors. "Is this where you work?"

"Sometimes," I respond.

He jokingly sighs. "Do you ever give a straight answer?"

I shrug. "That depends."

"Well, at least I'll know where to find you *sometimes*." He tilts his head toward the library and turns on his heel, walking back the way we came.

"And why would you need to find me later?" I shout after him.

He turns to answer as he walks backward. "So I can ask you out on a date."

I smile again. "Raven!"

He stops in his path. "What?"

"My name is Raven." I don't wait for his response as I open the door and head inside to finish my shift.

Mystic River has a cancer, and I plan to eradicate it, but I just might enjoy myself while I'm here.

CHAPTER SEVEN

RAVEN

Leaving Noah with someone else for the first time since I got him back was not as easy as I thought it would be. I may trust Kat, but there is something about walking away from your child that stabs you in the heart. I have a feeling that will never go away.

I put on a simple plum-colored tank top, Chucks, and a pair of cutoff denim shorts for tonight's work uniform. The shorts cover my ass, but with legs like mine, these shorts could be Daisy Dukes.

Oh well. That's my lot in life.

If worse comes to worst, I'll pull out the self-defense moves Dahlia taught me. Pierce beat her bloody when he found out she did that. Anthony was ready to put her in the ground, but Pierce stepped in and reminded him that she was worth more alive than dead.

Parking toward the back of the lot to leave room for customers, I stroll across the gravel. When I came by to fill out paperwork the other day, Griffin asked that I get here before the rush starts.

Entering The Wandering Raven, I'm met with the same dismal ambience. A couple of tables are occupied, and again, Benny sits at the bar with a drink in hand.

Griffin gets a mischievous look in his eye when he spots me, dragging his gaze up my exposed legs and across my barely there cleavage. "How's it goin', Raven?"

"Good. Ready to get started," I tell him enthusiastically while hiding the butterflies swarming my stomach. This is my second first day, and it doesn't help that my boss is hotter than any man I've ever seen.

His smile is wide. "Perfect. Come on back here," he instructs.

I round the bar to the far corner and come up next to Griffin. Being in his proximity makes my brain go all fuzzy. Standing this close to him rids me of the earlier butterflies and causes an overwhelming need to roll through me. When he turns his back on me, my eyes wander south.

Hot damn. He fills his jeans perfectly.

I've been with plenty of men. Ninety-nine percent of them were not by choice. But I'd definitely choose Griffin to ram me into the headboard.

"Know how to make a drink?" He turns around, raising a brow, and I know I've been caught.

Shoving my embarrassment out the window, I tease, "Yes. Need a stiff one to get through my training?"

Griffin crowds my space, forcing me to back up into the counter and shelves behind me. His hands go to the wooden counter, resting on either side of me, less than an inch away from my body. "I got something stiff, alright."

Smirking, I return fire. "Is that the best you got, Griff?"

"Not by a long shot, Sunshine," he says with another smirk.

Don't kiss the boss. Don't kiss the boss.

He moves his hand, reaching up to a higher shelf, but his

eyes remain fixed on me. As he reaches, he leans in closer. His lips are a breath away from mine. Then he steps back with a bottle of whiskey in his hand.

"Can you make a Manhattan?" Griff questions as he hands me the bottle.

That's one way to douse the fire.

"One Manhattan, coming right up," I proclaim as I toss it frivolously.

I move around the space, grabbing what I need. Vermouth, bitters, a mixing glass, and a maraschino cherry.

"On the rocks?" I ask over my shoulder.

My question is met with silence. Turning my head, I find Griffin's eyes glued to my backside. I clear my throat, and his eyes snap up to mine. He gives me an unapologetic shrug and answers, "However you want to make it, Sunshine."

Shaking my head, I dismiss his shenanigans. "On the rocks it is."

At Euphoria, I wasn't just a dancer and plaything. I also had to help out with waitressing and bartending. Seven years at that horrible place, and thankfully, I walked away with more skills than just being able to do the splits.

I stir the mixing glass until it's cold to the touch. Griffin places a stemless glass on the counter next to me. I add the ice, then pour the drink in.

"One Manhattan on the rocks."

Griffin takes the drink from my hand. "Bottoms up." Then he downs the cocktail like it's a shot and doesn't even wince.

"That's good," he says to the glass with an impressed expression on his face. "Okay, let's go for another. Margarita on the rocks with a twist."

"Oh, come on. Give me something hard," I reply in jest.

I clean my mess and gather the next set of ingredients. Griffin hands me another glass when I'm almost done mixing.

I salt the rim, add the ice, and the drink. And once again, Griffin downs the cocktail like an experienced frat boy.

"Let the girl be, Montgomery," Benny butts in. "She's passed inspection. It's not like the folks here are going to order anything more complicated than that. Most are gonna order a Bud Light and call it good. Now let her pour me another whiskey."

Griffin gestures to Benny. "You heard the man. Pour him a whiskey."

A warmth spreads through my chest at their acceptance. "You got it, Benny, my friend."

Pouring the dark liquid into a short glass, I keep my attention on the task at hand but direct a question to Griffin. "So. Anything I need to know before tonight? Seating, tables, restocking. Any of that?"

"Customers seat themselves. We don't do table numbers. We're not that rigid here. And I can show you the rest."

After Benny gets his whiskey, Griffin shows me around. I learn how to put in a food order, close someone's tab, clean the tables, restock the bar, and so on. Once I've proven that I'm more than competent, he shows me the stockroom, his office, and the kitchen.

In the kitchen, the equipment is all silver, and the floors are plain white tile. There's a door on the far end that I assume leads to the outside and the dumpster.

A man stands at a fryer removing potato wedges from the basket. He's average height with light blonde hair.

Griffin introduces us. "Camden, this is Raven. Raven, this is Camden."

"Raven?" Camden's brows rise in humor.

"Yeah, yeah. Corny, I know," I reply before he can crack a joke like Griffin did the day I met him.

Griffin gets an odd look on his face and chimes in before Camden can say anything else. "Camden is the cook. Don't touch anything hot, but you won't have to worry about that. You won't be back here much anyway." He places his hands on my shoulders and steers me back out into the bar.

"I know not to stick my head in the oven. I'm not five."

"Trust me, Sunshine. I've noticed."

My stomach flutters at his implication.

Damn. I'd climb this man like a tree.

He keeps pushing me until I'm back where we started, standing opposite Benny.

Whirling around on him, I place my hands on my hips. "What was that about?"

"I don't know what you're talking about." Griffin makes an innocent face and changes the subject. "I'm sure you'll meet Knox at some point tonight. He might be held up in the office all night, though."

"Knox?"

"My partner."

A light goes off in my head. "Oh. Ohhhhhhh." Of course, a man as good looking as Griffin is already taken.

Reading my expression, Griffin shivers. "Uh, no. Knox is my *business* partner."

I raise my hands in a defensive gesture. "Hey, I'm not judging. Live your life. Seriously. There's nothing wrong with loving who you love. I know we're in Texas, but I'm not that kind of Texan."

Folding his arms, Griffin adds, "Knox is also my brother."

So there are two people in this world who look like *that*? Heaven help me.

Even though I know he's telling the truth, I decide to have some fun. "Okay, dating your brother is weird," I tease, making a disgusted face.

"Ha, ha. Very funny," Griffin says sarcastically.

Griffin reaches to pinch my side, but I swat his hand out of the way, wagging my finger at him. "Nuh-uh."

"Ticklish?"

"No," I respond too quickly.

"Right," he replies, disbelieving. "I got your number, Raven. Remember, payback's a bitch." He winks, and on his way to the back hall, he turns and walks backward. "Poke around the bar. Familiarize yourself with where everything is. There's a cup of quarters right there by the ice machine if you want to change the song on the jukebox."

"Does it only play country?" I shout back, but he's already turned the corner.

"Unfortunately," Benny grumbles.

Placing my elbows on the counter in front of him, I tilt my head and give him my best endearing smile. Now that I have a moment, I take in his features. Weathered skin, salt and pepper hair, hazel eyes.

"It's Benny, right?"

He grunts his affirmation.

"We haven't been properly introduced. I'm Raven." I stick my hand out to him. He stares at it like he forgot what a handshake is.

When he finally takes my hand, he gives me a half-hearted comment, "Nice to meet you, Raven." Then he goes back to staring at the TV behind me on the wall.

Ignoring his dismissal, I continue, "I take you for a soft rock kind of guy."

He grunts again.

"You're right. Soft rock is too cliché." I pretend like I'm thinking really hard. "I got it! Jazz. Definitely jazz. And I bet you listen to funk when no one else is around."

There's a slight wrinkling at the corners of his eyes, letting me know he's paying attention to everything I say and he's finding it amusing.

I place my hand on my chest and gasp as he takes a sip of his drink. "Why, Benny! We just met! You can't ask me something so personal as to what type of music gets me hot and bothered!"

He chokes and spits the whiskey back into his glass.

I giggle at the mess I created, swipe a coin from the cup Griffin told me about, and make my way to the jukebox across the bar. Trace Adkins drifts from the speakers, and I wrinkle my nose. I'm in the mood for a faster beat.

The coin goes in through the slot, and I pick a song I vaguely recognize. Trace Adkins is replaced by Luke Bryan, and I feel the beat resonate in my chest. For the first time in a long time, I let the music flow through my limbs and dance my way back to the bar. I sway and move my arms as I move behind the bar and explore, taking note of where everything is.

The song ends, and another takes its place. Still fast paced so I'm able to continue. Eventually, I forget what I'm doing, and I let the song take me away.

Georgia Kelly used to make me practice my routines until I'd collapse from fatigue. She herself was a ballerina, but her dream never took off. So, obviously, that meant I had to fulfill it for her. Then along came Anthony, and I was yet again forced to dance. He'd snap his fingers, and I would have to dance until he said stop. Being tired wasn't an option. I was their puppet.

But the day I was rescued, I promised myself that I would cut the strings and do what I want when I want. And right now, I'm choosing this.

Feeling eyes on me, I pause mid-spin and snap my attention to Benny. His mouth is hanging open with his glass half lifted and his gaze trained on me. It's not a predatory gaze. I know what that looks like.

"You got talent, kid."

A blush takes over my cheeks, and I suddenly feel exposed. "Thanks."

Benny gives me an honest-to-God smile and goes back to watching the TV.

It's different when I'm complimented as I'm forced to dance on a pole. These movements came from my soul.

And it felt…freeing.

Out of the corner of my eye, a dark figure shifts in the hallway, but when my head snaps in that direction, there's no one there.

I need to get a grip. Seeing things that aren't actually there is not a good sign.

CHAPTER EIGHT

RAVEN

It's nine p.m., and The Wandering Raven is in full swing. The pool tables and dart boards have a queue, and every table is full. The bar has a solid wall of bodies surrounding it, waiting to place drink orders, and Benny has yet to give up his seat. Griffin is filling the role of waiter, running food orders all over the room.

The jukebox is getting a good amount of use, and some customers have created a dance floor while they two-step to artists like Garth Brooks and Brad Paisley. Most of the men are wearing their nice flannel, cowboy hats, and boots, while some of the women wear a more feminine version of the same attire.

There are a few women with jean shorts, cowgirl boots, and cute tops that Griffin seems to be purposely paying little attention to. Their hair and makeup are flawless, and they keep shooting come-hither glances in Griffin's direction.

The Wandering Raven is clearly the place to be on a Friday night.

I don't know how Griffin and Knox did this before by

themselves. It's a madhouse in here. Kat had mentioned the people in town treating Griffin and Knox differently, but from what I can see, they're more than accepted.

"Two Bud Lights, please," a kind middle-aged woman orders.

"Coming right up!" As I fill two glasses with beer, I spot a couple walking down the back hall. "Here you go," I say with a smile as I hand the drinks over.

My eyes go back to the hallway. Throughout the evening, I've seen people wander back there, but not a single one has returned. Sometimes Griffin walks out the front door, but I have no idea what he'd be doing out there in the parking lot.

Should I be worried? Kat said this place was run-down. She didn't mention sketchy shit going on in a backroom. Although I haven't the slightest clue as to where they're going. I've been down that hall. There's a men's restroom, a women's restroom, and an office. I want to take another look, but I can't while the bar is in full swing.

"Excuse me?"

"What can I get you?" I ask the next cowboy in line, who looks like he barely started shaving last week.

"Five Budweisers and open a tab," he answers.

"Can I see some ID, please?"

He sets his elbows on the counter, leans in conspiratorially, and lowers his voice. "You don't need to see my ID, sweetheart." He finishes off with a wink that I'm sure he uses often.

I mimic his position and respond in kind, "Yes, I do, *sweetheart*. No ID, no beer." Ending my sarcasm with a wink, just like he did.

His expression flips to annoyed. "Griffin and Knox serve me all the time without having to see my ID."

"You shouldn't lie. My mom always said that liars go to hell." I actually don't know for sure if he's lying. Griffin didn't explicitly say, "Don't serve minors" when I got my brief training earlier, but I figure it was implied.

"Listen here, my business has never been refused before. I don't know why you gotta act like a bitch with a stick up your ass. I got rights, you know."

Shaking my head, I respond mockingly, "Whew. Such big words for such a little boy. But my answer is still the same. No ID, no beer."

His hand whips across the counter and wraps tightly around my wrist, pulling me toward him. "What did you just say to me?"

Up close, I can see the spots where he still can't grow facial hair. His behavior speaks to his entitlement.

His hand squeezes even harder, but I don't let the bite of pain show in my face. If he wants to make me hurt, he has to work harder. I've had worse than this.

I ball my other hand in a fist, ready to send it flying right at this punk's nose. Before I can carry out my plan, a shadow falls over me, and a large hand encircles my fist, blocking me from breaking any noses.

The complex scent of deep soil mixed with falling rain overwhelms my senses, like vetiver, but richer.

The kid across from me releases his hold immediately, and his lips become slack as terror enters his face. Everyone around him takes a step back, giving the kid a wide berth.

Following his line of sight, I almost have to break my neck to find the face of the shadow hovering over me. My eyes glide up a sculpted chest and strong neck. I have to blink a few times when I see his face. It's identical to Griffin's except for his eyes and a couple of scars decorating his face. His eyes are an enchanting meadow green that swirl with tempered rage as he directs that anger at the kid trying to manhandle me.

Knox Montgomery.

The scars slicing through his lip and brow draw me in, and I have to physically stop myself from reaching up and tracing the discolored skin.

I want to know more about him. I want his light green eyes to consume me. I want to know what it feels like when he runs his rugged hands over my skin.

My pussy throbs as I imagine what it would feel like to be with him. Would it be soft and sweet or hard and punishing?

He growls at the boy in front of me. "Did you just lay hands on my bartender, Huck LeBlanc?"

CHAPTER NINE

KNOX

Huck has always looked just like his dad and now acts like him, too. And he touched *her*.

Raven Henry.

Her resume didn't state that she looked like…this. Griffin came downstairs a few minutes ago to swap places with me and said that I need to introduce myself to our newest employee. I figured I would come out here and help, avoiding Raven the entire time. But instead, I find Huck acting like an entitled little prick.

The rest of the bar continues their reveling as my hand darts out, gripping the collar of his shirt. I pull him closer, bringing him halfway over the bar. Raven doesn't take a step back but attempts to wedge her sexy curves between me and Huck and places her hand on my bicep.

"I'm okay. It's okay. See?" Raven holds up her wrist for my inspection, but I don't find everything okay. It looks like someone dipped their hand in red paint and grabbed her wrist. I can see Huck's distinct finger marks that will later turn into bruises.

Raven finally sees what I see and attempts to cover it up. I grab her arm, just below the red skin.

"This looks anything but okay, Darlin'."

Her nostrils flare. "I had it handled."

"Sure, you did."

Her glare becomes more furious. "Don't patronize me!"

Huck interjects into our side argument, "Look, Montgomery, the chick says she's fine. No harm, no foul. Right?"

"Chick?" Raven exclaims indignantly.

"I'd stop while you're ahead, bud," Benny throws in.

Our attention snaps to Huck, and my words come out threateningly as I release Raven. "So, not only are you assaulting my employees, but now you're resorting to insulting them? And on top of that, you lied."

"I didn't lie. I swear," he proclaims as he waves his hands.

"So, you didn't say that you've been served here before? You're nineteen. We'd never give alcohol to someone underage."

"I was just kid—" he starts.

My fist squeezes tighter. "I don't recommend lying to me again, Huck."

"Hey, now. What's going on here?" Griffin sprints to my side.

"Your brother is a murdering psycho, that's what!"

Huck's insult hits its mark. Griffin and I have been over this a million times. We don't need the town's approval. All we need is the bar and each other. But to be called a murderer in my place of business will not stand.

I feel a crunch under my fist as it connects with his face. Huck falls to the ground, howling and clutching his face. Benny slinks from his seat and hauls Huck to the front door. Benny may be old and a bit of an alcoholic, but he serves as our unofficial bouncer when needed. For every person he has to throw out, he gets a free drink. And for a guy who seems to be trying to forget their past, free drinks are essential.

"What was that for?" Griffin demands.

Balling my fists at my side, I answer, "He hurt Raven."

"What?"

"It's nothing," Raven argues again.

"It's not gonna feel like nothing when your wrist bruises," I contend back.

Griffin steps between us. "What bruises?"

"Those." I motion to Raven's wrist, and Griffin grabs her hand, raising it to examine the injury. He looks at me and we read each other's faces instantly.

Huck is banned for life.

With a nod in agreement, Griffin takes over the bar, and I lead Raven into the kitchen. We pass Camden, who is putting together a plate of a cheeseburger and fries. "You're going to have to wait tables for a bit," I inform him.

Camden's eyes dart between Raven's wrist and my knuckles. He knows I'm quick to anger but also knows I wouldn't hit someone without cause. "I'm on it," he assents and exits the kitchen with a tray full of orders.

I step into the walk-in freezer and grab an ice pack. When I return to Raven, I find her with her hands on her hips. "You can drop the tough girl act."

"It's not an act," she argues.

Real smooth, Romeo.

I'm not used to carrying long conversations with a gorgeous woman. I'm who women come to when they want to walk on the wild side. It's a transaction and nothing more. We fuck and they get to go back to their gossip circles, claiming they had a wild night with one of the Montgomery twins. Griffin still partakes in such transactions, but I'm tired of the emotionless fucking. It's not for me.

Reaching for her arm, she steps away. It's like a shot

straight to my chest. I assume she doesn't know mine and Griffin's history or what the Montgomery name means, and her rejection hurts more than normal. But I don't let it show.

"If my wrist gets treated, then so does your hand," she insists.

You know what happens when you assume…

She wasn't disgusted by me. She was making sure I got help as well. That's new.

Too stunned to reply, I stand there with a blank stare.

Raven takes my silence as consent. "I'll grab the first aid kit." She's out the door and back before I can even form words. She sits at a stool beside the stainless-steel counter and motions for me to join her.

Sitting on another stool facing her, I lay her hand flat and gently place the ice pack on her wrist. Now that the adrenaline is gone, I can feel the softness of her skin. My cock begins to harden in my jeans. Her hair is pulled back into a messy ponytail, and her midnight-black waves cascade down her back. My eyes wander over her full breasts and thighs. Fresh ink peeks out from under the thick straps of her tank top: two small crowns side by side.

Her spirited blue eyes meet mine, and I watch as her pupils grow. Raven's breathing increases, and I decide to push my luck. I flip her hand, exposing the inside of her delicate wrist, and run the pads of my fingertips over her pulse. She lets out a small gasp, and goosebumps spread over her skin. Holding back the smirk that attempts to take over my face, I place the ice pack back on her wrist.

Raven clears her throat. "So, you must be Knox."

"Must be."

"I'm Raven," she declares and holds out her hand for me to shake. I oblige and command my dick to calm down when her eyes roam my face and she bites her lip.

"Nice to meet you, Raven."

She smiles. "Nice to meet you too, Knox."

The sound of my name on her rosy lips just about has me undone. No woman has ever had me this mesmerized. I'm thirty-eight years old and can honestly say I've never longed to know how a woman's skin tastes or how she sounds when she comes.

The energy around her is addictive. I could easily lose myself in Raven Henry. Her fire, her heart. It's beautiful. I want to capture that beauty and whisk her away to keep it all for myself.

But she's an employee. The Wandering Raven doesn't need a sexual harassment lawsuit attached to its name.

"It already feels better," Ravens claims, removing the ice pack. "Your turn." She opens the first aid kit and pulls out the supplies she needs. As she touches my hand again, guiding it to her face to inspect the injury, my body develops a mind of its own. My thumb runs circles over the back of her hand, and her breath hitches again.

Forcing myself to stop, my muscles go rigid.

Being around her is going to be more difficult than I anticipated.

"That kind of thing doesn't normally happen."

Her brow raises. "You punching someone in the face?"

Raven's sass drives a laugh out of me. "No, I mean employees being harassed and assaulted. Underage kids never ask for drinks because we know who is of age and who isn't."

"Huh," she says more to herself than she does to me as she runs an alcohol wipe over my broken skin. "Word must have gotten out that you hired a new bartender."

My shoulder raises and lowers. "Probably. That's small towns for ya."

"Guess so." She shakes her head. "But I had it handled."

My answer is to give her a look of disbelief.

"I've worked in a bar before, and it was more dangerous

than The Wandering Raven." She rolls her lips inward as if she's said too much.

My head angles to the side. "Where? It wasn't on your resume."

Her jaw tightens for a moment. "It was a long time ago, and the owner wouldn't give me a good reference even if he remembered me. He didn't like me slapping customers when they were drunk and wanted to play a game of grab ass."

"Sounds like an asshole of a boss," I comment.

"You don't know the half of it," she replies as if an ugly memory floated to the surface.

I hesitate for a moment, unsure of what to say here. Usually, Griffin is the one I have this type of conversation with. He's been my best friend and confidant my whole life. That's what happens when all your friends disappear from your life at age sixteen and refuse to acknowledge you.

"Umm. If you want to talk about it, I'll listen."

"Thanks, Knox. But I don't know if that's an appropriate boss-employee conversation." She smiles teasingly.

"Consider it team building," I quip.

Raven's melodious laugh drifts from her lips to my ears, and I feel myself doing an unfamiliar movement.

I smile back.

As Raven goes back to tending bar, Camden goes back to the kitchen, and I head to the back hall. The wainscotting does its job, hiding the secret door located right next to our office.

When I open the door, I'm hit in the face with boisterous clamor and an unmistakable herbal smoke. The narrow steps down to the basement are hazardous, and we don't have any plans to change them.

Hitting the bottom step, I scan the room. Five of the six poker tables are full, each dealer in our employ is busy officiating the games at their assigned tables, and the bar on the right side of the room is at more than capacity as people gather around to watch various sports that they have all placed bets on. Multiple flatscreen TVs are streaming live events like the NHL, NFL, MLB, and NASCAR.

Griffin is standing in the corner with a repeat customer, the mailman, Ernie. I'm not sure where the poor, scrawny guy Ernie is from. He just kind of showed up in town one day and got the job as the Mystic River mailman. I'm not sure how he keeps his job. He constantly delivers mail to the wrong address. I swear he does it on purpose because it's only certain people who get their mail mixed up. So, it's either intentional or he's taking one too many hits of the rolled-up buds before he clocks in for work.

Ernie and Griffin make their exchange, and Ernie makes a beeline for the exit. He doesn't stick around for cards or sports. He shows up once a week, buys a bag, then dips. As Ernie passes by, Griffin and I make eye contact, and I nod my head, giving him the go-ahead to head back upstairs.

Our "little" side business is more rumor than common knowledge. Sheriff Jackson has never been able to get enough evidence to secure a warrant, and anyone who does utilize our services wouldn't dare snitch. Not only would the rest of our customers go after them, but we'd make sure they were never seen again.

I begin circulating the room with keen eyes, walking by each and every player. Most are too focused on their hand to pay attention to me. Cheating doesn't happen often, but it's not uncommon. And there's always a sore loser that we have to set straight.

We don't have much down here. People can place bets on sports and races, or they can play poker at the tables. And we may not have the appropriate licenses or permits, but that never stopped our grandfather, great-grandfather, or great-great-grandfather. So, it sure as hell isn't going to hold back Griffin and me.

Once I'm done with my inspection of the tables, I don't have to fight my way through the crowd to get to the bar. Everyone parts like the Red Sea, so my path is clear.

"Hey! Back already, Knox?" Florence Baker, the local librarian, greets me. Florence tended bar upstairs when Pops ran The Wandering Raven, and she insisted she continue when we took over. We didn't hesitate to take her up on her offer. But we knew Florence well before The Wandering Raven. She's been the librarian since I can remember, and she's one of the few people in town who didn't shun Griffin and me.

"Yeah, just had a small teen problem upstairs," I answer her.

"I hear you hired a new bartender." Florence peeks at me out of the corner of her eye as she fills another glass with Bud Light and hands it to a customer.

"That we did," I confirm.

A round of boo's flood my ears as the Nets score another three-pointer against the Rockets, ending Florence's line of questioning. I ignore her pointed looks, prying for more information, and busy myself filling drinks.

"So?" The woman is like a dog with a bone.

"Her name is Raven. She's new in town," I concede.

A flicker of approval crosses Florence's face. "Good hire," she praises in a monotone voice. "She works for me at the library, too. Hard worker. Talks too much, though."

Turning my head toward her, I make a face conveying my annoyance at her hypocrisy.

"Don't give me that look, Knox Montgomery. You have no room to talk."

We go back to serving up drinks, and an hour later, the Rockets have won, and spirits are high. Well, most of them. There's always at least a few who lose out on money. That's the way it is here. The basketball fans begin to clear out after they collect their winnings or walk away empty-handed.

A fist slams on the far poker table, and someone shouts, "Aw, come on! This bitch is obviously counting cards!"

My feet are moving before I notice who is causing the scene.

Graham LeBlanc.

Like uncle, like nephew, I guess.

I don't give him a warning as I grip the collar on the back of his shirt and lift. Graham lets out a choking sound as he tries to get his feet under him. I don't wait for him as I drag him behind me and shoot off a text to Benny. Once again, a path is cleared as I lug this asshole out of the room and up the stairs.

By the time I'm in the back hallway, Graham is standing and letting some vitriol fly. "You piece of dumb shit! Get your grubby hands off me! I want my money back! That game is rigged!"

It takes everything in me not to take him out right here, right now. This man's brother is the reason for the scars I carry. He's smaller than Frank and a major prick just like his brother. But he doesn't deserve my wrath. Frank is smart enough to never set foot in The Wandering Raven. He wouldn't walk out alive. But that doesn't stop Frank's wife, son, and brother from coming.

Benny comes around the corner and I hand Graham over to him. Benny may not look like much while sitting at the bar, but he's just as big as I am. And every time he has to throw someone out, it's like he sobers up in ten seconds flat.

Graham has yet to cease with his insults, but they're like water on a duck's back. But before he gets tossed out the back door, I interrupt him, "I expect your balance to be paid in full by tomorrow. I'm giving you the night because I don't want to see your punchable face for the next twelve hours. As for the game, you knew what you were signing up for when you walked in. It's no one's fault but your own that you suck at playing cards."

I nod at Benny, and he hauls Graham out the back door. He'll rough Graham up a bit and send the idiot on his merry way. He'll have a couple of black eyes and maybe a broken arm, but he'll be fine. Benny is good at handling this type of thing. Griffin and I prefer to handle collections ourselves, so this arrangement works out perfectly.

Pinching the bridge of my nose, I release a large exhale. The letter is burning a hole in my pocket. I told myself I would keep it close just in case, but I was only lying to myself.

I head into the office and plop down in the rolling chair, letting out a groan. Back problems have become my daily companion, and they serve as a reminder that I'm not twenty-five anymore. A few months ago, Griffin said we needed something with good lumbar support and bought the chair along with some cushy mats to put on the floor behind the bar. I will never admit to him that he was right and that his purchases might be the only reason I'm not crawling out of The Wandering Raven every night.

I pull the letter out of my pocket and drop it onto the desk. Ignoring the letter hasn't done me any good. It's become a silent obsession—a dark whisper in my ear.

"Fuck it," I say to myself and tear open the envelope.

Dear Knox,

I knew you'd be the one to open my letter. Your heart is pure, unlike Griffin's. He's never forgiven me, but I know you want to. It'll lift a burden from your shoulders, one that never should have been there because

I'm innocent. I finally figured out how all that evidence wound up in my truck, but I can't tell you in a letter. Come see me and we'll talk.

Amos Montgomery

My fists clench the letter, wrinkling the paper. My sneer could burn a hole right in the middle of the page.

I let him get to me. Again. He's always been able to get me to do what he wants. A few well-placed words and I'm bending over backward to make him happy.

Not this time.

For all I care, the state of Texas can give him the needle, and I won't miss a wink of sleep.

CHAPTER TEN

RAVEN

Drumming my fingers on the steering wheel, my leg bounces. The façade of the building is exactly how I remember it. They've added a few more hedges, but other than that, nothing has changed.

The five-story building is set back about fifty yards from the road, giving a sense of wealth from all the greenery between it and the road. Umber-colored bricks make up the exterior walls. Pointed arches surround the entrance. The steep roof creates a vertical emphasis. Long lancet windows covered with bars give a peep into every room.

Rooms that I'm all too familiar with…

Mystic River Psychiatric Hospital is just as harrowing as ever.

After running into Dr. Whitlock the other day, the urge to drive by the hospital clogged my throat. The plan was to drive by, make a U-turn, and head home. But I've been parked across the street for an hour now, and I can't seem to shift my car into drive.

I don't know how I'm going to get what I need when I

can't make myself step foot inside. The thought of being trapped in there again short circuits my brain. I contemplated posing as a volunteer, but the risk of being identified is too great. People in town won't know me because I'm not from here. But in there? Chances are much higher. If there weren't patients in there, I'd set the whole place on fire. I'll just have to dig up the dirt the old-fashioned way.

Dropping my head back against the seat, I massage my temples with my fingers.

Moving the black round tile diagonally, I stare blankly at the checkerboard in front of me. I'm not even sure I know all the rules of checkers, but it beats the game of cricket some of the other patients are trying to play outside. It's too hot out today.

"Your move," my opponent, Riley, informs me, but I have no idea what piece he moved. He could've moved one of my own, and I wouldn't notice.

That's how invested I am in this game.

Riley tried explaining the game once, and I pretended to understand. I think he can tell I have no idea what I'm doing but he doesn't care.

"Is that a shiv, Hoyt?"

My hand drops the piece I was about to play as my attention is drawn to the commotion on the other side of the rec room. My mouth forms into an unpleasant twist.

Leonard, an orderly who's always on a power trip, yanks Hoyt out of his chair as an unsharpened plastic spoon falls out of Hoyt's lap. Hoyt is in his eighties and has been diagnosed with PTSD from his time serving in Vietnam.

On the table in front of his chair is a half-eaten cup of red Jello. Leonard grabs the front of Hoyt's shirt with both hands and pulls. Hoyt cries out in pain.

Leonard is always stirring up trouble. He enjoys dishing out our punishments.

The breath in my lungs grows thin and ragged.

"Don't," Riley warns.

But it's too late.

I'm up and out of my seat, barging right for them.

With his back to me, Leonard isn't aware of my approach, and I use his heedlessness to my advantage.

Jumping on his back, I circle on arm around his neck and use my other hand to rapidly hit him in the head. Hoyt scrambles away, leaving his snack behind. Leonard flips me over his shoulder, dropping me onto the hard tile flat on my back. Staring up at the empty white ceiling, I wheeze in an attempt to get air back in my lungs.

Leonard looms over me with a vicious grin on his face. "Dr. Whitlock is going to have so much fun with you."

Cold sweat bathes my skin in foreboding disquiet.

My hand reaches to turn my key in the ignition, when a candy red Ferrari California comes zooming down the road. The windows are tinted, preventing me from being able to see who's in there. I duck my head down as the driver passes me and barely slows as it turns onto the drive of the hospital.

I peek my head up just enough for me to see the car screech to a stop in front of the entrance. Dr. Whitlock comes charging out the doors while the man from the grocery store exits the sports car.

Scrambling, I grab my phone, open the camera app, zoom in, and start recording. I keep my head low in the hope that they don't see me or my phone.

Lewis Whitlock marches right up to the man and slams his palms into the man's chest, pushing him backward. The man stumbles back a few steps, holding his hands out at his side. Dr. Whitlock gets in the man's face, pointing a finger and turning red with anger.

I wish I was closer so I could hear what they're saying. Whatever they're discussing, the good doctor isn't happy about it, but the other man looks like he doesn't have a single worry in the world.

The man pulls out a stack of folded cash from his pocket,

calming Dr. Whitlock. His face is still flushed, but he stops yelling. Whitlock fishes out a small bag from his own pocket and tosses it at the man. The bag hits the man in the chest as Whitlock snatches the cash. He gives the mystery man another yell and storms back into the hospital.

After Dr. Whitlock marches up the few steps leading to the door, he looks back at the man, telling him something else I still can't hear. Before he goes back inside, he looks directly at my car. My heart pounds, the rhythm echoing in my ears. There's no way he can see me in here, but it's as if he can see me through my phone. It's as if he knows it's me in the car.

He once told me I was his favorite as he held me down. He said he liked my struggle. He liked how I fought back.

Dr. Whitlock finally goes inside, leaving me with the memories I never asked for. The ones I wish would leave me alone.

I focus back on the man as he opens the small clear bag, grabs something out, and pops it in his mouth. Then he hops in his car and peels back the way he came.

Ending the recording, I replay it a few times, hoping I will suddenly learn how to read lips, but that wish doesn't come true.

This isn't exactly the proof I was looking for, but it's a start.

CHAPTER ELEVEN

RAVEN

I really should've thought it through before I accepted a day job *and* a night job. I got a few hours of sleep before I had to be up to get ready for the library. At least I can take Noah with me to this one.

Florence has a hard exterior, but I've seen her with the kids who come into the library. She's like a grandma waiting to spoil her grandchildren. When I told her that I needed to bring Noah with me on Saturdays, she almost seemed excited.

Noah and I had a quick breakfast and then headed out. I made him bring his backpack, which he did begrudgingly. After all the work we did catching him up with the other kids, I don't want him falling behind again.

At the library, Noah went straight to the kids' section and curled up in a beanbag chair with a book he randomly pulled from the shelf, while I got to work shelving books, sending emails about overdue fines, and so on.

Rolling my sore neck, I turn in my computer chair to Florence. "I'm finished with—"

"Shelve those books next," she interrupts me while staring at her own computer a few feet away. I'm pretty sure she's playing solitaire.

Instead of barking back, I push the rolling cart out in front behind the circulation desk and start with the romance novels. As I replace these books on the shelves, I make note of the ones that look intriguing so I can add them to the list of books I want to read. *Gifts* by Brynne Asher, *Find Me* by Ashley N. Rostek, *Cuervo's Carnival* by N.J. Weeks, and *The Diavolos* by Nouha Jullienne.

Looks like I'll have something to do in my downtime.

"Got any good recommendations for me?" a voice says from behind me.

Jumping, I let out a yelp as the book I'm admiring drops from my grasp, and a hand covers my mouth. My heart picks up speed.

"Shhh. Don't want to get in trouble with the fossil that is Mrs. Baker." The man behind me chuckles.

I whirl around with my fist at the ready, but I'm met with familiar sunset hair. I relax my hand at my side as he smirks and bends down, picking up the book.

"*Ice Planet Barbarians*," Jed reads the title to me and follows with a questioning raise of his brow.

"Gotta keep it interesting," I defend sarcastically.

"And blue ETs with horns and bizarre dicks is what does it for you?" he teases but his voice has an edge that is off-putting.

"I'm trying to broaden my horizons." I shrug, adding the same edge to my own tone.

Jed places the book on the cart. "There are other ways to do that."

I take a closer look at Jed. His shirt is slightly rumpled, and his hair is disheveled under his cowboy hat. The dark circles under his eyes are faint, but I can still spot them. He doesn't have the same flirty demeanor as the first time we met.

"What can I do for you, Jed?" I fold my arms and lean onto one leg, attempting to appear calm, but I'm observing his every move.

His eyes wander the shelf behind me as he answers, "Would it be cheesy if I said I just wanted to see you again?"

"Yes," I respond immediately, all playfulness gone.

A switch flips, and he brings back the man I met the other day. "Then let me prove it to you."

Keeping my face passive, I respond, "And pray tell, how might you accomplish that?"

"Come to dinner with me tonight." His gaze looks eager, like he'd eat me up if I let him.

Would I?

Maybe.

Still determined to give him a hard time, I don't let him off the hook so easily for his judgmental comment. "That didn't sound like a question."

His forehead scrunches. "Huh?"

"If you want to take me to dinner, then you need to *ask*. It's the gentlemanly thing to do." Toward the end of my reprimand, my lips curve.

Jed's smile matches my own. "Raven, may I please take you to dinner tonight?"

"I have to work, but I might be free on Monday."

He makes his confusion known again. "You're working at the library at night?"

"No, I have a second job."

"Oh. Where? Maybe I can come see you tonight." Understanding dawns his face.

"The Wandering Raven," I answer, and continue before he can crack the joke. "I know, I know. Raven working at The

Wandering Raven. Ha ha. Trust me, you're not the first person and you won't be the last to think it."

A muscle in his jaw ticks, but he smooths it out before I can address it. "I may not be able to make it there, but I'll see you Monday." He turns and stalks back down the aisle. His shoulders are tense, and his boots hit the carpeted floor harder than necessary.

"Wait," I call out, but he either doesn't hear me or he's ignoring me.

Great. The first time a guy asks me out and I've already been rejected.

Welcome to life, Raven.

"Fuck!" I kick the right rear tire on my car as rays from the sun heat my skin, only furthering my frustration.

"Mom, you shouldn't say 'fuck,'" Noah reminds me as he pokes his head out the car window.

I give him my back as I take a deep breath.

On our way home from the library, one of my tires popped. I was supposed to buy a jack and a tool kit before we even drove to Mystic River from New York, but I had other things on my mind. So now, here I am with a spare tire, but no way to change it. We live about twenty minutes outside of town, which in an area such as this is quite the distance. We were halfway there when I both felt and heard the tire practically explode. I don't want to make Noah walk in this heat the rest of the way home, and somehow, I don't have fucking service in this one damn spot. I can't leave Noah here by himself. I may be new to full-time momming, but I'm not dumb. And I haven't seen a single damn car drive by.

This is just for a moment. It's not forever. I'm going to breathe for a minute, then I will figure out a solution. I always do. I have no other choice.

I can do this.

With renewed determination, I turn back to Noah. "I'm sorry. You're right."

"If I can't say 'shit' then you can't say 'fuck,'" he tells me very seriously.

The laugh that comes out of me is an uncontrollable reaction. I wipe away tears that I'm not sure are from laughing or frustration or a mixture of the two. "You're right. If I won't let you say 'shit' then I can't say 'fuck.' You're very right about that."

Noah looks at me like I've grown a second head.

The crunch of tires on gravel coming from behind me reaches my ears. Relief and terror flood my system.

This better not be some asshole.

When I turn around, I find a disarming smile that I recognize flashing at me from inside a dark green Ford F-250, a car that I've seen in the parking lot of The Wandering Raven. I'm not sure if my boss coming to my rescue is worse or better than an asshole being my Good Samaritan.

Griffin hops out of his lifted truck, and his work boots hit the rocky pavement. His arm naturally flexes as he shuts the door, and I feel my panties grow wet as I witness the movement. I didn't think I had a type. I've never been able to explore that, but I'm quickly realizing that I crave a man with strength.

As he approaches me, Griffin's look of concern as he eyes my shattered tire punches me in the gut.

When was the last time someone looked at me like that? Like they cared for what my situation was.

"What happened to your tire?"

I nibble on my lip, unsure of how to feel about all the

emotions this man brings out of me without even trying. "I'm not sure. It decided it didn't want to be my tire anymore when we were almost home, and I still haven't bought a jack," I joke.

"Mom?"

My eyes widen in alarm. I haven't introduced Noah to many people. I'm not ashamed of my son. I'm just used to people using his existence against me, something I can never let happen again.

I run to Noah's car door and get him to put his head back inside the car. "Just wait here, okay? Stay in the car until I say it's safe to come out, little king."

"Moooom," he groans.

I ignore his protest of his nickname and turn my attention back to Griffin. My arm rests on Noah's open window.

"You're a mom," he states. It's not a question.

"That I am," I confirm, all playfulness gone.

Griffin's eyes assess me, and not in an appreciative way. He looks like he's determining how to best approach a cornered animal, and I'm sure that's what I look like.

"I'm not going to hurt you, Raven."

He says it so matter-of-factly. I know it's meant to reassure me, and it's said in a way that makes me feel like he doesn't mean just now. He's telling me that he would never hurt me.

How long has it been since anyone said that to me?

Never.

Clients didn't care to calm me down or put me at ease. They paid for their time with me. They could do whatever they wanted. Even when I was locked up, I was never told I wouldn't be hurt.

Part of my brain is screaming at me to grab Noah and run. Fuck my plan and what I came here to do. Noah's safety and well-being will always come first.

But a much louder part of me is telling me that I can trust

Griffin. He may ruin my panties every time he gets close, but he would never raise his hand toward me with the intention to do harm.

Letting out the breath I didn't realize I was holding, I nod. If he opened his arms right now, there's a ninety percent chance that I'd run right to him and welcome the embrace. I'm so damn tired, but I can't let that be the reason I let my guard down completely.

"Let me help you, please," Griffin pleads.

Bringing back some of my sarcasm to ease the tension, I quirk a brow. "Do you magically have cell service?"

He scoffs, feeling my apprehension begin to deflate. "No, but I have a hitch, a tow bar, and chains so we can get you and your son out of this heat."

His mention of the sun reminds me that I'm probably already sunburnt.

Great.

"Do you have what we need to change the tire instead? I think that would be easier," I suggest.

"I left my jack at home." Griffin shrugs.

I sigh. "Okay. A tow would be great. Thank you."

Even though I've calmed down, Griffin still walks toward me with caution. When he gets to my side, he peers inside. Noah looks at Griffin like any curious child who has been through a shitshow would. Skeptically.

"Who are you?" Noah's distrust is obvious.

Griffin's eyes soften as his gaze roams over Noah. I suddenly know what he sees. Noah's scar. I stiffen, waiting for the shameful comments.

Instead, Griffin holds his hand out to Noah. "I'm Griffin. What's your name?" Each muscle in my body slowly melts.

Griffin Montgomery, everyone. Sexy as hell and good with kids.

Lord, help me and my panties, please.

CHAPTER TWELVE

GRIFFIN

She's a mom. Fuck. Raven is a mother. She had sex, got pregnant, and made a whole fucking human in her body.

Why does the thought of her having sex with another man make my blood boil? I have no claim over her, and I'm not a caveman.

When I stumbled upon a car on the side of the road with its hazard lights blinking, I didn't think I'd find Raven. Not to mention the fact that she's wearing a pair of jeans that look like they were tailor-made to show off her ass in a way that makes me want to get my hands on it.

Noah puffs his chest up at my gesture, wanting to meet my sign of respect with robustness. He puts his hand in mine and replies, "I'm Noah." He studies me further. "You look like my friend."

"Who's your friend?" I ask.

"Knox."

When did that happen?

My eyes catch on the scar lining the side of his face again, and I feel the same pang I felt before cut through my chest.

"Knox is my twin brother," I inform him with a smile. "That's why we look alike."

"When did you meet Knox?" Raven questions Noah with a frown.

"He taught me how to throw a football." Noah smiles proudly.

When did that happen?

Raven must be thinking the same thing because her frown deepens. But Noah speaks before she can ask more questions. "I'm in first grade."

I exaggerate with my response. "Wow! First grade? That's practically a grown-up. That makes you the man of the house, doesn't it?"

Is it bad that I'm hopeful his father isn't in the picture? I don't think Raven would have flirted with me the way she did if she had a partner, but you never know with these things.

Noah scrunches his brow, mulling over my words. I can see the moment he decides that I'm right as resolve takes over his expression. "Yeah." He nods to himself. "Yeah, I am." He looks me straight in the eye, letting me know he's made of tougher stuff than most. Much tougher than any other six-year-old should have to be.

"You know what that means, right? It means you need to protect your mom and take care of her."

"I can do that," Noah assures me.

"Good man." I smile at him again. Out of the corner of my eye, I see Raven pursing her lips together. Her eyes are shining brightly with unshed tears, and her lips tremble.

"Thank you," she whispers to me.

I don't answer her but instead turn back to Noah. "How about you and your mom hop in my truck so we can get you and your car home."

Noah crowds my personal space as he leans his head out the window to get a good look at my truck. He makes a great effort to keep his face composed, but his eyes widen for a moment. "Yeah, I guess we can do that," Noah says nonchalantly and gathers his books, placing them in his backpack.

"Sounds good, my man," I say with an amused smile. This little boy is something else.

I lead Raven and Noah to my truck and get Noah situated and buckled in the back seat.

Raven plants her feet firmly on the ground beside the open passenger door. Hands on her hips, she offers her help. "What can I do?"

"Get your pretty little a—" My attention flashes to Noah, who is watching our interaction closely. "*Behind*. Get your pretty little behind in the truck. It'll go by faster if I can just get this done."

She holds strong. "I'm not some princess waiting for a knight in shining armor to rescue her. I don't sit on the side while shi—" She looks back at Noah as well. "*Things* need to get done."

"You can't say 'shit,' Mom," Noah reminds her.

The deadlock between me and Raven dissolves as we both fail to hold in our laughter. I never thought hearing a child swear would make me laugh so hard that my abs hurt.

Once I've caught my breath, my attention snags on the beautiful smile on Raven's face. I've seen her flirt, I've seen her smirk, and I've seen her angry. But I've never seen her smile like this. Her smile is one that men would go to war for. Raven's eyes sparkle with humor, and the light air that surrounds her is one that I know I would follow anywhere.

I swear all the blood in my body rushes to my cock, and I curse myself for getting a boner in front of a child.

Spinning on my heel, I stalk to the back of my truck to busy myself. A door slams shut, and I hear footsteps follow me. Raven doesn't even give me a chance to refuse her help as she holds up a hand to silence me before I can ask her to get in the cab. Folding this round, I get back to grabbing what I need. Her keen observation of my movements is almost unsettling, but I quickly realize that she's watching so she can learn.

"Your dad ever teach you how to change a tire?"

Raven's shoulders stiffen for half a second before she forces herself to relax. "No. He didn't," she grits out.

Oops. Dad is not a good topic of conversation.

I continue the small talk, attempting to dig myself out of this hole. "Where are you from?"

Raven quirks a brow in my direction. "What is this? Twenty questions?"

I chuckle and turn toward her, resting my hip on the open tailgate of my truck. "Just trying to get to know you, Sunshine."

Her nose wrinkles in a way that can only be described as adorable, and she refuses to look at me. "That's not necessary."

"Come on," I implore. "How about this, a question for a question."

I want to know more about this woman with the long legs, round hips, and a smile that would melt hearts all around the country. I'm playing with fire, but I can't help myself.

Raven tilts her head slightly as she studies me. I see the moment she decides that she's just as curious as I am. "Okay, but I get five passes." She mirrors my stance and crosses her arms right under her round tits, unknowingly emphasizing them.

"One."

She narrows her eyes. "Two."

"Done," I accept. Before she can take it back, I reach my

hand out to seal the deal. But when she places her hand in mine, I feel the calluses on her palm, and something primal beats in my chest.

Acting on instinct, I grip her hand and pull her close. Our bodies are perfectly aligned, not an inch of space between us. No doubt she can feel the effect she has on me. Her eyes widen, and her chest rises and falls with shocked breaths, but she doesn't pull away.

Pushing my luck further, I raise my free hand and tuck a lock of hair behind her ear. "Where did you live before New York?"

"Pass."

An amused smirk turns my lips upward. "That was an easy one. Are you sure you want to waste a pass?"

"Yep." Her face is confident in her decision.

Tracing her plump lips with my finger, I push again. "Tell me a secret, Sunshine. Tell me something no one else knows about you."

She bites her lip again, and I can't help but be jealous that it's not my mouth nibbling on her plump, rosy lip.

"I named Noah after my brother," she admits in a whisper.

"I don't understand how that's a secret. Wouldn't your brother…" I trail off, feeling like I've dug myself into another hole.

Raven's eyes grow sad, but she's brave as she keeps her gaze locked with mine. "He's dead," she reveals.

Shit.

My brows scrunch together in confusion. "But your parents—"

A muscle in Raven's jaw ticks, and she interrupts me, "They're dead too."

THROUGHOUT THE ENTIRE PROCESS OF GETTING RAVEN'S CAR hitched to my truck, she continues to insist on being an active participant. Once the SUV is loaded up, Raven and I get into the cab and find Noah content in the back seat.

"Address, Sunshine."

My request seems to snap her out of the daze our discussion put her in. "What? Why?" she asks incredulously.

"I need your address so I can take you home," I explain slowly and point to the GPS screen.

Noah chimes in, rambling off their address, and I smile to myself, realizing how Knox and Noah met. Raven moves to enter it in, but I cover her hand with mine. "No need. I know where we're going."

Understanding dawns on her face. "Oh. Right. Small town."

Little does she know…

I let Raven choose the music on the radio for the short drive to her house, curious to see what she'll choose. She flips through a few stations and lands on one playing AC/DC.

This little spitfire never ceases to surprise me.

Watching her out of the corner of my eye, I find her mouthing the words and subtly dancing in her seat. In my rearview mirror, Noah is bobbing his head and doing the same. Something settles in the center of my chest.

Happiness.

I rub my sternum. I never thought myself *un*happy, and I definitely never thought I'd want to date a single mom.

One of my rules in life has been to never involve kids. It's not that I hate them, but in my experience, when kids are involved in things like relationships, things can get messier.

No one wants to hurt the kids, but they always end up being the collateral damage.

But Raven is a woman wrapped in mystery, and I've never been so intrigued by a woman like this.

Turning down the correct street, I maneuver my truck and her SUV to back into her driveway.

Whistling with a smile on my face, I hop out of my truck and circle the front end to open Raven's door. Noah is out and waiting for his mom when I make it to the other side.

Opening the passenger door with a dramatic flourish, I grab Raven's purse and guide her out of the car with my other hand. "Here we are, Sunshine," I say to her with a wink.

"Thank you, Griff," she says genuinely.

The use of my nickname draws my eyes to her lips, and my mind conjures up the image of how they would look wrapped around my cock.

Not now, little Griffin. This is not the time or the place.

"Mom, it's hot," Noah informs Raven as he pulls on his shirt, trying to cool himself off.

"Sorry, li—Noah. Here." She pulls out her keys and hands them to Noah. "Go on inside." He snags the keys from her hand and runs up their lawn. Barely pausing to unlock the door, he hurries inside.

Raven fans herself as she watches. A drop of sweat slides down her neck and disappears beneath her shirt.

Is it the time and place yet?

I gulp, swallowing down the saliva that has formed in my mouth from just looking at her. "Why don't you go ahead and go inside. I'll get your car unloaded."

She waves her hand. "No, no. I'll help."

"Alright then," I comment.

I don't know if I'm going to be able to keep little Griffin

under control if she keeps sweating like that. Like a damn goddess.

Thankfully, we get her car unloaded without Raven noticing the boner in my jeans. I swear my cock is hard enough to pound nails.

After we're done, I pluck her purse up from the hot concrete and walk her to her front door. I may sleep around a bit, but I'm still a gentleman.

I hand over her purse and slide my hands into my pockets, attempting to keep my mitts to myself.

She turns and leans against the door. "Thanks for rescuing us today. Noah isn't used to this heat," she says with a small chuckle.

"And you are?" I tilt my head to the side.

"I am what?"

"Used to the heat."

"Oh. Umm…" Breaking eye contact with me, she takes a deep breath. Her mouth goes tight, and a crease forms between her brows as she thinks something over. Coming to a solution, she nods her head and says, "I've acclimated."

I don't understand why that would be a difficult thing to admit to, but I don't let my confusion show. "Did you live anywhere else besides New York?"

"I've lived various places." A cloud very briefly passes through her eyes.

I know what secrets look like. I shouldn't push and pry, but I want to know everything about Raven. I need to know. I can't accept anything less than consuming her from the inside out.

Caging her body with my own, I place my forearm above her head and lean in. Our eyes connect, and I feel myself drowning in her like I did the first time we met. Her chest rises and falls in quick succession as her breathing picks up. I smirk, noticing the effect I have on her.

I hold myself still, even though I'm dying to get a taste. Again, I'm a gentleman—a damn consent king.

Raven's consent comes when she places her hands on my stomach. My muscles contract on their own as she slides her hands up over my abs and pecs. She grips my neck and pulls.

She couldn't have made her intention clearer if she tried, and in all honesty, neither could I.

I dip my head but keep my movements slow, drawing out the anticipation. Raven pulls harder, but she's a small thing. I have more muscle in my right pinky.

When our lips meet, I swear it's like a damn romance novel. I get that feeling in my chest again. A feeling that seems to only happen with her.

Our lips move together in a progressive rhythm. I'm desperate to touch her, to feel the way her tits would bounce when I thrust into her. But I know that if I were to touch her now, I wouldn't stop, and her son is inside.

Instead, I put my other forearm on the door, allowing me to lean in further. But I keep a minuscule amount of air between my body and hers. I can't rush this. I don't *want* to rush it. So, I bask in the moment. I relish the soft feel of her lips and the passion behind them.

Breaking our connection, I rest my forehead on hers. My breaths are coming out faster now, matching hers.

We don't say anything. No regrets and no embarrassment. Just two people savoring the spark between them.

When I finally get my faculties under control, I lean my head back far enough to see her deep blues. "Welcome to the neighborhood…neighbor," I say with a smirk.

Her mouth gapes wide. She lives in the corner house, so it's not hard to figure out which house is mine.

"So, you live there," she deduces and points. "And I live here." She points to her own house.

"That's right."

Raven's lips round as she says, "Oh."

I finally pull back all the way, spin on my heel, and aim straight for my truck. It feels ridiculous starting my car only to drive over one house. But I can't block her car in her driveway.

Turning off the engine, my eyes wander to Raven's front door. She's still there, but she's staring right at me. Her eyes impossibly wide and her hand over her mouth.

That's right, Sunshine. You're not gonna get rid of me that easily.

CHAPTER THIRTEEN

GRIFFIN

Cracking my neck, I walk through the entrance into The Wandering Raven. Knox and I just got done with another *guest* in the barn. I was more of an active participant this time around, which isn't something I do often. But this one had a mouth on him, and I wanted to send a message. Don't fuck with the Montgomery brothers.

However, the soreness of my muscles is a reminder that I'm not twenty anymore.

A quick glance around the room shows me that a few customers have wandered in for a late lunch. But there's a certain spot that's vacant, and it shouldn't be.

My brows draw together as I stomp right for Benny. "Where's Raven?"

Benny rolls his eyes. "No need to fly off the handle."

I don't heed his advice. "Where?"

Benny nods his head toward the hallway, and I follow his direction. I'm about to turn the corner when I hear Raven talking, and she doesn't sound too happy.

"What do you mean there's nothing you can do?"

Her pause fills the hallway with suffocating ire.

"When I send my son to school, I am putting him in your and the school's care. And that doesn't just mean his physical safety. It includes his emotional and mental wellbeing. I—"

What the hell is going on? Is Noah okay?

Raven takes a deep breath. "Mrs. Burke, if you would just work with me on this, I know we could come to a resolution. One where Noah isn't being bullied, and your classroom has a peaceful atmosphere."

Bullied. My God. Nothing changes.

"He's very self-conscious about the scar on his face. There was an...accident when he was little. So, hearing that he's being made fun of for it is distressing. Not only that, but the bully is encouraging other kids to participate in the bullying as well."

Oh, hell no.

Noah is being bullied because he has a scar, and it sounds like his teacher is refusing to intervene on his behalf.

Knox and I know all too well that people don't like someone who's different. They act as if diversity is going to kill them. They see danger instead of what diversity actually is.

Beauty.

It's cliché to say this, but it's true. If we were all the same, then no one would be unique. We wouldn't have the things we have or be able to live the lives we live without diversity.

This fear will never go away if we don't teach kids that diversity is good.

"I'll think over what you've said and get back to you... Yep...Sure...Have a good evening."

Assuming she's ended the call with that awful teacher, I peek my head around the corner.

Raven leans against the wall with her head tilted toward the ceiling. She releases an exhale and closes her eyes. Her lips begin to tremble, and a single tear falls from the corner of her eye.

I hate seeing her like this. I hate not being able to look in her eyes.

Remedying that, I step out from my hiding spot. "Hey there, Sunshine. Are you okay?"

Her head snaps in my direction, and she pushes off the wall. She sniffles and wipes the wet streak on her face. "I'm fine."

"Is there anything I can help with?"

She straightens her shoulders, clinging to her pride. "I have it handled. Thanks." Raven avoids my reply by leaving the hall as fast as she can.

I spin, following her path with my eyes, and watch as she and Knox bump into each other.

"Whoa, hey. Sorry. I didn't see you there." Knox places his hands on Raven's shoulders.

"No problem." Raven ducks under Knox's arms, slipping out of his way, and returns to the bar.

Knox looks at me while running his hand through his hair. "What happened?"

My arms cross in front of my chest. "We need to talk."

CHAPTER FOURTEEN

KNOX

Sometimes Griffin's ideas are one can short of a six pack. And to be fair, mine can be the same way. But I have to admit, this one has some merit.

Waiting by the pool tables, I pretend to straighten things even though it's already tidy over here.

Griffin walks behind the bar, switching Raven's focus from wiping down the counter to him. "Hey, Raven! Could you come with me, please? I need some help in the kitchen."

"Sure thing, boss man," she returns and follows him.

I march right for the shelf under the bar where I know she stores her purse. Benny watches as I bend down but ultimately ignores me for whatever is on the TV.

God, please don't strike me down for doing this.

I've never gone through a woman's purse, and I know it's a major do-not. But sometimes you gotta do what you gotta do.

Keeping my eyes averted, I dig around and pause when I feel jagged metal. I pull her keys out but cannot figure out which one is the one I'm looking for.

Why does one person need more than two keys?

"She's gonna figure it out," Benny comments.

I continue to flip through all the keys, searching for an indication that tells me I've found it. "This doesn't concern you."

Benny sighs and mutters, "Kids these days."

The kitchen door cracks open but doesn't open further. I freeze, waiting to see who it is.

"Should I check the storeroom?" I hear Raven shout from the doorway.

Fuck it. I'll just take the whole thing.

With swift movement, I shove the keys in my pocket and stride to the cracked door. My hand grasps the edge, pulling it back to reveal my presence. "Need help with something, Darlin'?"

Raven's gaze is over her shoulder, but when I speak up, her attention snaps to me and she jumps back. With a hand on her chest, she says, "Good God! You can't sneak up on people like that."

"I didn't sneak. Did I sneak?" I direct my question at Griffin with a smirk.

Griffin returns my expression and crosses his arms. "Not at all."

Raven scoffs. "You two are the worst. Double the trouble."

Double a lot of things.

Something inside my rib cage yearns for me to reach out and touch her. I need a connection. Any connection. As long as it's her.

But I don't reach for her. I can't. Not yet.

Holding myself back is one of the hardest things I've ever done.

I clear my throat. "Did you need help with something?"

Griffin chimes in, "No, we're good. Do you need help?" His question has a meaning Raven doesn't understand.

"Nope. Just heading out to the locksmith."

Raven, out of the loop, scrunches her face and ping pongs her focus between Griffin and me.

"I'll be right back." I don't give her the chance to ask questions and head for my bike.

"WHY ARE WE DOING THIS AGAIN?" I QUESTION AS I APPLY WD-40 to the hinges.

Griffin's head and arms are under the kitchen sink, so his response is dampened. "Because she needs the help and is either too prideful or too untrusting to accept it."

After I got a copy of each of her keys from the locksmith, Griffin made an excuse to leave The Wandering Raven and met me here with our toolbox in hand. It took us a minute to figure out which key was the right one, but once we were in, we got to work.

We already secured the laundry connections, which were loose. Then Griffin went for the kitchen sink to fix the drip, and I headed for the door. This front door would scare the boogeyman with the noise it makes, hence the WD-40.

I finish up with my task and turn for the kitchen. "Do you think she'll notice?"

Her house is a smaller replica of ours, minus one bathroom. She has decorated the first floor with scattered accents of violet, such as the throw pillows on the couch and the curtains on the windows. However, it's missing photos. Not a single personal photo in sight.

"Done," Griffin claims and slides out. "Anything else we should do?"

"I think we got it all."

Griffin raises his brow. "Same time next week?"

"Same time next week," I confirm.

CHAPTER FIFTEEN

RAVEN

Wiping down a recently vacated table, I sigh through my nose. Lunch at The Wandering Raven isn't nearly as busy as it is at night, but still busy, nonetheless.

I told Kat about my car troubles to let her know I wouldn't need her to watch Noah for my shift. She insisted I use her car and wouldn't take no for an answer. When I got here before opening, Griffin's lips pinched together in a hard line, then he poked his head outside, scanning the parking lot. He came back inside, satisfied, and we got right to work.

Blinking away my puzzlement, I take the tub of dirty dishes to Camden in the kitchen, then return to the bar. Knox and I are the dynamic duo running the place today. I didn't ask what Griffin is up to. I didn't want to seem eager or clingy.

It was just a kiss. I need to calm down.

As I'm refilling Benny's glass, I let the question slip. "Why do they go out in the front sometimes?"

"Why don't you ask them?" Benny grumbles.

I slide the glass on the counter in front of Benny, but

when he reaches for it, I slide it away. His glare might make lesser women shiver, but Benny's the kind of person who projects a hard exterior. I've faced real evil, and Benny isn't it.

My brow raises. I know he knows what I want.

Benny rolls his eyes and spills the beans. "They have a barn down the dirt road that leads away from the parking lot."

"What do they do there?"

Benny doesn't answer me. He stands, grabbing his drink out of my hand.

As Benny drops back onto his stool, three women walk in through the front door, letting in too much light. I thought I would get used to that when customers arrive, but I don't think that day will ever come.

When my eyes finally adjust, I notice the women have taken the table I just cleaned. A shot of annoyance makes my eye twitch. It doesn't help that these women look like fucking Karens. They each wear their hair styled to perfection. Their clothes look like they've been freshly dry cleaned and pressed, and their makeup looks pristine. They pretend to read the menus that we leave on the table, but their eyes wander the room. The one with bright blonde hair spots Knox as he exits the kitchen, and her eyes flare with interest.

My eyes roll as the blonde pulls on the front of her shirt, exposing more of her cleavage. She sees my annoyance and smirks.

"Hey, Knox!" she calls to him. When he makes eye contact, she bats her lashes and continues, "We're ready to order."

Knox doesn't show an inkling of emotion.

Is this the type of woman he prefers? Skinny and manipulative?

I look down at myself, observing how the width of my hips is bigger than hers. I know men want me. Many have paid for access to my body. But would a man as caring and protective as Knox want me?

Instead of answering the customer, Knox turns his head to me. "Raven! Table four needs your help."

Table four? I know for a fact they don't have a numbering system for the tables.

Brushing off my confusion, I grab my pad of paper and a pen, then switch into waitress mode. "Hi, ladies! Thanks for coming in. What can I get for you?" My smile is fake, my tone is fake, and my welcoming attitude is fake as well.

Knox isn't mine by any means. I didn't leave New York just to come here and dive into a serious, committed relationship, and that's assuming Knox is even interested in me that way. Then throw Griffin into the mix, and shit gets all sorts of confusing. But all of that aside, I don't have to like watching women flirt with them.

The blonde sneers at me. "We'll wait for Knox." She's clearly the ringleader of this trio.

Fake smile still in place, I attempt to kill them with kindness, and if they die, then I'll consider it bonus points. "Knox is busy at the moment. I'm more than happy to take your order."

The blonde looks me up and down, and her friends follow suit. I don't know what they're looking for. I'm wearing my normal work attire. Cut-off denim shorts, a tank top, and tennis shoes. I know their stares are meant to make me shake in my boots, so to speak. But I've faced scarier people than them. It'll take a lot more than the judging eyes of a few pathetic women to make me flinch.

My eyes search out each of their left hands.

One…two…three wedding rings.

"I know you're new here, honey, so I'll let you in on a secret. You're not woman enough for him. Either of them, really. You're how old? Eighteen?" She adds a half-smile.

My eyes widen. "Twenty-five."

"Still too young. He needs a woman more…" She tilts her head side to side as she gives me another once over. "*Experienced.*"

The muscles along my jaw clench. Placing my hand on the table, I lean into their huddle of three, so it looks like we're sharing a secret. "No offence, *honey*, but desperation doesn't look good on you."

The two other women gasp, and I swear I hear a chuckle turn into a cough somewhere behind me.

The blonde's eyes sharpen, and her mouth grows tight.

I don't wait for her comeback as I spin on my heel and head straight for the kitchen.

"Ughhh," I growl at no one in particular.

Camden snorts as he assembles the burger in front of him on a plate. "I take it you met The Vultures?"

"The who?" Camden's question snaps me out of it, and I snigger.

"That's what I call them. Kaitlyn, Nicole, and Heather. They've lived here their whole lives, as well as their parents, grandparents, and so on."

"Ahh. I see." I know the type. Walter and Georgia were the type as well. They think that since they have old money, a recognizable last name, and a fake body, they can do whatever they want and say whatever they want. There usually aren't consequences for people like them.

"Yeah," Camden says with a sad smile. "They come almost every day for lunch, and flirt with Knox and Griffin."

"Good to know," I comment.

I turn back to the door and sigh. Flipping back around, I inform Camden, "I didn't get their orders, and I don't think I can go back out there and ask."

Camden laughs at my situation. "I got you, girl. They order the same thing every time."

I place my hands together in front of me like I'm praying. "Thank you, thank you, thank you! Any chance I can hide in here until their food is done?"

"Oof. You could, but Knox will probably come looking and drag you out himself."

My heartbeat picks up at the thought of Knox putting his hands on me.

A tempting thought.

Sighing again, I admit, "You're right. And that's not a good way to impress the boss." I give Camden a mock salute and push myself out the door.

Kaitlyn and her group don't notice my entry, and I spot the three drinks in front of them. A grain of guilt pokes at me, realizing that Knox served them when he had asked me to take care of it.

Knox is filling a few glasses with beer behind the bar, and I head straight for him.

"Hey. Sorry about—"

Knox snags my upper arm and hauls me into the stockroom.

"Let go of me," I protest as I shove his shoulder, but he shows no sign of registering my objection.

He ignores me and slams the door behind us.

"Seriously, Knox. What the hell?" I throw my hands up in frustration. I know I wanted his hands on my body, but I was picturing something very different.

Knox doesn't respond to my outburst. I back up into the shelves when I notice his wild eyes and flared nostrils. His chest is puffed up, and his breathing is rapid. He looks like a bull ready to charge.

"Knox?" My voice sounds small.

His hands clench and unclench at his sides. His gaze starts at my feet and travels up my long legs. He lingers for a moment at the junction of my thighs, causing me to squeeze them together. The resulting groan from his throat is long and primal. I feel it reverberate in my core.

Knox's eyes continue their path up my stomach and across my breasts. Now I'm panting with him. I want him to repeat the journey with his hands, his tongue.

I can feel the lust rolling off of him, and it fuels my own. But I can also feel his hesitation. I should heed the nagging thought at the back of my mind that this would be a bad idea. Potentially catastrophic.

But I want to know what it would feel like when my need is so strong that I can't think of anything else but the pleasure we give each other.

Curiosity wins as I open my hand and offer it to him. He looks down at it and back at me. He raises a brow, and I know I've made the right choice. He's asking for my consent. I offered it, and he still asked. That's all the confirmation I need.

I give him a single nod, and he explodes.

Knox closes the small distance between us. The force of his momentum pushes me further into the shelves at my back, and his chest collides with mine. He grips my ponytail with one hand and my hip with the other. He tugs on my hair, forcing me to crane my neck, and he dips his head. I rise onto my toes, eagerly meeting his lips, but his hold on my hair doesn't let up. I revel in the pull as I loop my arms around his neck.

He doesn't waste time as he nips at my lips, encouraging me to open my mouth. The first swipe of his tongue and I'm a goner. I can only imagine what his tongue would feel like shoving into my pussy. My panties flood with arousal as we continue to taste each other.

Needing me closer, Knox bends down, picking me up by the back of my thighs, and lifting me so my center is perfectly aligned with his hard length.

Hot damn. He's huge.

My legs instantly wrap around his waist. He groans into my mouth as my fingers dive into his shoulder-length waves and my nails scrape the back of his head.

I roll my hips, grinding up and down his thick cock and applying the right amount of pressure to my clit. It's my turn to moan into his mouth, and he greedily swallows it down.

He moves his hips with mine and breaks our kiss, placing his mouth right next to my ear. "You're gonna have to be quiet for me, Darlin'. I don't want to have to rip Benny's ears out because he heard your sweet sounds," Knox growls.

Double hot damn. He's got a dirty mouth, and he's an expert at using it.

"I can try," I assent breathlessly.

His hips keep the same rhythm, driving me higher and higher as he replies, "Baby, I don't think you understand. *No one* gets to hear you. Not a single goddamn soul. Your moans, your sighs of pleasure, are *mine*."

On his last word, he tilts his head and sinks his teeth into my neck. I open my mouth to sigh in pleasure, but he lifts his hand and covers my parted lips, effectively trapping the sound.

"Mine," Knox growls before he attacks my mouth again with his. Our tongues move against each other, and he nips at my lower lip, sending a small jolt of pain through me. But it's pain that I welcome, and it spurs me on.

He kisses his way down the front of my throat, sucking and nipping at my skin as he goes. When he gets to the top of my breasts, he sucks and nips some more. He pulls the front of my top down, snagging the cups of my bra with one hand, and my tits slip free. He grunts. "Fuck, you're perfect." Then he lifts one and he sucks my stiff peak into his mouth. Hard.

This time, I hold in my cry of pleasure, biting my lip. I

run my fingers through his hair more as I bask in the way he praises my body.

I slide a hand down his chest and taut abs, letting the feel of his firm muscles urge me further. When I finally run my hand over the front of his jeans, I rub up and down on his cock. He grabs my wandering hand and brings it above my head, trapping it there.

"You keep touching me like that, Darlin' and I'm gonna come in my pants like a damn teen, and I'm too old for that shit."

Shit shit shit. The thought of that happening makes me even hotter.

With my head thrown back, I hear the springs of the doorknob as it turns. My body stiffens, and I pull at Knox's shirt to get his attention.

Knox feels the shift in my body and stops immediately, lifting his head from my chest. "What's—"

The door opens, and a body steps into the cramped space, shutting the door behind them. "Well, well, well. This is not what I expected to find. Not at all."

Shit on a cracker. This isn't good.

CHAPTER SIXTEEN

KNOX

Of all the cockblocks in the world...

When I heard what Raven said to Kaitlyn and her miserable minions, I wanted to fall to my knees before her. There have been plenty of people to stand up for Griffin and me over the years, and I stopped looking for that protection when I was sixteen. But hearing the fierceness in her voice, the grit—it was more than enough to make sixteen-year-old Knox feel safe. I didn't think that wound needed healing, but I was wrong.

Then she walked right up to me, and I couldn't keep it together. I needed to touch her, taste her. I still tried to hold back, but she offered herself to me, and I wasn't going to pass up that opportunity.

The first swipe of her tongue, and I was done for. The feel of her under my hands was better than I imagined it would be. Not a single fantasy lives up to the real deal.

Enter Griffin...

I keep Raven's exposed tits covered with my chest and release my hold on her legs. She drops them and slowly slides down my body. I hold in a final groan as her delectable pussy rubs over my desperate dick. She goes to tuck her breasts back into her bra, but I knock her hands out of the way and do it myself. It's an excuse to get my hands on her one more time, and she lets me.

Tucking away each beautiful globe, I do my best to remember Raven just like this. Flushed cheeks, swollen lips, and messy hair. It's a sight that makes me want to let the caveman out again and pound my chest in triumph.

Swiping my thumb across her plump lip, I instruct, "Try to keep customer insults to a minimum. Yeah?"

A sassy smile curves her lips. "I make no promises."

Unwilling to lose our contact, I don't move as she shimmies her body around mine. Griffin opens the door for her and gives her a wink as she exits. He shuts the door once more and turns to me.

"Hypocrite much?" he accuses while blinking in disbelief.

"It's not like I planned this." I rub the back of my neck and sigh, tilting my head to stare at the ceiling.

Griffin pummels me further with his comments. "Clearly. In the liquor closet? Seriously, man?"

I right my head and give him a deadpan glare. "If I'm a hypocrite, what does that make you? You kissed her, too."

He shrugs a shoulder, unconcerned. "A rule breaker. Duh." He scoffs. "And I'm not your damn dog. You can't just snap and expect me to do whatever you want."

"You're right. You're not. A dog would be easier."

He crosses his arms and glares back. "Woof."

After a minute of silence, he drops his arms and exhales loudly. "Did you hit your head or something? You're not usually like this."

Rubbing the space between my eyes, I face the truth of his words. "I know. She just…brings out a different side of me. I can't seem to get her out of my head."

"I know the feeling."

"I know you're attracted to her too," I point out.

He doesn't deny it and chooses to deflect instead. "I should've called dibs," he pouts.

I won't let him off easily. "Don't do that. We can talk about this."

"We don't need to." His jaw clenches.

Griffin isn't comfortable with talking about his feelings. It's like pulling teeth, but that won't stop me from pushing.

"Yes, we do." I take a step closer and place a hand on his shoulder. "We've done this before."

"You mean…" His brows furrow.

"Yep," I answer definitively.

"But would she…"

"That's up to her to decide."

"But she has a…"

"I know. You told me that last night."

He keeps his forehead scrunched as he thinks it through. "Fuck it. Why not? What's the worst that could happen?"

I shrug my shoulders. "She could freak the fuck out, quit her job here, and file a harassment report with the police."

"Your optimism is inspiring."

Fuck optimism.

Raven is ours.

CHAPTER SEVENTEEN

RAVEN

That did not happen. Nope. Not at all.

Did I kiss my boss?

Yes.

Did I expect his brother, whom I kissed yesterday on my front porch, to walk in?

Absolutely fucking not.

Do I regret it?

Jury's still out on that one.

Enjoying my time in Mystic River has not been a priority, and it should stay that way. Distractions are just that. Distracting.

I busy myself, wiping down the counter while I gain my composure. That kiss, if it could even be called that, was something else. I've never experienced that kind of raw lust. My panties are uncomfortably wet, and the more I think about what happened in the stockroom, the wetter I'll get. If I can avoid the discomfort of wet panties for the rest of my shift, that would be great.

Scanning the tables, I check to see if anyone needs help. Everyone seems content for now, and thankfully, Mrs. Queen Bee and her posse have vacated the bar and left cash on their table to cover their bill.

Benny is dutifully on his stool, staring at the TV behind me. I look over my shoulder and find the reporter Sherry Jenkins on the screen. Something about her aggravates me, but I can't tell what it is. She sits poised behind a table in her finely pressed navy-blue suit. Her blonde bob frames her face in a way that's flattering, but I can't help but notice how even as she looks at the camera head-on, it's almost like her nose is turned up at the audience.

I snatch the remote and turn up the volume.

"Another woman was found dead in her apartment this morning in Chelsea. Authorities are unwilling to comment at this time on what has been found on scene…"

Don't say Dahlia. Don't say Dahlia.

"But sources say the state in which Lena Hill's body was found is eerily similar to murders that occurred over a decade ago. John Bartlett, also known as the serial killer John the Baptist, is currently serving life in prison without the possibility of parole."

Thank God.

"With the discovery of this body, we have to ask ourselves, 'Is this the work of a copycat? Or did the police arrest and convict the wrong man?'"

Me: What's this I'm seeing about a John the Baptist copycat?

Dahlia: Don't worry, Mom. I'm being safe.

Me: I'm serious. The original went after prostitutes.

Dahlia: I'm not a prostitute.

Me: I know that, but who knows if a serial killer will care?

Dahlia: I promise I'll be safe and lock my door at night.

Me: You're not locking your door at night?!

Dahlia: Kidding! Like Declan would ever let me leave my door unlocked at any time.

Me: Does that mean he's been sleeping over?

Dahlia: New subject. How's the double dick going?

Me: Nice try, but I got the hint. I'll talk to you later. Love you, babe. Please be safe.

Dahlia: I will. Love you too.

That woman is going to put me in an early grave just from worrying about her.

The channel changes to sports analysts debating football plays and who is the better quarterback. I turn to find Benny setting the remote down on the wood between us.

I give him a questioning look, to which he answers, "Got tired of hearing that shit." Then he goes back to nursing his drink.

Odd how he always seems to be drinking but never actually shows signs of being drunk...

Spotting a few empty glasses, I make my rounds refilling

drinks and closing out checks. I'm resetting the balls on one of the pool tables when Griffin and Knox finally come out of the stockroom. Their eyes immediately find me, and I freeze. One set of forest greens; the other set golden brown. Each filled with a heat that causes a stirring in my stomach.

If I thought I was drenched before, I was so wrong.

My motto is to expect the worst and hope for the best. I expected them to yell or throw a couple of punches, and I hoped they would shake hands and call it good. Whatever they discussed in there, it didn't dampen the heat in their eyes. If anything, they look more determined.

My gulp is audible, and I squeeze my legs together, drawing their attention to the apex of my thighs.

Our moment is broken when Camden exits the kitchen with a tray full of food. Griffin takes a direct route to the kitchen while Knox strides right by me for his office. With both of them gone and the lunch rush over, I return to my safe space behind the bar.

Benny lifts his glass to his lips, pausing before taking a drink. "You're in deep shit."

A sigh mixed with a laugh escapes me. "And don't I know it."

I'm learning quickly that when The Wandering Raven is busy, it's *busy*. But when it's slow, it's dead.

When everything slowed down, Griffin disappeared down the hall behind Knox. Benny asked for a refill one time, then I got everything ready for the nighttime rush. But now, it's crickets.

When I took this job, I was hoping I'd be able to get

insider information from some of the locals. I'm well aware of how loose-lipped drunk people can be. Benny clearly isn't drunk, but he'll have to do.

Bending to rest my elbows on the bartop, I sigh. "Tell me something about yourself, Benny."

He raises a brow.

Letting out another sigh, I shrug my shoulders. "I'm bored."

Benny lifts one shoulder, brushing me off and returning his attention to the TV.

"Is your real name Benny? Or is that a nickname?"

The crickets have formed a damn choir.

"What is there to do around here?"

Benny crosses his arms and places them on the bar, leaning only a couple of inches toward me. "Why don't you just tell me what you're fishing for so I can finish watching the debate on whether or not Tom Brady is a better quarterback than Brett Favre."

One side of my mouth lifts. "What makes you think I'm fishing?"

He scoffs. "Oh, please. You've practically got your bait on the hook and are miserably waiting for a bite."

"I don't even know what you just said." My nose wrinkles.

His look turns deadpan. "I wasn't born yesterday, Raven."

Our gazes fix intently on each other, assessing.

I'm about ready to cave when the front door flies open and bounces off the wall with a bang. The sound sends a jolt to my entire being. I have to physically stop myself from diving onto the floor. Benny just sat up straighter, and his hand disappeared under the bartop like he was grabbing something.

A whistle of appreciation comes from the doorway as the sunshine is cut off and we are once again swathed in a dusk-like glow. Two men are strolling toward me. The same two men I met at Mystic Beans.

The one with the world tattoo on his throat speaks up first. "There you are, sweetheart. I was starting to think you were avoiding us." His teasing tone is in juxtaposition with his powerful walk. A man like this doesn't doubt himself. He makes hard choices and sticks with them.

Finally. An asshole I can deal with.

"To avoid you, I'd have to care where you are first." I rest a hand on my hip and pop the other out.

His hands come together and cover the left side of his chest. "Straight through the heart. Give a man a break."

"What do you want, Atlas?" Benny snaps.

The other man stands slightly behind Atlas. He's just as big and scary-looking as Atlas, but he lacks the jocular air that Atlas throws out like free candy.

Atlas lifts his hand, and hot damn, even his fingers are tattooed. I finally notice the duffle bag. "Delivery. Bas and I wanted to bring it personally."

My eyes bounce from the bag to Benny's hidden hand to the bulges at the other men's hips and back to the bag.

Shit.

"You just wanted an excuse to harass Kat," Benny accuses.

"What we do could hardly be categorized as harassment."

"I'm sure Kat would beg to differ," Benny shoots back.

Atlas's smile turns fierce. "Kat will beg, alright."

"Ugh! My ears!" I interrupt and make a gagging sound, easily breaking the tension.

Atlas crosses his arms. "I didn't take you for a prude, sweetheart."

Raising a brow, I respond, "Hardly. But the talk of sex in relation to you? Ew. No."

"Aw, come on. We could have some fun together."

I open my mouth to refute his claim, but a shout cuts me off. "The fuck you will!" Heavy footsteps pound across the bar. A peek over my shoulder shows me Griffin and Knox with thunderous looks on their faces and aiming them right at Atlas and Bas.

"What the fuck are you doing here?" Knox spits out at them.

Atlas lifts the bag again. "You asked us to."

Griffin narrows his gaze. "Where's Hermes?"

"Busy," Bas answers, speaking for the first time. His voice is gravelly and warm.

Griffin and Knox keep untrusting looks on their faces, but Knox's leans more toward rage.

"In the office," Griffin directs and turns on his heel, expecting to be followed. Knox steps aside and waits until Atlas and Bas have passed him to trail behind.

Not once do they glance my way. Not once do they seem worried about me. I'm not sure if I should take their lack of concern as a compliment or an insult. Maybe they think I'm capable of taking care of myself, or maybe they knew Benny had it handled.

Once they've disappeared down the hall, Benny relaxes his shoulders a fraction, but not completely. Both hands come back to the bartop, and he resumes watching the TV.

I open my mouth, but Benny interjects, "Not now."

Rolling my eyes, I decide to join Benny in watching the boring-as-hell show.

That was hardly the first drug deal I've witnessed, and clearly, it's not going to be the last either.

I shouldn't ask questions because I don't need anyone asking questions about me either. But I can't stop curiosity from trapping me in her tangled web.

Jumping up from my relaxed position, I announce, "I'm going to see if there's anything to snack on in the kitchen."

Benny grunts, his eyes never straying from the screen.

On light feet, I walk to the kitchen door but turn and head for the back hall at the last minute. Fingers crossed Benny doesn't notice. But when I step into the shadows of the poorly lit hallway, I swear I hear Benny let out a sigh.

Gliding my back against the wall, I tiptoe to the office door. Hostile voices fall from the room along with a single stream of light. The door is open barely an inch. When I'm right next to the door, I crouch down and listen intently.

"We weren't due for an order for another week," Griffin says plainly.

"Well, I can't let the good people of Mystic River go without," Atlas jokes.

"Our supply is fine," Knox informs curtly.

There's a small creak, like someone took a step or leaned in a chair. "Have you been buying from another supplier?" And that's the second time I hear Bas's voice. I take it he's not a talker.

Griffin's voice is adamant. "Absolutely not. Our word is as good as gold. We told you that you would be our exclusive source, and we've stuck to that."

"Then what seems to be the problem?" Atlas asks.

"We've run into some…competition."

"What kind of competition? Our bud is top of the line. You shouldn't have any competition." Atlas sounds slightly insulted but mostly annoyed.

So, Griffin and Knox buy weed and sell it.

Thank God.

I was worried it was something like fentanyl.

Griffin sighs. "A new player is offering a different product, and it's getting people hooked quick and bad. Once a customer goes to the new dealer, they don't come back to us."

Now that guy is the one with shit like fentanyl.

"I see," Atlas grumbles.

"We're working on it," Griffin assures him.

Atlas offers, "Let me know if you need help dealing with it."

There's a scraping of chairs, and I take that as my cue to leave.

CHAPTER EIGHTEEN

GRIFFIN

Sneaky little minx.

Raven thinks she blended in with the shadows, but you can't hide something as precious as her. I almost didn't see her, but I know every nook and cranny of this place. I could walk around blindfolded perfectly fine. So, when a shadow barely a shade darker than the hallway moved by the door, I knew it was her. Knox saw it too.

When Knox and I got a text from Benny, telling us that Atlas and Bas, the president and vice president of the Ferrymen, were here with a delivery, we dropped everything immediately and came running. I don't care if Raven knows about our real business. She was going to find out eventually. And if she can't handle it…well, that's too damn bad because I wouldn't let her leave if she tried.

I don't care what she overhears. She's stuck with us.

Raven can fight it all she wants, but we're inevitable.

But her covert tricks are going to earn her a spanking—or ten. Just picturing her ass in the air and red from my hand has me getting hard. Now all I want is to bring her in here, bend her over the desk, and make her scream.

The scraping of chairs on the wood floor erases my fantasy.

"Actually..." Knox stops Atlas and Bas before they can leave our office. We exchange a look, communicating an idea. He opens a drawer of our desk and pulls out one of the confiscated bags, handing it over to Atlas. "Here. We haven't been able to find out much about these. Every dealer we find is too afraid to talk to us."

"We can make them talk," Atlas offers.

"They're not exactly *around* anymore," I admit.

Atlas smirks. "Ahh. I see. Well, we'll hand these over to Einstein. If anyone can figure out what these are, it's him."

I nod, accepting their help, and watch them leave.

"Do you think they'll be able to get us answers?" Knox nudges me with his elbow.

"What other choice do we have? The only information we've gotten so far is that the head honcho is someone they call 'The Alienist,' which isn't much to go on." I rub my eyes, tired of this whole thing. It's like we're trying to complete a puzzle, but half of the pieces are missing.

"Should we wait for the Ferrymen before we make our next move?"

Shoving my hands into my pockets, my face goes hard. "Absolutely not."

"Then should we——"

"Yep," I interrupt.

"What about Raven? She heard the whole thing."

I smirk. "She'll have to deal with it."

Raven's changing everything. She's already brought Knox out of his shell. I'm used to making sure he doesn't get hurt or get himself into trouble. And I try to get him to loosen up every now and then, so he doesn't forget to have fun.

But Raven does both for Knox without even trying. When Raven saw how Kaitlyn and her two stooges act toward us, she didn't hold back. And Raven makes him smile. I haven't seen Knox like this…ever.

So, where does that leave me?

Raven has done more than just mix things up. She's brought a peace to our lives that we haven't known in so long.

Yeah, she's hiding something, but who isn't?

Raven's secrets won't get rid of us, and I won't let ours drive her away either. She can try to push us away, but it won't work. She's already cemented herself in our lives. Losing her would be like losing a piece of my soul.

She doesn't get to leave.

CHAPTER NINETEEN

RAVEN

Setting the last bag of trash by the back door, I sag against the wall. I knew this job would be a lot, but oh my, do the people of Mystic River sure know how to party. There wasn't a single dull moment tonight. Camden finished up in the kitchen an hour ago and went home, which apparently isn't far.

Must be nice.

An exhausted groan makes its way through my limbs and out of my mouth. My phone vibrates in my back pocket, and I pull it out.

Dahlia: How's it going working for two hunks of man meat?

Shaking my head, I laugh to myself. I shouldn't have told her about Griffin and Knox the other day.

Me: Just fine and dandy.

Dahlia: By "fine and dandy," do you mean you get to admire up close just how fiiiiiine their dandies are?

Me: What kind of euphemism is that? What does that even mean?

Dahlia: Don't gatekeep. You know exactly what I mean. Dandy. Dick. Cock. Schlong.

Dahlia: Wait…did you get double-dandied?

Me: Now you're just saying words.

Dahlia: Don't play dumb.

I sigh through my nose and allow myself to admit the fears that have been circling my mind.

Me: They're different. I don't know what to do with that. An asshole, I can handle. Sexy, protective men with a sweet side? This is new territory, and they have secrets.

Dahlia: Hey, I know what we lived through was shit, and it's warped how we view men in general. But I promise you, they're not all bad. There are good ones who will wrap you in their arms, and suddenly the world won't seem so bad.

Me: Is that how Declan makes you feel?

Dahlia: …

Me: You don't have to answer that.

Dahlia: Yeah. He does.

She's right. They're not all bad, and I'm learning that firsthand.

Looking back at the bags of trash, I force myself to pick them up to toss in the dumpster. I shouldn't have asked to work a double today. But after my...*rendezvous* with Knox in the closet, I needed to work off the tension in my body, and Kat was more than happy to hang out with Noah a bit longer. And I can't even touch what happened with Griffin on my doorstep yesterday.

Not to mention, my panties were uncomfortable as fuck all day today. I should've gone home during my break and changed them, but part of me wanted the reminder of how hot it got between Knox and me.

Griffin appears at my side out of nowhere, causing me to jump and drop the trash.

"Jesus Christ! I'm gonna put a bell around your neck!"

He smirks. "Does it come with a collar?"

My jaw becomes unhinged.

Did he just imply he'd wear a collar for me? Sexually? Sans clothing? What am I supposed to say to that?

Griffin keeps his smirk perfectly in place and says, "Don't worry about those. I'll take care of them."

"Are you sure? We finished up everything else in there." We silently worked in tandem, sweeping and mopping the floors, cleaning up the bar, wiping down the tables, putting all the billiards back in order, and restocking the bar.

"Yeah, I got this." He hits me with a wink, effectively incinerating my panties.

I'm going to have to start a stockpile if I'm going to spend much more time around these Montgomery men, and seeing as how I work for them...

I'm fucked.

Blowing a breath through loose lips, I hang my head. I'm tapping into my energy reserves and bleeding them dry. I've had it worse several times before. This is nothing. But God, I'd give just about anything to be magically transported to my bed right about now.

"If you're sure, then I'm going to head out." My sneakers slap against the tile as I put one foot in front of the other.

"Hey! And have Benny walk you out to your car," Griffin instructs as he easily loads his thick arms with the bags of trash.

Hot damn. I'm a sucker for a man with big arms.

"Sure thing," I confirm half-heartedly.

"I mean it. Don't be a brat, Sunshine," Griffin emphasizes.

"I said I would, didn't I?" I reply with an ounce of sass.

When I step through the kitchen door, I notice right away that Benny is no longer in sight.

It's fine. This is the twenty-first century. I can walk myself to my damn car. I'm an independent woman. A *tired* independent woman, but independent, nonetheless.

I snag my purse from where I left it behind the bar and trudge across the hardwood and out into the open air. The temperature hasn't dropped much since night took away the sun, but the sky is blanketed in bright stars. I let the heat fill my lungs as I revel in the clarity in the air. I missed this about Texas.

A few steps into the gravel parking lot, and all the oxygen is stolen from my lungs. I pause, frozen in place. A cold sweat coats my skin, and every part of my body begins to shake.

A small figure waits for me by my car. He's what I imagine my son will look like in a few years, except he's missing the scar, and his eyes are an exact copy of my own. I hold in a whimper as he steps into the moonlight.

Noah Kelly.

The crown of his Kingdom Hearts shirt reflects in the moonlight. Noah raises his arm toward me, revealing the belladonna in his hand. He opens his mouth, but no sound comes out. Everything goes quiet, then his young, innocent voice crashes into me.

"I needed you, Raven. You weren't there."

Tears stream down my face, and my lips tremble. "I'm—I'm so sorry," I somehow manage to choke out.

"Why weren't you there?" His head tilts to the side as he asks his question, only it doesn't stop. As his cheek gets closer and closer to his shoulder, blood trickles out from his nose, eyes, and ears.

"You weren't there," his voice cascades over and over, the words never ending.

"No!" I shout as his head continues to turn like the hands on a clock.

My legs finally begin to work of their own accord. "No! No! I'm sorry!" My knees slam into the tiny rocks on the ground, slicing into my skin. I reach for his face to correct the contortion, but all I grasp is empty space. He's gone.

It's as if he never existed. As if he never lived. As if he never loved.

My voice is hollow. "No, no, no, no, no. Please. I'll make it right. I tried to make it right."

"Raven! Raven!"

I failed. I didn't protect him like I promised I would. I thought I had made it right. I need to make it right.

"Raven, Darlin'. Look at me. What happened?"

A small sniffle and the aroma of vetiver enters my system. "Knox?"

I finally register his hands cradling my face. Blinking the tears obscuring my vision, Knox's face comes into view. His brows are deeply furrowed.

Another sniffle. Bergamot and sea salt.

"Griffin?"

"I'm right here, Sunshine."

Arms envelop my upper body, and I realize I'm sitting on someone's lap.

"Baby, what happened?" Knox asks again.

How do I answer that? I'm not even sure of what happened. But I know why. I know what I need to do.

Shaking my head to clear the fog, I move to stand back up, but Griffin just tightens his hold. "Absolutely not. You're staying right here until we make sure that you're okay."

"I'm fine," I insist.

"I would beg to differ," Knox argues and makes a pointed look at my knees. A quick glance down, and I find blood dripping down my legs.

Whoops.

"Let's get her back inside and make sure she doesn't need to go to the hospital," Knox directs.

"No!" I refuse a bit more firmly than the situation warrants. "I mean, no. No hospitals, please. I'll be fine."

They both give a look of suspicion.

Knox narrows his eyes slightly. "We'll see." It's neither a yes nor a no, but I'll take it.

Griffin adjusts me in his arms and smoothly rises to his feet.

I startle at the way he does it so effortlessly. "Whoa, hey! I can walk."

"I told you before, Raven. Don't be a brat," he growls.

Sweet Baby Jesus. His grumbly demeanor should negate the shiver that zips down my spine and shoots straight for my core. I was practically catatonic not five minutes ago, and all these two have to do is breathe and my pussy is ready to party.

Something is seriously wrong with me.

CHAPTER TWENTY

KNOX

I don't know what the hell just happened. One minute, I'm ordering more inventory, and the next, I'm running outside with Griffin. Raven's scream had the hair on my arms standing on end. I'll never forget it as long as I live.

"This is ridiculous," Raven complains.

I've seen Griffin carry many people, and not one of them has ever complained.

"How unfortunate for you," I quip.

The glare Raven shoots my direction does little to intimidate me. It's more adorable than anything else.

Benny holds the door open as we cross the threshold. "Shit," he mutters when he gets a good look at the blood on Raven's legs. "Do I need to call an ambulance?"

"No!" Raven answers immediately.

Griffin's tone is unmistakably serious when he says, "If we need to call an ambulance, we're calling an ambulance."

"No. Hospitals."

Raven said the same thing outside, but it was more of a

plea. Now, it's a command. Her voice is unshakable, the complete opposite of how we found her outside.

The staring contest between Raven and Griffin is tense. But it ends abruptly when Griffin sighs. "Fine."

"Thank you," Raven says with a sassy head nod.

I snag the first aid kit from behind the counter as Griffin sits Raven on the bar. When I go back to the other side to stand in front of her, I grab a stool and sit my ass down.

Scooting forward leaves little room for Raven's long legs. I'm a big guy. It is what it is. But then I realize our position…

Fuck me.

I accidentally moved the stool too far forward, and now I'm literally in between her thighs.

Lifting my head, I catch Raven's gulp and watch the way it makes her slender throat move. Hopefully she swallows like that with a dick in her mouth…

My cock is already hard and ready for her. The zipper of my jeans becomes wildly uncomfortable. I wouldn't be surprised if my dick breaks through. It's practically desperate for her.

I'm desperate for her.

But she's bleeding.

So, I turn my attention away from the tempting view and get to work using wipes and bandages to clean her up.

Griffin plops onto the stool next to me and doesn't miss a beat. "What happened out there, Raven?"

Raven clears her throat. "I saw a rattlesnake."

My head whips in her direction. "Come again?"

"A rattlesnake?" Griffin furrows his brows in disbelief.

"Yep." Raven pops her lips as she answers and doesn't bother to explain more.

"And you screamed bloody murder because…" Griffin leads Raven to give another answer.

"It scared me." She shrugs a shoulder.

"So, you dropped to the ground to…what? Slither on the ground so it would think you're a snake as well?" I question.

She frowns lightly. "Something like that."

Griffin sets his elbow on the bar and tips his body to the side. "Where did you say you were from again?"

"New York," Raven replies a little too quickly.

Griffin and I exchange a look.

"Anywhere before that?" Griffin presses.

"New York," Raven repeats, but slowly this time. Her blasé attitude doesn't seem genuine.

I squint my eyes. "And in New York, they pretend to be snakes to scare them off?"

"Indeed." Raven nods.

"Liar, liar. Pants on fire," Griffin sings like we're back in third grade.

"I'm no such thing, Griffin Montgomery," Raven shoots back as her eyes turn to slits.

I'm not a fan of liars. Never have been. But I get the feeling Raven isn't lying to gain something. This seems more like a lie of necessity.

Raven glances down at me. My hands are resting on her thighs, and I'm still between them.

"Oh, look! You're done. Thanks! I feel all better, Dr. Montgomery." Raven places her hand on my shoulder to guide me backward and give her space. Instead, I stand up and put my hands on her waist, lifting her up off the bar and setting her on her feet on the floor.

"Oh. A doctor and a gentleman," Raven teases.

Griffin scoffs behind me.

"I'll be whatever you need me to be, Darlin'," I tease back with a wink.

An adorable pink hue brightens her cheeks as her eyes widen.

Raven clears her throat again. "Well, this has been fun!

But it's late. See y'all tomorrow!" She snatches her purse and is out the door before we can say bye.

We're left behind like a pair of monkeys scratching their heads. Griffin steps up to my side, and we both continue staring at the door, dumbfounded.

"Did you believe…" I start.

"Nope." Griffin pops his lips like Raven did earlier.

"She said…"

"Y'all." Griffin nods.

"So, New York…"

"A lie," he confirms.

"Are we gonna…"

"Yep," Griffin confirms again.

"Glad to see we're on the same page."

"Always."

My ride home from the bar was short-lived. I need the open road. I need the wind whipping around my body as I breeze down the pavement. I need that reset.

But today was not the day, and tonight is not the night.

Griffin got home about thirty minutes before me. I'm sure he's asleep by now. That man can fall asleep at the drop of a hat, and he sleeps like the dead.

I drop the keys to my bike on the little table as I trudge through the entryway. My boots practically dragging across the plain-tiled floor, and I stomp my way up the stairs to my bedroom. When I walk through the first door on the left, my bedroom, I begin shedding my clothes.

Stripping all the way down to nothing, I fall into bed, groaning. Sometimes, I wonder how much longer I can keep doing these extensive workdays. I've lived a life that hasn't been easy. It's been brutal to my body. So when I lie down in my bed at night, every bone, joint, and muscle cries in relief.

"What a day," I say to myself. And what a day it was indeed.

Raven's soft moans and sighs have been playing in my head on repeat. It's a soundtrack I never want to lose.

The way she rubbed her warm pussy against my length has me itching to make that happen again. But this time, Raven would drop to her knees in front of me, undoing my pants and tonguing each inch of my newly exposed skin. Her tongue is warm and wet, causing all my blood to rush straight to my dick.

"Shit." I rip my sheets off and wrap my hand around my thickening cock. I move my hand up and down, the friction all too perfect as the scene continues to play out in my mind.

Raven would pull down my pants to my lower thighs, allowing my dick to spring free. It would already be hard and dripping. Her tongue would peek out and lick my precum.

My thumb swipes across my slit at the end. I thrust my hips up into my hand, and the moan in my throat echoes around the room.

In my mind, Raven wraps her plump, sweet lips around my shaft and takes more of my length into her mouth as her tongue slides along the underside.

"Shit, shit, shit." My hips pump faster, and my fist squeezes, adding a pinch of pain to my pleasure. The bite pushes me over the edge, and ropes of my release shoot from my cock as I pump harder.

When I come back from the high of pleasure, I look down and take in the large amounts of cum all over my stomach and thighs. Reaching my hand over the side of the bed, I snag the first piece of fabric I can and use it to wipe up my mess.

It's official. Raven Henry is going to be the death of me. Death by fictional blow job.

My phone begins buzzing, but I ignore it, opting for sleep instead. But sleep proves to be elusive after the third time my phone goes off.

"This better be important," I mutter to myself.

Jumping out of bed, I find my jeans on the floor and pull my cell phone from the front pocket. Caller ID says "Unknown." I tap the green button and hold my phone up to my ear.

"Who the hell is this?"

"A concerned third party. Did you read your father's letter?" The voice is deep and almost sounds electronic, as if the person on the other end is using something to disguise their voice.

If they know about the letter, then they probably work for the prison or maybe even the post office, but I'm betting on the prison. "I don't know what you're talking about," I lie easily.

"I know you got it. When you read it, remember that you shouldn't believe everything you're told." The mysterious voice ends the call before I can ask more questions.

Whoever that was, they're not on Amos's side. They want him to stay in prison. But does that mean Amos is telling the truth? Does he really have proof that he's innocent?

I blow out a heavy breath, knowing what I have to do next—wake up Griffin. Never a fun task.

CHAPTER TWENTY-ONE
RAVEN

*R*uby *liquid trickles down the polished wood stairs of our house. My eyes trace its path backward up the winding staircase to find the source.*

"Mom? Dad?" My call echoes down the marble floors, but there's no reply, which isn't out of the ordinary. Mom is probably out shopping, and Dad is probably at the country club.

My foot touches the first step, and a tingle creeps up my neck. I take the second step, and my mouth goes dry. Every bone in my body is begging me to turn around, to run out the front door, and call the police.

But I can't look away.

I need to know.

When I'm halfway up the staircase, a body comes into view. It's upside down with the face buried in the steps. But I don't need to see his face to know who it is.

I know that hair. I know those clothes.

"Noah?"

Little hands, cold on my warm body, wake me with a

start. Opening my eyes, I find Noah, dressed for school with his backpack on and everything.

The dizziness from my sleep accompanies me into day and pushes to transform into nausea. My muscles feel weak. My brain is still exhausted.

I need coffee and something chocolate.

"Mom," Noah says, tapping his foot. "I need you to wake up."

"What time is it?" Blinking, I search my bed and night-stand for my phone.

"It's 7:30."

"Oh sh—crap! Sorry, little king. I didn't hear my alarm go off." I swing my legs out from under the covers and sit up.

I knew working nights would be difficult with having to get up in the morning. But I should have also factored in that my bed is made of clouds that were blessed by God himself. Usually, I get good sleep, with last night being the exception. I'm going to need to do something in order to actually wake up in the morning.

Rubbing my eyes, I let out a larger-than-life yawn. "Let me get some clothes on, and I'll grab you a quick breakfast to eat in the car."

"I already had a Pop Tart."

Dear Pinterest Moms, please don't come for my head. Sometimes, Pop Tarts are just easier.

"Shit," I curse as I check the time again, noting I only have a few minutes to get Noah to school on time. I let myself slide with that one. Desperate times call for profanity. Sue me.

Noah bites his lip, holding back a laugh at my groggy swearing.

"Grab me a Pop Tart. I'm getting up," I instruct Noah.

Two minutes later, I meet Noah downstairs. I forgot to rotate the laundry last night, so all I have is a Mudhouse sweatshirt from New York and my sleep shorts. My bridge troll chic look won't be winning any awards, but it will have to do.

Noah hands me my Pop Tart, and as I'm opening the front door, he asks, "How are you getting me to school?"

I really need to do something about my quality of sleep.

Groaning, I step outside, hoping a solution will appear in my driveway. But what I find is a whole new reason to swear.

"Holy shi—"

Noah covers my mouth with his hand. When he pulls away, he'll probably have drool covering his palm because in my driveway are two men.

Two *shirtless* men.

Specifically, my bosses.

Knox is kneeling on the ground with a lug wrench in hand, tightening bolts on the front passenger tire of my car. Griffin is in the same position but working on the back wheel.

The heat of the morning has them dripping with sweat in a way that's completely pornographic.

Griffin's jeans hang low on his hips, giving me a glimpse of that sexy V-thing I thought was only achievable in Photoshop. I think the phrase "abs of steel" was made for Griffin. I spy black calligraphy on the side of his rib cage, but I can't make out what it says. The waves in his hair look like they were styled at a high-end salon, although I'm positive he wakes up looking like that. The way his arms flex with each turn of the wrench has my core weeping for attention.

Knox's ass is nice and snug in his jeans. I've never stared at a man's ass before, but Texas is proving to bring on a whole slew of new experiences. His torso is like that of a Greek statue. He has all the muscles I didn't know existed. His hair is pulled into a bun, but small pieces of hair at the front have fallen, highlighting the strong lines of his face. Knox's back is covered in ink. The face of a skull with hollow eyes is surrounded by flaming trees. It's a work of art.

My pussy clenches, making my need grow. I didn't think bodies could look like that. Now I know what people mean by "eye candy."

Lord, have mercy on me, please.

Griffin drops the wrench, swiping a rag hanging from his back pocket and wipes the sweat from his face. "I win!"

"It's not a race," Knox grumbles back.

"Yes, it is."

"No, it's not," Knox retorts, setting his own wrench down on the pavement.

Noah drops his hands and gives me a confused look. "Why are you staring, Mom?" His question gets the attention of both Knox and Griffin. My toes curl, and my face turns crimson.

Caught red-handed.

"Uhh…" I'm interrupted before I can come up with an answer.

"Good morning, Sunshine." Griffin beams at me. The mischievous look in Griffin's eyes gives me a picture of what he would do to me right here, right now if we were alone.

"Mornin'," Knox greets with a smirk. A flutter in my chest travels to my core as Knox gives me a once over.

They jump up from the ground and head right for me, snagging their shirts along the way. And thank heavens, they don't put their shirts on.

My brain finally pushes through the drowning thoughts of sex and realizes what they were just doing.

"Knox!" Noah exclaims.

"Hey, Bud," Knox greets back with a single wave.

"He's my friend who taught me how to throw a football," Noah informs me with a smile, pointing at Knox.

"Sure did," Knox confirms with pride. He reads my expression and answers my question before I can voice it. "It was the other day. Noah accidentally threw the football at me, so I showed him the correct way to throw it." He looks from me to Noah. "Have you been practicing?"

"Yes," Noah returns with a smile.

My mouth goes dry as my chest tightens. He…they…I can't put this ache in my chest into words.

I clear my throat, but my voice still cracks with emotion. "Did y'all change my tires?"

"Yep. All four." Griffin is shining with pride.

My eyes blink rapidly. "I only had one flat."

Knox shrugs, but Griffin is more than happy to explain. "That is true, but we wanted to be sure you wouldn't get another flat like the other day."

I swallow the emotion building in my throat. "Let me know how much I owe you for your time and the tires."

"No compensation necessary. We were happy to do it," Knox replies.

My knees grow weak as something inside me begins to right itself.

Is this what it's like to have people in your corner? Is this how it feels when someone does something for you because they want to and not because they expect something in return?

Walter and Georgia didn't have a charitable bone in their bodies. Growing up in their homes taught me that love is conditional. If I did what was expected of me, then I was rewarded. But my little brother didn't understand that. He didn't fit into their mold of what they wanted him to be. Walter wanted a son who didn't show emotion, liked football and golfing, and got good grades. Noah Kelly didn't live up to those expectations. Georgia wanted a daughter who danced ballet, played tennis at the country club, and looked pretty while doing it all. I made myself small. I folded in on myself to fit that rigid idea of who I should be.

After my ballet recitals, Georgia would buy me a Hermès

purse. After I'd defeat our neighbor's daughter in singles tennis matches, Georgia would buy me jewelry from Tiffany's. After I won Miss Teen Texas, Georgia bought me multiple designer dresses.

But my brother didn't get the same treatment.

When Noah failed his math test, he didn't get dinner. When Noah wanted to play video games at home rather than football at school, Walter broke all the electronics in Noah's room. And when Noah cried, Walter used his fists. It's no surprise that Noah became depressed.

But now, I have two men in my life who care and want to help. And I didn't have to do anything to get their help. They give it to me freely.

"Thank you so much," I whisper as tears swim in my eyes.

"Happy to do it," Griffin responds.

"Moooom," Noah whines.

"We're going, we're going," I assure him. "Sorry, I gotta get Noah to school." Grabbing Noah's hand, I step to move around the tempting brothers in front of me, but I'm stopped in my tracks. Literally. Knox steps in my way.

"We can take him," he offers.

"Oh, you don't have to do that." I release an exhausted laugh.

"It's no problem," Griffin insists.

"Ooo! Please, Mom! Please!" Noah jumps up and down, pulling on my arm. "Can we take your motorcycle?" Noah asks Knox.

"That's up to your mama," Knox answers.

I tilt my head. "You have a motorcycle?" I should be more worried about my son riding a motorcycle, but I'm still a bit muddled by the half-naked bodies in front of me.

I think I've found my weakness—the lickable muscles on my boss's bodies.

Knox nods. "Yeah, I park it in our garage."

My focus goes back to Noah. "How do you know he has a motorcycle?"

Noah's ears turn red. "He rode it after he showed me how to throw."

Forcing my mom brain to turn on, I think over letting Knox take Noah to school and pinch the bridge of my nose.

"Pleeeeeeease," Noah begs. He folds his hands together and holds them in front of his face, wearing his best puppy eyes.

I nibble on my lip and turn to Knox, making up my mind. "No speeding."

"Of course."

"He has to wear a helmet," I add.

"That's a given," Knox confirms.

"No weaving around cars."

"Wouldn't think of it," Knox soothes.

Releasing a heavy sigh, I look down at Noah. "Listen to everything Knox says, no talking back, and no asking to stop at Mystic Beans." Kat has gotten Noah hooked on the pastries there. Every time we go, she gives him one for free.

"Thank you!" Noah exclaims with a huge smile on his face and takes off toward Knox's garage.

"I'll keep him safe, Darlin'."

The unease in my gut settles. "Thank you."

Knox takes a step closer, and it's like every nerve in my body is humming. I want no space between us. But my front yard is not the place for the kind of things my body wants.

He gently grips my chin and bends down. His lips grace my cheek. So soft, so tender. He doesn't wait for my reaction. Instead, he turns and strides off after Noah, slipping his shirt on as he goes.

My cheeks flush again when Griffin clears his throat. He

has yet again been privy to an intimate moment between his brother and me. His *twin* brother.

"Go back to bed, Sunshine. There's still time before the library opens. We'll get Noah to school."

Griffin mimics Knox's step forward. But instead of my cheek, his lips touch my forehead, lingering. I close my eyes and allow the peace he gives me to spread through my limbs. The gesture feels intimate. He's not even really kissing me, yet I feel like we need to find a private room. Like this public display of affection would make an old woman clutch her pearls.

"Sweet dreams," he whispers against my forehead. He swiftly steps away, pulling his shirt over his head and stalking to his driveway, where Knox has already fitted Noah with a helmet.

My stomach tangles itself in knots.

It's just for fun. They wouldn't want me if they knew everything. Don't get attached.

Knox starts the engine with a kick and heads down the driveway on his motorcycle at a slow pace with Noah tucked safely in front of him. When they pass, Noah wildly waves goodbye, and I return the sentiment by blowing a kiss to him.

They stop at the stop sign, but don't move forward. I'm about to call out to them and ask if everything is okay, when another engine fires up and Griffin exits their garage.

Of course, they both have bikes.

When Griffin pulls up next to Knox and Noah, Griffin holds out his fist to the side, and Noah meets it with his own, giving Griffin a fist bump. Griffin whoops, and they all take off.

Standing there, dumbfounded, I realize that Noah is going to ask for rides every day for the rest of his life, and if we move, there won't be anyone to do that with him.

CHAPTER TWENTY-TWO

GRIFFIN

All eyes are on us as we pull up to Mystic River Elementary. Knox and I are used to people staring. We've grown immune to the judgment. But Noah fidgets under the pressure of all the watching people.

Coming to a stop side by side, Knox and I kill the engines. Knox helps Noah remove his helmet and guides him off the bike. Knox pulls out a luggage net, securing Noah's helmet to the back of the saddle.

"Thank you for bringing me to school," Noah articulates while looking at his feet. When we rise from the saddles of our motorcycles, Noah's head rears back slightly. "Are you coming to school too?"

Knox and I bend down on one knee in front of Noah. I straighten his backpack on his shoulders as I ask, "Noah, do you know what it means to be brave?"

Noah raises his chin. "It means you don't have nightmares because you're not afraid of anything."

A sad smile curves Knox's mouth. "Kind of. You don't

have to be fearless to be brave. Being brave means you stand up to the things that scare you, even when you feel afraid."

Noah rocks back and forth on his feet. "I'm not brave."

"Yes, you are," Knox refutes.

"No, I'm not," Noah opposes in a low voice, his eyes cast downward.

"Hey." I wait for Noah to look at us again. "You are. I promise you are. And I need you to be brave right now."

Noah's chest expands on an inhale, and he nods as he releases the air from his lungs.

I raise my brows. "I know there's a kid here who hasn't been nice. Could you look around and let me know if you see him?"

His eyes scan the people milling about. Instead of using his voice, Noah points to a kid who is talking to his dad. Knox and I recognize the father right away.

"Thanks, Bud. That was very brave," Knox praises. We stand back up together, and Knox directs Noah. "Let's go inside."

"My mom usually just drops me off here and leaves."

Knox's voice deepens maliciously. "We need to have a little chat with your teacher."

"Mrs. Burke?" Noah blinks repeatedly like he can't believe anyone would want to talk to that grumpy woman, and I don't blame him.

Shrugging, he doesn't ask any more questions and leads us to the doors. We check in with the receptionist, and Noah guides us to his classroom.

I feel like a giant monster amongst all these mini humans. Some scurry away from Knox and me like they're afraid we're going to stomp all over them, and some stop and openly gape at us. And honestly, I'm scared I'm going to accidentally step on one of them.

"It's that one." Noah points to a door at the end of the

hall decorated with cutout paper traffic signs that say things like "learning zone" and "do your best."

As we approach the room, Noah grabs mine and Knox's hands. Knox and I make eye contact over Noah's head. His expression matches my own.

I grip Noah's hand, infusing the connection with all the care my heart can muster. The more I give, the more my chest tightens.

Noah's tenderness is going to break me.

He releases our hands, ducking into the classroom and starting his morning routine. The bell rings as the last of the kids remaining in the hallway scurry into their respective classrooms.

"Excuse me. Can I help you?" A woman in Noah's class-room glowers at us. Her dress makes her look like a Pepto-Bismol bottle. Her hair is only a few inches long yet somehow curled. A pair of delicate reading glasses rests on the tip of her nose. The nametag pinned on her chest tells us her name.

I give her a vicious smile. "Let's have a chat, Mrs. Burke."

"Pull out your reading books. Twenty-minute reading starts now," she instructs the class. Stepping into the hallway with us, she shuts the door and confronts us head on. "Do I know you?" The wrinkles around her beady eyes become more prominent as she glares.

"No, ma'am," I reply.

Mrs. Burke rests her hands on her hips. "You both need to leave."

"You're going to want to hear what we have to say, Dorthea." Knox's voice is cold.

Her shoulders tighten. "How do you know my name?"

My sneer darkens my face. "We know a lot of things. Like what dear Charles does every Sunday night."

"I don't know what you're talking about. My husband

goes to church on Sunday nights." She scoffs to cover her denial.

I lean an inch closer, my height swamping hers. "He's in the hole ten large, Dorthea. How long do you think it'll take to pay up if thirty percent interest is added onto his total?"

It finally clicks in Dorthea's mind who we are. "Knox? Griffin?" Her focus jumps all over, trying to merge the image she has of us from when we were students in her classroom. Her lip curls. "You two were always more trouble than you're worth."

An icy calm glides over my chest. "Should I up it to forty percent?"

Her nostrils flare. "What do you want?"

Knox folds his arms. "For you to do your damn job."

"I do." She makes an annoyed noise in the back of her throat.

I tower over her more. "No, you're not." She finally shrinks back from us. "Make the bullying stop."

"There's none of that in my classroom."

Knox's jaw tightens. "Don't lie, Dorthea. We'd hate to have to bring this discussion to Charles and take what we're owed in blood."

"You wouldn't dare," she gasps.

"But we would." I tilt my head to the side. "So, what's it going to be? Stop the bullying, or does Charles need to make an appointment with the ER?"

Her skin turns ashen. "I'll make it stop."

"Wise choice," Knox responds.

"We'll be in touch." I open the door for her like a gentleman, and she darts away from us.

When the door shuts again, we make our way back to our bikes. Before putting on his helmet, Knox turns to me. "An appointment with the ER?"

"Super badass, right? I gave myself chills with that one."

Knox and I laugh together and take off out of the parking lot.

We've always been close. We've had to rely on each other for strength to continue. But now, we share more laughs than ever before.

KNOX HOLDS THE LEVEL STEADY. "DON'T YOU THINK SHE'LL notice that her table doesn't wobble anymore?"

"Who knows?" I mark a cut line on one of the longer table legs.

"Well, won't she figure all this out?" Knox juts his head forward with his brows lifted, conveying his annoyance.

Setting the pencil down, I sigh, aggravated. "Let me ask you this. If Raven found out that we copied her key, break into her house regularly, and fix her stuff, what would you do?"

Knox blows out a breath, thinking his answer through. "Beg?"

Snorting, I shake my head and get back to the task at hand. When we're done evening out the legs, we place everything back on the table the way we found it.

Standing back to admire our work, Knox peers at the arrangement. "Was the stack of napkins right there? Or was it over here?" He moves the pile over a few inches.

"No. It was here." I move the stack to the other side of the table.

Knox picks up the napkins again and a few other items. "No. The file was right there."

Scratching my head, I scrutinize the positioning. "Do you think she'll even notice?"

Knox's wish comes out more like a question. "Hopefully not?" He shrugs, tilting the folder in his hands, scattering its contents on the floor.

I gesture to the jumble all over the floor. "Now *that* she'll notice."

Knox gets down on his knees and starts gathering the array of papers and pictures. "Aw, shit. Help me pick this up."

"Fine," I groan.

The pictures I'm loading up catch my eye, and I peer closer.

Knox gives me a scolding look. "Hey! Don't dally. We gotta finish this up so we can head over to the bar."

I flip the image around, showing Knox. "Why does Raven have a surveillance photo of Lewis Whitlock?"

Knox's eyebrows drop over his eyes, and he studies the picture closely. Then he digs through his own pile. "They're all of Lewis. What is Raven doing following Lewis around?"

Examining the photos, I catalog each one in my mind. Lewis at the grocery store, Lewis shaking hands with Frank LeBlanc, Lewis walking into the psychiatric hospital.

My head drops to a concerned angle. "I don't know, but I sure as hell am going to find out."

CHAPTER TWENTY-THREE

RAVEN

"Shit. Shit. Shit," I mutter to myself as I practically sprint across the parking lot to Mystic River Elementary next door.

Yesterday, when I picked up Noah from school, he handed me a flier from the PTO. They're in need of volunteers for their annual Halloween carnival. I figured that getting more involved at his school might help with the issues he's been having, so I texted the number on the flier saying I was excited to help.

I may have been a bit overly enthusiastic in the text, and to be honest, I'm nervous as hell. A room full of moms? That's a hard pass.

But I'll do anything for Noah. Sitting through a meeting and helping out on Halloween is hardly cause for suffering.

Approaching the main doors, I slow to a fast-paced walk, and fuss over my hair and clothing, making sure everything is in place.

The woman sitting behind the welcome desk is typing away on her computer. Her glasses are perched on the end of her nose, and her frosty short hair lies flat. Her buttoned-up blouse and fitted sweater add to the haughty air around her.

"Hi, I'm here for the PTO meeting," I say with a smile, and sound slightly out of breath.

Without turning from her screen, her eyes give me a quick once-over. She sighs as if actually having to speak and do her damn job is the worst. I can commiserate, but seriously?

"Sign in on the clipboard and grab a visitor's badge. The meeting is down the hall that way in the cafeteria."

Her monotone greeting is full of school spirit…not really.

Doing as she says, I sign in, grab a badge, and hope to the good man upstairs that I keep my cool and don't punch the old lady square in the nose. Damn this stuck-up small town and all the prejudiced people who live here.

Thankfully, there are signs to guide me right where I need to go. As quietly as possible, I open the door, but it's like the hinges haven't been greased in a million years. The creak is like a crackling sound, and there's nothing I can do about it.

I slip inside and hope that no one noticed, but I must be all out of luck today because every single head in the room is turned and staring right at me.

"Sorry," I mock-whisper, and plop down in the nearest open seat, which is unfortunately in the middle of a full row. "Sorry. Excuse me," I continue to murmur apologies as I step on toes and purses.

"We started promptly at two o'clock," a prissy voice says to me as I take my seat. I look up and quickly regret my "I should get involved campaign."

It's the snobby blonde from The Wandering Raven.

The one I told off.

And she's at the front of the room leading the meeting.

Shit on a stick.

"Got it," I return with two sarcastic thumbs up, even though I would really love to give her two other fingers.

Her displeased smile is unable to rattle my cage, leaving her unsettled. She's someone who is used to getting their way. What a shocker.

She resumes the meeting, and I pay attention. I'm not gonna let Prissy Pants rain on my campaign.

"So, it looks like we have someone for every booth except one…" The blonde's gaze goes directly to me.

They already gave out assignments? I wasn't *that* late.

"Looks like our newcomer has the honor of manning the dunk tank this year," she announces all too gleefully.

Ain't no way…

"Thank you so much for offering to do that," she thanks me with the fakest of all fake smiles.

She's pulling my leg…

She looks down at the pad of paper in her hands and continues, "Now, onto the bake sale…"

I'm starting to regret this. Getting dunked in water as people throw baseballs at a target does not sound like my kind of fun. But I'm not going to let Miss Manners and her high school bullying techniques work on me. I'm going to be the best dunker there ever was.

Dunker? Dunked? Dunkess?

Whatever.

At least it's still hotter than Satan's oven in October or else my tits might give everyone a show that is not appropriate for a school function.

At the end of the meeting, everyone disperses, but the three-woman welcoming committee heads right for me. They're like clones, wearing the same style of outfit.

I stay in my seat and take up a relaxed position. I'm not afraid of a few mean girls who peaked in high school.

"Hi, we weren't properly introduced the other day. I'm Kaitlyn LeBlanc. I'm the PTO president. My husband is

Frank LeBlanc. The mayor." She holds her hand out to me, but I don't take it.

LeBlanc? More like LeBitch.

"How nice for you," I return with a sad smile. "I'm Raven Henry."

"This is Nicole Harlow and Heather Davis," Kaitlyn introduces.

"Nice to meet you," Nicole and Heather say at the same time.

"That's so cute. You two must rehearse that often. The delivery was spot on," I comment while giving a sarcastic nod.

Kaitlyn's eyes narrow, and her lips purse. She lowers her voice so no one else can hear. "I know you're new around here, honey, so let me explain how this works. What I say goes. What I want, I get. You won't like what happens when you get in my way."

I finally stand, putting us on the same level. "Katie, was it?"

"Kaitlyn," she corrects as her nostrils flare.

I don't lower my voice when I reply. "Right. Well, Katie. I feel sorry for you. Pining after men you know will never want you back. I understand that you're probably lonely because Frank is too busy boning his secretary. But going to their place of business day after day is just sad. I don't know what you did to make them hate you, and I don't want to know. So, let's just not, okay? You can threaten me all you want, but you've got nothin' to intimidate me with. I've faced scarier monsters than you."

Kaitlyn is about ready to explode. Her face is redder than a tomato, and I saw her eye twitch a couple of times. Her minions are so astonished, they look like their eyes are about to pop out of their heads.

"Give me the dunk tank. Give me all the jobs you don't

want. Because, *honey...*" I place my hand on her upper arm in a caring way that doesn't match my words. "I don't flinch." I give her arm a friendly smack and turn, heading for the exit.

Mean girls don't change. They grow up mean, and they stay mean. But they all can be shut down the same way. Some might advise to kill them with kindness. But I'd rather just kill them.

CHARGING OUT OF THE ELEMENTARY SCHOOL, I HEAD BACK TO the library. Noah doesn't have long before school is over, but I needed some air. The air in there makes me want to punch Kaitlyn, and the air outside is too hot. So, the library it is.

Walking on the sidewalk leading to the library, the same red Ferrari that I saw outside Mystic River Psychiatric Hospital speeds through the school zone. The car passes me on the street, but when it's only twenty feet ahead, the brakes screech as the car stops. The driver shifts the car into reverse and backs up toward me.

The driver in the front seat is the same man I saw with Lewis, but with him so close, I can actually make out his features.

His deep honey hair is swept to the side with extensive amounts of hair gel. His face is clean-shaven, and his eyebrows are pristine, like he just had them waxed. His slate-gray eyes are too calculating as they wander up and down my frame.

He coasts alongside me in his car as I keep walking. "You must be new?"

How original.

"Yep." I give him my answer without looking at him.

He hangs his arm out of the car window. "Would you like a ride somewhere?"

My voice is clipped. "I'm good."

"It's okay. I'm the mayor." He says that like it means I should trust him based on his title.

That's a good joke.

"Good for you." He either doesn't pick up on my mocking tone or chooses to ignore it.

"I'm Frank LeBlanc."

The dots connect in my brain, and I stop in my tracks, turning to face him. "Kaitlyn's husband."

Frank stops his car next to me, shifting into park, and winks. "That's me."

I feel as if my counterfeit smile conveys how I feel about him, but again, Frank ignores it.

"What's your name, sugar?"

When I had the thought that I could have fun here, I didn't mean with this slime ball who resembles a Bergen.

"It's Raven. Not sugar."

"Oh. So, you're the new bartender."

"Yes, I am."

"How about that ride, sugar?" His own smile is smarmy, giving me chills.

A small snort leaves my mouth as I step up to his car door. He leans toward me as I place my hands on the weatherstrip. "Franklin—"

"It's Frank," he interjects as his smile flashes menacingly for a moment.

"Sure, Stank. You're married, yet you're still hitting on me in front of your kid's school? You know your wife is just inside, right?"

"She doesn't have to know."

"But that's assuming that I'm willing to go home with a guy named Funk."

"Frank," he corrects.

"You see, Tank, I don't think it's a good look for the mayor to be hitting on the newest constituent of Mystic River in front of the elementary school. That's not a great way to get votes."

Frank's face turns a deep red as his breathing gets harder and his mouth contorts. He throws his car into drive and zooms away, not waiting for me to even step back.

Waving my hand in the air, I call out after him, "Bye, Skunk!"

Maybe outside air is exactly what I needed because I feel much better.

CHAPTER TWENTY-FOUR

RAVEN

Shoving the book on the shelf a little more forcefully than necessary, I end up knocking a couple off the opposite end.

The book did nothing wrong. I need to calm down.

But Kaitlyn's words are replaying through my head over and over while I finish my shift at the library, and it's making me ready to go off on her all over again.

Picking up the books that have become a victim of my temper, I try to nicely place them on the shelf.

"What I say goes. What I want, I get."

Another slam and another thump on the ground.

"Woah. What did those books ever do to you?"

My head turns in the direction of the teasing comment, finding the man who is still one big mystery to me. The cowboy. He's wearing his easy smile and typical southern getup. Boots, jeans, and a flannel.

Jed is a handsome man, but I'm starting to realize that my type leans more toward a specific pair of twins.

Is it wrong to want both brothers?

Sighing, I crouch down to pick up my mess again. "Nothing. I shouldn't be taking out my frustrations on the works of…" I flip one of the books over to get a look at the cover. "Lo Gold."

Jed crouches down with me, gathering up books. "Everything okay?"

"Just fine. Nothing to stress about." We stand together, and he hands me the books to return to the shelf.

"Are you sure?" Jed asks with a tight expression.

My raised brows are all he needs to give up on his line of questioning. He twists his lips to the side like he's mulling something over.

"Do you need help finding a book or something?" I watch as he shoves his hands in his denim pockets.

"No, I'm good." His lips press into a thin line.

"You keep showing up here without checking out some books, and Florence might ban you," I tease.

The rigidity in his body releases. "I'm sure she'll forgive me." His half-smile makes me feel like I'm having deja vu, but I can't pinpoint why.

"Actually…I came to find you," Jed reveals, rocking from his heels to his toes and back again.

"Okay…" I trail off as I finish shelving the abused books.

Some of that tension creeps back. "Do you want to go to dinner on Friday?"

"Oh." My hand covers my mouth.

It feels like hours before I can even formulate a thought, and all I can think is that I would have preferred a different man to ask me. Or rather, two different men. But it's not like we gave each other promise rings or something. We've only shared a kiss. They were both very intense kisses, but that's beside the point. I don't owe them anything, and they don't owe me. So, I shouldn't feel guilty about being asked out by another man.

"I have to work on Friday," I tell him.

"Oh, okay. That's alright." He nods his head and starts to turn.

I reach for his shoulder before he can turn away fully. "But I'm free tomorrow night," I blurt out.

Jed's eyes practically sparkle, spinning back to me. "Tomorrow night? Yeah! I mean..." He clears his throat. "Yeah, tomorrow night works."

I hold in the chuckle that wants to burst free at his attempt to look cool. "Great."

"I'll pick you up at six," he informs me.

"Okay," I agree and give him my address.

I'm ready for this—putting myself out there. I need it. This is part of moving on and leaving what happened in New York back in New York. A date doesn't mean we have to get married. It's just a free meal and hopefully some good stimulating conversation.

God, I hope this isn't a horrible first date.

CHAPTER TWENTY-FIVE

RAVEN

"I'll be back no later than eleven o'clock," I inform Kat as I double-check to make sure I have all the essentials in my purse.

"Don't worry. I have everything covered here," Kat assures me as she grabs my hands, halting my nervous fidgeting.

I spent way too long getting ready for this date. Just figuring out an outfit was hectic enough. My entire wardrobe is currently strewn about my room. I settled on a cute pair of skinny jeans that hug my curves in all the right places, a loose but flattering white tank top, and a pair of flats. My makeup is simple as well, and I left my hair down in its natural waves.

Sighing, I give my friend a half-smile. "Seriously. Thank you for this."

"Don't mention it, babe," she brushes me off.

"But I want—"

I'm interrupted when I get a text from Jed, letting me know that he's here. Kat sees the text as well and pats my arm. "Go have fun."

"Okay." I relax my shoulders and call out, "Be good for Kat, Noah!"

He comes running into the entryway. "Can I make popcorn?" Noah's eyes almost bug out of his head. "Woah, Mom! You look really pretty."

I wrap him in a hug and kiss the top of his head. "Thanks, little king."

He looks up at me curiously. "Where are you going again?"

"Umm. Out…With a friend."

Noah tilts his head. "What friend?"

"Uhhh…"

Kat comes to my rescue. "Hey, Noah! How about we watch a movie while we eat popcorn?"

"Yes!" Noah lets go of me and runs into the kitchen.

Kat leads me to the door and practically shoves me outside. My jaw becomes unhinged when I see what is waiting for me in my driveway. Jed is leaning against a motor-cycle, wearing a brown leather jacket, medium wash Levis, and a plain red tee. He's texting on his phone, so he doesn't notice my approach.

Yes, he looks attractive, but am I expected to get on the bike? I've always wanted to ride a motorcycle, but not with someone I barely know.

When I'm finally within a few feet, Jed tears his attention away from his screen. His perusal of my outfit doesn't make my heart go *pitter-patter* like I want it to.

"You look amazing," he compliments.

"Thanks." I tuck a piece of hair behind my ear.

He leans to look behind me. "Where's your son? What's his name again? Nolan? I'd love to meet him."

Kat and I discussed what I would do when I decided to start dating, and the first thing I said was that the men I date wouldn't meet Noah until I was sure about them. And I'm sticking to that now.

"Umm…Are we taking this out?" I question and point to the motorcycle, distracting Jed from his inquiry.

"Yeah!" he answers excitedly and hands me a helmet to put on.

"Oh. Thanks. It's just that I've never…"

"Ridden a motorcycle before?" he finishes for me.

"Yeah," I confirm.

"You have nothing to be afraid of. I know what I'm doing. I've been riding for years. We'll be perfectly safe. It's not like there's traffic here in Mystic River," Jed points out.

Unease spreads from my gut and up my chest. "True. But still. I think…"

Jed stands up, takes the helmet from my sweaty hands, and places it on my head. "I got you. Just hop on after me."

Proving he has done this before, he easily slips onto his bike and starts it. My heart takes off in a sprint. Jed is oblivious to my current state as he takes hold of my hand and guides me onto the seat behind him. He revs the engine, turns around, and we take off.

The rush of wind around my body mixed with the discomfort inside does nothing to ease my fears.

What have I gotten myself into?

"AND HE SAID, 'WHY THE HELL WOULD I CARE? IT'S NOT MY cow.' So, I said back…" Jed cuts himself off as he takes another bite of his spaghetti.

I think this will go in the record books as the worst date

ever. We rode to the next town over for dinner at this Italian restaurant. When we arrived, every part of my body was cold, especially my arms and feet. I don't know how my purse didn't just blow away, and my hair was a rat's nest. I tried combing it out with my fingers, but that did little to tame the mane.

Then, when I told Jed what I was ordering, he asked if I was sure that's what I wanted…

This man isn't getting a second date. That's for damn sure.

At our table, my seat is positioned perfectly under a vent, and the air conditioning is on full blast. I'm pretty sure my goosebumps have goosebumps.

Jed continues to talk, even with food in his mouth, and I nibble here and there at my chicken alfredo. It's not that I don't like farm animals. I think cows are adorable. But for the last forty-five minutes, Jed has ranted nonstop about his frustrations with his vet.

I'm all for getting things out and venting. But since this is our first date, this doesn't feel like a good get-to-know-you topic.

Discreetly, I slip my hand into my purse, fishing for my phone. When I feel the silicone case, I drag my hand out and keep my phone and hand in my lap.

Me: Get me out of here!

Kat: That bad?

Me: Probably worse.

Kat: Need me to call?

Me: Yes, please!

Jed just keeps on going and somehow is almost done with

his plate. "He tried saying that I still owe him the full two-fifty—"

My phone vibrates in my lap. "One sec." I hold up a finger, interrupting his *riveting* tale. "Hello?"

"On a scale of one to dumpster fire, how awful is this date?" Kat whispers.

Gasping, I exclaim animatedly, "Is Noah okay?"

"Oh, so it's a triple forest fire."

Injecting worry in my tone, I reply, "I'll be right there. Thanks for letting me know." I end the call and face Jed. "I'm so sorry, but I need to go. Noah just threw up everywhere and is running a fever."

Jed shakes his head. "Kids are resilient. I'm sure he'll be okay."

Is he…is he not going to take me home?

"I need to go home now," I state sternly.

"But I wanted to take you to see this new horror movie. It has great reviews."

I ignore his plea and repeat myself, "I need to go home now."

He looks up at the ceiling and sighs. When he looks at me, his whole attitude has shifted. "Fine." He quickly gets the check and pays. I absently watch as he signs the receipt, but don't realize until we're out the door that he didn't even leave a tip.

Asshole, indeed.

CHAPTER TWENTY-SIX

GRIFFIN

"And that one looks like a butterfly," I say to no one in particular. Literally no one.

Tonight is the first night I've had off in years. Knox and I decided that The Wandering Raven will be closed on Mondays from here on out. And it's weird. So here I lie on my memory foam bed, staring at my ceiling and finding outlines of things in the texture.

I need a hobby.

Well, there's one hobby I wouldn't mind exploring, but sex with my employee slash neighbor isn't exactly easy when she's a single mom caring for her kid and working overtime. Knox decided to go for a ride on his motorcycle.

Pulling out my phone, I shoot off a text.

> Me: You suck.

> Me: Why didn't you ask if I wanted to go for a ride?

> Knox: ...

> Me: Don't text and drive.

Knox: I'm not. I'm at the gas station.

> Me: Grab me a candy bar.

Knox: No.

> Me: Pleeeeeease.

Knox: No.

> Me: Why not?

Knox: Because you can get one yourself.

Giving up, I toss my phone aside and go back to staring at the ceiling.

Thud. Thud. Thud.

What the hell?

Thud. Thud. Thud.

Is that the front door? No one knocks on our front door. I think the last person was a kid fresh out of high school, trying to sell us pest control. Because of him, we put a "No Solicitors" sign outside.

Thud. Thud. Thud.

"Ugh," I complain as I sit up. My feet touch the cold hardwood floor, and I instantly regret not putting on more than a pair of sweats and a tank today. The cold is not for me.

Thud. Thud. Thud.

"Yeah, yeah. I'm coming!" I shout. Taking the stairs down two at a time, I feel my limbs waking up. As I swing open the door, I find what could arguably be the last person I expected to see.

"Katarina?"

"Kat," she corrects me, firmly, and pushes past me to get inside.

"Uhhhh…" Leaving the door wide open, I spin to face her.

She folds her arms across her chest. "I need your help."

"Okay?" I massage the base of my neck.

Kat falls into her explanation seamlessly. "I'm babysitting Noah next door, but there's an emergency at the coffee shop. Tyler called and said that the espresso machine is on the frits again, and my other machine is already jacked up. The company I bought them from said someone would come today to fix the first, but no one showed—"

"Kat," I interrupt. "What does any of this have to do with me? I don't know espresso machines."

She sighs. "I need to leave, but I'm supposed to be babysitting Noah. Could you go over and watch him until Raven gets back?"

Gets back?

I didn't even notice her car was gone. It's true that I haven't gone outside today, but I feel like I would've heard her leaving. Unless she left while I was in the shower…

"Where's Raven?" I know my tone is a little hard, but Kat doesn't flinch.

She tries to hide her smile. "On a date."

What. The. Fuck.

I give Kat the go ahead to leave and take care of her emergency, and she gives me a rundown on putting Noah to bed. In a sprint, I hurry to Raven's house next door.

"Noah?" I call out when I open the front door.

"Griffin?" Noah responds and comes running down the stairs with wet hair and dressed in pajamas that have trains all over them. "Miss Kat said that you'd be coming." He snags my hand and drags me up the stairs after him.

Before she even asked me?

I chuckle and shake my head. "Oh, did she?"

"Yeah! So I set up my train set so we could play with it."

He leads me into his room, where he has a little table adorned with a small town and train tracks. Noah scurries over to the table, still dragging me along. He pulls me down to sit on the floor and hands me a plastic red tub.

"These are your trains." Then he produces another red tub. "And these are mine." He goes on to show me each of the trains in his bucket and mine, informing me of the back-stories he's created for each one. I nod and smile at each explanation, asking questions and making comments when he pauses.

Kat told me to get him in bed when I got here, but I can't seem to say no to this kid. His heart is so pure and innocent. He wants what we all want.

Love and acceptance.

Knowing that my words and actions could affect Noah and his outlook on the world makes me nervous. That's a lot of power to hold over someone so small. It's daunting. But Raven has trusted me to be around her son, and I don't want to break that. I mean, it can't be too hard. I have enough counterexamples in my own childhood, so I can think of what Amos might do in a situation and do the opposite.

It doesn't take long for me to notice Noah's yawning and drooping eyes.

"Let's get you in bed, little man," I suggest.

Noah startles. "No, I'm awake. I'm not tired." His claim is followed by him rubbing his eyes.

Holding back my smile so as not to provoke him, I reply, "You seem pretty tired to me."

"But I'm not." Water fills his eyes, and he sniffs.

Shit. What would Amos do? Probably mock Noah for showing emotion.

The opposite it is.

Gently, I remove the tub from his lap. He's too groggy to even put up a fight. I pick him up and set him on my lap. As if I've comforted him a million times before, he leans into me, placing his head on my chest.

"I know you want to play. And I promise we will, but we can't right now. You need to sleep. If you don't get enough sleep, then your body won't have the energy to play tomorrow."

Leaving his head where it is, he asks, "I won't be able to throw my football?"

"Yeah. You need sleep first."

He's quiet for a few long moments, making me think he's fallen asleep. But then he says, "I don't want you to leave. Mom says I can't talk about it, but I used to live with bad men. They hurt Mom."

My arms automatically wrap around him.

What happened to Noah and Raven? Did they even live in New York? The mysteries surrounding these two keep multiplying.

"I'm so sorry, Noah. No one should hurt your mom."

Water dampens the front of my shirt.

"They hurt me too," he admits in a small voice.

That's my final straw. A tear trickles from my eye, and I use my arm to wipe it away.

What kind of monster would hurt this little boy?

I hold him closer for a second, then pull away so he can see my face. His cheeks are wet, and his chin wobbles. "I won't let that happen ever again. No one will hurt you."

He nods, then leaps forward, wrapping his arms around my neck. "Thanks, Griff."

"Anytime, little man. Anytime."

And I mean it. If the monsters who hurt Raven and Noah aren't dead already, they will be. Soon.

A couple of minutes later, and he's out cold. As if I'm

holding thin glass, I carefully maneuver Noah into his bed and under the covers. I wait to make sure he's peacefully asleep, then quietly leave.

That little boy deserves all the love and protection in the world. He should always feel safe in his home. He shouldn't have to worry that someone is going to hurt Raven.

When I set my foot on the first step to head downstairs, my stomach drops at the shout I hear coming from outside.

"I said, no!"

I know that voice. That's the voice of my Sunshine.

Whipping out my phone, I shoot off a quick text to Knox and run down the stairs.

"Raven!"

CHAPTER TWENTY-SEVEN

RAVEN

Half an hour later, Jed parks in my driveway. I hop off the seat and shove the helmet in his direction before rushing to my front door. I try the handle, but nothing happens.

Locked. Shit.

As I dig in the bottomless pit also known as my purse for my keys, a hand slaps against the door next to my face.

"Now, how about my thank you kiss?"

Like hell.

Jed grips my shoulder and spins me. His head dips, and my hands come up to shove him away as I turn my face to the side.

"Jed. No," I grunt, using all my strength to keep him away.

He pushes his body closer. The heat of his breath is heavy on my skin. "Mmm. Yes, just like that."

My chest squeezes, making it hard to get air into my lungs. This isn't the first time someone has tried forcing themself on me. And with the way the world is, this likely will happen again. But I'll never forget the first time.

"I'm told you're refusing to take your medication." Lewis's smarmy expression freezes my entire being.

"I don't like how it makes me feel," I reason with him.

"That's too bad." He locks his office door and strolls to his desk, opening the drawer where he keeps the syringes. "This is a special medicine," he enlightens me as he presses slightly on the plunger and flicks the needle, sending droplets everywhere. "After this, you won't give the orderlies a hard time."

Dr. Whitlock's smile is still in place as he approaches me. I lean as far away from him as possible, but I don't get far because of the restraints on the chair. I fight against their hold, but they don't give.

"Shhhh," Dr. Whitlock hushes as he swipes my hair to the side. "I know you just wanted to see me again. But you have my attention now." He sticks the needle in the side of my neck and injects me with the liquid.

Concrete fills my veins over the next couple of minutes. Each muscle in my body relaxes to the point that I can't move. Dr. Whitlock strokes my hair over and over.

I know what happens next.

A tear escapes my eyes and rolls down my face.

"You're so beautiful," Dr. Whitlock praises as he wipes my tear away.

But that was then, and this is now. I have control of my body.

"I said, no!" I shout as I thrust my knee up as hard as I can and shove Jed backward.

Reflexively, Jed's hand flies up, hitting me in the face as he groans and stumbles away hunched over. "What the fuck!" he yells back.

A metallic taste fills my mouth. "No means no, you asshole."

Jed glares up at me. "You were with *them*. Why them and not me?" He laughs, shaking his head. "You're just like the rest of them, wanting to play at being their little slut. Is that how you like it? You like being a whore?" He sneers at me.

My brows crinkle.

What does that mean?

"Raven!" someone bellows from inside my house.

Was that…

Easily finding my keys this time, I fish them out of my purse, unlock the deadbolt, and rush inside. Resting my back against the door, I click the deadbolt back in place and calm myself down, but my hands shake uncontrollably as adrenaline rushes through my body.

"Raven?" Footsteps bounce off the stairs, and my boss, or one of them, appears at the bottom.

"Griffin? What are you doing here? Where's Noah?"

"In bed. Was that you screaming outside? What happened to your lip?"

"That was hardly a scream," I scoff, pushing off the door and crossing my arms to hide the quiver in my hands. I ignore his question about my lip. It's still numb so I'm sure it's split.

"What was going on out there?"

I take a few steps forward. "Nothing," I lie.

Griffin marches toward me. With each step, the muscles in his legs flex. I finally notice the fact that he's not in his usual get-up; instead, he's wearing gray sweatpants and a white tank top. A flutter moves through my stomach, and I suddenly feel overheated.

Hot damn. Can you say, "eye candy?"

Scratching at the lock on the front door has me spinning around in alarm. But before I can scurry over and hold the door closed, the bolt unlocks and Knox steps inside.

My lips twist in a muddled frown. "Knox? How did you just—"

"I texted him," Griffin interjects.

"But he just—"

Knox sounds out of breath. "Everything okay? You texted me '911,' so I rushed over."

Double hot damn.

I finally take in Knox's wet hair dripping all over his shoulders. He's wearing an outfit almost identical to Griffin's. This many men in sweatpants cannot be good for my health.

"Raven was screaming outside," Griffin explains.

Knox turns to me. "Why were you screaming? And what happened here?" His hand grips my chin lightly, tapping the cut with his thumb.

That fluttering from earlier ramps up, and I feel my core tighten. They're my bosses. I don't know why that's not sinking in. My brain gets it, but my damn pussy hasn't gotten the memo.

Ignoring the pull I have to them, I fake annoyance. "Oh hell. For the last time, I wasn't screaming."

"Sounded like screaming to me," Griffin mumbles, then frowns. "Didn't you hear it?"

Knox points to his head. "I was in the shower. But back to the original question." He looks at me again. "Why were you screaming?"

They're like dogs after a bone.

Throwing my hands up, I stomp past them. "I'm not doing this."

Knox stops me with a hand on my arm. I try to brush him off, but he grabs my wrist and holds my hand up for inspection. When he sees the tremble, he shows Griffin. They make eye contact and exchange a brief nod. The two of them spring into action, and before I know what's happening, Knox scoops me up in his arms and carries me to the couch. Griffin heads into my kitchen, and I hear him opening and closing cabinets.

"I can walk. I don't need to be carried."

"But I'm just so good at it," Knox quips.

"You're impossible," I sigh out.

Knox flops down on the couch with me still in his arms, settling me in his lap. I try to swing my legs off so I can sit on the cushion next to him, but Knox's reflexes are quick. He wraps his hand around my thighs and stops me from scooting away.

"I can sit by myself."

"But I make a better seat," he says simply as if he's stating a fact.

"Got it," Griffin announces as he walks into the living room. He carries a shot glass filled to the brim.

"Is that my Don Julio? Are we turning this into a party or something?" I give him a skeptical look.

Griffin hands me the small glass. "Bottoms up, Sunshine."

When I still don't drink it, Knox explains, "For the nerves, Darlin'."

"Oh. Right." I down the shot, ignoring the sting of the alcohol as it connects with my bleeding lip, and give the glass back to Griffin. He places it on the coffee table, then sits on the edge. He hands a damp cloth to Knox, and he uses it to dab at the blood on my mouth.

"Who were you on a date with?" Griffin questions.

Knox rears his head back. "You were on a date?"

Well, this just became even more awkward than I thought possible. Kissed one brother, then the other, and went on a date with someone else. I'm not ashamed, but having to talk about it with my bosses, aka the two brothers I kissed who are also my neighbors, is beyond weird.

"Just a friend," I finally answer.

"And you had to shout 'I said, no' at him? What did he do?" Griffin's expression is serious.

"Give us a name," Knox growls. "All we need is a name."

Placing my hand on Knox's chest, I feel the thundering of his heartbeat. "Look, I'm fine. I handled it. He got a knee to the balls. I'm sure the ride home on his motorcycle was more than painful."

Griffin grasps my free hand in his. "Proud of you."

"Thanks. But again, I'm fine. He's the one who was limping away."

Knox's touch is soft as he grasps my chin like he did earlier, tapping my lip again. "But he drew blood, he touched you when you said no repeatedly. That's not okay."

"Well, he might've lost a testicle, so all is right with the world. Besides, he didn't do anything that…" I stop myself from finishing that thought.

"Anything that what?" Griffin repeats, searching for the end of my statement.

I clear my throat and swallow, but keep my mouth shut tight.

"Anything that what, Raven?" Griffin questions again. He pushes closer, invading my space. But the move isn't to intimidate, it's to provide comfort. To me.

"Anything that hasn't happened before," I finish.

Knox's mouth pinches shut, and Griffin's nostrils flare.

"I've dealt with men like this my entire life. The first man to…" I stop myself again. Dammit. It's like my filter just flies out the window around these two.

"Let's start with the man from tonight. Just tell us his name. Please," Knox implores.

I drop my shoulders. "Jed."

Griffin squeezes my hand, and Knox sits up straighter. The mood in the room shifts from care and concern to guarded and on edge.

"Did I say something wrong?" My eyes bounce back and forth between the two brothers.

"Are you sure?" Griffin asks.
"Yes. Why?" I lean toward Griffin.
"Because that's our dead grandfather's name."

CHAPTER TWENTY-EIGHT

KNOX

That 911 text from Griffin just about ended my life. He didn't even say where he was. So when I found his bedroom empty, I looked up his cell phone location, and it showed that he was next door.

I ran out of the house as fast as possible. When I got outside, I saw a man hunched over on a motorcycle speeding away. I thought nothing of it until now.

Whoever that man was, he's messing with us. After the letter from Amos and the cryptic phone call the other day… there's no such thing as coincidences.

"Your dead grandfather?"

"Yep," Griffin answers, less upbeat than usual.

"Why would someone steal your grandfather's name, lie to me, and then take me on a date? I'm not connecting the dots here." Raven's face scrunches.

Now probably isn't the best time to tell Raven how we feel, so I pull an excuse out of the air. "Because you're our neighbor."

As Raven turns to me, Griffin looks at me over Raven's head, wrinkling his eyebrows and frowning.

Raven stares off to the side. "That doesn't make any sense." Then she spins back around to Griffin, and his scolding expression disappears.

Griffin fills his cheeks with air and exhales, formulating a reasoning for my explanation. "Well, I don't know if you've noticed, but most of the people in Mystic River aren't our biggest fans."

"Because of…" Raven cuts herself off.

Griffin bites his lip and nods his head. "Someone told you."

Raven grimaces. "I may have gotten the Cliff Notes version from Kat."

I shrug a shoulder. "At least you got the information from someone who doesn't act like we're the spawn of Satan."

Raven's head drops to an angle, and her mouth pinches as she contemplates something. But it's not hard to figure out what's on her mind.

"Just ask,' I prompt her.

Raven reluctantly reveals what she's thinking. "You two dated her at the same time? Knowingly?"

"Yes." Griffin, nonplussed, drags out that single word.

Raven's cheeks pinken. "Interesting."

Griffin and I look at each other wearing identical smirks. A thousand words silently passing between us.

"You two do that a lot," Raven interrupts.

I frown. "Do what?"

"Y'all always have these silent little conversations. Is it a brother thing or a twin thing?"

Griffin shrugs. "A bit of both."

"Want to fill me in a bit?" Raven cocks her head.

"Yes, Scarlett was our high school girlfriend," I start.

Raven's eyes widen comically. "Were people accepting in the eighteen hundreds?"

"Brat," Griffin comments as he pokes her side.

I continue the story. "Actually, no. We got a lot of shit from the town for our less-than-conventional relationship. We were sixteen and having fun. Then Scarlett didn't show up to school. Her father led a huge search across all the neighboring counties, and what was found was her blood in a truck, her clothes in the bed, and a shovel with her blood on it as well."

Raven gives me comfort by placing her hand on my shoulder. "Your father's truck, right?"

I guess it's a good thing she already knows that detail of the story. If it bothered her, she wouldn't let me hold her right now.

I nod my head. "Yes. Amos, our father, was convicted of her murder and sentenced to life in prison. It was a big deal because he was convicted without a body."

"Scarlett's body was never found?"

"Never," I confirm.

Raven's focus goes to her hands, searching for answers. "But what does Jed have to do with all of this? It's possible that it's a coincidence."

"I don't believe in coincidences," I reply.

"Plus, the letter from Amos claiming his innocence and the phone call the other night," Griffin adds.

"Wait. What phone call and what letter?" Raven rubs her head, and we explain both to her. Neither answer satisfies her. She jumps up from my lap and paces the room. "I don't understand what any of this has to do with me. I'm just your neighbor."

"*Just* the neighbor?" Griffin asks incredulously.

Raven rolls her eyes. "You're right. I'm also your bartender."

"You're more than that, Sunshine."

Raven blinks excessively. "This isn't how it was supposed to go."

Griffin stands from the coffee table and blocks Raven's path. When she tries to go around him, he gets hold of her wrists, keeping her in place. "What do you mean?"

"Mom?"

We all turn towards the stairs, where a bleary-eyed Noah stands half asleep.

"Hey, little king," Raven coos, rushing to his side. "Did we wake you up?"

He shakes his head.

"Let's get you back to bed." Her head turns to us and says pointedly, "Griffin and Knox were just leaving."

"We were?" Griffin asks sarcastically.

"Yes," Raven answers with wide eyes, daring us to contradict her in front of Noah. With her hand held out to her side, she directs us to the front door.

I get up from the couch, my knees popping as I go, and follow Griffin to the entryway. In the open doorway, I turn to find Raven right on my heels. She gasps as I bend, putting my mouth against her ear. "You can go on whatever dates you want, Darlin'. But we both know they'll all lead you to one place." Grabbing her wrist, I guide her hand to my chest, right over my heart.

I need her to feel the cadence of my soul and know that it's all for her.

"Us." My lips press to her cheek quickly and earnestly. I step back, allowing for Griffin to take my place.

He cups her cheeks and places a kiss on her forehead. She closes her eyes, basking in the heat. "Sweet dreams, Sunshine." His hands fall away from her face, and he steps back.

We stand together on her porch and don't allow her to

break our gaze as she shuts the door and turns off the outside light, draping us in the stillness of the night. Neither of us move from our post.

Griffin taps his fingers at his side. "We still need to…"

"We will," I finish for him.

"She seemed…"

"I agree." My head dips in a single nod.

"Do you think she'll…"

"We'll convince her."

CHAPTER TWENTY-NINE

KNOX

Before the sun lit up the sky, I was up and on my bike despite my lack of sleep the night before. Griffin and I have a lot of questions. We weren't able to get answers out of Raven last night, but today, I plan on getting answers from somewhere else.

The journey takes a couple of hours. I use that time to prepare myself and build up the thick concrete walls around me. All too soon, I'm pulling into the prison parking lot, killing the engine.

Sitting on the saddle, I stretch my neck. My eyes roam over the red brick façade of the Huntsville, Texas State Penitentiary. The process of checking in and getting to the visitor room is extensive.

Once I'm in the room, it's like something out of a movie. Everything from the glass partitions to the cord phones. I'm not the only visitor in here, but the room is hardly full. I'm directed to a small stool that seems fit for a toddler and not a thirty-eight-year-old man.

A loud buzz sounds from the room on the other side of

the glass, and a large door opens. In walks a guard followed by a line of men in orange jumpsuits.

The moment Amos passes over the threshold, his eyes go straight to me. A cocky smile lifts the corner of his mouth. It takes all my willpower not to smash my fist through the glass and wipe that smug look off his face.

With a confidence he shouldn't have, Amos sits down and picks up the black phone, raising it to his ear. I do the same, internally grimacing at how sticky it is.

"It's good to see you, son," he greets me.

I let the title of son roll off my back. This man hardly deserves the title of father, which means I'm not his son. Jumping straight to the point, I respond, "You said you had proof. Where's your proof?"

"You know, I've been here for over twenty years, and you haven't visited me once," he says, acting offended.

But I won't play his game. "The proof."

Amos's knuckles holding the phone turn white. "You know, if it wasn't for me, you'd have been living on the street. When your mother didn't want you boys, I fed you and kept a roof over your head. You should be thanking me."

"Griff was right. This is a waste of time." I pull the phone away from my ear and move to hang up.

"Wait!" Amos blurts out. "Wait," he repeats more calmly.

I return the phone to my ear and sweep my hand out in a motion that cues him to get on with it.

"I didn't kill Scarlett Whitlock."

"The proof, Amos," I prompt again.

"She's alive."

I hunch forward, my voice menacing. "What? Is this your idea of a joke?"

"Why would I lie to you?"

"I have a laundry list of reasons," I deadpan.

Amos holds his finger up, scolding me. "I'm your father, boy. Watch it."

"You have done nothing to earn being called that." I scoff.

"I didn't kill your girlfriend," he tries convincing me, but his argument is thin.

"Where's. Your. Proof." I pound out each word at him.

He finally answers my original question, "It's safe with a friend."

Rolling my eyes, my head shakes. "Which is another way of saying you don't have shit. Nice try. Enjoy rotting in here." Slamming the phone down, I stand from the stool and inform a guard that I'm ready to go.

"Wait! Wait! Get your ass back here!" Amos shouts at my back, but I don't turn around. "She's been living in Boston! She's been alive this whole time! And she's coming back!"

"That's enough!" a guard barks. "Calm down, Montgomery!"

"Watch your back! She's coming!"

The guard leads me back to the entrance. Not once do I look over my shoulder. I keep my focus fixed ahead, leaving behind Amos and his lies.

CHAPTER THIRTY

RAVEN

Ever since my date from hell, I've tried to keep my distance from the Montgomery twins. But they find excuses to stop by the house and to be right next to me at The Wandering Raven. Even now, Griffin is on my ass. The only reprieve I get is at the library.

As I wipe down the counter, waiting for the night crowd to shuffle into The Wandering Raven, Griffin restocks the liquor. "You can go take care of your boss man things, you know. I don't need a babysitter."

Griffin continues to shelf the bottles. "I'm not babysitting."

"Could've fooled me." My tone is bland, conveying my sarcasm. "Why can't Benny be my babysitter?"

"I'm not a babysitter," he quips without looking away from the TV.

"Benny's busy," Griffin adds.

Spinning toward Griffin, I throw my hands up. "Benny's never busy." Over my shoulder, I add, "No offense."

Benny's attention is still locked on the screen. "None taken."

"Stop acting like a brat," Griffin replies, yet again not looking at me.

Groaning dramatically, I go back to wiping the bar.

Fine. I'll just pretend he's not here. Simple enough. I can ignore my sexy boss for one night, even if every time he's near and I get a whiff of his sea salt and bergamot aroma, my core aches.

Since my rescue, I haven't had sex. It's just been me and my toys. Maybe I'm just going through a bout of hysteria like women in the nineteenth century. I've been deprived of orgasms and just need a release.

It's not long before a few customers wander in. I take their drink orders and quickly get them filled behind the bar. Griffin doesn't follow me, which is a relief. Maybe I need to focus more on the tables tonight so I can breathe.

When I approach the last customer with his drink, I rethink not having my shadow with me. He's the type who looks too put together. Like he's trying too hard to convince everyone around him that he's a nice guy. But nice guys don't lurk at a booth in a bar, staring at every woman who walks in.

As I hand him his Bud Light, he grazes his fingers over mine and shoots me a wink.

Bleh. I'm going to need a shower after this shift.

I scurry away and contemplate staying behind the counter. But then Griffin is right by my side again.

Ugh. Nowhere is safe.

After only a few minutes, I'm ready to burst. Griffin is just trying to be nice. I know. But give a girl some space.

Needing some respite, I grab a quarter from the cup and march over to the jukebox to pick a song. No one has started dancing yet, but maybe this will do the trick. I haven't line danced in years, so it takes me a moment to remember the steps. But once I have the hang of it, I'm able to have some fun.

To the right. To the left. Right heel. Left heel. Repeat and turn.

A couple of women join me, falling into step easily. We laugh and sing along to the Luke Bryan song about country girls "shaking it."

After the first chorus, a large set of hands land on my hips and dance with me. Glancing over my shoulder, I expect to find a certain face with warm amber eyes. As frustrated as I am with him, my pussy still wants to have some fun. But instead of Griffin, I find the "nice guy" I served earlier.

My insides twist, knowing it's his hands on me. I didn't ask for him to touch me. I didn't even secretly wish for it.

I grab his wrists and remove his hands from my waist. "No, thanks."

"Aww, come on. Don't be like that." He reaches for me again, but I step out of the way.

A yelp and breaking glass have me turning toward the bar, where I find Griffin storming for us. The way his muscles and veins strain tells me he's furious.

Holding both hands up to the customer, I warn him, "You should go."

"Not without a dance." His smile is demanding.

When I can feel Griffin's footsteps shaking the wood floor, I know he's close. As he reaches me, I place my hands on his chest and stand in his way. "Dance with me."

Griffin wasn't expecting my invitation. He glances back and forth between me and the customer, trying to decide what to do.

I try again, "Dance with me, please." By now, others have joined in and are line dancing away.

Griffin's muscles flex under my hands, and my stomach flutters. Biting my lip, my eyes roam up and down his body.

He catches me admiring and smirks. Griffin waves to

Benny, who is standing behind him, and Benny marches past us to the handsy customer. Griffin makes a hand gesture, and Benny, understanding the meaning, grabs the man by his upper arm and hauls him off toward the back hallway.

I watch the whole scene with concern, but Griffin distracts me. He grabs my right hand and places his arm around my waist, pulling me so we're right up against each other.

"Know how to Texas Two Step, Sunshine?" His fury is gone, and in its place is a sultry man.

I try to keep my mouth closed because drooling right now would be so unattractive. "It's been a while, but I think I remember."

He winks seductively. "Let's see what you got."

Griffin takes two quick steps forward, and I follow his lead by taking two steps back. We flow with the music as he spins us around the make-shift dance floor. He never breaks eye contact with me. He stares purposefully as if my eyes will tell him everything my mouth can't.

My body pushes as close as I can get, wanting to feel his heart beat against mine. His erection grazes my thigh as I step between his feet in a spin. Color rises in my cheeks, realizing he's just as turned on as I am.

When the song ends, the dancing couples stop and clap. But Griffin doesn't feel like doing the same. He snags my hand and drags me away. The bar has filled up since the start of the song, so Griffin has to move people aside to get through the crowd.

I try pulling back on my hand, but he doesn't let go. "Where are we going?"

He marches me past the bar and into the kitchen. Camden is at the stove top, pulling a burger off the grill. When he sets the patty on the bun, he notices us and frowns.

Griffin tilts his head toward the door. "Customers need your help."

"Okay?" Camden's compliance is full of confusion as he steps out.

Griffin locks the door as soon as Camden exits and backs me up against the wall. Unlike our first kiss, his body touches mine everywhere.

Do I want to do this?

Yes.

In this moment, I'm going to be selfish. I'm going to allow myself to find bliss in Griffin's body and enjoy myself.

Griffin's voice deepens with lust. "You had a glimpse of the other side of the fence. The grass isn't greener over there. You're meant to be here. Right here. With me. Where you belong."

My mind blanks.

I've never been with someone who wanted me on such a primal level, who wanted to keep me because they knew me. Griffin may not know about all the skeletons in my closet, but he and Knox have seen more than most.

Griffin doesn't wait for my response. He bends and locks his lips with mine, groaning as he tastes me. The push and pull of our kiss is filled with all the pent-up emotions we've been dancing around since we met.

My hands eagerly find the hem of his shirt and tug upward. Griffin steps back for a brief moment to pull the material over his head. My eyes snag on the black ink on his ribs that I saw the other day. The script reads, "over my dead body."

My brows scrunch. "That's a bit dramatic."

Griffin glances down at the quote, then smirks at me. "I would argue that it's not dramatic enough."

My only response is to give him a questioning look.

"It's a reminder that I won't let someone take anything

from Knox and me without a fight. Knox is the one with the short fuse, but that doesn't mean I won't do what's necessary."

I tilt my head. "What are you afraid someone will take?"

"You."

Griffin doesn't give me a moment to process his confession. He pushes my body against the wall with his as our mouths meet again, and our tongues aggressively slide against each other's.

Needing to feel every muscle, my hands roam up his abs and over his arms. He's so firm and solid. I'm sure I could bounce a quarter off his pecs.

He grabs the side of my neck and uses his thumb to tilt my head back further, deepening the kiss. His other hand grips my hip as he grinds his steel length into my stomach.

A moan echoes through me when I roll my hips, dragging my core against him.

Griffin removes my tank top, and with one hand, swiftly finds the clasp of my bra. The straps loosen, and I break our kiss, looking him in the eyes as I let the material fall from my chest. My nipples grow taut under his gaze.

His eyes darken, and his fingers lightly pinch each stiff peak. My hands grip his biceps as that small pinch sends a jolt of need to my pussy.

His hands shift, cupping my breasts as his thumbs swipe back and forth over the tips. He dips, placing his mouth on my neck and takes his time kissing his way up to my ear.

"Tell me another secret, Sunshine. Tell me something else you've never told anyone."

I freeze, and he feels my hesitation.

Griffin slides his hand down my stomach, leaving goosebumps behind, and undoes the button and zipper of my denim shorts. He reaches in and cups my center. My hips move of their accord, pushing my wetness further into his hand.

"Tell me and I'll make you come like a good girl."

Holy shit.

My pussy drips with arousal, soaking Griffin's hand. His proud smirk sends a flutter to my center.

"You're soaking my hand, Sunshine. Tell me a secret, and I'll make the ache in your cunt go away."

It's hard to think with one hand in my pants and one on my boob. He's driving me crazy.

"I've never had an orgasm during sex."

The color of Griffin's eyes turns predatory—determined. "I can fix that."

He hooks his finger around my panties and moves them to the side, then dips a single digit inside me, but not all the way. He teases me, circling my opening and making me pant harder. His thumb doesn't stop rubbing my nipple. Every swipe and every circle make the ache, the need to come, grow stronger.

"Please," I whimper. "Please make me come, Griff."

He growls, thrusting his finger the rest of the way and attacking my g-spot. My hips bounce up and down as I lose myself in the pleasure. He slips another finger inside next to the first. The delicious stretch makes me want more.

I don't notice as he releases my breast and unbuttons his own pants, letting them drop to his thighs. His fingers keep time with my thrusts as I rush to my release while he slips his boxers down his thighs with his pants.

I look down at the glistening head of his cock, thick and hard without me touching his shaft at all. He's big. Very big. Maybe too big.

My eyes widen, and he smirks.

"It'll fit, I promise."

"I'm not so sure," I reply.

Griffin chuckles, and I continue staring, dumbfounded.

With my past, I've had sex many times, and I've seen many dicks. Short dicks, skinny dicks, limp dicks, uncut dicks, and even crooked dicks. I've been forced to endure them all.

But my curiosity has me reaching for him, wondering what it feels like when I actually want the person I'm getting naked with. Before I can get my fingers around him, he grabs my wrist and brings my hand above my head against the wall.

"Not yet, baby. If I let you touch my cock right now, I'm going to come way too early. Just touching you already has me so close to the edge."

My heart melts.

I know how to please a man. I know how and where to touch him to get him off. But I've never had a man get so turned on from bringing me pleasure.

He's everything.

I guide his hand out of my pussy and kick my shorts off. "Pick me up, Griffin, and sit me on your dick. I need you inside me."

Griffin moans at my commanding tone, lifting me by the back of my thighs. He presses me into the wall and hands me a condom. I speedily rip open the foil and glide the rubber over his girth. He guides my opening to his cock and presses inside.

"Fuck. You're so tight, Sunshine. So warm and wet." He keeps pushing in further and further. My head falls back, banging against the wall, and my eyes close.

When he's completely seated inside, my pussy pulses around him. "I'm so full," I whine, loving the feel of him.

With one hand under my ass, Griffin uses the other to guide my face to his. He dominates my mouth, and I willingly submit. He doesn't move anything else except his lips and tongue. I squirm, in desperate need of friction, and Griffin swallows down my responsive moan.

Griffin moves his lips to my ear, using his tongue and teeth. "What's next, Baby? Tell me and I'll make it happen."

My heart cracks wide open.

How does he know what I need him to say without me knowing it myself?

"I need you to move. I want to come, Griff. Please, let me come."

"Hold on."

That's his only warning before he picks me up off his cock and slams me down on his length as he thrusts up, hitting the perfect spot inside my pussy. When another moan builds in my throat, he slams his lips on mine.

"Give it to me, Raven. Give it all to me."

My legs wrap around his hips, and I use the leverage to thrust my hips with his. My body takes over, desperate for a release.

The sound of his dick moving in and out creates a slick sound that bounces off the walls. It's obscene. It's vulgar. But it's so sexy.

My pulse flies as does Griffin's. A bead of sweat rolls over his temple and down his cheek when he hammers his hips harder into me.

"I'm so close. I'm so damn close," I pant.

"Play with your clit, Raven. Make yourself come all over my dick. I want to feel your cum dripping down my balls."

I do as he says, rubbing my bundle of nerves with my index finger.

The grand ascent of my climax hits its peak.

"Come for me, Baby."

Griffin's words push me over the edge. My pussy flutters, squeezing his cock, pulling him in deeper. His hips stutter, and I feel his length pump his seed into my channel.

Griffin slumps, crushing me into the wall, and I love it. "Fuck, Raven. You're going to kill me with your pussy."

Tracing his spine with my fingertips, I rest my head on his shoulder. "Maybe I shouldn't be having sex with an old man, then."

"Such a brat," he quips back.

There's a pounding on the kitchen door, causing me to yelp and hide my face in Griffin's neck.

"Guys! Let me in! The mozzarella sticks are going to burn!"

Griffin tries hiding his grin behind his fist, but his laugh still breaks free. "Just a sec!"

I keep my face hidden. "Oh my God. I just had sex with my boss."

"Good thing there isn't a company policy against it," he teases.

CHAPTER THIRTY-ONE

RAVEN

"And here's the last one: *Martial Arts for Dummies*." I pass the book to the gentle older woman.

"Thank you, dear," she says softly and adds it to the stack in her frail arms. Her neck is craned forward, and her shoulders are hunched. Her delicate sweater practically swallows her whole.

"Do you need any help carrying those out to your car?" I offer.

She quirks a brow at me. "I may be old, but I'm not dead." Giving me her back, she walks slower than a sloth to the circulation desk to check out her new books.

I chuckle at her sass.

She showed up earlier and asked for all the books we had on "kicking ass." Her words, not mine. I happily looked up the list of books in our system and pulled them for her. Normally, Florence would have helped the woman, but Florence is at a doctor's appointment.

After scanning the woman's books, she takes the stack and is on her merry way. Possibly to kick some ass.

I'd pay to see that.

My mind drifts to yesterday at The Wandering Raven and what Griffin and I did in the kitchen.

I still can't believe we did that, but I can't find it in me to regret it either.

A book drops on the counter in front of me, causing me to almost jump out of my seat. "I'd like to check this one out, please."

Every inch of my skin becomes hyperaware, and my hands form fists on my lap. My nails create crescent indentations on my palm as I restrain myself from grabbing Dr. Whitlock's collar and slamming his face against the desk.

A false smile curves my lips, and I control my tone. "I can help you with that." I slide the book and his library card closer then begin the process.

"How's your son?"

The vein at my temple pulses with my rushing blood.

"Great," I reply, adding phony politeness in my voice.

Dr. Whitlock doesn't take note of the vibrating rage sweating out of my pores. "Florence told me you're new here. How are you liking Mystic River?"

"Just fine," I answer, as I finish with the computer and slide the card and book back to him.

He picks it up while staring at me. "You know, you look familiar."

The lie rolls off my tongue with ease. "I get that a lot."

"You remind me of—"

"Have a nice day," I cut him off, dismissing him in a backhanded way that southern women do.

He glares but thankfully picks up on the hint and leaves.

A whoosh of air exits my lungs when he's finally out of sight. I'm going to have to avoid Dr. Whitlock from now on. He was about to recognize me, and that would ruin everything.

The electronic bell on the front door chimes, and a man who looks like he's had a rough go of it enters. His pants look like scrubs, and his upper body is covered in a hoodie. The front pocket is full, and whatever he has in there, it's heavy. I can practically see his skull with the way the skin on his face hugs every bone. He looks like he hasn't had a proper meal in years.

His profile looks familiar. As if I know him, but that's impossible. There's no way he could have gotten out.

Patting his pockets, his eyes jump all over, but when he catches sight of me, he flexes his fingers and doesn't look away.

"Seth?" I whisper in disbelief.

The bags under his bloodshot eyes are dark and heavy. He runs one of his hands over the buzzed hair on his head. His mouth moves, but he's too far away for me to hear what he's saying.

He pulls something the size of his fist out of his pocket and stomps right for me. I roll my chair backward until I hit the wall, while the man brings his hands together, and a small click meets my ears when he parts his hands again. Then, with excellent aim, he tosses the fist-sized thing in his hand at me.

It lands on the floor at my feet with a small thump and a roll. The object is dark green and has grid impressions over the whole thing.

It's like something straight out of a movie. I don't have time to think. Only act.

Kicking the object toward the desk, I take off as fast as I can. Before I can warn the other people in the library, the circulation desk explodes. The force knocks me off my feet, and I fall onto the unforgiving carpet. Bits of laminate, wires, and plastic rain down on my back.

To say the library turns into chaos would be inaccurate.

Screams and cries toll around me. Moms escape with their small children out of the exits with other patrons right behind them on their heels.

But above the wailing, a tune whistles in the air. Searching for the source of the melody, I groan. My body aches from the grenade explosion.

Seth leisurely strolls toward me and sings a nursery rhyme, but it doesn't sound quite right.

"Hickory Dickory Doc,
The girl got hit by a rock.
The clock struck one,
The girl ran off,
Hickory Dickory Doc."

Flipping on my back, I crab walk backward as fast as I can. A full smile takes over Seth's face as he tracks my movements. The red surrounding the irises of his eyes gets bigger as he reaches into his pocket again.

"Hickory Dickory Doc,
The madman threw the rock.
He scared them off,
Got her alone,
Hickory Dickory Doc."

I jump to my feet and run for the emergency exit in the adult fiction section. When I hear that same click, I know I only have moments before another explosion. The grenade whizzes by me and lands right in front of the exit door.

Making a sharp turn in the opposite direction toward the computers doesn't protect me from the blast. I'm knocked off my feet again, but this time I land on all fours. More debris hits me then a heavy wooden shelf gets me right in my lower back.

The stench of smoke invades my nostrils, but the alarm doesn't go off. I know exactly where the extinguisher is, but I don't think I can get to it with Seth chasing me and fucking throwing grenades all over the place.

Hopping to my feet, I face him and defensively raise my hands. "Seth," I plead with him. "It's me. It's Raven." But my appeal falls on deaf ears.

He approaches me and whips out his hand to grab mine. His hand is cold and feeble. His fingers are like thin bands of steel digging into my hand. With a strength I didn't think possible, he applies pressure, and an agonizing pop jolts up my arm. I bite my lip to stop myself from crying out in pain. I pull at his wrist with my free hand, attempting to get him to let go, but he doesn't budge.

"Please, Seth," I try again. "Remember me? I gave you my vanilla pudding." It was only one time, but I'm praying he recalls the gift.

It's like my words don't register whatsoever. The deranged smile is still plastered on his face as he reaches back into the front pouch of his hoodie.

No, no, no. I'm not dying here like this.

With my free hand, I stiffen my palm and thrust upward at his face. The flat of my hand connects with his nose, and a reverberating crunch rings out. The force of my hit whips Seth's head to the side, throwing him back. He lets go of my injured hand, and I take off for the children's section. Crouching down behind the last row of books, I look around, forming a plan in my head.

Maybe I can just run for the front door. I'm not sure where Seth is, but I need to get out of here. Who knows how many more grenades he has on him.

Whistling continues and gets closer. Another click, another bang. This time, coming from the entrance to the library.

"Hickory Dickory Doc,
The girl stopped the rock.

The clock struck two,
The girl ran off,
Hickory Dickory Doc."

A chill trickles down my spine. The lyrics of the remixed nursery rhyme feel like a message; however, decoding it will have to wait. But the "got her alone" line makes my stomach turn into a tight ball.

I can get through this. I just need to make it to an exit. If I find an exit, I'll be okay.

There's a clank against the windows, and a few moments later, the glass shatters into tiny pieces, shooting in every direction. Tucking my face into my knees, I cover the back of my head with my hands.

My jaw clenches when a sharp object slices through my hand. A thick, warm liquid dribbles through my hair and down my neck. When I peek up, I find a piece of glass sticking out of my broken hand.

Seth's whistling resumes, now closer than before. The hairs on the back of my neck stand straight up. His shoes appear at the end of the aisle. He stops, easily spotting me on the ground. His nose is crooked, and blood flows over his lips, down his chin, and drips onto the floor.

The expression on his face is positively giddy. When he smiles this time, his teeth are covered in red.

"Hickory Dickory Doc,
The madman gave me the rock.
The room was blown,
Got her alone,
Hickory Dickory Doc."

My limbs shake, and my breath gets trapped in my lungs.

"Freeze! Texas Rangers!" Two men in white dress shirts, slacks, and cowboy hats stand on both thresholds that lead into the children's section. Their feet are planted and both men have a gun raised at Seth, but he doesn't pay either of them any attention.

"I said, freeze!" the one on my right orders.

Seth pulls out another grenade, and each ranger acts fast. Seth stumbles backward with each bullet that pierces his body. When he is riddled with bullet holes, he falls backward onto the child-sized bean bag.

One ranger cautiously approaches the body, his gun still fixed on Seth, and the other rushes to my side. "Let's get you out of here. Can you walk?"

But I can't move. I can't speak. All I can do is stare down at the bleeding body of the man who used to be a scared boy. A patient of Mystic River Psychiatric Hospital.

CHAPTER THIRTY-TWO

GRIFFIN

"Ninety-two bottles of beer on the wall, ninety-two bottles of beer! Take one down, pass it around. Ninety-two bottles of beer on the—"

"If you keep singing that fucking song, I'm going to throw *this* bottle of beer at you," Knox threatens.

"I'd like to see you try," I goad.

We're supposed to be discussing the current outstanding balances for the gamblers downstairs. And what do you know? Graham LeBlanc made the list.

Knox points to the list on the desk. "These two are supposed to pay up tonight, but this one," he points to Graham, "may need a more…personal visit."

"We can find him—"

Camden bursts through the door, panting and sporting wild eyes. "You need to get to the library. Now!"

"What's going on?" Knox's lips purse.

"It's Raven. Something's happened at the library."

That's all he needs to say to get us to spring into action. Knox and I are up and running to my truck.

"Benny, you're in charge," Knox shouts as we pass the bar.

"Everything okay?" Benny calls to us. But we don't have time to satisfy his curiosity.

Knox and I are in the cab and peeling out of the parking lot in under a minute. The good thing about living in a small town is that it doesn't take more than fifteen minutes to get from one end of town to the other. It's just our luck that the library is on the same side of town as The Wandering Raven.

"What do you think happened?" Knox asks.

"I think we're about to find out," I say as I nod to the parking lot full of police cars, firetrucks, first responders, and lookie loos.

A team of firefighters have a hose in their hands, aiming it at the library. Smoke billows out from the broken windows, and…is that a hole in the side of the building?

"What the hell happened here?" Knox questions in awe.

"I have no idea," I respond.

"Do you think Florence is okay?"

"She may not have even been here. She has her monthly appointment with her cardiologist today, remember?"

Parking my truck in the elementary school parking lot, we hop out of the truck and jog into the fray. We shove our way through the crowd, ignoring the police tape barrier. It's chaos all around. An EMT tends to a mother and her child who have little cuts and bruises sprinkled over their arms and faces. More people wait on the side to have their wounds treated. Firefighters in full gear are running into the burning building. Police officers fight to keep a perimeter around the mess.

"There." Knox points to Raven sitting up on a gurney at the back of the ambulance. An EMT holds her hand in his as he looks her over. When Knox catches sight of it, he cracks his knuckles and juts his chin forward.

We weave in and out of the bedlam that lies between us and Raven. When we're only a few feet away, someone steps in our path.

"What the hell are you two doing? Get back behind the tape before I tase your asses!" Sheriff Asshole Jackson hollers in our faces.

Knox steps up so he's toe to toe with the Sheriff. Knox is significantly bigger, taller, and stronger than the sheriff. I think it's part of what fuels the animosity between them. I'm no doctor, but I'd say Sheriff Jackson has a bad case of Short Man Syndrome.

Knox narrows his eyes and smirks. "No can do, Sheriff."

Sheriff Jackson's lips thin in a flat line. "Are you threatening me, Montgomery?"

"Hush up, Clayton. You're all bark and no bite. Leave them alone." Florence smacks the sheriff on the arm.

"Not now, Flo." Sheriff takes a step back and holds his hand out to get Florence to stop.

She smacks him again. "Don't you dare 'Flo' me!"

"Knox! Griffin!" Raven brushes past the EMT in front of her and leaps down from the ambulance.

We step around the sheriff, and Knox catches Raven in his arms, lifting her off the ground. They embrace each other, arms wrapped tight. When they pull back, instead of setting her back down, Knox passes Raven to me. And just like she did with Knox, Raven wraps her arms around my neck. She buries her face in my neck, and I take the time to relish in the way she clings to me. It's like we're her lifeline. We're her haven.

I feel warm liquid heat the skin on the back of my neck. What the hell?

Raven pulls back so we're face to face. Blinking and a quick shake of her head, she says, "I need to get Noah." Then she tries to push away to get me to put her down.

Like that will ever happen again.

As long as I'm breathing, Raven will be in my arms.

"Raven." I try to get her attention. "Sunshine!" She stops her struggle. "Let's finish getting you checked out, then we can go get Noah, okay?"

She nods her head in agreement.

"Hey! Are you deaf? I said get back behind the tape!" Sheriff Jackson approaches me from behind.

If it wasn't for Raven flinching at his yelling, I would ignore him. But he scared her. He made her afraid. And after whatever the hell she just went through? I can't let that stand.

Between Knox and me, I'm usually the one with a level head. But with this woman, I'll do anything to make her happy and keep her safe.

Setting Raven on her feet, I cup her soot-stained cheeks in my hands. She attempts to encircle her hands around my wrists, but I'm not a small guy. Her fingers and thumb don't even come close to touching. Then I get a glimpse of her eyes when they connect with mine, and it's all I need. The desire to be in her presence solidifies into a vital need required to live.

Sheriff Jackson's voice gets louder and bolder as he continues to yell. "I'm not gonna tell y'all again! Get back behind the tape!"

My hands drop from her face, and I spin my fist cocked back and ready to smash into Sheriff's face. But two sets of hands pull at my clothing, restraining me.

"Not here, Griff. He's not worth it," Knox grunts as he struggles to keep his grip on me.

One set of hands lets go, and Raven steps in front of me, her back plastered to my front. "They're here for me."

Sheriff Jackson angles his body, using the few inches he has on Raven to intimidate her. But she doesn't back down. She keeps herself planted between him and me.

A small droplet of something dark falls from Raven's hand. She's bleeding. She's in pain and bleeding but puts me before herself.

I stop fighting Knox, and he finally lets go. Pulling my shoulders back, I puff up my chest, trying to get the sheriff to back off.

"Family only," Sheriff Jackson informs Raven in a harsh voice.

"They're here. For me," Raven repeats slowly as if he didn't catch her explanation the first time.

Sheriff raises his finger, pointing menacingly at Raven. I swear, I'm going to break that damn finger off his hand.

"I don't give a shit. They're troublemakers. Always have been, always will be. I don't need them messing with my scene." He looks her up and down, aiming to make Raven feel small. "And I have some questions for you concerning all of—"

"Hey! Sheriff!" A man with a bolo tie, cowboy hat, and a Texas Rangers badge pinned to his chest strides right for us. "Where the hell have you been?"

"Doing my job," the sheriff barks back.

"I'm not a newborn calf, Jackson. I told your deputy to inform me when you arrived. What took you so long to get here? And why were my rangers on scene way before you and your men?"

The sheriff's face turns the same shade as a ripe tomato.

Snaking my arm around Raven's torso, I spin us in the direction of the ambulance, leaving the sheriff to get his ass chewed out. "You're hurt, Sunshine. Let's get you patched up."

CHAPTER THIRTY-THREE

KNOX

If I hadn't stopped Griffin, the sheriff might be dead right now. I saw how Raven twitched when the sheriff raised his voice. I was gearing up to go but quickly changed directions when I saw the way Griffin went impossibly still and curled his hand into a fist. If Griffin is ready to throw punches, then I know it's bad.

But as much as I'd love to beat Sheriff Jackson bloody, Raven's health and safety come first.

I step up into the ambulance and narrow my eyes at the EMT who had his hands on Raven earlier. "Out," I bark at him.

The man recoils and shields his face with his hand. I grip his upper arm and guide him so he's standing.

Leaning so I'm closer to his face, I repeat myself, "Out." He doesn't waste time as he scrambles out the back.

Griffin helps Raven up, and I grip her hips and lift her onto the gurney.

"You didn't have to scare off the professional," Raven jokes.

"Yes, I did," I reply.

"Why?" Raven's brows scrunch in question.

Because I came close to putting him in the hospital.

Because no one else gets to touch you.

Because I need to be the one to take care of you.

But none of that comes out of my mouth. Instead, I gently hold Raven's injured hand in mine, assessing the cut on the back of her hand.

"What happened?"

"A piece of glass. The EMT removed it, and he got the bleeding to stop, but I think I opened it up again."

I dig around the drawers and cabinets for the supplies I need. Tossing a wipe and gauze to Griffin, I instruct him to clean Raven's cut and slow down the bleeding. When I find what I'm looking for, I sit back down on the bench in front of Raven and reassess the cut.

"It seems you're always around when I need a doctor," Raven jokes again.

"I'd rather it be me taking care of you instead of some… person," I explain.

"You mean 'man?'" Raven asks with raised brows.

I disregard her accurate assessment. She doesn't need to know the extent of my obsession.

I ask, "Are you okay with needles? I need to numb the area."

"No drugs," Raven demands.

Griffin gapes. "But Sunshine—"

"No," Raven insists again.

"Okay, no anesthesia," I concede reluctantly. Pinching my lips together, I get to work suturing her wound instead of answering her question.

"What happened here, Raven?" Griffin questions.

"Not right now, please. I just—I can't—" Raven rolls her lips inward. She hops up from the gurney and jumps down from the ambulance. "It's time to pick up Noah. I better get going." Then she takes off.

Griffin and I hasten after her and catch up easily. The pandemonium out here has calmed considerably because the firefighters were finally able to extinguish the fire. Although the nosy crowd has multiplied.

Griffin stops Raven with a hand on her shoulder. "Hey, I'm not so sure you're okay to—"

Raven spins around abruptly, jerking back from Griffin's touch. From me. "I don't have any other choice. I'm a single mom. I'm the only one Noah has. It's all on me to make sure he's fed, he's safe, he's clothed. I can't afford to be anything but okay."

Grasping her shoulders, I spin her to me, making sure her eyes are only on me. "Darlin', ever heard that saying, 'it takes a village?'"

"Yes."

"Well, you're part of our village now. You and Noah. Griffin and I may not be experienced in childcare, but we're here." I bend and rest my forehead against hers, lowering my voice. "You're not alone in this. You'll never be alone like that again."

A tear trickles out from the corner of her eye. Raven's voice is high-pitched with emotion. "Don't make promises you can't keep."

"I would move heaven and earth for you, Darlin'. Don't doubt that."

Another tear.

Her eyes search mine for the lie, but she won't find it. Because I'm not lying. Raven and Noah aren't on their own anymore.

"Okay," she whispers. That one simple word makes me feel like I've won the Texas lottery. That four-letter word is another foot in the door, another step closer to convincing her that she's ours.

"Miss Henry?"

Raven takes a step back, but I grab hold of her hand and intertwine our fingers together. And she lets me.

The man who was handing Sheriff Jackson his ass earlier stands next to us, a concerned look on his face. I want to shield her body with mine, but she wouldn't like that.

"What can I do for you, Officer?" The exhaustion in Raven's voice is apparent. Griffin notices it too. We nod at each other, solidifying our plans for the rest of the evening.

"Officer Langston, ma'am." He tips his hat politely. "I know this isn't easy, but I need to ask you a few questions."

Griffin steps in. "Could the questions wait? Raven needs to get her son from school."

Raven's shoulders relax at the idea that she won't have to repeat her story all over again. I'm not even sure how she's still standing. The adrenaline has left her body by now.

"Miss Henry?" Langston asks, wanting Raven's input.

"Yes. My son Noah is just at the elementary school right there." Raven uses her thumb to point over her shoulder. "Would it be possible to be interviewed at my home? I-I can't be here anymore."

"Of course, ma'am."

"Thank you, Officer."

Raven breaks our connection as she turns to head to Mystic River Elementary. But I quickly take hold of her other hand, and once again, she lets me. Griffin drapes his arm across Raven's shoulders, and we walk together.

The knot in my chest eases a fraction. This feeling, this sense of home. It's like this is how it was always meant to be.

Raven, Griffin, and me.

CHAPTER THIRTY-FOUR

RAVEN

"Can we have burgers every night?" Noah asks, but it's muffled.

"Don't talk with your mouth full," I chide him.

"If you want," Griffin answers Noah's question, but that earns Griffin a punch in the arm from Knox.

I can't lie, sitting around the table together is nice. It's something I could easily get used to.

Knox said I'm not alone. I don't want to get used to not being alone, but I can't stop the warmth that spreads through my chest, easing the damage done by so many who came before.

After signing Noah out of school, Griffin steered us toward his truck. My keys are in my purse, which is still in the library and probably burned to a crisp. On our way to my house, Griffin pulled over and picked up dinner from Mystic River Grill. He and Knox thought ahead and ordered online while I got Noah.

Noah has asked questions about what happened, but I have no idea what to tell him. I don't want to lie, but I'm not sure if he needs the full truth right now. He's young, and he's already seen too much of the dark and ugly the world has to offer.

I don't want to revisit what happened in the library, but controlling the thoughts in my brain is difficult with how tired I am. The adrenaline has worn off and left me fatigued.

Seth's face flashes in my mind. Trying to push the image away brings about the start of a headache. His whistles ring in my ears along with the ominous rhyme.

Seth said, "The girl got hit by a rock." But Seth didn't have rocks. He had grenades. Is the rock supposed to be a symbol, or did he *think* he was throwing rocks at me?

Seth also said, "The madman threw the rock," but then later, "The madman gave me the rock." My first assumption is that Seth is the madman. But Seth didn't give himself a rock. So does the madman change meaning at the end, or is the madman someone else the whole time?

I fucking suck at poetry.

Noah swallows his food. "Mom?"

"What? Oh. Umm." I pretend to think through the question. "I don't know if burgers and fries every night for dinner is a good idea." I shake my head.

"Aww, man," Noah complains, and takes another sip of his soda, passively. But when he sets his cup down, he places it on the side of his plate, something that makes my eye twitch.

Every time he does that, I swear on everything I own, he accidentally knocks his drink over. Then it's a whole fiasco, complete with pouting and sometimes crying. So, to prevent the issue, I usually ask Noah to move his cup, or I just do it for him. And today, I decide to move it for him. But it doesn't go unnoticed. Griffin and Knox watch me with puzzled looks on their faces.

"Knox, can you teach me how to drive my own motorcycle?" Noah blurts out.

Knox is thrown off guard. "Uhh…" And that is the way of kids.

"Noah…" I place my hand on his arm.

"Motorcycles aren't just fun toys. They can be very dangerous. If you want to learn when you're older, you're going to have to talk to your mom about that." Knox's answer is perfect. He didn't lie. He didn't make promises that he might not be able to keep. And he didn't brush off Noah.

They're better with kids than they think.

"Mom?"

"Let me think that one over, little king." I know my only experience on a motorcycle wasn't pleasant. I might have enjoyed it if it weren't for Jed being a total asshole.

"So, Noah, how's school going?" Griffin asks. When Noah appears to shut down, Knox punches Griffin in the arm again.

"Fine," he answers with his head down.

Griffin keeps going. "Do you have a best friend at school?"

Noah sinks further into himself. "No."

Knox dishes out another punch, and Griffin acts like he's going to punch Knox back. But Knox widens his eyes and tilts his head toward Noah. Griffin makes a frustrated noise.

He's going to have a nasty bruise later.

Griffin keeps trying. "That's okay, bud. I didn't have a best friend either. Do you know why?"

Noah shakes his head.

"No one liked me." Griffin shrugs a shoulder.

Noah's eyes widen. "What? But you're so cool!" His disbelief is adorable.

Griffin's smile is small but full of affection. "Thanks. But my family was different. Knox and I were made fun of a lot."

"You didn't have a best friend either?"

Knox shakes his head.

"No way," Noah says to himself. I can see the thoughts flying through his brain. "How was your family different?"

Griffin clears his throat. "Well, our mom wasn't around. And—"

"Like she worked a lot?" Noah interrupts.

Guilt wraps itself around my heart and squeezes. I feel bad that I can't give him what every other child has. If it were possible, I wouldn't work at all. I've already missed so much of his life. I don't want to miss anymore. But life costs money, and money isn't free.

"No. Our mom decided she didn't want to be a mom anymore, and she left."

Noah takes a minute to digest the new information. "My mom would never do that to me. But I'm sorry your mom left."

Knox and Griffin both wear a sad smile. Noah's innocence has them both charmed.

"Thank you, Noah. And you're right." Griffin's eyes meet mine. "Your mom would never do that."

His confidence in me bolsters my dwindling belief that I'm not messing this all up. He thinks I'm a good mom. He believes in me.

"So, because your family was different, kids were mean to you," Noah deduces.

"That's right," Griffin confirms.

"I don't like that," Noah states.

Griffin nods his head. "I didn't like it then either. I had to defend myself a lot. Bullies aren't actually all that tough. They'll leave you alone if you stand up to them."

Noah sits back, staring at his mostly empty plate. "May I be excused?" Noah asks me.

I nod. "Clear your plate, then brush your teeth and head for bed, please."

Pushing out his chair, Noah stands with his plate in hand.

"Love you, Mom," he says as he walks by and gives me a small kiss on the cheek.

It's like I suddenly turned into a damn fountain because, for the millionth time today, tears gather in my eyes. "Thank you," I whisper to Knox and Griffin.

Knox repeats his statement from earlier, "You're not alone."

There's a knock at the door, and both men jump to their feet. Knox nods to Griffin and exits the kitchen, heading for the front door.

I stand to go with him, but Griffin keeps me back. "Let him answer the door, Sunshine."

"But it's my front door," I argue.

"Don't be a brat. You went through something traumatic today. I think it's safest if—" Griffin cuts himself off when he hears the door open and Knox starts talking.

"Hello, Officer Langston. Come on in."

The front door slams shut, and footsteps tread to the kitchen.

Langston removes his hat and greets me with a handshake. "Sorry for the late hour, Miss Henry." He's dressed in a denim shirt and denim jeans. The white in the scruff on his face and in his hair is an indication of his age. His tired eyes speak to the long hours he works.

"Not a problem, Officer. And, please, call me Raven."

He nods and turns to the other two men in the room. "I didn't catch your names earlier."

"I'm Knox Montgomery, and this is my brother Griffin."

"Nice to meet you. And how do you know Raven?"

"We're her—"

"Neighbors," I interrupt forcefully. "They're my neighbors."

Griffin and Knox share a secret smirk.

"Please, have a seat." I offer one of the wooden chairs to Langston. "Would you like a cup of coffee?"

"No, thank you, ma'am," he replies as he sits down.

The rest of us occupy the empty chairs and scoot in.

Langston pulls out a pen and a small notepad. "Could you tell me what happened today, Raven?"

"Yeah, sure," I agree, but my stomach is rolling at the thought of having to relive it all over again. Griffin drags his chair so there's no space between us and places his arm around my shoulders. Knox discreetly reaches for my hand under the table, tangling our fingers together and resting them on my thigh.

I'm not alone.

I recount Seth entering the library, his disheveled appearance, the pocket full of grenades, the creepy rhyme he recited, and the way he didn't register when I was trying to talk to him. I recall every sound, every scent, and every word.

I keep my story factual. I know I'm distancing myself from what happened. My eyes don't fill with tears, and my voice is monotone through the whole retelling.

However, the same can't be said of Griffin and Knox. Griffin's shoulders move up and down as his breaths get shallower and closer together. Knox tenses but is careful not to squeeze my hand. But neither interrupts me, nor do they lose control.

By the time I'm done, a cold sheen of sweat covers every inch of my skin.

"Thank you, Raven. I know that wasn't easy," Langston acknowledges.

"No problem." The smile on my face is forced.

Langston positions his pen on his notepad again. "I have a few more questions if you're up for it."

I swallow. "Sure."

"Did you know your attacker?"

"No."

He flips a page. "According to a few witnesses, his name was Seth Beauregard. Does that name sound familiar?"

"Um. No. I can't say that it is." I shake my head.

"And this poem—"

"Nursery rhyme," I interrupt. My heart races as I try to remember what he said. "It was Hickory Dickory Dock, but he changed the words. He said something about a madman and rocks, but…he didn't have rocks."

Griffin strokes my upper arm, and Knox surrounds my hand in both of his. I lean into their touch as a pleasant glow softens my disquiet.

Langston looks at me intently. "Do you have any idea who this madman is that he referenced?"

"No," I lie.

"Well, thank you for your time. I'll get out of your hair." Langston places his hat back on his head and stows the pen and notepad in his pocket.

Knox leads Langston back to the door, and I head upstairs to check on Noah. I peek in his room to find him out cold.

"Goodnight, little king," I whisper as I shut the door quietly.

I almost jump out of my skin when I turn and find Griffin right behind me. My outraged whisper doesn't properly convey my frustration. "What are you doing? You scared me half to death!" I slap his shoulder in the same spot Knox punched him earlier.

Griffin's smirk is like gas on a flame. "We said you wouldn't be alone."

Waving my arms, I whisper-shout again, "We're in my house, you dummy! You don't need to attach yourself like a Siamese twin!"

"Agree to disagree." Griffin snags my hand and leads me

back down the stairs. We go all the way to the kitchen, where we find Knox cleaning up after dinner.

Scurrying over to help, I gather trash and dirty plates. "You didn't have to do this."

"It's not a problem," Knox says simply.

Griffin joins, and we have the kitchen clean in no time.

"Thank you for coming today."

"You don't need to thank us."

Fidgeting with my hands, I contradict Griffin, "But I do. You rushed to my side and stayed with me. You fed Noah and me, you held me while I was interviewed, and…" A sob catches in my throat. "And you reached Noah in a way I haven't been able to."

Instead of giving me words, they give me what I'm starting to crave. Support. Griffin stands at my back and snakes his arms under mine and around my torso. Knox stands at my front and gently holds both of my hands in his, minding my stitches and bringing our hands to his chest.

When my body starts to sway, the day catching up with me, Knox releases my hands, and Griffin sweeps me into his arms. I'm too tired to argue like normal as I'm carried upstairs and to my room. I don't even argue when Knox digs through my drawers and finds a pair of sleep shorts and an oversized tee, handing both to me and leading me to my connecting bathroom. They at least leave me alone to dress. And when I'm done, I walk out to find both of them dressed down to their boxers. I'm so tired that I can't even appreciate the beautifully sculpted bodies in front of me.

Fatigue makes my limbs and eyelids feel heavy. I can't even take the few steps to fall into my bed.

Knox takes me by the hand and leads me to the bed and lifts the comforter. He urges me to slide to the middle, and I comply. Knox slides in after me while Griffin lies down on my other side.

Their hands move my practically lifeless body, positioning me on my side facing Knox. Griffin wraps himself around me from behind while Knox plasters himself to my front. Their warmth is irresistible, and effortlessly, I drift away into unconsciousness surrounded by a bouquet of vetiver mixed with sea salt and bergamot.

CHAPTER THIRTY-FIVE

RAVEN

*S*printing the distance between us, I crash down to my knees. Adjusting his head so I can see his face, it's like the rug is ripped out from under me. The feeling like I'm free falling down a dark hole racks my body.

Shaking his shoulder, tears gather in my eyes. "No. Noah, wake up." But no matter how much I jostle him, he doesn't wake. "Noah!"

Rolling his body all the way over, I get a better look at his injuries. The bruise on his cheek from last week has faded to a light green, but there's fresh bruising. A necklace of purple skin mottles his neck. Blood leaks from the corner of his mouth and nose. But the most concerning wound is the large bleeding gash across his forehead.

"NOAH!"

My body curls over his. My tears mix with his blood.

"Please don't be dead. Please don't be dead," I repeat over and over. Sitting up, I find my shirt wet with blood. I scan his body and realize his shirt is damp. Lifting the cloth, I find a single large stab wound in his stomach.

Naturally, my gaze swings to the top of the stairs, curious to see if the cause of his fall is in plain view.

And it is.

Or rather, he is.

Rising from my huddle, my hands ball into fists. "What did you do?"

My voice is filled with promise—a promise of revenge.

Sleep coats my eyelids, making it difficult to open them. Maybe I can squeeze in a few more minutes before I need to take Noah to school. So I nestle further into the warmth under my cheek. My hand runs up and down my body pillow. It's so nice and…hairy?

What the hell?

Rubbing my eyes, I finally blink into a conscious state of awareness. All too aware.

Maybe this is just a dream. A very erotic dream because if I'm right, I'm sandwiched between two very attractive half-naked men.

I'm lying on my side with my head resting on Knox's chest. His very sexy chest. In my sleep, I've attached myself to his side like a damn monkey. Knox's arm is buried under my pillow, and his other arm is tucked behind his head.

And then there's Griffin. If I'm a monkey, then this man is a boa constrictor. His leg somehow slithered between mine and my legs, having a mind of their own, gripped his in a vice. I can feel Griffin's breath on the back of my neck, telling me his face is nuzzled in my hair.

I'm surprised he hasn't suffocated.

Griffin's thick arms are wrapped around my torso with his hands resting on my stomach. My very bare stomach. Apparently, my shirt decided to shimmy up my body, but thankfully, stopped just under my boobs.

If this isn't a predicament, I don't know what it is.

The blackout curtains in my room are doing their job,

completely blocking out the light, so I have no indication of what time it is. And my phone is nowhere in sight.

A mental groan resounds in my brain as I try to figure out how to get out of this odd game of Twister.

I hope they're not light sleepers.

My hand slides on top of Griffin's, lightly grasping and pulling apart his grip. I move his hand a few inches when he breaks my hold and secures his hands back together.

"Nope. Go back to sleep, Sunshine."

I guess that answers that question.

"I need to take Noah to school," I whisper, hoping not to wake Knox, but my attempt at politeness fails.

"School was canceled today. Besides, he's still asleep." I feel his words vibrate through his chest and against my cheek.

"How do you know that? Do you have my phone? I need to check my email to make sure." I stretch my arm across his body, trying to reach my nightstand.

With his eyes still closed, he shakes his head. "I checked. It's canceled."

I frown. "How?"

"I unlocked your phone. It wasn't hard. By the way, you need to turn off facial recognition."

"What!" I exclaim.

Knox continues as if I'm not outraged. "You never know what someone might do with access to your phone." His voice is too vexatious for my liking.

Propping myself up on my elbow, I jostle Knox and Griffin in the process. "What did you do?" I question with narrowed eyes.

Griffin sniggers behind me, while Knox smirks with his eyes still closed.

Tired of the mystery, I lunge for my nightstand, snatching my phone. Griffin and Knox protest my swift movement, but I don't pay them any mind. With my legs sprawled across

Griffin and my torso smothering Knox, I open my phone and search for anything amiss. No bizarre texts sent, and my background hasn't changed.

Did they…No. They wouldn't. But maybe…

Tapping on my photo app, I find a handful of new pictures of the three of us, but I'm dead asleep.

"What!" I screech for the second time this morning.

I open each picture, ripping off the band aid. In one, Griffin is giving the camera a thumbs up and a goofy smile from behind my head. In another, they're both faking sleep. And in another, my mouth is wide open with my cheek on Knox's chest.

My body shakes from their laughter. I glower at each of them over my shoulder, but that only makes them laugh louder and harder. Pretty soon, the noise is boisterous, and I feel the light of their humor flow through me, infecting my heart. The suppression of my smile fails, and I flip, sitting up between them. I smack them both on the chest.

"You two are menaces to society!" My insult makes Griffin clutch his stomach from laughing so hard, while Knox buries his face in the pillow.

"Mom?"

Shit.

Turning around, I spot Noah in my doorway, dressed in his pajamas and rubbing his eyes. I jump out of bed and stand to the side, wincing. "Did we wake you up?"

I never wanted Noah to see something like this. Nothing happened and nothing was going to happen, but after our history, I want him to feel safe here at home.

Knox waves his hand, motioning Noah forward. When Noah finally realizes who's here, he lights up. He dashes for my bed and jumps on it.

"Did you guys spend the night? On the next sleepover,

can you sleep in my room?" Noah unleashes a barrage of questions and random statements.

Griffin gets his attention by tickling Noah's stomach. "Are you hungry?"

Noah looks down at his stomach as if it holds the answer. "Yes," he responds with a smile.

"How about we make some breakfast?"

I scoff. "Do you know how?"

Noah grimaces and positions his hand to block his words from my ears, but I still hear him. "Mom usually burns the food."

Knox coughs to cover his chuckle, and I shoot him a glare. But he doesn't seem the least bit remorseful as he sassily smirks.

Griffin slaps his hand on his bare chest and makes a pained expression. "Do I know how? Don't insult me, little man." Griffin's ruse ends on a smile.

Noah laughs at Griffin's jesting.

Griffin slaps his lap with both hands and climbs out of my bed. "I'll tell ya what. How about we make a breakfast feast fit for kings and prove to your mom that I'm an amazing cook."

"Yes!" Noah pumps a fist in the air and cheers.

Griffin leans forward, scooping Noah up in his arms, and they begin chanting together. "Fit for kings! Fit for kings!" Their new mantra follows them out of my room and down the stairs.

My hand covers my mouth as tears swim in my eyes.

This. This is what Noah needs. What *I* need.

Vetiver floods my senses as Knox encompasses me in his arms and rests his chin on the top of my head. I let myself lean into him. His warmth seeps into my bones, soothing all the places inside me that have been cold for so long.

Knox's folded arms rest just under my breasts. I resist the

urge to guide his hands to cup them. A pulse starts up in my core, dampening my panties.

I could find refuge in Knox. I could discover a pleasure that's just ours.

But would this all be ripped away if they knew?

My feet carry me forward out of his embrace, and I excuse myself. "I need to get ready for the day." His footsteps follow me through my bathroom and into my closet. I walk all the way inside, while Knox halts at the threshold.

I wanted to be alone for a moment. I need to think things through logically without the haze of their care clouding my brain. When they're around, I want things I never thought I could have.

"Raven."

The tugging in my chest begs me to turn around.

"Darlin', look at me." Knox's voice is pleading.

I cave.

My feet shift me to face him. My eyes wander from his bare feet up his strong legs and chiseled abs. His gaze searches mine. Breath saws in and out of my lungs as I clench my thighs together. Knox bites his lip when he notices the tension in my body and extends his hand, offering himself to me.

Maybe they'll leave. I can't control their choices. But I can control what I do and what I feel.

And right now, I choose to feel this with him.

CHAPTER THIRTY-SIX
RAVEN

I take a few long strides and jump. Knox easily catches me, grabbing my ass with both hands as I wrap my legs around his waist.

Our mouths fuse together, his soft lips gliding over mine. Using my teeth, I gently bite down on his lower lip, and the vibration of his groan rumbles in his chest.

My hands slide from his beautiful locks to his neck. The tips of my fingers graze a bit of raised skin, reminding me of the ink on his back.

I break the kiss and question, "What are the skull and trees for?"

"You want to talk about this *now*?" His disbelieving shock is almost comical.

My shoulder lifts in a shrug. "I'm curious."

The indecision on his face makes me feel like I'm asking for too much. Just as I'm about to take my question back, he blurts out his answer. "I got it at a time in my life when it felt like I had nothing going for me. I felt dead inside and like my world was burning down around me."

My chest cracks with understanding and pain on his behalf. I know what that's like. I know what it feels like to want to give up, to want to just curl in a ball and pass away.

I nibble at my lip. "And now?"

"Well, this beautiful woman and her son moved in next door to me, and now my life is full of light."

It takes great effort to hold back the tears that want to fall.

"No more questions. I need to feel you, Raven."

Knox swings me around, setting me down on the bathroom counter, never breaking our kiss. His hands travel under my shirt and up my stomach. The graze of his fingertips causes me to tremble. I push my hips forward, seeking relief.

His hands engulf my globes and knead them. My core weeps for his touch as his tongue aggressively invades my mouth.

Knox growls, "Show me those tits, Darlin'. I want to see what's mine."

I whimper and do as he says, whipping off my shirt and tossing it aside. I lean back, resting my weight on my hands, and let him look his fill.

The vein in his neck tenses as he grips the edge of the counter. My nipples pebble as Knox ogles my chest.

He bites his lip and slams my bathroom door closed, turning the lock. "I'm going to do everything I've been dreaming about doing to your body, and I don't want to be interrupted."

"Wh-What do you want to do to me?"

Knox approaches me with power in each step. He nudges my knees apart with his hips. "First, I'm going to suck on these." He circles my nipple with the tip of his finger, sending a jolt to my center. "Then I'm going to taste you here." His hand cups my center over the thin material of my shorts. "And then I'm going to fuck you until your squirming and dripping all over my cock."

The moan that works its way up my throat is full of need. "Please."

"I love hearing you beg."

Knox uses his hands to push my breasts together and lifts them up to his mouth. His tongue swirls around one peak and sucks it into his mouth, causing me to cry out and run my fingers through his hair. He releases my nipple with a pop and switches to the other one, giving it the same attention.

My panties grow wet as my pussy clenches. "Please, Knox. Oh God. Please, I need you."

He ignores my plea and drags his tongue from one nipple to the other and sucks again, using his tongue to flick the tip of my breast.

"Please. Please. Please."

"Because you said 'please,'" Knox says with a sultry smirk.

He kisses, licks, and nips his way down my chest and over my stomach. He bites the edge of my shorts and drags them down my legs. Lifting my hips, I help him get my shorts over my ass.

Knox licks his lips as he stares at the apex of my thighs, my pussy glistening with arousal. He pulls my hips forward, bringing me to the edge of the counter. He presses his nose to my curls and inhales. "Fuck, Darlin'. You smell so sweet."

His breath fans across my core, and I pant, desire spreading through my body. I open my thighs even more, giving Knox a better look at me.

Knox pushes his face between my pussy, licking my opening. My head falls back against the mirror, and my eyes roll to the back of my head.

"Look at me, Raven. Watch me eat your cunt," Knox commands, and I comply.

He laps at my wetness like a starving man, teasing my

entrance. I rub my pussy on his face, and he moans. It's better than all my vibrators combined.

Knox grabs my arm, guiding my hand to the back of his head.

Oh fuck. I'm not going to survive this.

"More, Knox. I need more."

He moans harder and louder when I push his head into my pussy. He uses both hands to grab my ass as he shoves his tongue inside me as far as he can.

Knox lifts his head for a brief moment. "Suffocate me, Raven. I want to die right here between your thighs with my tongue in your cunt."

I'm going to need his dirty talk from now on.

He doesn't wait for my response and goes back to tonguing my center. But this time, he circles my clit. His tongue attacks every bit of my pussy.

The tension low in my belly builds with each swipe of his tongue. My hips move faster, fucking his face.

Knox flicks my bundle of nerves then sucks on it hard. My ass lifts off the counter as he takes me to a higher plane of bliss and pleasure. I bite my hand, muffling my cry as my climax hits me.

But Knox doesn't let up. He causes wave after wave of beautiful ecstasy. When he finally stops, I feel like I can breathe again.

"Shit, Knox. You're going to kill me."

He stands, his face shimmering with my cum. His tongue peeps out of his mouth, licking my essence from his lips.

"The sweetest honey."

I whimper as my core pulses with aftershocks.

Knox pulls at the waistband of his boxers, shoving them down his legs. His cock springs free, a bead of precum leaking from his tip.

He's going to rip me in half with that thing.

He wraps his hand around his shaft and pumps a few times, causing more precum to spill. "I'm not going to be able to hold back. Are you sure?"

"Yes. I want you. I need you inside me." I scramble for the drawer next to my knee, opening it and pulling out a condom from the brand-new box.

Knox rips the condom from my hands. "Who did you buy the condoms for, Raven?"

My eyes blink in confusion. "What?"

He grits his teeth. "Who are the condoms for?"

"You. You and Griffin. I just bought them the other day."

"Good."

He growls, gripping my chin and pressing his lips to mine. He thrusts his tongue in my mouth, forcing me to taste myself. I moan in his mouth, reveling in the rich flavor.

I retrieve the condom from his hands, rip it open, and roll the rubber down his length.

Knox's fingers dig into the flesh at my hips, holding me still as he drives forward and seats himself all the way inside me.

"Damn, Darlin'. I'm going to need this every day. Promise me, I'll get this cunt every day. I'm already addicted."

My mind spins, basking in the way my pussy stretches around his thick length. He digs his fingers in harder, demanding a response.

"Yes. Everyday. Move right now, and I'll let you come inside me every day."

Knox smirks. "Deal." He moves his hips back and thrusts forward, repeating the motion.

"Shit, shit, shit," I chant.

My already primed pussy flutters around his cock. Sweat drips down my spine as we move together. He pistons his hips faster and harder, staring at my boobs.

Knox groans, "Your tits look so pretty bouncing like that for me."

A whimper escapes my lips, and I squeeze his waist harder with my legs. My inner muscles tighten, and he groans again.

"Squeeze that cunt around my dick."

His dirty words bring me closer to my release. I'm so close, and he knows it.

Knox snakes his hand between our writhing bodies and easily finds my clit. His fingers pinch my bundle of nerves, setting off fireworks in my core.

His other hand covers my mouth as my pussy contracts, squeezing his length. Knox moans as he empties his own release inside me. He continues to fuck me, drawing out my orgasm.

With a final pump of his hips, we both collapse. Knox rests his forearm against the mirror above my head. His hair and chest are wet with perspiration.

"Damn, Raven," he pants.

"I'm ready to go back to sleep," I admit.

"I was going to suggest we go again," Knox teases with a wink.

I huff. "Good joke."

Knox dips his head, kissing and sucking my neck. "I'm serious," he mumbles into my sensitive skin.

"Well, they do say to obey your elders." I smile at my own joke.

Knox gently bites my neck, and I yelp, scooting away. His dick glides from me, and we both groan. Knox plants his lips on mine, the kiss heating up quickly.

Faint cheers drift through the door. "Ride the bikes! Ride the bikes!"

Knox and I break apart, chuckling.

"We should go check on them," Knox suggests, and I nod in agreement. He helps me off the counter and dresses me.

My chest ties up in knots at the gentle way he slides my shorts up my legs. His touch is gentle and attentive. My eyes water as my throat clogs with emotion.

Fun is starting to look more like forever.

CHAPTER THIRTY-SEVEN

GRIFFIN

Noah opens the walk-in pantry and exuberantly runs inside. Not even a moment later, he pops his head back out. "What all do we need?"

"Let's have a look." I follow behind him and point out everything we need. Noah dutifully carries each ingredient and sets them on the counter. "I think that's everything."

"Wait!" he exclaims, then runs back into the pantry. He returns with two aprons. The small one is covered in trains, and he hands the other to me. It's purple with embroidered words that read "No Bitchin' in my Kitchen."

"Uhh…" I stutter.

"Put it on," Noah demands.

The things I do for this kid…

Aprons on, we work together to mix the batter and turn on the stove. He's a top-notch sous chef. I show him how to pour the batter, and we go over the rules around the stove. Once I'm satisfied that he understands, we get back to it.

"How do we cook the other side?"

"Like this." I slip the spatula under the pancake and toss

it in the air so it'll land back on the pan. It's a move I perfected in my early twenties, but I must have forgotten the trick because the pancake doesn't flip.

Noah looks down at the pancake, then at me, and back at the pancake. "I think that's not how you do it."

Some time and many more failed attempts later, Noah scrutinizes the pancake batter on the ceiling. "I thought you said you knew how to cook."

"I did." Grimacing, I pour more batter onto the pan. The new pancake sizzles a little too much. "It's been a while."

Noah hops off the stool I pulled up to the counter for him so he could help and moves to my other side where the stack of finished pancakes sits. "They're really brown."

Scratching the back of my head, I examine the pile and realize he's right.

Okay, time to pivot.

Turning off the stove, I sweep Noah up in my arms and spin in circles. "You mean you're not going to eat the perfectly burned pancakes we slaved to make?" He giggles and grabs for me, afraid he'll fly out of my grasp.

"Okay! Okay! I'll eat them! Put me down!" Noah yelps in between his laughter.

I sit him back on the stool and ruffle his hair. "I'm just pulling your leg."

Noah blinks repeatedly and glances down at his lap. "No, you're not."

My lips pinch, holding back my grin. Clearing my throat, I explain, "It's an expression. It means that I was joking."

Noah squints. "What does joking have to do with legs?"

"Well…that's…a good question. I actually have no idea. It's just something people say." I shrug.

Noah does the same. "So, what now?"

"Now, we get you changed out of your pjs and go out for breakfast."

"Can we ride the motorcycles?" Noah squeals, reaching a pitch I've never heard before in my life.

Oh, hell. I don't know how to say no to this kid, but I can't give him a definitive answer. So, I come up with the next best thing.

"If your mom says it's okay, then yeah. We can take the motorcycles."

He squeals again, jumping at me and hugging me around my neck. I return the hug so he doesn't fall. Noah pulls back but keeps one arm around me. Thrusting his fist in the air like we did before, he creates a new chant.

"Ride the bikes! Ride the bikes!"

I join in with him, and his smile grows.

"What's going on down here?"

We stop our shouts, and my eyes snap to the bottom of the stairs. Raven and Knox stand together, observing the mess Noah and I have made.

Raven's jaw drops. "What did you do to my kitchen?"

Noah points his finger at me. "Griffin did it."

"Hey!" In retaliation, I poke his side, causing him to giggle again. I face Raven and Knox. "I guess I lost my magic pancake touch. We need to go get breakfast."

Noah raises his fist again. "Ride the bikes! Ride the bikes!"

Raven's shock turns into a reluctant grin. "Fine. But this mess needs to be cleaned up before we go."

Knox sighs and strides past us, grabbing the cleaning supplies from under the sink. Raven wrinkles her brow.

Shit.

We're not supposed to know where those are.

I step in Raven's view of Knox. "Why don't you go back to bed and relax, Sunshine. Pull out the book we found in your nightstand, *Letting Go* by Liz Colbert, but don't touch that other thing we found." Her face turns an adorable shade of pink. "We'll have this place cleaned up soon."

"Sure." She nods her head, but her expression doesn't change as she heads back upstairs.

"Knox," I whisper with force. I raise my brows and jut my chin forward.

He brushes me off. "She'll find out eventually. It's inevitable."

"But maybe we should decide when that is," I reply slowly.

Knox ignores me and gets to cleaning, and Noah and I follow suit.

Raven might hide from us when she gets an idea of the full picture. But she's already in too deep. The moment she walked into The Wandering Raven, she sealed her fate.

CHAPTER THIRTY-EIGHT

RAVEN

"N̲o."

"Yes."

Griffin crosses his arms. "No."

"You're not the boss of me." I dig my heels in.

Griffin raises a brow. "Actually, I am."

I was caught in the act. The act was getting ready for work. Griffin acted as if I were kicking puppies, but I was just putting on mascara. So, we commenced in a standoff and neither side has backed down.

My nostrils flare on my exhale. "It's been a week since the library…incident. I want to get back to work."

"And I'm telling you no." His tone almost feels condescending.

Knox appears behind Griffin's shoulder. "What's going on here?"

Griffin gestures to me. "Raven wants to go to work tonight."

"Griff…" Knox breaths through his teeth awkwardly.

"No," Griffin repeats.

Relaxing my shoulders on a big exhale, I step up to Griffin. My hands clasp together around his neck, and the shift in his mood is immediate. The hard lines etched in his face soften, and his muscles loosen. His arms drop, and his hands land on my hips. Griffin's amber irises find my blue, and a wave of peace lulls us both.

My hands tangle in his hair and massage the back of his head. He groans and tips his head backward.

My fingers still. "I know you're worried. But I'm okay. I'm safe. The man who attacked me is dead."

Griffin's jaw tenses at my mention of Seth.

I offer more reassurance, hoping it'll give him the calm he needs. "He's not coming back. The Wandering Raven has you, Knox, Benny…I won't be by myself."

Griffin's focus sways between Knox and me. "You don't go anywhere without one of us. Not even the storeroom. I want someone to have eyes on you at all times."

In hopes of cracking a smile, I salute him. "Sir, yes, sir."

He squints and smacks my ass.

"Hey!" I cry out.

Griffin raises his finger, scolding me. "Don't be a brat." His seriousness cracks and a smirk makes its way through.

"No promises," I mock.

Shaking his head, he walks away, but he shouts, "We leave in twenty. And I'm driving!"

"He just worries about you," Knox explains.

"I know." My body leans back against my bathroom counter.

Knox steps up to me. "We both do."

Without thought, my thighs spread, and Knox steps closer. He reaches under my ass, lifting and setting me on the cold quartz.

He dips his head, and my lips meet his eagerly. The jolt to my core has me rearing to go, wanting a repeat of his first performance in my bathroom. But his hands don't move from where they rest on either side of my hips. I lift my leg to wrap around his hip and pull him closer, but he breaks our kiss and steps back.

"Don't want to distract you," he says with a wink.

I push out my lower lip in a pout. "But I like your brand of distraction."

He leans forward. His mouth finds my neck and sucks hard. I cry out as his hand reaches between us and covers my pussy. Knox releases my neck with a pop and growls, "I'll teach you to crave it. Crave me." He releases his hold and swiftly exits.

Panties soaked.

Nipples hard.

Core aching.

I think it's safe to say I'm addicted.

"Benny!"

"Raven!"

That big softy. He definitely missed me. And in the blink of an eye, I know he'll go right back to pretending to be annoyed by me.

Griffin and Knox walk off to get to work, and I fill my spot behind the bar. And just like I predicted, Benny won't look my way again. As always, he's watching the TV behind me.

At least some things don't change.

And that saying holds true an hour later when The Wandering Raven is packed. You'd think that after someone throws grenades around the public library, the community would be too afraid to leave their houses. But I guess not in Texas.

With a tray in hand, I meander around the bodies all over the bar, handing out drinks and food orders. Knox and Griffin have taken turns back and forth helping out. Sometimes they're both on the floor with me. And Griffin is always sure to find me.

But at the moment, neither Griffin nor Knox is out here helping, and I'm getting swamped. I saw both of them walk out the front, but that was twenty minutes ago.

Dropping my tray behind the bar, I grab the keys to Knox's bike and stomp to the kitchen. "Camden, you got orders!" I leave him there with a perplexed expression on his face and march to Benny. "You're on drinks. I'll be right back."

Benny watches me leave a trail of smoke in my wake as I march out to Knox's bike. I've ridden it with him enough in the last week to know what I'm doing…I hope.

After a few minutes of failing to start it, I give up and set out on foot. I don't know how long the walk is, but we'll see.

Benny and Camden are going to have to hold down the fort a little while longer.

The tire tracks are easy enough to follow, and the full moon lights the path for me. The further I walk, the taller the grass becomes, and the louder the rattle of the cicadas gets.

A chill snakes up my spine, making my muscles go taut. My arms fill with goosebumps, so I hug myself to stave off the sudden cool breeze.

The cacophony of the cicadas blends together to create one sound. One word.

My name floats around me. I turn in a circle in search of the source but find nothing. I spin one more time and pause. Someone stands a few yards back down the path.

Raven. Raven. Raven. Raven.

"Hello?" I call to them, but they don't reply. They don't move. It's like they didn't hear me at all.

Raven. Raven. Raven. Raven.

My name breaks into a million voices whispering over each other.

I swing my head from side to side, but still nothing. My focus goes back to the figure on the road, but I find him closer than before.

Gasping, I jump back. "Who are you?"

Still no answer.

Raven. Raven. Raven. Raven.

As my hands become clammy, I fish in my back pocket for my phone. Turning on the built-in flashlight, I point it in front of me.

"It's not real. It's not real." I fail to convince myself, and my stomach flips. Illuminated in the beam is the person I miss the most.

Noah Kelly.

He looks just like he did when I found him on the stairs, but without all the blood. The dent in his head is there as if that's how his head is shaped.

His mouth opens like it did a couple of weeks ago, but his voice sounds like he's talking underwater. His lips don't move to shape each word, but I know it's him speaking. "You weren't there."

My lips quiver. "I-I'm sorry. I'm so sorry. I should have s-stayed home that day."

Noah's voice becomes clearer. "You're not done."

"What?"

"You're not done, Raven." Noah lifts his arm, presenting me with the belladonna clutched in his hand.

I step closer, taking the deadly flower from his grasp.

"You're not done, Raven."

"What are you talking about?"

"You're not done."

His mouth stretches wider, forming creases in his cheeks. But he doesn't stop. His chin stretches closer to his chest as the skin at the corners of his mouth separates, splitting his face in two. Little creatures with tiny legs trickle out of the hole in Noah's face.

The sight of spiders gets my feet working again. I shove my phone back in my pocket and hasten down the road in the direction of the barn.

My shoe catches on the tip of a rock, causing me to fall to the unforgiving dirt. A tickle scurries up my leg. A glance down reveals that a few spiders have caught up with me and are climbing up my body.

Scrambling backward, I brush off the spiders, clamber back to my feet, and take off in a dead sprint.

The further I get from Noah, the warmer the night becomes. Sweat rolls down the side of my face, and the muscles in my legs begin to burn, but I don't stop. I don't stop when my chest starts to ache. I don't stop when I spot the lights of the barn.

A pained shout bleeds from the structure, and I finally skid to a stop.

What the hell?

CHAPTER THIRTY-NINE

RAVEN

Creeping up to the barn, I keep my footsteps light. Even with the gravel beneath my feet, I'm able to remain silent.

The red painted wood of the barn is half gone, weathered away by the elements and time. There aren't any windows that I can see. The only entrance and exit are the double doors at the front, which are cracked open.

Inching as close as I dare, I peer inside without being seen. The barn lacks the stalls you would typically expect to find in a barn. Instead, it's just one huge room. In the middle, a man is strapped to a chair. The cut on his cheek and his split lip drip blood down his face and onto his shirt. A light hangs above his head, doing little to light the barn. Griffin and Knox stand facing him, so their backs are to me.

"I didn't even hit him that hard," Knox claims.

Griffin shakes his head. "I keep telling you that you need to pull your punches."

The man in the chair raises his head, meeting Griffin's

and Knox's scrutiny with a glower of his own. He spits a wad of blood, and it lands at their feet.

"Let's try this again." Griffin sighs.

Knox balls his fist and punches the restrained man right in the eye. The man's head thrusts back from the force of the hit and groans.

Griffin dangles a small plastic bag with deep red pills in front of the man's face. "Where did you get these?"

My hand flies to my mouth, covering the gasp that wants to slip free.

Where did they get those? They look like the pills I saw Dr. Whitlock with. Why do Griffin and Knox have them? Are they dealing with Whitlock as well as those bikers?

A tremor ripples through my muscles, causing my foot to slip and kick the door.

Shit. Shit. Shit.

"Who's out there?"

I don't wait for them to find me out here and run back the way I came. Hopefully, the spiders are gone by now, but I can't let arachnophobia slow me down.

"Raven!"

Their bellows are accompanied by pounding footsteps on the road. I take a hurried glimpse over my shoulder and find them closer than I would like. I push my stride to lengthen and my feet to hit the ground faster. My arms ache as they swing in time with the movement of my legs.

"Raven, wait!"

The trip back is faster than the one I took out to the barn. The sultry words of Jason Alden radiate from the bar along with hoots and hollers of people having a good time. I give myself a split second to choose between the bar and continuing to run down the road.

Dark and dreary road or crowded bar?

The saying "strength in numbers" still lives on for a reason.

My feet carry me through the parking lot and up the steps of The Wandering Raven. I burst through the door and into the fray of line dancers, people doing shots, and billiards. The revelers enjoying their evening relish in their ignorant bliss.

Benny yells over the raucous partyers, "Raven! You're finally back! Get over here! I need your help!"

Does Benny know? Does he know what Griffin and Knox do out at their barn? Is he in on it too?

Shaking my head at him, I dash into the hallway, searching for a hiding place.

Bathrooms? Too obvious.

Office? Too close.

A single sliver of light cuts through the wall right next to the office door. The peculiarity draws me closer. I slid my fingers into the crack and pull. The wall peels away easily, revealing a secret door and a hidden descending staircase.

A basement? Should I try hiding down there? Do I have a choice?

My name sails through the air over the carousing of the bar. "Raven!"

Fear propels me forward, closing the door behind me and flying down the stairs. Reaching the bottom, I'm hit with an atmosphere I didn't expect to find. There are people sitting around tables playing cards, and more people crowd a bar off to the right, shouting at the array of televisions hanging on the wall. Various sports games and entertainment are streaming live on the screens.

My brain can't even begin to form theories. All I can think is "hide."

Strolling across the floor to the rambunctious spectators, I act like I'm supposed to be here. I slide through the cheering and shouts and find an empty seat. Tucking my elbows into my sides, I try to make myself smaller. But being a tall woman with hips, that task is nearly impossible.

The man on my right is shouting at a TV with a basketball game, and the man on my left cheers for some type of fighting match on another screen. A few behind me are arguing about the stats for a professional sports player that I've never heard of.

A woman in a long-sleeved tee tends the bar like she belongs there. She stands at the end with her back to me, dealing with a few rowdy customers. Her small stature is misleading because the attitude and sass she slings all over the place lets everyone know that they shouldn't mess with her. There's something about her that seems familiar, but I can't put my finger on it.

She approaches me, throwing a towel over her shoulder. "What're you havin'?"

My eyes comically pop out of my head. "Florence?"

"Oh, howdy there, Raven! Funny seein' you down here."

What universe have I landed myself in?

My head spins. "You're a bartender?"

I peek over my shoulder, looking for Griffin and Knox. They must not have figured out I'm down here because I don't see them anywhere. Hopefully, they don't put two and two together at all.

"Sure am. Librarian by day and bartender by night. Just like you." Her smirk is knowing, but I'm not sure what she knows that I don't. "Well, no library right now." She shrugs. "Anything to drink?"

It's like an out-of-body experience. "I'll have a vodka tonic, please." I need to be alert, but not that alert. If I get any more aware of my surroundings, I'll explode. Maybe I can hide out here for a bit, and when a large group of people leaves, I'll file out with them.

Florence pours my drink and sets it down in front of me. Without a second thought, I grab it and down it like a shot. The burn hits my throat, and I hold back a cough.

"Rough night?" Florence asks with raised brows.

Wiping my eyes, I set the glass back on the counter. "You could say that." Another glance tells me I'm still in the clear. I exhale a steadying breath, forcing my shoulders to relax.

Florence rolls her lips inward. "I have a feeling you're in for the night of your life."

"What?"

I follow her line of sight to the staircase and spot two identical furious men. They separate, scanning the room. Sitting forward on my stool, I rub my chest. Maybe if I sit perfectly still, I won't draw their attention…

Dumbest idea ever. I'm not an ostrich burying their head in the sand.

Okay. I need a plan.

I'm faster than they are. I could bolt for the stairs, taking them by surprise.

Is there another option?

No.

Here goes nothing…

CHAPTER FORTY

KNOX

Worst night ever.

Maybe we should've been more transparent with Raven, but now that's just wishful thinking. And unfortunately for her, we're not giving her a choice in this. She's not going anywhere.

When Griffin and I chased Raven down the road, I questioned if she'd been a runner in a previous life. I was just happy to see Raven run for the bar and not head for town. That would've been dangerous running down a road like that into town. And she would have been in a world of trouble if she had chosen that route. Just the thought of Raven in danger has the edges of my vision tingeing with red.

I was only a few seconds behind Raven, but when I got through the entrance of The Wandering Raven, she was lost in the flood of people having a good time. Griffin and I searched every inch of the place, leading us to the conclusion that there was only one other place she could be…

Downstairs.

Once again, I had an "I told you so" moment with my earlier self. We should have been more forthcoming. But we are where we are, and from here on, we will make it perfectly clear to Raven that no matter what, she can't get rid of us. There's nowhere she can run; there's nowhere she can hide that we won't find her.

Now, Griffin and I are searching for Raven amongst the many gamblers of our hidden basement.

Griffin meanders between the poker tables while I inspect the bar. With each step closer to the bar, the stronger the ache in my chest becomes.

She's here. I know it.

Letting my instincts be my guide, I elbow my way through the rowdy people watching the games and races on the TVs. It doesn't take me long to find her. Raven's long hair is unmistakable.

I watch as she plants her feet on the floor, placing her hands on the bar. Her shoulders move up and down, readying herself. I smile at her tenacity.

Sorry, Darlin'. Not this time.

Stepping backward, I keep my eyes on her as I leave the crowd. She wants to make this a game? We'll make it a game.

I nod to Griffin, then tip my head in Raven's direction. He reads me easily and comes right to my side. He raises his brows in question, and I reply with a smirk. Griffin draws his head back, blinking, and I nod my head again. He smiles with a shake of his head.

Most don't understand our nonverbal communication. That's okay. They're not meant to. We've always been this way. It's just something we do.

We creep over to the staircase, positioning ourselves on either side of it in the shadows. And just like I predicted, Raven slips from her perch on the stool and shoots for the stairs. When her foot touches the bottom step, Griffin and I make ourselves known. Griffin grabs Raven from behind, covering her mouth with his hand, and I step ahead to open the door at the top. Raven struggles, yelling behind Griffin's restraint and kicking her feet out. Her thrashing is meant to throw Griffin off balance, but it doesn't work. He's too solid.

Once we're out, I help Griffin get Raven into the office. Griffin slams the door shut with his back, not breaking his hold on Raven. I stand in front of them, deciding how to keep Raven from hurting herself.

"Let go of me," Raven grunts as she refuses to give up the fight.

Her shoe grazes the outside of my thigh, and her hand whacks me in the head. Griffin chuckles when I duck out of the path of Raven's other hand.

"That's enough," I growl.

Griffin uses a leg to wrap around Raven's and then the other. I grab Raven's wrists and switch my grip to one hand. Lifting her wrists above her head, I push them against the door. My body leans into her, securing her hips between mine and Griffin's to prevent her from throwing her weight around.

Raven's heavy breathing pushes her breasts into my chest. My free hand twitches, needing to feel the weight of her soft globes in my hand again. I watch as her nipples pebble.

"Mind telling us what had you wandering out to the barn, Sunshine?" Griffin queries.

Raven raises her chin. "I needed help in the bar, and both of you disappeared. I'm sure Benny and Camden are swamped now. How about you put me down and we can all go pitch in out there?"

"Nice try," I snort. We let go, then she'll run, and we'll never see her again. That's not happening. That's *never* happening.

Raven still tries to convince us. "If we don't, you'll probably lose customers."

Griffin smiles as if she's telling a joke, which she might as well be. "People come for the atmosphere, not the service. And we're the only bar in town. We basically have a monopoly."

Raven rolls her eyes.

I raise my brows to emphasize my demand. "Now, tell us why you ran. Don't bother denying anything."

Her fingers flex in my grasp. "I thought it was just weed."

Understanding dawns on Griffin's face. "Ahh. I see."

"Well, this is insulting," I comment.

"Offending you is the least of my worries," Raven snarks.

Time to set the record straight. "You were right. We do sell weed, but…"

"We don't sell pills," Griffin corrects her.

Raven remains unconvinced. "Uh-huh. Sure."

"This," I pull the plastic bag from my pocket that Griffin handed me earlier at the barn, "is what we found on the dealer, who is the man you saw tied up in the barn. Dealers selling these pills have been popping up all over the area."

I can see the hesitation in Raven's eyes. She's mad and doesn't want to believe us, but she does.

Griffin and I exchange a grin, and Raven eyes us suspiciously.

"Don't you dare," Raven warns.

But we don't listen.

Griffin's hands glide up Raven's stomach and cup her tits. Raven squirms, rolling her lips in to trap her moan inside.

I smile at Raven mischievously, earning me a glare. I undo her denim shorts and slip my hand inside but stop just before I reach the apex of her thighs. "Say it again. Tell us how you don't want this."

Raven groans in frustration, gyrating her hips to push my

hand lower. But I keep my hand where it is, infuriating her even more.

As Griffin massages her globes, I push Raven's shorts and lacy thong down her legs, knocking off her shoes as well. Rising back to my feet, I trace my fingers up her luscious legs, causing a shiver to roll through her.

She's so responsive. I love it.

I swipe my fingers back and forth right above her center. Her breathing picks up its speed as I ratchet up her need.

I want her desperate for us. I want her out of control and lost in desire.

Griffin drags his teeth over the column of Raven's neck. "Are you gonna lie to us, Sunshine? Are you gonna tell us to stop?"

Her whimpers cause more blood to rush to my dick, making my shaft impossibly hard. I could come in my jeans just from listening to her sounds.

Griffin smoothly rips Raven's top over her head and unhooks her bra. Her boobs spring free, giving me the best view. They're so full and round. The urge to suckle her alluring pink tips is difficult to suppress, but I need her begging.

I slide my hand over Raven's slit, her arousal gathering on my fingers and pushing it back. Griffin uses one hand to tug and twist her stiff peak while his other slides between their bodies. He reaches for her opening from behind and uses her cream to lubricate her back hole.

Raven stiffens, apprehension clear on her face.

"Trust me," Griffin implores. Raven's lack of response is answer enough.

Working together, Griffin and I tease both of Raven's holes, and we don't stop until she's panting so hard that her tits jiggle with each breath.

She growls in irritation, but neither of us penetrate her openings.

"Got something to say, Darlin'?"

"Fuck you!" she grits out.

"That can be arranged," Griffin jokes.

I give her a small taste of what she wants, dipping the tip of my digit inside her pussy. Her mewls become more frequent.

She may think this is punishment, but it's just as torturous for us.

Raven finally caves. "Ugh! Please! Just…Please!"

"Please, what?" The sensuality in my voice adds to my own need.

"Please, fuck me! I want to come!"

"Sure thing, Sunshine," Griffin growls in her ear.

Simultaneously, Griffin pushes his finger past Raven's tight ring of muscle, and I thrust two fingers in her pussy.

"Fucking finally," Raven sobs. She becomes an active participant as she wraps one arm around my neck and reaches behind her to Griffin with the other. She uses her grip on us to help her move up and down, fucking our hands.

Scissoring my fingers, I play with her g-spot.

"Yes! Right there. Oh my God. Right there." A dot of sweat trickles down her neck, rolling between her breasts. Her tips are pointed upward, as if they're begging for my mouth.

And who am I to turn down the wants and needs of the most perfect pair of tits I've ever seen?

Dipping my head, I suck one nipple in my mouth, flicking and swirling my tongue around her pink tip. The sound that builds in her throat is one of pure pleasure, so I continue my ministrations.

When I feel her inner muscles clench around my digits, I know she's close. Griffin and I nod at each other and double our efforts.

"Shit, shit, shit." Raven freezes, her entire body tensing up as she reaches the peak of her orgasm. Her moan echoes off the walls as she plummets into ecstasy.

Griffin and I continue stroking, easing Raven through her climax. Raven slumps when the last ripple leaves her, her entire body relaxing.

"That was just the start, Sunshine."

"What?"

I grin at her shock as Griffin and I lead Raven over to the desk. Hastily, we undress and watch as Raven's eyes widen with every piece of clothing we remove. I hop up on the desk, guiding Raven to straddle my lap.

My erection easily slips between her wetness, and we moan together. I reach behind me to open a drawer and fish for a condom, but Raven places her hand on my cheek, turning my head to look at her.

"I don't want anything between us." Her other hand rests on my chest, right over my heart. She looks over her shoulder at Griffin. "Any of us."

Griffin groans.

"Are you sure?"

She nods. "I have an implant in my arm. We don't need it."

"Fuck. You're amazing." My lips capture hers, sucking on her bottom lip. My hands spread under her ass. "Put me inside you, Darlin'."

Raven raises to her knees, gripping my length. She brings the tip of my cock to her entrance, then falls down to my lap, impaling herself on my dick. She drops her head on my shoulder, biting down to muffle her moan. Her pussy spasms around my length.

Gritting my teeth, I desperately instruct, "I'm gonna need you to move, Raven."

She lifts up on her knees, sliding her warm heat along my

shaft, then drops back down. Her muscles tense as she moans in pleasure. She repeats the motion and easily finds a rhythm bouncing on my dick. She rests her hands on my shoulders to help her move faster. I grip her hips, thrusting my hips to get myself deeper.

I need her to take every inch. I need the feeling of her surrounding me.

Each jiggle of her flesh makes it more difficult to hold back my orgasm. I run my hands over every inch of her skin, loving the feel of her curves shaking with the force of our thrusts.

Griffin moves closer, grabbing the globes of her ass. Raven falters as she looks over her shoulder. Her back arches, brushing her breasts against my chest.

I quickly reach for the same drawer and pull out the bottle of lubricant, handing it to Griffin. He squirts out a good amount into his hand and massages Raven's other hole.

Raven's thrusts become harder as her need escalates.

"Relax for me, Sunshine," Griffin rasps in her ear.

Raven nods and does her best to hold still in my lap. He places his hand in the middle of her spine and steers her forward. She leans into me and immediately reaches for my lips with her own. I give her what she wants, distracting her with a kiss. She clutches onto my shoulders, needing to find purchase.

I can feel Griffin push himself in Raven's ass as her fingers dig into my skin. She whimpers in my mouth as Griffin and I fill her together.

"I'm so full. It's too much." A drop of sweat forms on Raven's brow as she scrunches her face.

Griffin sweeps Raven's hair over one shoulder and licks up her neck. "Breathe, Baby. We'll take care of you."

Her whimper is answer enough.

Griffin lifts Raven by her ass as I lift her by her thighs. As we bring her back down, sheathing our cocks in her holes, we pump our hips, drilling in further.

We repeat the movement, and Raven moans, tilting her head up to the ceiling. Griffin turns her face to the side, capturing her lips with his own.

Spurred by Raven's response, we keep going. She becomes slicker with every thrust. Her arousal drips down my dick and over my balls, creating a puddle on the desk.

Raven's pussy contracts, and Griffin and I feel it, letting us know she's getting close to her release.

As Raven and Griffin keep their mouth sealed together, I dip my head and cover her pink nipple with my mouth. Her answering groan vibrates through her as her whole body tenses, and she explodes with pleasure.

Her pussy tightens and sucks the cum right out of my dick. I moan with her tit still in my mouth, drawing her orgasm out longer. Griffin erupts with a groan of his own as he reaches his climax.

Coming down from the high of our release, we all have a hard time regulating our breaths and heartbeats. Ever so slowly, Griffin pulls out from Raven, both of them groaning at the movement. Reluctantly, I stand from the desk, allowing Raven to slide down my front and my dick to slip free from her warmth. We moan together, a shiver rippling through her body.

My attention goes to the apex of her thighs and the mixture of cum leaking from her holes.

"Shit, that's hot," I curse, ready to go again. Instead, my index finger tips her chin, giving myself her sweet lips. The kiss is chaste but intense.

When our lips part, Griffin runs his fingers through the mess we've made on her inner thighs. He turns her head to the side, and without being told, Raven opens her mouth, sucking Griffin's fingers clean.

Another groan rumbles in the back of my throat.

Raven opens her lips, running her tongue along the underside of Griffin's fingers as he pulls them from her mouth.

"Let's get you cleaned up, Darlin'." I need to do something, or else we're going to go another round, and I'd rather let her rest. Griffin and I were fairly rough.

I find the extra shirt I keep in here for emergencies and drop to my knees in front of Raven. She looks down at me, blinking her eyes and frowning. Her confusion is adorable while simultaneously infuriating.

Has no one ever kneeled at her feet? Has no one ever taken care of her after sex?

Raven is the type of woman who was made to be worshipped. I'd make a blood offering at her altar multiple times a day if she'd let me. She has the body of a real woman. Her ass, her breasts, her hips.

She is perfection.

Once I'm done, Griffin helps Raven dress back into her clothes, while I search for my own. When we're all clothed again, Raven's gaze roams around the room. She looks everywhere but at us.

"Sunshine," Griffin addresses her.

"Hmm?" Raven responds but still won't make eye contact.

Griffin tips his head, a sign for me. I round to Raven's back and circle my arms around her middle, while Griffin steps up to her front and rests his hands on her hips. We sandwich her between us, not a whisper of air between our bodies.

"Raven, are you okay?" Griffin tries again.

Her answer is hurried. "Yeah, I'm fine."

I tilt my head to the side to get a view of her profile. "Is what we did okay? Did we push you too far?"

"What?" Raven's mouth pops open. "No. Not at all. I loved every second of that."

"Then what's on your mind? You're not here." I lift my hand to tap her temple, then fold her in my full embrace again.

She bites her lip pensively. "I've seen those pills before."

That is not what I was expecting.

Griffin rushes to inquire. "What do you mean? Where?"

"I saw Dr. Lewis Whitlock doing a sale at the grocery store with a man and then again with the same man outside the psychiatric hospital."

I scoff. "Well, that's quite brazen of him, but I'm not surprised. Most people love him, and some steer clear of him." Shaking my head, I continue, "But to deal those pills in public? That's a whole new level of audacity."

Griffin's focus is cast downward as he thinks through the new information. "I'm not surprised. He's always been that way." He finally looks up, asking Raven for more information. "Do you know who the man was?"

"Yeah, I met him outside the elementary school when he tried to pick me up." Raven makes a disgusted face. "He said he was the mayor and that his name is—"

"Frank LeBlanc," I finish for her.

That man. That goddamn man. There are plenty of people I don't like in Mystic River, but him? I'd relish in the slow death I'd give him. I'd use his blood to paint the walls. I'd record his screams so they could lull me to sleep every night.

I drop my arms away from her body as the twitch transitions into a shake, and the onslaught of adrenaline causes my heartbeat to race. My hands pull at my hair as I shout to the room, "Fuck!"

"Knox? What's wrong?" Raven tries to take a step toward me, but Griffin holds her back.

"Give him a second," he instructs her.

"That motherfucker!" Sweat dots my skin, and my breaths become shallow and quick. I spin with my fist at the ready and send it flying through the drywall.

I'll end him.

CHAPTER FORTY-ONE

RAVEN

The muscles of Knox's back remain tense as he faces the wall, his fist covered in white dust. He's almost manic.

I try to step forward, but Griffin holds me back again. "Raven," he warns me.

Spinning in his arms, I level him a firm look. "Trust me."

He fights his indecision, but eventually gives in. His arms fall to his sides, freeing me, and I use caution in approaching Knox.

Knox would never hurt me. Of that, I have no doubt. But right now, he's not himself. Underneath all the rage is someone who's hurting, someone who needs a gentle touch. We all mask our pain. No one wants the people around them to see beneath the layers. Because under all those layers is where we are most vulnerable. And when we finally find that person or persons who we feel safe enough to show them the pain, it's scary.

Tentatively, I place my hand on his shoulder, causing him to flinch. Keeping my hand on him, I circle to his front and squeeze myself in the little space between him and the wall.

The hole he created lines up perfectly with my head. My other hand lands on Knox's other shoulder, and I slide my hands up to his neck. His eyes squeeze shut.

His agony penetrates my chest, making tears well up in my eyes. This type of pain isn't from a single event. This is from a lifetime of rejection and hurt.

"I'm here," I whisper to him. "You have me and Griff. We're here for you."

Knox's clenched jaw twitches, and a single tear drips from the corner of his eye, and I use my thumb to wipe it away.

I repeat myself one more time, "I'm here."

Knox's knees give out, and he falls. Griffin darts forward to catch him. I drop down beside Knox, whose shoulders shake with each sob that leaves him. Cradling his head in my lap, he turns to me and holds on to me like I'm his lifeline. Griffin's face crumbles as he watches his brother break. My hands run through Knox's hair, brushing it out as I whisper affirmations and comfort.

The weight of the air in the room is heavy. But I won't crumple under the pressure. I can hold this for him, for them. Whatever happened was more than traumatic. It was branded on his soul.

When I find the man who caused Knox and Griffin this pain, I'll make sure he takes his last breath on this earth.

Knox's body calms, and his breathing returns to normal. I lean forward, placing my lips on his damp cheek. I grab the edge of my shirt and use it to dry his face.

"Frank hated Griffin and me after Scarlett died. Probably before then, too."

I need to start adding all these names to a list. Frank is already someone I avoid, but now, I'm thinking he may need a good punch to the groin.

"He and his friends came to our house the night after Amos was arrested. We hadn't been picked up by CPS yet, because our grandpa said he'd take over guardianship. We didn't have anything more than locks on our doors and windows, and they broke those easily."

I don't like where this is going. Please, don't let this story turn out how I think it will.

"Pops was here at The Wandering Raven working. So they pulled Griffin and me from our bed and dragged us out back."

My stomach sinks, and my mouth goes dry.

"There were six of them, so they easily held us down while Frank beat us. He seemed to focus on me more, though. He'd just gotten done with his knife on my face when Sheriff Jackson showed up and scared them off."

"They weren't arrested?"

Griffin chimes in, "The sheriff claimed he couldn't see who it was and said that because it was so dark, our testimonies wouldn't be credible."

My face turns an incandescent shade of red. I feel like it's my turn to punch a hole in the wall.

"And now that piece of shit is the mayor," Griffin adds.

Who the hell would vote for someone like that?

The way this town has chewed up and spat out these two is despicable. I could set fire to Main Street and not feel the least bit of remorse.

"Scarlett was like the rest of them. She just wanted a story she could tell her friends about the Montgomery brothers, something I wish we would have found out before we decided to date her." Griffin sneers.

If that bitch were still alive, I'd rip her heart out of her chest with my bare hands. People aren't prizes. I know that better than anyone. People have feelings, dreams, and goals. They're not inanimate objects that were made for another's pleasure and entertainment. When people are treated like they're nothing, they eventually believe that they're nothing.

Griffin and Knox aren't nothing. They're worth more than all of Mystic River a million times over.

Knox's head still rests in my lap, but his eyes show me that his mind is somewhere else. The color leeches from Griffin's face as he stares down at his brother.

I want to take this away from them. I want to carry this load for them. I can take it.

The sound of glass breaking, followed by inebriated laughing, slips into the room. Griffin looks to the door, then back at Knox.

Placing my hand on his arm, I reassure him, "You can go. I got this."

Griffin hesitates, moving to stand but glances back at me. "Trust me."

He nods and takes off, leaving Knox and me behind.

We don't move from the spot on the floor. We don't even speak.

As I have difficulty swallowing, I continue to brush his hair with my hands. The stabbing in my chest grows the longer Knox seems empty.

Eventually, a tear falls down my face, landing on Knox's cheek. He blinks, coming back to this moment with me. I don't want this to be about me because it's not. Our pain is different, and one isn't greater than the other. But I can't stop the swell of emotion building in my heart.

Knox sits up, his features softening when he finds my face wet. "Don't cry for me, Darlin'."

My voice comes out soft. "But you're worth crying for."

Knox circles me in his arms and holds on tight, communicating what he can't express with his words. With his chin on my head, Knox's voice is soft. "I'm not worth it. I know it."

Pulling back, I stare up at him, disbelieving. "What are you talking about? What kind of self-talk is that?"

"Look at me, Raven."

"I am." I frown at him, offended.

"No, really look, Darlin', look closely."

Something must have hit him on the head because Knox is talking nonsense.

My frown deepens and my voice grows louder. "I am."

Knox's tone is firm. "No, you're not. Because if you were, you'd see how unevenly matched we are. I don't deserve you."

This better not be about what I think it's about…

Blinking incredulously, my jaw unhinges. "I'm going to sound like a broken record here, but…What the hell are you talking about?"

Knox's jaw tightens. "Do I really have to say it?"

"Yes." My cheeks flame.

"My scars, Raven!"

Nailed that one, and I hate that I'm right.

"What about them?" I exhale in exasperation.

"They make me—they—" He's too flustered to form a complete sentence, but I'm not letting him off easy.

"They what?"

"They make me ugly!" he shouts.

My heart cracks. I wanted him to admit it out loud because it needed to be released. But it hurt.

"If your scars make you ugly, then what does that say about Noah?"

Knox's eyes blow wide. "It's not the same."

"How?" My lips thin into a hard line.

"Because it's not!"

My voice hardens. "You're wrong. It's exactly the same. Neither of you asked for someone to take a knife to your face. Neither of you had a choice in the matter. You both were young and innocent and have to carry the weight of someone else's cruelty for the rest of your lives."

Knox's mouth opens and closes, unable to come up with the words.

He breathes heavily as I frame his face with my hands and force him to look at me. "Your scars are not ugly. They're part of you. They're proof of your strength, your resilience, and your life. I don't want you any other way."

He grabs my cheeks, his gaze searching my face. "You're perfect."

My tears spill from my eyes.

Knox opens his mouth to say something else, but he holds his words back. Instead, he pulls me into him, wrapping me in his embrace and refusing to let go. My chest permeates with a sense so strong and unfamiliar that I freeze.

Is this what it feels like to be loved by someone?

CHAPTER FORTY-TWO

GRIFFIN

"Can I take the blind fold off now?" Raven huffs in the middle seat of my truck between Knox and me.

"Nope," Knox answers with a shit-eating grin.

Raven crosses her arms and pouts.

Yesterday, Knox and I decided that we needed to take Raven on a proper date. Especially after the shitty one she had with "Jed." So, we arranged for Kat to babysit and surprised Raven. We put on the blindfold and wouldn't tell her where we're going.

"I'm not a big fan of surprises."

I snort at the little tantrum she's throwing. "You'll get over it."

I pull up to the spot Knox and I picked out, and I throw the car in park, shutting off the engine.

"Wait here," Knox orders Raven.

Raven gestures to the fabric covering her eyes. "Not like I can go anywhere."

Knox chuckles, and we climb out of the cab together. We

rush to put everything together. We're halfway done when Raven opens the passenger door.

"Are y'all almost done?"

"No," we respond in unison.

Raven groans incensed and slams the door again.

When we're finished, Knox and I guide Raven out and to the back of the truck. I rip off the blindfold, and Raven blinks, her eyes adjusting to the light.

Her mouth forms a silent O as her hands clasp together against her chest. "Y'all did this for me?"

"Of course," I answer.

Raven takes in everything from the blowup mattress in the bed that we covered with pillows and blankets to the projector on top of the cab and the screen we set up at the tailgate. She runs her hand over the soft fabric and picks up the two bouquets of white chrysanthemums we laid out for her. She brings them to her nose, inhaling, and turns to us, smiling.

"They're my favorite. Thank you," she chokes out.

"Let me help you up." Knox enthusiastically grips Raven by her hips and lifts her over the side of the truck. He helps her remove her shoes, then does the same for himself.

I move to the other side of the truck and hop in.

Raven snuggles between Knox and me with a bright smile on her face. "What movie are we watching?"

"Florence gave us a recommendation, but we've never watched it before," I reply.

Raven vibrantly wiggles side to side. "Let's watch."

As the movie plays, we learn quickly that Raven is one of those people who likes to talk through movies, and she notices everything. And I really do mean *everything*.

"Was no one driving that log truck?"

"Why is Emmett carrying a bag of eggs? I thought vampires don't eat."

"Were they supposed to be kicking a soccer ball or passing a hacky sack? Because there was nothing there. They were kicking air."

"Why does Bella blink so much? Does she have dry eye?"

"Does anyone else think Edward looks like a disco ball?"

Knox and I can't stop laughing at her commentary. Her lack of filter reaffirms how far we've come together in such a short amount of time. When we first met, Raven was flirty, sure, but that wasn't really her. Her real deep thoughts are not ones she shares with everyone, so seeing her like this makes her even more sexy in my eyes.

"Would you let me be a spider monkey and carry me around on your back?" Raven's frown is pensive.

Knox and I can't help but bust a gut laughing at that one.

"I'm serious," Raven claims, shoving at our shoulders. But that only makes us laugh harder.

Raven narrows her eyes, then changes her tune to indifference, poking the beast. "It's okay. I wouldn't want to hurt your fragile backs. Old men shouldn't lift that much anyway."

Knox and I sober abruptly.

"Who are you calling old men?" Knox shoots Raven a predatory expression.

The sly smile on Raven's face has me feeling jittery. "I mean, think about it. You're closer to fifty than you are twenty. It's not like you can go chasing me through the trees."

Knox plays into her hands. "I resent that. I could track you anywhere."

"Prove it."

Knox's eyebrows slide up his forehead slowly in puzzlement.

"Chase me." She turns to me. "Both of you."

I have a feeling I'm going to like where this is going. "Why?"

"First to catch me gets a blow job."

My dick reacts to that idea.

Knox quells his own reaction. "What about the second?"

"They get to fuck me from behind."

Fuuuuuuuuck. Is this woman even real?

Knox sits up straighter. "That doesn't sound like a bad second place prize."

"I think I'm the one who wins either way." Raven stands, removing her shirt and flinging it our way. "I'll even make it easy for you and leave some clues behind." She bends down, caressing my face. Her breasts almost spill out of her plum-colored bra. "Wouldn't want you to strain your eyes."

My hand reaches for her perky mounds, but Raven pulls back, well aware of the game she's playing, judging by the sultry smile on her face.

"Cover your eyes and count to thirty." Raven hops down from the truck and heads for the trees, not in any hurry. She glances over her shoulder. "Oh, and you might want to hurry. If you take too long, I'll have to start without you."

We both ignore her directive and watch as she unsnaps her bra, letting it fall into the grass at her feet.

"Shit," Knox curses.

A growl rumbles up my throat. "If she's not going to play fair, then neither am I."

"Same."

We silently count, but Kox hops out of the truck before I'm anywhere near thirty.

"Hey!"

He shouts over his shoulder, "Sorry, not sorry, brother!"

Following his lead, I take off after him. The thrill of the game Raven has set up makes my cock swell with blood. Running with a boner is no simple task, but for the chance of sex with Raven outside, I'd do it every day.

She's unlocking fantasies in me that I didn't know I had.

We pass Raven's bra first and search for the next article of clothing. Her little white cutoff shorts rest on brush a good twenty yards ahead. I make it to those first, but Knox finds her matching lacy thong before me. He sprints ahead with me right on his heels.

Raven waits for us in a clearing surrounded by trees. She's kneeling on the ground with her knees wide apart. Her head is thrown back in pleasure as one hand twists and pulls at her nipple, and the other spears in and out between her pussy. With every reveal of her fingers, they glisten more and more with her arousal. Her cries and moans are breathy.

Knox and I can't seem to move our feet. We're transfixed by this siren.

My mouth waters, needing a taste of her.

Breaking the spell, I march for her and drop to my knees. I clasp her wrist, pulling her fingers from her channel. Raven doesn't resist as I bring her digits to my mouth and suck them clean. Her sweet honey slips down my throat, and I immediately become obsessed to her taste. I moan around her fingers and watch as Raven's pupils dilate.

"I'm going to need a taste of that every day, Sunshine."

Her mouth pops open, and I swipe my own fingers through her slit. "Taste yourself, Raven. I need you to understand how addicting you are."

Raven sticks out her tongue, and I shove my fingers inside. Her tongue glides and swirls around my digits, making my cock twitch in my jeans.

I pull my fingers away, leaving Raven panting.

"You weren't first, Griff. I'm going to need you to move behind me and watch as I suck Knox's dick."

Knox's groan echoes in the trees, and I do as Raven instructs. I scramble behind her, removing my clothes in a frenzy.

I position myself at Raven's back as Knox advances, his clothes already gone. Raven peers up at him from under her lashes. "Lie down."

Knox clambers to comply, and Raven crawls over him, bracing herself on his thighs. She exposes her silky ass to me as she bends her arms and dips her head, taking Knox's erection into her mouth. His hips lift off the ground, and he lets out a long moan.

"Take me all the way in. Let me feel you gag on my dick." Knox's deep rumbles follow Raven's submission.

"Do that again," Knox thunders.

Raven pops her mouth off his length and peeks at me over her shoulder. "What are you waiting for? My pussy needs to be fucked."

This commanding woman is going to kill me, but death by pussy would be a great way to go.

Raven goes back to driving Knox wild as I guide my dick to her entrance. Her juices drip onto my shaft, making it easy for me to push inside.

A groan of delight cuts through my chest as her core constricts around my dick, sucking me further into her heat. I allow myself to relish in the feel of her cunt stretched around me.

"I want to live my life just like this, balls deep in your cunt."

Raven hums her consensus.

Unable to resist any longer, I pull my hips back and drive forward, repeating the motion. Raven actively participates, rocking back and forth, meeting me thrust for thrust.

Every time I pound into Raven's pussy, the flesh of her ass jiggles. The sight is so satisfying, so arousing that precum leaks from my tip.

The sloppy sounds of Raven moving her mouth up and

down Knox's girth merge with the squelching of my dick sliding in and out of Raven's pussy. The slapping of skin on skin adds to the refrain.

Raven's inner muscles tremble, squeezing my cock and bringing me closer to completion.

Using my mouth, I wet my index finger and play with her puckered hole. Raven's moan of glee encourages me to breach her tight ring of muscle. I time the hammering of my hips with my finger, sliding in and out of her ass and cunt. Her pussy spasms, forcing her to the edge of oblivion.

Bending over her back, I murmur provocatively in her ear, "Is this what you needed, Raven? You need to be fucked in all your holes? Is my good girl good turning into a slut?"

My words set Raven off, throwing her into a violent paroxysm of pleasure. She moans and writhes through her orgasm. Her muscles pulsate around me, causing my own explosion of euphoria as I fill her with my seed. Knox joins us over the edge, roaring with his climax.

Raven sinks down, burying her face in Knox's stomach. My body automatically follows her, not wanting to lose her heat. Her center quivers with aftershocks as her muscles visibly relax.

My heart still hammers in my chest, but an overwhelming sense of tranquility fills my body, telling me that this right here is all I need.

I pepper Raven's spine with kisses, and she hums in satisfaction.

"Come on, Sunshine. We need to clean you."

"Hmm?" Her languid body is easily malleable as I stand, bringing her with me. My dick slips out, and we moan together.

There's a splat on the dirt floor. I look down between Raven's feet to find my cum dripping from her.

"That's so fucking sexy, Sunshine."

"I'm leaking," she whines, trying to close her legs.

I stop her by crouching down to my knees and holding her inner thighs apart with my hands. I force her to spread further, giving me the perfect view of her opening. More of my cum drops, and she squeals.

But I need Raven to know how feral this makes me—how much I need to see this. So I shove my face up, eating her out from behind. Her squeals turn into moans as she can't help but grind her cunt on my face.

Knox stands in front of her, holding Raven steady as I feast on our combined releases. The mix of sweet and salty explodes on my tongue, becoming my new favorite flavor. Raven soaks my face, drowning me in her cream.

I drag my tongue up her backside and lave at her asshole.

Raven cries out, bending her knees and almost collapsing to the ground from the jolts of pleasure.

"Come on his face, Raven. Let my brother eat your ass."

I slurp and lick and taste as if this is my last meal. I switch back and forth between her holes, swirling my tongue and dipping inside.

Raven's legs shake from her impending second orgasm. She rocks her pelvis against my face and chants my name. Her entire body tenses, pushing her into a tornado of bliss. She shudders, moaning as I guide her through her climax.

When I'm done, Raven starts to tip, but Knox sweeps her up, carrying her in his arms as she hums completely satisfied. We walk back to the truck as I gather our clothing along the way.

Knox sits Raven on the tailgate, and I use my shirt to wipe all the fluids from her body.

Soon, I'll make her wear our scent all night. But for now, I want her to know what it means to be taken care of.

I move Raven to the cab, buckling her seatbelt, then join

Knox in putting everything away. When we climb in on either side, we find Raven fast asleep.

Knox looks at me over her head, emotion churning in his eyes, and I know exactly how he feels.

She is everything.

She is home.

CHAPTER FORTY-THREE

RAVEN

My eye twitches as I listen to Kaitlyn LeBossy drone on and on about the Halloween carnival at the PTO meeting that I debated skipping. I should be paying better attention, but with every word that leaves her mouth, all I can think about is how she's used her words to hurt people.

Kaitlyn is just like the girls I grew up with. They walk around with their noses in the air as if no one else matters. Like we all live to serve her majesty, Queen Kaitlyn. Now that's one monarchy that I would happily overthrow and party at their beheading in the town square.

The elementary cafeteria probably isn't the best place to be spewing hatred with my eyes, but this is my outlet, and I'm taking it.

As I'm distracted plotting Kaitlyn's demise, a woman plops down in the seat next to me. Her gorgeous appearance doesn't distract me from the abnormality of the situation. No one has sat next to me at the last two meetings. I'm pretty sure Kaitlyn and her minions have threatened every other mom into making me feel ostracized. I hope this brave soul doesn't get backlash for not obeying the creed of Dictator Kaitlyn LeBitch.

I study her with my guard up. You never know what may happen when you're in a room full of vultures, as Camden would call them. It doesn't help that this woman looks as if she were cut from the same cloth as Kaitlyn. Bleached blonde hair, lip fillers, orange skin. Her eyes are hidden behind Gucci sunglasses, and her nails are painted blood red.

"Raven, are you sure you have everything you need for the dunk tank?" Kaitlyn inquires, drawing me from my observation of the new woman. Her brow is raised, like she's throwing down a challenge.

Sitting up in my chair, I'm unwilling to let her see me as anything but what I am—Montgomery retribution. "In the last email, you said the PTO already has the tank, baseballs, and everything else. So, I guess the real question is, are *you* sure you have everything for the dunk tank?"

I see your challenge, and I raise you an insult.

"I assure you, we do." Kaitlyn's fake smile wouldn't fool a blind person. Her frustration crawls up her shoulders as she addresses someone else about their assignment, like the good micromanager she is.

"My hat is off to you," the woman next to me whispers with a smile on her lips.

"Thanks," I respond. "All in a day's work."

My potential new friend continues the conversation, "She stuck you with the dunk tank?"

"Yeah, I was late to the first meeting," I explain.

Kaitlyn's glare turns deadly in my direction. "Anything you'd like to share with the rest of us, Raven? We're always open to new ideas."

Rolling my eyes, I don't bother to hide the motion. Public humiliation doesn't faze me. I open my mouth, prepped with a quip, but my neighbor interjects.

"Now, now, Katie. No need to pitch a hissy fit." Then she lowers her sunglasses and gives Kaitlyn a wink.

Kaitlyn flinches, blinking rapidly. She flounders for a response, then clears her throat. "Anyway, setup will begin promptly at noon."

Tuning out Kaitlyn's redundant information dump, I lean so I can whisper lower. "It seems it should be me taking my hat off to *you*."

She smirks. "I've known Katie for a long time. She's always been one to go on power trips."

"Why am I not surprised?" I snort.

"You handle her just fine," she promises me. "Not everyone is brave enough to take her down a peg. The fact that you are is a good thing."

"Well, someone has to."

She leans my way, lightly bumping her shoulder with mine. "I'm Ruby, the way."

"Raven," I return.

"Hey, you're the new bartender at The Wandering Raven, right?"

"That's me."

"Those Montgomery twins are a nice little snack, right?"

A visible flush colors my cheeks as spots dot my vision. If it wouldn't get me arrested, I'd knock this bitch out right here, right now.

I loosen my tightened jaw to respond. "Have you had them for a...*snack*?"

"Oh, yes." Ruby smiles to herself as whatever memory she has of them comes forward.

Cage the rage. Cage the rage.

She gives me a smirk. "Have you had a taste?"

Maybe this woman doesn't know how close she is to death right now.

Ruby does a small hop in her seat, angling her position to

face me. "You little slut! You totally have. We should compare notes."

Okay, no. This has to stop.

"Just because we've had sex with the same people doesn't mean that we're in a club."

Ruby's face pinches, filling with tension. "And it's a wonder why no one sat next to you." With her parting jab, she stands, slinging her bag over her shoulder, and stomps out of the meeting in her extremely high Prada heels.

I don't want to admit that her hit landed, but in a way, it did. Am I that obvious? Do I have a sign on my back that says, "Loner but not by choice?"

I can't let it show that she got to me. I'm in a room full of sharks, and they're just waiting for me to bleed.

As soon as Kaitlyn ends the meeting, I'm out of my seat and down at the front of the school, waiting for the bell to ring. Thankfully, I don't have to wait long, and I'm able to make myself look busy as the other moms exit the school by staring at my phone, pretending to text and scroll. But really, I'm playing Wordscapes.

Droves of children rush down the hall, excited for the end of the school day. They laugh with each other and play around, causing even more chaos. I'm searching for Noah when I finally notice that he's one of the frolicking children. He's caged in by two boys his age on either side of him.

Is one of those kids his bully?

But...he's laughing genuinely. His smile spreads from ear to ear, and the other two boys laugh with him. Noah's shoulders are loose, not stiff. His eyes are full of light, not trepidation.

Witnessing this monumental step passed his obstacle has my throat clogging up and my eyes watering.

When Noah finally notices me, he says bye to his friends and runs straight for me, waving around a piece of paper.

"Mom! Guess what? Today, I made a map of the United States out of noodles."

I swallow my emotions to reply to him. "That's so exciting, little king! Do you—"

"Miss Henry." Noah's teacher, Mrs. Burke, stands behind Noah with her arms folded.

Tucking Noah into my side, I plaster a fake smile on my face. "Mrs. Burke, how are you?"

Her eyes dart from side to side. "Tell them I did what they asked. It stopped."

I blink, shaking my head. "I'm sorry, what?"

"Just tell them," she emphasizes again.

My mouth opens and closes. Is this a practical joke? "Tell who?"

Mrs. Burke frowns, chastising me. "Don't act dumb."

"I honestly have no—"

"Tell them," she interrupts me and walks away.

I look down at Noah. "Do you know what she's talking about?"

Noah shrugs.

What is with the people of Mystic River today? It's like there's something in the water. Cranky teachers and horny former hookups out here just slinging their attitudes all over me.

Speaking of which…

Someone has some explaining to do.

Taking anger out on my laundry isn't the most mature, but it's productive. And hopefully, I don't break anything in the process. I thought the dryer door was broken after I slammed it shut, but after careful inspection, I concluded that it would survive. Folding made me angry all over again because there isn't a way to angrily fold the laundry. The laundry ends up just being another heap of jumbled clothing.

After the PTO meeting, I waited for Noah to be done with school and went home. I explained to him that I wasn't in a good mood and needed to work through it. My heart broke and dissipated some of my fury when he asked if he had done anything wrong. The last thing I want is for him to feel responsible for my emotions.

But then we got home, and I saw the guys' motorcycles in their driveway. I told Noah that I needed to be alone for a bit, and he scurried off to do his homework so he could go outside and throw his football.

So here I am, putting away the clean laundry and slamming the dresser drawers because this is finally therapeutic.

Stack of shirts. Open the drawer. Set them down. *SLAM!*

Pile of leggings. Open the drawer. Set them down. *SLAM!*

"Raven!"

"Noah!"

My front door opens, and the objects of my sour mood walk right into the blast zone.

Sleep shorts and shirts. Open the drawer. Set them down. *SLAM!*

Little feet scamper across the hardwood floors downstairs. "You're here! Are you here to throw my football with me?"

Denim shorts. Open the drawer. Set them down. *SLAM!*

I can hear the confusion in Griffin's voice. "Uhh. In a bit, my man. Knox and I are going to check on your mom."

"I don't think that's a good idea. Mom said she wants alone time."

Bras and panties. Open the drawer. Set them down. *SLAM!*

I don't listen to the rest of what they're saying. The more

I think about them, the more I remember Ruby and every-thing she said.

With no more clothes to put in my dresser, I huff and kick it as if it told me I look fat in my jeans.

"Whoa. What did the dresser do to earn your wrath?" Griffin jokes.

My muscles tremble as a flurry of emotions swirl around my body. "I can't do this with Noah in the house. I don't want him to hear."

Knox fills me in. "We sent him outside."

I'm officially in the clear to let it all out. But should I?

My calming breath doesn't do its job. So, I try again. And again.

"Darlin'?"

Nope! Not today!

Whirling on them, I ball my fists at my side. "Don't you dare Darlin' me!" I pinch of guilt gnaws at me. It's not their fault. I know it's not. But it's like today was the straw that broke the camel's back.

Blinking, Griffin pipes up, "Maybe you're the one who has done something to earn her wrath."

Pointing my finger, I add, "I'm not too happy with you either, Griffin Montgomery."

"She last named you," Knox says with lifted brows and a ghost of a smile.

Griffin squints, taking in every aspect of my body. Rigid posture, red haze in my eyes, tight jaw. "What happened today, Raven?"

Sarcasm isn't a good look in times like these, but I need to protect my wounded heart somehow. "I'm so glad you asked. I met a lovely woman today who felt inclined to let me know she's fucked you both and wanted to compare notes."

I'm not sure what I was expecting. Frustration? Guilt? But

I get neither. The undiluted rage that rolls from them leaves me dumbfounded.

Knox widens his stance and crosses his arms. "First of all, and I speak for Griffin and myself in this, fuck that woman. Not literally. I mean that she can die for all we care."

A vein pulses at Griffin's temple. "Second, we had different lives before you. We're almost forty years old. Did you think that we've been celibate that whole time?"

"Of course not," I return with a little more fervor than I mean to.

"We were going on dates while you were still learning how to walk, a fact I don't like to dwell on because it makes me feel like a damn predator." Griffin shakes his head, and Knox winces at his words.

I roll my eyes. "You're not predators. And I'm an adult. A *consenting* adult. I know how to say no. Y'all aren't some evil beasts taking advantage of my innocence. That went out the window a long time ago."

The pain of that memory is like a knife to the gut.

"That's exactly my point. You had a life before us, too," Griffin points out.

Not much of a life.

"I know that." I cross my arms, not yet willing to let go of the injustice of today.

Griffin makes another point. "You've definitely had sex before us. You didn't arrive in Mystic River as a virgin."

Not by choice.

Another knife.

"Who was it? The woman," Knox inquires.

"She said her name was Ruby."

Griffin rears his head back, and Knox frowns.

"We don't know anyone named Ruby," Griffin informs me.

I still can't let the argument go like a real mature adult

would. "Are you sure? You could've gotten drunk and taken her home."

"No way." Knox shakes his head. "We don't sleep with the same woman separately. If I go home with her, Griffin avoids her. The only time it's the same woman is when it's together, and that isn't something we do regularly or while drunk. So, we remember their names."

My pulse picks up at the thought of them in bed with another woman, but I can't keep lashing out. That's not fair to them.

Knox tips his head. "Then what's the problem?"

"I would like some kind of warning, so I'm not blindsided by women wanting to boast about bagging the Montgomery twins. And you're right, we all had lives before whatever this is started," I wave at the space between us, "But if the situation were reversed, you'd probably kill the men who talked to you like that woman talked to me."

"That's true," Griffin says with a shrug. Neither of them bothers trying to deny it at all. "And as for this," Griffin makes the same waving motion, "Call it what it is. A relationship. It may be considered unconventional to some, but that's what we have. We're building a life together."

Knox's expression is open and sincere. "We're all in, Raven."

Why do they have to hit me right in the heart every single time? It's like they know what I need when I need it. My eyes bounce back and forth between them as my throat clogs with emotion.

"Before you two, I'd never…" I trail off, realizing what was about to come out of my mouth, but they won't let it go.

Griffin steps up next to Knox. "You'd never, what?"

Pinching the bridge of my nose, I squeeze my eyes shut. My truth sits on the tip of my tongue, waiting for me to let it free. A part of me wants to keep them in the dark because then they're more likely to stay. But I know that's denial whispering sweet nothings in my ear.

They say that the truth sets you free. But what if the truth was never my prison? My cage was made up of people who sought to control me and use my body for their own profit. They may be out of my life, but part of me that they hurt is still held in a cage. Will breaking the lock on that cage help or hurt me more?

I've never been able to talk about this with anyone. I have my fellow survivors, but we've never discussed it. We lived it together. We don't need to bring that back into the space between all of us. And Noah is my son. I'm supposed to shield him from things like that.

So, if not Griffin and Knox, then who?

Along with their gift of discernment, it's like they also have the gift of mind reading or something. They're always able to look at me and just know.

Griffin picks up on the secrets I'm still holding close to the vest. "There's something else."

Do I tell them? What will they think of me?

"Whatever it is, you can tell us. We're not here to judge. We're more like the last people who could ever judge someone." Knox's solace gifts me with the remaining courage I need.

My heart swells as I realize that I trust them. I trust them with my secrets. I trust them with Noah. I trust them with my heart.

Dropping my arms to my sides, I face them, ready to set this part of my soul free. "My life in New York wasn't what you'd imagine it to be. I didn't go walk down Saks Fifth Avenue searching for the perfect dress. I didn't explore Times Square or take the ferry to the Statue of Liberty. I never stood at the top of the Empire State Building to admire the beauty of the city lights at night. My life was full of things no one should ever have to go through."

"Well, you had Noah when you were only nineteen. That couldn't have been easy," Griffin sympathizes.

If only that were all…

They did the math correctly on that one. That's usually the first thing people do when they find out I have a son and that I'm only twenty-five.

Blowing out a breath, I respond, "Yes, that was part of it." I swallow and lay it all on the line. "When I was eighteen, I was kidnapped. My captors took me to New York and forced me into prostitution."

The temperature in the room goes up as Griffin and Knox start to lose their cool.

I scramble to finish explaining, biting the bullet. "I got pregnant with Noah right away. My captors realized that if they let me have the baby, they could keep him as leverage. Eventually, they found out about my training as a ballerina and moved me to their strip club, Euphoria."

Griffin's breath gets heavier as Knox's fists clench and unclench.

"Almost two months ago, we were all rescued. I grabbed Noah and got out of dodge." I pause, waiting for them to say something, but they stay quiet. I shuffle my feet. "So, that's how I ended up here."

"You were trafficked?" Knox questions.

"Yes," I clarify. Griffin still doesn't speak. He walks over to my bed and sits on the edge. He rests his hands in his lap, studying them closely.

Knox poses another question. "Noah was the product of rape?"

"Yes," I answer again, waiting for all the anger stewing inside them to turn to me, but that doesn't come. It never comes. I should've known better. Griffin and Knox would never do that to me.

Knox furrows his brows. "Were you part of that human trafficking ring that was run by Anthony Cole? It was all over the news."

"It was Anthony Cole and Pierce Murphy, but Pierce was able to get away in the raid on Euphoria. Law enforcement is still searching for him."

"So, he's alive?" Griffin finally chimes in.

I nod. "Yes, but he's probably not even in the country anymore." Neither brother is satisfied with that answer. Knox treads back and forth.

"He's still breathing?" Griffin tilts his head up to look at me.

"Yes, but he's on the run. He doesn't control me anymore. It's okay." I hold my hands out, palms up in a placating gesture. Knox stops his pacing and looks at me incredulously.

Griffin's eyes turn fierce. "It's okay? What about any of this is okay?"

"Everyone else is either dead or in prison awaiting trial. They got what they deserved," I rush to explain.

Griffin jumps to his feet. "They got what they deserved?" Both brothers stomp toward me with puffed-up chests.

Stumbling a step back, I'm thrown off balance by their temper. But I force myself to hold my ground. "Stop repeating everything I say!"

Griffin throws his hands out at his sides. "I just find it hard to believe that you're okay with this because I sure as hell am not!"

"Me too," Knox adds. "These people basically tortured you. They didn't just facilitate your rape. They treated you like a slave!"

Griffin shakes his head. "I think they're getting off too easy. Death and prison aren't enough."

"I agree." Knox cracks his knuckles. "Maybe we need to dish out a little justice of our own."

Griffin tilts his head in agreement. "I'll look at getting flights. Maybe we can—"

"Stop!" I interrupt. "No one is going to New York. No one is getting beat up."

Griffin faces me. "Why aren't you just as angry about this as we are?"

Something takes over me and unleashes everything. "You think I don't get angry about it?" My voice gets louder and louder with each word. "They took everything from me! I would go months on end without seeing Noah. It's a miracle he even recognizes me as his mother!" My shoulders lift and drop with a deep breath. "But anger doesn't change anything. Anger doesn't give me back the years they took from me. Anger doesn't make up for all the moments I missed with Noah. I'm done with being angry at them. It takes too much from me. I'm not giving them any more than what they've already taken from me."

When I'm done, all the energy leaves my body. My shoulders sag, and my head bends down.

Griffin steps right up to me as his hands find my face, guiding me to make eye contact with him. The sweet amber of his eyes opens up to me, allowing me to feel every ounce of his passion. His fury on my behalf, his despair for the pain I experienced, and his adoration for the woman I turned out to be. My own azure eyes fill with tears.

Griffin's thumbs sweep across my cheeks. "You're so strong." His lips crash down on mine. We move together in perfect synchronicity. My arms wrap around his middle, pulling him closer. This kiss isn't for release or to get lost in each other's bodies.

It's comfort.

It's home.

Our lips break apart, and Knox steps to my side. I turn to him, and Griffin's hands drop from my face.

Knox cages me in his arms, sealing our bodies together, and I drape my arms around his neck. The tug in my chest that nips at me when he's around settles. It's soothed by his touch. His tone is reverent. "I'm in awe of you. You've been through so much, and yet you still get out of bed every day and keep going. You're amazing."

Knox dips his head, and our mouths connect in a seamless kiss. His passion pours into me. The pieces of my soul that have broken over the last seven years begin to take shape again.

I know there's still more I need to tell them, and I will. But first, I need to make sure they won't be caught in the crossfire of my battles.

CHAPTER FORTY-FOUR

KNOX

"Why are we here again?" Raven eyes the talking pumpkin nervously.

"Because Halloween is around the corner, and you don't have anything to decorate your house with," Griffin replies.

Yesterday, Griffin came home and announced that we were taking Raven shopping for Halloween. Apparently, the idea was inspired by the town decorating Main Street, which they do every year.

Griffin and I normally don't go crazy for Halloween, but we decided to lean into it this year. Halloween is typically a big night at The Wandering Raven, so we're not home to hand out candy or anything. We don't even decorate. But this being Raven's and Noah's first Halloween, we want to make it a good experience for them. Plus, that's what the parenting blog we've been reading said to do.

We've been leaving Camden in charge more and more recently, and he has risen to the occasion. So, we had no problem with leaving him in charge today and taking Raven to Abilene, while Noah is in school, to do some shopping.

The Halloween store we found seems to pop up every fall and has all the things one could possibly need to fully celebrate Halloween. It has everything from laughing skeletons to fog machines. However, I'm not a huge fan of the life-size scarecrow that popped out at me when we walked in.

"You don't have a costume either," I add as I dig through the rack.

Slutty nurse? No.

Slutty schoolgirl? No.

Slutty librarian? Possibly…but no.

"Oh no. No, no, no, no. I'm not dressing up." She steps up to my side and pulls the costume I have out of my hands. "Wonder Woman?" Her outrage is amusing.

"Why not?" Griffin questions.

Raven throws her hands up. "Because this is ridiculous."

"When's the last time you dressed up?" I look down at her.

"When's the last time *you* dressed up?" Raven throws back at me. "Besides, I'm manning the dunk tank at the carnival, so a costume is pointless."

Griffin tilts his head. "What carnival?"

Raven sighs. "The Mystic River Elementary Halloween Carnival. That's why I've been going to those PTO meetings."

My forehead wrinkles. "Isn't Kaitlyn LeBlanc in charge of—"

"Yep," Raven answers irritated.

"Oof," Griffin grunts.

Rubbing my chin, I question, "Isn't the dunk tank where people throw balls at a target, so you'll drop in the water?"

Raven nods. "Yep."

Griffin gives Raven a hard look. "We're going to ignore the fact that you weren't going to include us in your Halloween plans and focus on the dunk tank."

Raven returns the look and changes the subject, her stubborn side coming out. "How about we focus on Noah's bully?"

My eyes dart around. "What about him?"

"Mrs. Burke told me to tell 'them' that she did what they asked. Do you know who she's referring to?" Raven crosses her arms.

Griffin and I are silent.

"What did you say to her?"

I blurt out, "Dorthea's husband may have an IOU with us."

Raven's mouth falls open. "Did you blackmail an old woman?"

"A crotchety old woman," I mumble.

Raven covers her face with her hands and paces for a second. She mutters to herself in her hands.

Even if she's not happy with it, too bad.

Raven stops in front of us and places her hands on her hips. "You two are something else."

Griffin grabs Raven's chin. "Act like a brat and I'll treat you like a brat."

Raven bites her lip as her breathing speeds up. A beautiful rouge crawls up her chest and over her cheeks. Her nipples harden into stiff peaks.

Hell. She's perfect.

Griffon and I give each other a look, forming a plan. I grab a random costume off the rack, and we usher her to the dressing rooms. We guide her into the room labeled "family" and shut the door.

"What are you two doing?" Raven spins around sharply when she realizes that we're in the room with her.

I hold the bag toward her. "We want to watch you try on the costume."

Raven's eyes roll with annoyance. "You just want to watch me take my clothes off."

"That too." Griffin sits on the long bench that takes up the entire wall and leans back, letting his legs spread.

Raven's tone is brisk. "No funny business."

I sit myself on the bench a little over from Griffin. "We would never."

"I'm serious."

"So am I," I insist, but the wicked lilt in my voice gives me away.

Raven tries to scold me with a sharp glare, but the anticipation of where this could lead overpowers her chiding.

An impish glint sparkles in her eye as she gives us a half grin. "If you're going to be in here, then I'm going to need some assurances."

Griffin's smile flips into a bemused frown. "What kind of assurances?"

"First, hands to yourselves."

"Done," I agree for Griffin and me.

"Second, you can't touch yourselves either."

"That's pushin' it, Darlin'."

Raven quirks a brow. "Do you want to see me try on," she picks up the bag, reads the label, and grumbles, "this librarian costume?" She faces us again with confidence in her tone. "It's only two stipulations. Either agree or wait outside."

Our ambivalence makes Griffin and me hesitate, but we finally assent.

Raven gives each of us a swift kiss, then grips the bulges in our jeans. My cock twitches in her hand. "Good boys."

She releases her hold and spins, adding a sway to her hips as she walks back to the costume bag. She leaves her tempting ass in the air as she bends over and removes the contents.

Raven rights herself and turns her back on us, placing the

costume on the clothing hooks in front of her. Removing her cropped tee, she reveals that she's not wearing a bra.

A groan rumbles in my chest, and I realize she isn't going to be wearing one the whole drive home either.

Raven peers over her shoulder, keeping her soft globes hidden from view. "Shh. We don't want to get kicked out."

Turning back, she grabs the blouse off the hook and slides her arms in, buttoning up the front.

Then Raven unfastens her frayed shorts, loosening the waistband. She grips the front and slides them down her milky, lean legs, bending forward. Each inch lower reveals another slice of her black strappy panties. When her shorts are at her ankles, and she's completely bent in half, her swollen pussy is on full display.

Fuck. She's wearing crotchless panties.

"Brat," Griffin comments in a strained voice.

"You planned this," I accuse.

Raven stands, grabbing the pleated mini skirt and sliding it on. The skirt leaves the bottom of her ass cheeks on display.

No fucking way is she going to be allowed to wear that out in public.

She looks over her shoulder again, a sensual tilt to her lips, and shrugs in response to my allegation.

Griffin's jaw tightens as he repeats himself, "*Act* like a brat and you'll be *treated* like a brat."

Raven turns, giving us a full view of the costume. The deep blue blouse is only buttoned halfway, exposing her mouthwatering cleavage and barely hiding her nipples. The pert crests of her tits are rock hard, the outline of them pushing up against the material of her top. Her supple legs go on for miles.

Raven throws out her sass. "You can spank me later for misbehaving."

My length throbs, yearning to bend her over and turn her ass red with my hand.

"Ah ah ah," Raven berates playfully, pointing to my hand hovering above my lap. She drifts over to me, kneeling between my legs.

Her hands unbutton my jeans, pulling them halfway down my thighs and allowing my stiff erection to spring free. It slaps against my stomach, and Raven licks her lips. My cock twitches under her heated gaze.

Raven smirks, looking up at me. "A little birdie told me you cheated the other night."

I shake my head. "What?"

"You didn't count to thirty."

I glower at Griffin. "Way to be a sore loser."

Griffin gives me an unapologetic look.

Raven ghosts her lips up my cock. "You're going to have to wait your turn." She licks the slit at my tip and pulls away.

"Fucking tease," I groan.

Raven grins as she moves over to Griffin, removing his pants the same way she did with me. But this time, she wraps her lips around his length, sweeping her hair to the side so I can watch. Griffin chokes when his tip bumps the back of Raven's throat, and she swallows him down. She hollows her cheeks, sliding her alluring lips up his shaft. A pop sounds from her mouth as she releases the head of his dick.

Raven climbs up into Griffin's lap, lifting her skirt to give me a view of how Griffin's cock slips inside her.

The veins in Griffin's neck pulse as he holds himself back. Obediently, Griffin keeps his hands at his sides, but he balls them into fists.

Raven caresses his face, cooing, "That's my good boy." She keeps her eyes locked with his as she unbuttons her blouse. Her tits spill free, and my length twitches.

She cups the bottom of each and lifts one upward,

offering her turgid peak to Griffin's mouth. He attacks her globe with fervor. Raven bites her lip to refrain from crying out.

In her blissed-out state, she moves her hips, rolling and undulating.

Then she pulls her breast from Griffin and offers him the other. He moans around her nipple, sending a shiver through Raven's body.

"Yes, Griff. Just like that," she praises him.

Raven's movements become more frantic, and her other mound drops from Griffin's mouth. She bounces in is lap, and a drop of sweat dribbles down her slender neck.

Whispering something in Griffin's ear, Raven peers at me out of the corner of her eye. Griffin nods and adjusts his position as Raven holds onto his shoulders. He twists to the side and scoots back, resting against the adjacent wall.

Raven flips up the back of her skirt, presenting me with her rounded ass. I quickly realize why she had Griffin rearrange when she arches her back, pushing her large globes out further. She lifts on her knees, giving me a view of Griffin's dick spearing her channel. I watch as she repeats the movement.

I bite my lip, muffling my groan. "I've learned my lesson, Darlin'. Come sit on my cock."

"You're going to have to wait your turn."

Raven adds a roll to her hips every time she lowers herself onto Griffin. She speeds up, desperate for her release.

"Don't stop, Sunshine. I need your cunt to suck the cum right out of me."

Raven throws her head back, her mouth opening on a silent cry, and her body goes rigid. Griffin's muscles tense as they reach completion together. Raven sags forward, catching her breath with Griffin.

She only gives herself a moment, then flips her head up,

her hair whipping around with the movement. She looks right at me with satisfied but hungry eyes.

Climbing off Griffin's lap, she crawls to me, eyeing the precum dripping from my tip.

Raven's juices drop into my lap, covering my cock. She hovers her core above my lap, driving me wild.

"Please, Raven," I beg.

She cups my cheek. "Mmm. I love to hear you beg." Then she drops down, penetrating herself with my hard length. Her hand covers my mouth, smothering my moan.

Raven uses her hold on my shoulders to help her bounce up and down on my dick. She clenches her muscles around my shaft, pulling more of my seed out of my cock.

Her inner muscles clamp around me as she dips her head, biting my shoulder. Raven explodes, triggering my cum to fill her core.

Raven breathes heavily with me, basking in the bliss of contentment from amazing orgasms.

Griffin helps me move Raven from my lap. We take off the costume and use it to clean her up.

"Guess we have to buy that now." Raven giggles.

"I mean, we don't *have* to," I refute.

Raven's mouth falls open. "I'm not putting this back out there with our cum all over it!"

Griffin and I chuckle, letting her know we were joking.

Raven rolls her eyes but can't hide her smile. "Let's just buy our stuff and leave." She playfully pushes us aside and leaves the dressing room.

Griffin and I decide that we're going to surprise Raven with her Halloween costume and make our way through the checkout line with the new decorations and dirty librarian costume.

That woman has unlocked a fantasy I didn't know I had, and now I need a repeat performance.

Walking through the parking lot all together, the rays of the sun beat down on us. Griffin and I carry the bags, refusing to let Raven hold a thing.

"I'm not weak, you know." Raven folds her arms across her chest.

"We know." Griffin purses his lips, hiding his grin.

"Then—" Raven stops, frozen in place. Her attention fixed ahead. Before I can understand what she's staring at, Raven continues walking with a little more speed.

"Raven, is that you?" someone calls out.

Griffin and I scan the parking lot and find a woman awkwardly hurries toward us. She's wearing a white shirt with white shorts and a little blue scarf tied around her neck. Her heels click on the pavement as she scurries.

The woman waves her hand in the air. "Raven! Yoohoo!"

I dip my head so I'm sure Raven can hear me. "Do you know her?"

"No." Raven's answer is clipped.

"Raven! It's me! Madison Dempsey!"

"She seems to know you," Griffin replies.

We arrive at the truck, and Griffin and I load the bags in the back seat. Raven stands by the tailgate with her arms crossed, bracing for the woman, Madison, to reach her.

Madison grabs Raven's arm. "Raven! Girl! I haven't seen you since—"

Stepping away from Madison's touch, Raven cuts her off, "Do I know you?"

Madison laughs. "You're hilarious. Such a jokester."

Raven's shoulders tense. "I think you should leave."

Griffin and I step up behind Raven, staring down at the woman disturbing her. I don't care if Raven really does know Madison. She's made Raven upset. No one gets Raven upset.

"Is this a bit? Very funny, Raven." Madison's smile is a little too wide, a little to fake.

My tone is grave. "She asked you to leave, so leave."

"Who are these people, Raven? Your bodyguards?" Madison looks at Griffin and me like we're an inconvenience.

"Leave," Griffin growls.

Madison blinks affronted and leaves with a parting shot. "You need to hire better help." She huffs as she stomps away.

Griffin places his hand on Raven's shoulder. "Who was that?"

"Someone from a past life."

CHAPTER FORTY-FIVE

RAVEN

"Are you sure about this?" Dahlia's voice comes through my phone.

"I'm trying to do something nice," I hiss at her as I reach for a package of flour tortillas and drop them into my cart. "Besides, who doesn't love burritos?"

Dahlia snickers. "Oh, everyone loves burritos. But your burritos? That's a different story."

"Ha. Ha." I fake laugh bitterly.

I know I'm not the best cook, but I'm getting better. I successfully made edible grilled cheese the other day. And tonight, I want to do something nice for Griffin and Knox. They decided to officially close The Wandering Raven on Mondays, so tonight we're all getting together for dinner.

"I take that back. Double Trouble would do anything to eat your burrito." Dahlia laughs at her own joke.

"Oh my God!" I jump at the volume of my shriek, scanning the dairy aisle to make sure I didn't scare anyone else as well.

Dahlia keeps laughing on the other end of the line.

Shaking my head, I search for the right cheese. "I thought the euphemism for a woman's vagina was a taco."

"I'm pretty sure it's a burrito," Dahlia argues.

"If anything, a burrito would be a dick," I contend as I place the cheese in my cart and head for the next ingredient.

Dahlia won't let it go. "No way. The eggplant is a dick."

"I know an eggplant is a dick. But I swear the taco is a vag—" I choke on my dispute and drop the avocado I had in my hand. Frozen in place, my ears turn red as Florence Baker stares back at me.

I think I'm going to die right here, right now.

Dahlia tries to get my attention. "Raven? Are you there?"

Florence raises an eyebrow. "Eggplant dick. Taco vagina. Burrito blankets." She grabs her little bag of gathered avocados and heads for the bread aisle.

This humiliation will never leave me. Years from now, I'll be brushing my teeth, and I'll remember this moment and cringe.

"Oh hey, I just looked it up. Whoever that was, they're right."

"I'm going to kill you," I whisper indignantly into the receiver. "That was my boss from the library."

"You mean the library that burned down?"

"It didn't burn down. It caught fire," I correct her.

Dahlia makes a grim but valid point. "Right. Well. I think it's safe to assume you don't have a job there anymore."

"You might be right about that," I concede.

"So, what are you going to tell your boy toys about that bitch Madison?"

"Nothing," I hiss. "They don't need to know."

"Raven, babe, I know I'm not a relationship expert, but I recommend honesty. They're going to find out one way or another."

I rub my eyes, warding off a headache. "They'll think I'm crazy."

"You won't know until you give them a chance."

I don't like that she's right. I was hoping for validation, not the truth. But Dahlia isn't that kind of person. She's the friend who comforts but still tells you how it is.

"By the way, did you get my gift?"

I roll my eyes as I remember the way my mouth hung open when I opened the package from Dahlia. I'm still not over it. "Yeah. What the hell?"

Dahlia chuckles. "Just be happy I didn't get you a large. I ordered one to see what it was like, and I haven't used it. There's no way that monster is going to fit inside me."

My eyes widen. "You mean the one you got me isn't a large?"

"Believe it or not. That's the small size."

"What…I…What!"

Dahlia sighs. "I lost track of time. I need to go. August will be home soon."

"Give that little boy a hug for me," I request.

"Will do. Love you," she agrees and hangs up.

God, I miss that woman.

Placing my phone in my pocket, I push my cart around the store, finishing up shopping for the ingredients for dinner. When I'm satisfied that I have everything I need, I head for checkout.

The clerk scanning my items narrows her eyes at me, studying me and smacking her pink bubble gum. I've seen her a few times at the store before, but she never says two words to me. Her painted nails are long and decorated with rhinestones. Her thick hair is teased in the back, forming the hump that many women strive for. The bright red name tag pinned to her shirt says "Pam."

"Aren't you that new bartender at The Wandering Raven?" Pam's nose scrunches.

"Sure am." I smile half-heartedly.

Pam snorts and reads me my total as I load the bagged groceries in my cart and use my card to pay.

"You better watch your back," Pam adds before I walk away, pulling me up short.

"Excuse me?" I leer at her, tightening my grip on the shopping cart.

"They killed their girlfriend, you know," she says jeeringly.

Wow. I should've listened to Kat when she said that people here are assholes. I mean, that's now how she said it, but she might as well have.

"Wasn't their father convicted of killing her?" I try to correct her in a way that isn't outright condescending. My question also offers her an out because if she keeps going, I'm going to lose it.

"Everyone knows they did it and framed their dad. The twins hated him." Pam curls her lip.

I give up.

Deciding to put on a show, I cover my mouth and let out an unconvincing gasp. "Do you think they'll kill me too?"

"Probably," she comments, looking me up and down. "You're pretty enough."

I roll my eyes. "Here's an idea. Take your judgment and shove it up your ass so far that you choke on it. But you might have a hard time getting around the pole you already have stuck up there."

Pam's mouth hangs open as I stomp away and out of the store.

Well, this sucks. Now I'm going to have to get my groceries in the next town over.

Leaving my shopping cart at the entrance, I loop the bags

on my arms and load them in the back of my car. As I approach the driver's side door, something catches the corner of my eye. I stop, turning to the motion.

Sheriff Jackson and Dr. Lewis Whitlock argue between parked cars only a few yards away. One car is an SUV with the words "MYSTIC RIVER SHERIFF" on the side and emergency lights on top.

Ducking down, I keep my head high enough so I can surveil them through the car windows. Scanning the parking lot, I find other people wandering into the store, but no one pays attention to the conversation going on. I had to park toward the back of the parking lot to get a spot, and the sheriff and doctor are even further back than my car.

"They found scopolamine in his blood!" Sheriff Jackson says aggressively.

What's scopolamine?

Need to research that.

"What does that have to do with me?" Whitlock throws back, as if he's not worried at all. His open posture and uncrossed arms are a testament to his elevated confidence.

Yet another man living his life as if the consequences of his actions won't touch him. But if what they're saying means what I think it does, there's no way I'll let Whitlock get away.

I'll be his fucking consequence.

Sheriff Jackson's face fades to red. "Everything! Seth Beauregard was your patient. They're going to put it together."

Dr. Whitlock waves off the sheriff's concern, dismissing him. "Seth was troubled. It's not hard to believe that he was able to break out of the hospital and go on a killing rampage. I'll call it a psychotic break. Everyone will buy it."

Sheriff Jackson makes a frustrated noise in his throat. "I've seen his bloodwork. He wasn't even on antipsychotics.

That ranger, Langston, is going to get a warrant for Seth's medical records. He's too smart for his own good."

"Then we'll deal with it." Whitlock shrugs as if insinuating the murder of state law enforcement is an everyday occurrence.

"We?" The sheriff lets out a snide laugh. "There's no *we* in this. I didn't send Seth to the library armed with grenades."

Shit. I didn't want to be right about that. I hoped Dr. Whitlock didn't recognize me, but there was always a possibility.

The muscles in my legs begin to shake from my crouched position. Sweat dots my brow from the overbearing heat of the sun. Spying is not for the weak, that's for sure.

Whitlock gets in the sheriff's face, spittle flying from his mouth. "Is that what you think? You thought I put Seth up to that? That wasn't me. What reason would I have to destroy the library and terrorize the assistant librarian?"

Assistant librarian. That's me. So maybe he hasn't recognized me. But if he has, would he confide in Sheriff Jackson? He could be playing dumb. He could be masking his guilt with animosity. But if he really didn't…

"If it wasn't you, then who?" Sheriff Jackson pushes Whitlock back with a light shove.

Dr. Whitlock's eyes grow cold. "I don't know, but I'm going to find out."

"You do that. In the meantime, I'll be figuring out the personnel issue," Sheriff Jackson replies indignantly. He leaves on that parting shot, hopping into his police vehicle and speeding away.

Not very mindful of a police officer to be speeding through a parking lot, but whatever.

Whitlock watches the sheriff leave and climbs into his

own car, a dark sedan, and exits the same way. I follow suit as well, hurrying into my car and locking the doors.

My chest rises and falls dramatically as I pull out my phone and search scopolamine on the internet. The first result tells me that when scopolamine is used in its powdered form, it can be used to brainwash people.

I'm no medical expert, and I know not everything on the internet is factual, but if this is true, it means that Seth didn't know what he was doing.

A sense of dread fills my chest as I worry that Seth isn't going to be the only one dosed with scopolamine.

Information gathering has been slow-moving, and I can't let Dr. Whitlock continue *treating* patients.

But now I know that Sheriff Jackson and Dr. Whitlock are in on something together. Something that requires people to work for them. Maybe the pills or something else?

That may be the in I need—the key to the downfall of Dr. Whitlock.

CHAPTER FORTY-SIX

RAVEN

Ugh. All I want is to fall flat on my face into my bed and never get up. My shift at The Wandering Raven was long.

Pulling into my driveway, it takes every last bit of my energy not to fall asleep in my car. Maybe I should have let Knox and Griffin give me a ride rather than insisting I'm Miss Independent and don't need a man to drive me everywhere. I'm paying for that stubbornness now.

The only thing that gets me to move is the fact that my bed is way more comfortable than the driver's seat. So in all my zombie glory, I get out of my car and trudge up the sidewalk.

A shadow moves in my peripheral vision, and I turn my head to see what it is. Across the street in the empty lot is a dark figure blending in with the trees. My back tenses as my stomach twists. Squinting, I try to get a better view, but the person runs away.

As fast as possible, I unlock the bolted door and rush

inside, locking the door behind me. Resting my back against the wood, I breathe deeply to slow my racing heartbeat.

Glancing around, I find Lucy passed out on my couch, snuggled under a thick blanket. The only light on down here is the lamp on the side table, casting the living room in a dim glow.

Kat was right. Lucy is a godsend, and she's a very hard worker. She's a senior in high school and was more than happy to take on this babysitting job. She has only one more class to complete, which means she's on track to graduate early. She's slept here a few times but normally leaves when I get home.

"Lucy, I'm back." I tap her shoulder to wake her up, but she doesn't move. "Lucy? Are you okay?" She doesn't even blink.

I place two of my fingers on the side of her neck, checking for a pulse. When I find it, I rest the back of my hand on her forehead, and I check her temperature, which feels normal. The shadows on Lucy's face shift back and forth in time with her breathing.

Peeling back the blanket, I check for anything that looks amiss. In the rustling, something drops to the floor. I let go of the blanket and squat down, looking for the fallen object. Under the coffee table, I find an empty syringe.

My hand trembles as I reach for it. Every muscle in my body goes numb, and my stomach sinks as I pick it up and find the plunger pushed all the way into the barrel, leaving no trace of what was in here behind.

I scramble to check Lucy's arms, looking for track marks, but find none. I didn't think she'd have them, but you never know.

Above my head, a rhythmic creak echoes through the ceiling. A cold sweat coats my skin, and my pulse skyrockets.

Creeeak. Creeeak.

Automatically, I pull out my phone and send a quick text to Griffin and Knox, then dial 911.

With the phone held to my ear, I step carefully and slowly through the living room, scared I'll make a noise. My grip on my phone turns my knuckles white.

The operator answers quickly. "911. What's your emergency?"

Tremors rack my voice as I whisper my reply, "I just got home from work, and I think there's someone in my house."

Creeeak. Creeeak.

"What's your address?" Her tone is calm, a contrast to my own. I have to repeat my address twice because of the whimpers that I'm unable to hold back.

"Do you or anyone else need medical attention?"

"Yes, I think my babysitter, Lucy, was drugged. She won't wake up." I try to keep my rasping breaths mute but fail.

As I head up the stairs, the operator directs me. "Ma'am, I want you to go into a room and lock the door. Cops are on the way."

Creeeak. Creeeak.

With each ascending step, my stomach sinks lower and lower.

"I can't. My son, Noah, is upstairs." I keep my volume low.

"Police will be there soon," she assures me. "I need you to get somewhere safe."

"Not without Noah," I insist.

I reach the top of the stairs, and all the blood drains from my face as I realize the noise is coming from Noah's room.

"Where are you now?" she asks.

"I'm upstairs. I think the person is in his room."

"Don't go in there."

"I have to."

My head spins as I turn the doorknob and open the door.

It's like an out-of-body experience. I can't hear anything else the operator says. Words muffle through the speaker, but they don't register. Tears leak out of my eyes as I finally come to know the true meaning of fear.

My phone slips from my grasp, landing on the floor.

Noah's room is swathed in darkness, but small streams of light from the streetlamp outside illuminate bits and pieces. A breeze from the open window causes the light blue curtains to dance. A woman in a hospital gown sways back and forth in a rocking chair with a lump in her lap as she hums a familiar tune. As she rocks, the resounding creak reverberates from the wood of the chair. The poor lighting reveals the profile of her face, and I realize I know her.

"Alice? Alice, what's going on?"

I scan for Noah but find his bed empty. His covers are pulled back, and another empty syringe lies on his pillow.

No…

Alice begins to put words to her melody, and the chills covering my body become painful.

"Rock a bye baby, in the sweet bed,
When the man comes, the child will dread.
When the man leaves, the child will cry,
And down will come Noah, down from the sky."

Please no…

A step closer, situating me in the center of the room, uncovers what rests in her lap.

Noah.

And a gun.

One of her arms cradles Noah's head, and her other rests on his stomach with the small gun in her hand. The barrel points at Noah's sleeping face.

My hands stretch forward as I plead, "Alice, don't hurt him. Please. Not him." I'd rip my heart from my chest and serve it to her on a platter if it meant she'd let him go. But it's as if she can't hear me…

Just like Seth.

"Rock a bye baby, in the sweet bed,
When the man comes, the child will dread.
When the man leaves, the child will cry,
And down will come Noah, down from the sky."

With another small step forward, Alice's hand holding the gun swings in my direction. The black hole of the barrel aims at my chest.

"I'll give you anything you want. Anything. Just let Noah go."

Alice's head steadily turns to me. An ear-to-ear smile covers half her face as if someone permanently etched it into her skin.

Just like Seth.

Her eyes are blown wide, wider than what is normally possible. Healed cuts decorate her arms. Those weren't there seven years ago.

A crash from downstairs causes me to flinch. It's followed by shouts.

"Raven! Raven! Where are you?" Griffin's voice shines a tiny light on the fear darkening my sight.

I open my mouth to answer, but Alice brings the barrel of the gun to her lips, using it like someone would their index finger.

"Shhhhhh." Then she trains the gun back on Noah, standing with him propped against her shoulder and walking to the open window beside her.

A tremor vibrates through my body, weakening my knees. I have to lock them to keep myself from collapsing to the floor.

Heavy footsteps thunder up the stairs, but their tempo has nothing on my racing pulse.

"Raven, what's going…" Knox's words trail off behind me as he and Griffin take in the scene unfolding in Noah's room.

"Please, Alice. Hurt me. Point the gun at me. Not him."

She looks down at Noah and continues singing.

"From your slate rooftop, down to the wood.

By now you can tell, I'm up to no good.

One little shove is all it would take,

To see how sweet Noah's small neck would break."

Whimpers fall from my quivering lips. "D-don't. Take me. Please, Alice. Pl-please." I've survived so much, lived through so much. I've been able to keep going, but if I lose him, I won't come back from that.

I take another step forward, but she stops me with a shake of her head.

"Sunshine, walk backward toward me." His tone is gentle, but it doesn't calm me.

"No, no, I c-can't. Not without Noah." I can't stop the stutter in my words.

I have to make up for everything I missed, all the time lost. I need to see him ride a bike for the first time. I need to see him graduate from high school and college. I need to witness the happy life he builds for himself.

"Trust us," Knox implores.

Alice starts in on another verse.

"Rock a bye baby, in the sweet bed,

When his fate comes, the child will dread.

Oh, God.

My vision blurs, tears obscuring my sight.

When the night ends, the mother will cry,

And down will come Noah, down from the sky."

"Now," Knox commands. His demand sounds directed at me, but I discover quickly that it's not.

A million things happen in the flash of a second. Arms

wrap around my stomach and haul me backward into a solid chest. A powerful, large body bolts past me. Alice starts to let her body lean out of the open window. Her arms stretch out at her sides, and Noah is still resting on her chest. I lurch for Noah, but the steel bands caging me hold me in place. The person reaches Alice as her feet begin to leave the floor, ready to take Noah with her. His reach is just enough to snatch Noah from Alice, but he doesn't have time to reach for her. Alice wears that same smile all the way to the grass outside, her body is cast in flashing red and blue lights.

CHAPTER FORTY-SEVEN

GRIFFIN

Officer Langston scribbles on his notepad like he did the other night. "Did you recognize the attacker? Did she say her name or anything?"

Knox and I glance at each other. "No," we answer at the same time.

A lie, but we need to talk to Raven. Something we plan on doing as soon as everyone is gone. I thought we had already aired out all the dirty laundry, but she's still holding back. I don't want to make this about me because that's not fair, but I'm tired of the secrets.

The police lights are still blazing in front of Raven's house, where Langston is questioning Knox and me. I think I'm going to have blue and red dots permanently etched in my retinas.

"We were able to run the prints of the man from the library," Langston states as he flips back a few pages. "Seth Beauregard. It looks like he was a patient at Mystic River Psychiatric Hospital."

The hairs on the back of my neck stand up, but my face remains devoid of emotion.

Langston continues the interview, unaware of the colossal piece of information. "Are you familiar with anyone there? Patients or staff?"

Knox and I shake our heads in reply.

"If you think of anything else, give me a call," Officer Langston says as he pulls out his business card and hands it to me.

"Sure thing," Knox replies. Langston tips the rim of his hat and strolls over to a fuming Sheriff Jackson. Langston points a finger at Jackson, then pokes him in the chest a few times, pushing Jackson backward. Jackson grits his teeth and mutters something back.

Knox says exactly what I'm thinking out loud, nodding to the sheriff. "Langston got here first again."

Positioning myself at his side, I respond, "We need to figure out what's keeping the sheriff so occupied. Once is a coincidence. Twice is a pattern."

The coroner strolls by, pushing a stretcher. The lump inside the black body bag gives me chills. I've seen many dead bodies in my life, but Alice's dead body will haunt me for the next few decades at least.

When Alice fell, I handed Raven off to Knox, who was still holding Noah as well, and I ran to the backyard. I checked Alice for a pulse but found none. When the lights from the approaching emergency vehicles illuminated Alice's face, my body froze as my chest tightened. I could have handled the scary-as-fuck smile, but the lights showed me why her smile was so huge and why her eyes were still open.

They were sewn that way.

I cannot imagine the type of person who would sew the corners of their mouth into a smile. Then also sew their eyelids to their brows…the contents of my stomach stirred. Knox didn't believe me until he saw Alice's body for himself.

A police officer with latex gloves on walks by with clear plastic bags labeled "evidence." He takes them to Officer Langston, they have a short discussion, then Langston walks back to us.

"Have either of you ever heard of midazolam?" Officer Langston holds up one of the evidence bags. This particular one contains an empty syringe.

I answer his question with a question. "Isn't that a sedative?"

"Yes," he confirms. "It's usually used intravenously like this in a hospital."

A knot forms in my stomach.

Langston poses another question. "Do you know anyone who works in a hospital who might want to hurt Raven Henry?"

Not someone who would hurt Raven, but someone who would happily hurt Knox and me. Knox and I exchange a look. That one look validates he's thinking the same thing I am.

Lewis Whitlock.

"No," Knox and I answer together again.

Langston nods his head and offers his genuine appreciation. "Thanks for your help. Hopefully, we'll be out of here soon. I'm sure y'all want to check on Raven and her son." He sweeps his arm in the direction of the ambulance.

Raven sits with Noah in the back of an ambulance. He woke up not long after the police arrived, which was a relief to us all. Seeing him in the arms of a stranger lurking near an open window was enough to induce multiple heart attacks. And when I noticed he wasn't moving…I can't even think about that. And thankfully, Lucy also woke up en route to

Henrick Medical Center in Abilene. She's staying overnight for observation per her parents' request.

Noah has yet to be interviewed, but Officer Langston was kind enough to agree to wait. Sheriff Jackson didn't want to follow Langston's lead, but Langston threw his weight around and claimed jurisdiction.

Knox and I hurry over to Raven. Color has returned to her cheeks, and the terror in her eyes has left and been replaced with relief. We stand at the open doors, waiting for the EMT to give Noah the all-clear. He woke up before Lucy and was afraid to go to the hospital. The EMT reluctantly agreed to do Noah's examination here.

The EMT stumbles over his words, pushing the matter again. "We really should take him to Hendrick Medical Center with the other vic—patient."

Noah's eyes bulge, and the beeping of the heart monitor increases. "No! Mom, please. I don't want to go."

The distress on Raven's face bites at my chest. "What if I take him to urgent care as soon as they open?"

The EMT sighs. "That should be fine, but I strongly advise taking him to the hospital."

Noah shakes his head emphatically, and Raven gives the EMT a pleading look. The EMT unwillingly gives in to their request.

"Well, there's not much else I can do. A good night's sleep is the only thing left."

"Thank you." Raven nods as the EMT removes the wires and monitors from Noah.

When Noah is unhooked, Raven carries Noah from the ambulance and moves toward her house.

I jump in front of her, holding my hand up. "We can't go in yet. It's still a crime scene."

The weight on Raven's shoulders increases as she begins

working out the problem in front of her. For as long as I live, I will carry that weight for her.

Draping my arm across her shoulders, I steer her toward mine and Knox's house. Knox steps forward and takes Noah from Raven's arms. Raven doesn't put up a fight as we lead her and Noah in our house and up the stairs. Knox takes Noah to his own room and lays him down. As soon as Noah's head hits the pillow, he out like a light.

Then we guide Raven into my room. Raven lets us remove her clothes and slide one of my T-shirts over her head. It's like she's not really here with us. Her body is, but her mind is lost somewhere else.

Knox and I dress down to our boxers and usher Raven into my bed. Knox lies on his back, and we situate Raven in the middle, wedging her between us. I shift her onto her side, facing Knox, as I wrap myself around her from behind.

Raven breathes, amassing the gumption to answer all the questions we're holding back. She knows we want an explanation but won't bombard her.

"I grew up in Dallas," she starts.

That explains the woman we ran into at the Halloween store.

"My parents were all about appearances. The perfect house, the perfect marriage, the perfect children. Walter and Georgia Kelly. I changed my last name after I was rescued in New York. I didn't want to be connected to them anymore."

I bite my lip to hold back my commentary. Growing up in Texas, I'm well acquainted with people like that. I hate them. Parents who are more concerned about how they are perceived than whether or not their children become good people. They're the people who treat their children more like pawns on a chessboard instead of precious souls who need love and protection. Parents like Raven's are a dime a dozen. People like that shouldn't be allowed to procreate.

Raven places her hand over mine, seeking strength, and I'll always give it to her. I'd give her every bit of my soul. She could bleed me dry, and I'd still offer to give her my heart.

"I did everything they asked of me. Ballet, tennis, student government, debutante balls, perfect grades. I even dated the boys they wanted me to, which were always the children of business partners or people who would raise their social status."

It's like legal human trafficking.

I keep my breathing even. I don't want her to feel judged by my reactions.

"When I was eight, they had my brother, Noah. I'm still not sure what made them act the way they did with him. I don't know if he was unplanned, the product of an affair, or what. But they didn't welcome him home."

These people. If I didn't already know they were dead, I'd kill them.

"And Noah wasn't one who could be controlled. He didn't let our parents force him into anything. They wanted a son who liked football, but he liked computers." Raven sniffs, and Knox swipes his thumb across her cheek, wiping away her salty tears.

"I knew Walter would hit Noah. He said it was to 'teach him a lesson' and that he just wanted Noah to 'become a man.' Whatever that means. It got to a point where Noah didn't even have to do anything wrong. Walter would take off his belt and hunt Noah down just because he was in a bad mood. I did everything I could to intervene. But then Walter got smart and would wait until I wasn't home."

No child should feel unwanted. No child should know what pain feels like because of their parent. They're supposed to learn by falling off their bike or accidentally touching a hot pan. Children are supposed to be cherished. I don't have kids of my own and even I know that.

My fingers dig into my arms so hard that I wouldn't be surprised if I have permanent indents in my skin. But again, I don't want Raven to feel what I'm feeling, so I lean forward and press my lips to the back of her head.

"But Noah was strong. He was always stronger than me."

"Raven…" I growl. I don't like her talking about herself like that.

"He was though. He never gave in. No matter what Walter and Georgia did, he wouldn't do what they wanted. Lunch at the country club with the girl of their choosing, football tryouts, wearing their 'approved clothing.' Noah was unapologetically himself." Raven's tone is devoted. Her love for her brother is pure and unwavering.

"I'm sorry you lost him," I whisper in her hair.

"It was my fault," she chokes out.

"Impossible," Knox comforts.

Raven shakes her head. "I should have been there. He needed me, and I wasn't there."

"You couldn't have known he was going to die," I reassure her.

"But I did. I never should have left the house when I knew Walter was in one of his moods. When I got home, I found blood on the stairs." Raven swallows, bracing herself. "He—he had broken his neck, but he had been bleeding from a hit to the head and a stab in his gut. Noah was only ten."

He was stabbed? What the hell?

Raven's voice breaks. "I looked around for someone to help and spotted Walter standing at the top of the stairs with a bloody kitchen knife in his hand."

She shouldn't have had to live this. It never should have been her.

"He didn't even look remorseful. Walter said, 'He should've done what he was told.' And I just lost it. I started yelling, something I had never done before. I didn't even know I knew how to yell. Georgia came running out of their room on the second floor, and something in me just...snapped."

Raven blinks, shaking her head as if she still can't believe what she's telling us is what actually happened.

"They told me I was being disrespectful and ungrateful. But I was still stuck on the fact that Georgia was home. She heard my brother's screams and did nothing. She heard my brother, her son, in agony, and she didn't step in. He could've been crying for help or begging Walter to stop, and Georgia just kept going through her day as if her son being murdered was normal."

My vision narrows, and my heart rate speeds. My fingers ache to wrap around Walter and Georgia's throats.

I cannot imagine. It's one thing for Walter and Georgia to be frustrated or angry because Noah wasn't living the life they wanted. But it's something else entirely to take that indignation and take it out on their child. To act as if their child owes them a pound of flesh.

"In all the yelling, Georgia's hand connected with my cheek. It didn't even register that she slapped me. She kept yelling, but I couldn't hear a single word. It's like I acted on instinct. I ran right for her and shoved her. I just kept pushing and pushing until she fell over the railing. She landed on her back in the entryway."

Good.

"Walter was so furious. I think he was more angry at the fact that I was brave enough to fight back for once than at the fact that his wife was probably dead. He dropped the knife, grabbed me by the shoulders, and started shaking me and screaming in my face. I remember his spit hitting my face. He asked what was wrong with me, and I told him that I have a pathetic bastard for a father."

I'm so proud of her right now. Standing up for yourself

isn't easy, and even though she did it for Noah, she still did it. And she's right. Any adult who hits a child is a pathetic bastard.

"His fist rammed into my gut, and I doubled over. He started kicking and wouldn't stop. I just wanted him to stop. Even as I crawled away, he wouldn't stop." Raven's voice cracks on the last word.

The unfiltered sorrow in her words kills me. She shouldn't know what it's like to be afraid like that. She shouldn't know what it's like to have the wind knocked out of her like that. She shouldn't know what it's like to be literally kicked when she's down.

"I found the knife where he dropped it, so I grabbed it." Raven's tears don't stop. She opened Pandora's box, and she can't close it. "It's like my body took over, and everything I had been holding back came out. I just kept stabbing him over and over. Later, I found out that Walter had been stabbed nineteen times."

I don't blame her. A person can only be oppressed and controlled so much before they fight back. The oppressor is always shocked, like they didn't have it coming, but that's how it's supposed to go. Oppressors are always overthrown.

"Somehow, I ended up downstairs, and I heard Georgia still breathing. So, I did the same thing. I stabbed her nineteen times, too."

Again…good.

I can't change the past, but I wish I could've been there. Raven's hands shouldn't know violence. I'll be her fist, her knife, her shield. Every kill, every blow will be for her.

Raven's voice turns factual. "Georgia missed brunch with some of her friends, so they called the police to check on her. When the police arrived, they found me on the stairs with Noah's body. They said I was covered head to toe in blood. I remember having to be restrained when they tried to take

Noah from me, but not much after that. The doctors said I was catatonic, and when I didn't snap out of it, they deemed me unfit to stand trial."

Dear God.

I shake my head and hold her closer. Knox rolls onto his side and brings Raven's hands to his chest.

"And that's how I ended up in Mystic River."

CHAPTER FORTY-EIGHT

KNOX

Griffin's head pulls back as I frown at Raven's confession. "What're you talking about, Darlin'?"

Raven's voice drops to a whisper. "The judge issued a court order that sent me to Mystic River Psychiatric Hospital."

I knew Raven had secrets. We all do. But I didn't expect this. She's gone through more than anyone should ever have to, and she's still fighting.

My mouth remains agape, unsure of what to say.

"So, that's how you knew Seth and Alice," Griffin deduces.

"Yeah," Raven confirms. "We weren't best friends or anything, but I knew them. They never would have done anything like this on their own."

Raven's eyes are distant. "I wasn't there long, but it was long enough. Dr. Whitlock…he…he's evil. After a couple of weeks, he brought me to his office, and he injected me with something. It made my whole body feel heavy. I couldn't move."

I don't like where this is going…

"That was the first time he forced himself on me. I could feel everything, but I couldn't push him away or even talk. It became a regular thing. He'd call me his 'Blackbird.' One time, he saw me fighting with an orderly, so the next time I was in his office, he didn't drug me. He seemed to get off on my struggle."

My jaw tenses, but I force myself to relax so I can speak. "Do you think it's him that's behind all of this? Does he know you're in town?"

Griffin and I have hated Lewis for years. Then he became more of an inconvenience with the pills, but now…now, he's a dead man. He's living on borrowed time.

"I've run into him a few times. Once at the grocery store and once in the library, but I don't think he recognized me."

We all sit with that for a moment, debating if Lewis is out for revenge. He has a reason to hate each of us. Griffin and me for the death of Scarlett, and Raven for leaving, even though she was actually kidnapped. But there's nothing to indicate he's aware of that fact.

"What happened next?" I prompt her.

"I just wanted it to stop," Raven cries. "But I couldn't make Dr. Whitlock stop. Eventually, it felt like there was only one way out."

My stomach turns as my shoulders tighten.

Raven continues her story, which is quickly becoming my worst nightmare. "I was able to snag a pair of scissors and sneak them back into my room."

Griffin's breathing increases, causing his chest to push Raven further toward me. A sense of dread creeps up my shoulders to my neck.

"I cut my wrist once, but it wasn't very deep. That's all I was able to do before an orderly found me." Raven licks her lips as shame swathes her in a tight embrace.

I know how the story goes. I know her attempt wasn't completed because she's here, which is what I have to remind myself of, like a broken record. Keeping her hands on my chest, I slide one of my own to her chest. I lay my palm flat over the left side of her chest because I need to make sure it's working.

Raven is here. She's in my house. She's in my arms. She's alive.

Griffin props himself up on his elbow so he can see Raven's face better. "I know it's not what you wanted at the time, but I'm happy you were caught. It's selfish but fuck it. I'll be selfish. I need you here. I need your smile, your sassy attitude, and your sweet, sweet body."

I chime in, adding to Griffin's reasoning, "I need you to argue with me. I need the space you hold for me so I can unleash all my bottled-up feelings. I need to hold you at the end of every day as we fall asleep together."

Raven gulps and gives us what we're desperate for. "I need you too. Both of you." Her gaze flips back and forth between Griffin and me.

She clears her throat and finishes her story. "Then one night, I was taken from my bed. That's when I was kidnapped and taken to New York. Over the years, I was able to gather that my parents were trying to sell my brother. I think Noah found out somehow, and that's why they fought. Anthony Cole and Pierce Murphy were angry when Noah was murdered, so they took me instead."

My vision blurs, and my body feels cold. I never thought a single person could go through so much, but she has. She's leaped over every hurdle, knocked down every wall. She's so strong, so beautiful.

Mystified, Griffin asks, "Why come back?"

"I couldn't let him get away with it. I know I wasn't the only one. I came back to figure out how to shut down the hospital."

Leaning forward, I ask a question of my own. "Why not just go to the police or the press? You could've told your story."

"Who would believe me? I'd be labeled a crazy person, just like they're doing to Seth and Alice. No one believes someone with a mental health disorder." Raven shakes her head and looks down at her hands, avoiding eye contact. "So, now you know."

My eyebrows scrunch together. "Know what?"

"I'm a monster."

It's the final blow to my chest. Everything Raven has been through was done *to* her. She was reacting just like any other person would. And I'm man enough to admit that she has handled it all with more resilience than I ever could. Raven has more fortitude in her entire body than I have in my left pinky.

And she thinks that makes her a monster? Impossible.

"You're amazing. I must've done something right in a previous life because there's no way any deity would bring you into my life otherwise," I whisper reverently. "I love you."

Raven gasps.

Griffin uses his hand to sweep Raven's hair out of the way. "I don't deserve you, but I'm not letting you go. I know that makes me an asshole, but I don't care. I love you."

Raven's eyes widen, and her hand covers her mouth.

"But you both know everything now. How can you look at me and—"

Griffin grips Raven's shoulder and rolls her onto her back. "If you're a monster, then consider this my offering."

He lifts her shirt, revealing her lack of panties, and propels himself forward, digging his face in her pussy.

Raven gasps, her hands diving into Griffin's hair. She throws her head back, thrashing about from the onslaught of pleasure.

I sit her up and slide behind her. My back rests against the headboard as Raven lies on my chest. Her legs are spread wide, accommodating Griffin's broad shoulders.

Taking hold of the hem of her shirt, I lift it over her head. The cool air of the bedroom brushes across the tips of her breasts, causing them to pebble.

Raven moans as I slide my hands to her stomach and drag them up to her tits. Holding one in each hand, I stroke my thumbs over her tender peaks.

I create a path with my lip, exploring her shoulder and neck with my mouth. A shiver travels up her spine when I find her sensitive spot and give it extra attention.

Raven's breaths speed up, and she squirms as she gets closer to the pinnacle of her pleasure.

Griffin lifts his head, pulling her back from the brink of her release. "Tell me a secret, Raven. Tell me the secret I want to hear."

Outraged by her denial, Raven sends Griffin a withering stare. "What!"

Griffin drags a finger down her slit, flicking her clit. "Tell me and I'll let you come."

Raven bites her lip and clears her throat excessively. Her hesitancy is clear on her face. She squeezes her eyes closed, inhaling and exhaling, and when they open again, her anxiety is gone.

Raven sits forward and tilts Griffin's chin up. She brushes her lips against his and gazes into his eyes. "I love you." Griffin rests his forehead against hers, savoring Raven's words.

When they part, Raven reclines back, lying on me again, and cranes her neck to look at me. She places her hand on my face, guiding my mouth to hers. She coaxes my mouth open, her sweet honey exploding over my tongue.

Raven breaks our kiss, her ocean-blue eyes peering into

mine. With three little words, she gives me the most precious gift.

"I love you."

I attack her mouth, shoving my tongue inside. My fingers resume playing and teasing her nipples. She moans into my mouth as the slopping sounds of Griffin eating Raven's pussy reverberate in the room.

We quickly bring Raven to her peak. She curls her toes, arching her neck as she shatters into a million pieces.

When Raven's body relaxes, she reaches for my cock, but I stop her, grabbing her wrist. She whines, "I want to return the favor."

"I don't want reciprocation."

"But—"

Griffin cuts Raven off, "This wasn't about us, Sunshine. This was for you. Just you."

The confusion on her face is a stab to my chest. She's never had sex where it was for her or about her.

Griffin and I look at each other, the same thought circulating between us. Our nod is a vow. A promise to do stuff like this more often.

I extricate myself from Raven and grab a wet cloth from the adjoining bathroom. When I come back, Griffin has slipped the shirt back over her head. I push her knees apart and wipe away her glistening arousal.

I toss the cloth into the bathroom and lie back down in bed. Positioning Raven on her side, I pull her close, and Griffin wraps himself around her.

Raven rests her hand on my chest, and I envelop it with my own. I press my lips to her fingers, savoring the rapture of her afterglow.

A feeling settles in my chest, making everything feel right. With this feeling comes a truth that I believe with every fiber of my being.

Raven is our forever.

CHAPTER FORTY-NINE
RAVEN

Staring at the ceiling of Griffin's bedroom, I lie there unmoving. I woke up alone a while ago, unsure of where the guys went. Noah usually comes into my room to wake me up, but we're in a different house. Maybe he can't find me.

Sitting up, I scoot to the end of the bed to get up and find Noah. But I can't seem to get myself to stand.

I can't believe this is my life. Did I bring this all on myself? I was almost blown up, and then my son was almost thrown out of his window. Should I still try to shut down the hospital or is this task too much for me? Am I being selfish in wanting to shut it down?

Ugh.

Being left alone with my thoughts is never a good thing.

The bedroom door swings open, and Noah runs in, hopping on the bed. "Mom! We got yummies!"

Lifting him up in my arms, I sit him in my lap and rub our noses together. "Oh yeah? What kind of yummies?"

"The yummy yummies," Noah answers.

Unable to hide my concern, my forehead scrunches. "How are you feeling? Did you sleep good?"

"So good, Mama. I want to sleep in Knox's bed every night!"

I discreetly feel his forehead for his temperature. Noah seems fine, and he's acting normal, but I'm still taking him to the doctor later.

"Coffee and chocolate croissants are here!" Knox slides into the room with a brown bag and a to-go coffee cup in his hands, raised in the air.

Noah throws his hands up, mimicking Knox. "For you, Mama!"

Kissing Noah's cheek, I smother him in my embrace. "Aww, thank you, little king."

"I rode the motorcycle with Griffin. He got me my very own helmet!" Noah's smile is proud.

I smile back. "That's so awesome! Did you thank him?"

Noah puts on his thinking face. "I don't remember. I'll go tell him now." He jumps off my lap and bounds past Knox.

Knox walks over to me and kneels. He hands over the coffee and pastry, kissing my cheek. "Your breakfast."

"Thank you." I place a quick peck on his lips and grab the offered food.

Griffin joins us, sitting on the bed next to me. "Atlas called."

I squint. "The motorcycle guy?"

Knox's spine straightens. "What did he say?"

"His guy tested the pills. They're made of fentanyl."

"Shit," Knox curses. "How has no one overdosed yet?

I wave my hand. "Someone want to fill me in?"

Griffin nods. "We gave some of the pills we got off the dealers to the Ferrymen, Atlas and Bas. Atlas said he has a guy who can figure out what's in them."

"Ferrymen?" I frown.

"They're a motorcycle club. They're our suppliers," Knox clarifies.

My head cocks to the side. "Okay. So. The Ferrymen stepped in and helped out. And now we know Lewis Whitlock is selling fentanyl."

"We need to figure out our next step." Knox rubs his chin.

Griffin raises his index finger. "In time. First, I want to discuss something else."

"What?" I squint.

"It was something in Alice's rhyme."

My stomach plummets as my body grows tense. I'm on the verge of shaking and have to set my food and coffee aside to prevent it from spilling everywhere.

"Good God, don't remind me. That's going to fuel my nightmares for the rest of my life." Knox shivers.

Griffin stares at the wall, thinking over the puzzle before him. "She mentioned a madman. Just like Seth."

I rub my eyes, warding off a headache. "She said that the madman is watching me sleep. And something about a man coming and going, making a child cry."

"The child could be Noah," Knox theorizes.

"That's my thought as well," Griffin affirms. "And the madman has to be Lewis."

"I don't know." I purse my lips. "I mean, Lewis Whitlock is definitely mad. Only a madman could do the things he does to helpless people."

"I agree with that," Knox chimes.

"If he is the madman, then taking care of Lewis would be killing two birds with one stone," Griffin reasons.

I sit up a little straighter. "I'd call that a win."

"We could—" Knox starts, but Noah comes flying into the bedroom.

Literally. He has his arms spread out at his sides, tilting

them back and forth, as he makes zooming noises with his mouth. Noah crashes into Griffin, creating the sound of an explosion.

Griffin laughs. "Hey, little man! What's up?"

Noah pops up. "Will you and Knox play with me?"

Knox stands, taking Noah by the hand and leading him out of the room. "Of course, bud."

"Griffin! Are you coming?" Noah shouts.

"Yes!" Griffin replies, smirking at me. He gets to his feet, and hands me my coffee and pastry. "Enjoy your breakfast, Sunshine. Come downstairs after you've eaten and relaxed a bit."

He presses his lips to my forehead and follows after Noah and Knox.

A smile of affection curves my mouth as I bring the coffee to my lips, and giddiness spreads through me.

These men are going to spoil me rotten.

CHAPTER FIFTY

RAVEN

The last few days have been peaceful. After Noah's checkup at the urgent care in town, we've basically been living at Griffin and Knox's house. And the fact that my house is still a crime scene means that Noah and I have nowhere else to go.

Griffin and Knox's home is cozier than I thought it'd be, and they have fully adopted the southern hospitality charm. Noah became bored, so they bought him a new train set and a football. We ran out of clean clothes after day one, so they purchased a whole new wardrobe for Noah but only a few items for me. I think that has something to do with their inner neanderthal coming out when they see me dressed in their clothes.

The first time I walked out of Griffin's room in one of his shirts, he grunted something to Knox about playing with Noah and hauled me back into his room. He covered my mouth with his hand as he gave me screaming orgasm after screaming orgasm.

Later, I decided to test the theory that their sex drive was correlated to the wearing of their clothes. I walked out of Knox's room with one of his shirts on and was rewarded with more orgasms.

My vagina needed a break, so today I'm wearing my new clothing. A comfy tee and workout shorts.

Noah has been with Griffin in the backyard, tossing the football as I laze about on the couch with *Chasing Goldie* by Holly Roberds, another gift from the guys. I don't know where they got the book recommendation, and I'm not sure I want to know.

I'm about halfway through the novel when Griffin comes back inside with Noah in tow. "Get your shoes on, we need to go," Griffin demands.

Closing my book, I sit up. "Where are we going?"

"You'll see." He's being vague on purpose.

"Fine," I pout, sliding on my socks and tennis shoes as Noah does the same.

Griffin herds Noah and me into his truck and drives down the street. He lets go of the steering wheel with his right hand, driving with his left, and reaches for my hand. Curious to see what his goal is, I comply.

Griffin weaves our fingers together and rests our clasped hands on the center console. His thumb lightly traces the side of my hand, which does crazy things to my stomach. It's like he knows what he's doing to me because as we wait at a red light, he smirks and winks at me. I do my best to keep a straight face, but he sees right through me and chuckles.

This man. I don't know what I'm going to do with him.

My needy pussy has a few ideas…

After a few more minutes, I have a good guess of our destination. "The Wandering Raven isn't exactly a surprise," I say candidly.

"Just wait," Griffin instructs, shifting his truck into park, but doesn't cut the engine. He turns to Noah in the back seat. "With me, bud." Then instructs me, "Stay here."

I side-eye him. "What's going on?"

Griffin ignores my question and takes Noah inside. I'm alone for only a few moments when Griffin returns. He hops back in the driver seat and steers his truck down the dirt road I wandered the other night. I'm thrown around my seat like I'm a feather as we drive over all the bumps and rocks. A cloud of beige dust hangs in the air behind us. The tall grass and trees don't feel nearly as terrifying in the daylight.

"Noah is cooking with Camden in the kitchen. He's teaching him how to make fries. I wouldn't leave him somewhere he wasn't safe."

My head bobs up and down in affirmation. "I know." The thought that Griffin could be leading Noah into a dangerous situation didn't even cross my mind.

"I need your help with something. Actually, *we* need your help." He doesn't take his eyes off the road.

My head cocks to the side. "Okay…"

"Knox came across another dealer and has him tied up in the barn. We need you to be there while we try to get information out of him. You know things about Lewis Whitlock that we don't. We need to confirm that he's The Alienist."

I feel like I should be worried about this. Like I should be running away screaming. But I'm not scared. Not a single cell in my body is urging me to high tail it out of here.

Am I that fucked up?

"If you're not comfortable with it, just say the word. I'll turn around right now. We can pick up Noah, go back home, and you can finish your book while Noah and I play outside." He glances at me periodically, searching my face for clues on how I'm feeling.

The barn comes into view ahead of us, another thing that doesn't look so scary during the day. The paint could use a touch up, and the various plants around the barn could use some trimming. But other than that, it looks like an ordinary barn.

"I'll do it." It's an easy answer to give. If having me sit in on their little interrogation helps take down Whitlock, I'm all in.

And I'm not under the notion that their questioning is friendly. I saw the last guy. He didn't look like he'd just walked through a meadow or something.

Griffin stops a small distance back from the barn doors and turns to me, shifting in his seat and resting his forearm on the steering wheel. "Are you sure?"

"Yes."

Griffin unbuckles his seatbelt and mine then lifts me over the center console by my hips. I yelp as he sets me down in his lap and arranges my long legs so I'm straddling him.

My stomach does a somersault.

"Don't we need to—"

Griffin cuts me off as he places his hand on the back of my head and pulls my mouth to his. The kiss is simple but conveys everything he's feeling. I squirm in his lap, my core aching for more. But all too soon, he pulls me back and leads us out of the car.

No explanation as to why. No apology for getting me ready to go then pulling away.

Griffin has no trouble picking up on my frustration, which he finds amusing. He giggles like a little kid who just played the world's best prank as he grabs my hand, leading me into the barn.

My eyes narrow as I ascertain how to give him a terrible case of blue balls in retribution. But before my plan can take shape, we step inside.

Slivers of light bleed into the barn, painting a sinister and full picture. And interestingly enough, the inside of the barn is just as creepy as it was at night. I shouldn't be impressed that these two have mastered inflicting fear in the light of day, but here we are.

Guess I *am* that fucked up.

Knox leans against the wall dressed in his usual attire: a flannel, jeans, and work boots, twirling a pair of pliers in his hand.

Pinch me. That's sexy as hell.

Next to Knox is a worktable covered in various tools and objects.

And just as promised, there's a man tied to a chair in the middle of the room, but he looks nothing like the last man I saw here. He's clean, unblemished, and wearing scrubs. Another step closer and I'm able to read his nametag.

Leonard.

My entire body freezes, halting Griffin's steps. I try not to let my fear show, but a cold sweat dampens my skin, making my hands slippery.

I can't believe he's here…

"I want a turn with her," Leonard whines in the corner of Dr. Whitlock's office. He started sitting in on my "sessions" a couple of weeks ago.

I'm strapped to the chair again, liquid leaking between my thighs. I still can't move and probably won't be able to for another half hour or so.

Dr. Whitlock zips up his pants as he smooths his hair. "You're not ready yet."

Leonard stands his ground. "I know what to do and how to do it. You told me. I can do it."

"Alienism is an art. It's not something you can just rush into." Whitlock shakes his head.

"I know. You said that before. But there's only so much I can learn through observation. Just let me try." Leonard's attempt at reason doesn't sway Dr. Whitlock whatsoever.

Instead, Dr. Whitlock whirls on Leonard, slapping him across the face. "I said, no! Not my Blackbird!"

Leonard's head whips to the side as his cheek turns a painful shade of red. He glares at Dr. Whitlock, but he keeps his mouth shut.

Good. This is already a nightmare. I don't want anyone else taking advantage of me.

"Take her back to her room." Dr. Whitlock motions to me.

Being the obedient little prick he is, Leonard removes my restraints and moves me into a wheelchair. As he pushes me down the halls to my room, we pass several others. Orderlies, patients, and visiting family members. Not a single person asks if I'm okay.

And they never will. Who would intervene on behalf of a crazy person?

Leonard wheels me into my room and aggressively drops me onto my bed.

"I don't know what makes you so special. You're nothing but an experiment. One in a long line of experiments to keep him occupied." He sneers down at me.

I want to scream at him. Tell him that I'm no one's experiment. I'm not some plaything. But I still don't have control of my body, so I just lie there.

His hand lashes out, slapping my cheek. The sting causes instant tears in my eyes. They slip down my cheeks and directly onto my pillow.

Leonard moves my head so I'm looking up at him again. "I will have my turn soon enough."

The Leonard before me and the one I remember are similar, but this one has the beginnings of crow's feet at the corners of his eyes, and his hair is slicked to the side rather than the spikey mess he used to wear it as. He looks smaller sitting and tied down. He used to tower over me, but now it's me who has the upper hand.

Leonard's eyes glitter when he finally recognizes me. "It's been a long time, Raven."

"Not long enough." A surge of energy rushes through me, and I give in to my impulses.

Releasing Griffin's hand, I stomp to Leonard and kick him right in the sternum. The chair tips backward as Leonard wheezes.

Standing over Leonard, I hold my hand out to Knox, who knows exactly what my gesture means. Knox deftly places the pliers in my hand.

"Lenny, Lenny, Lenny." I tsk, circling the fallen chair so he can see me.

"Raven, Raven, Raven," he echoes back. "Just couldn't stay away, could you? I wooed you with my virility, and now you're back, begging."

Keeping my exterior calm, I crack my neck and straddle the prone half of his body. "Is that the only way you're able to fuck a woman? You have to drug her first?"

Leonard's nostrils flare.

I cross the arm holding the pliers over my chest and touch my finger on my other hand to my lips. "If you weren't able to incapacitate a woman, I think you'd be what people call an incel." Dropping my arms, I look down at Leonard with a vituperative smile. "It means involuntary celibate."

Griffin moves to stand next to Knox off to my right, and whispers not so softly, "Is it totally weird that I'm getting a semi watching this?"

Knox snorts.

I plop down, taking a seat on Leonard's stomach. My weight forces a rush of air to expel from his lungs.

Tracing his jaw with the tip of the pliers, I mock him, "I wouldn't let you stick your limp dick inside me even if you paid me."

My free hand winds back and goes flying across his cheek. Just like he did to me many times before. Every time Dr.

Whitlock wouldn't let him have a turn with me, Leonard would take it out on me when he got me back to my room.

Letting the pliers drop on his chest, I use my other hand to slap his other cheek. Leonard's head turns to the side. The burn of my blow has him breathing harder and faster.

After he gathers himself back together, he faces me again with an icy expression. "You hit like a girl."

"Better than hitting like a little bitch," I retort, digging my insult further into his injured pride with another slap.

Rising to my feet, I snag the pliers from Leonard's chest. I look to my admiring spectators and tilt my head. Griffin and Knox, knowing what I mean as usual, right the chair and double-check the duct tape holding Leonard in place.

They step back and assess my body appreciatively. Suddenly, my need from the moment in the truck earlier returns tenfold.

Questions first. Sex later.

Griffin and Knox stride around the chair and flank my sides.

"Let's hurry this along, shall we?" My polite grin disappears as quickly as it came. Stepping forward, I pinch Leonard's index fingernail between the teeth of the pliers.

"Stop! No! That fucking hurts! Stop!" Leonard's shouts barely register in my brain.

Wiggling his nail while pulling up at the same time, my movements cause a high-pitch screech to come out of Leonard. With a firm yank, I separate the nail from his finger.

Holding the pliers up, I examine the small nail. "Huh. That was more difficult than I thought it would be."

Leonard heaves, catching his breath. "You psycho bitch!"

Something inside my brain splinters. "Psycho bitch? I'll show you a psycho bitch." I repeat the process on his middle and ring finger, but faster than before.

"It's not a semi anymore," Griffin announces to the room.

Knox snorts again. "I'm right there with you."

Leonard has streaks on his face from his tears. "What do you want?"

"I'm so glad you asked." I sigh dramatically as if that's what I've been waiting for this whole time. Straddling him again, I sit on his lap and drop the pliers. "Tell us everything you know about the pills you've been selling. Who's the supplier, what's in them, all that stuff."

"Bu-But I don't know. I don't know!"

Shaking my head, I cup Leonard's cheek and frown. "So disappointing." Turning my head to talk over my shoulder, I casually ask, "What do y'all think? Thumb or pinky next?"

"Pinky," Griffin and Knox answer in unison.

Leonard's panicked breaths crowd my face. "Wait!"

Returning my attention to Leonard, I raise a brow. "Got something to say?"

"The Alienist. That's his name."

Standing back up, I pick up the pliers and rip off Leonard's pinky nail. He howls in agony.

My hand waves between Leonard and me. "We both know The Alienist is good old Lewis Whitlock. I want to know where *he* gets the pills from. How does he distribute them to you and the other dealers? How does he find dealers to work for him? That's the kind of thing we want to know."

"He-He leaves them in my locker at the hospital."

"See? Now we're getting somewhere," I say enthusiastically. "Dealers. Where is he getting them?"

"They're patients."

I flinch my head back. "Excuse me? What?"

"They're patients who plead insanity but aren't actually insane. They have an agreement. They get to come and go as they please as long as they sell Lewis's product."

My jaw clenches.

Lewis and these people are taking advantage of the system. Insanity plea is for those who actually need it. Not for criminals who don't want to face the repercussions of breaking the law.

Without warning, I take Leonard's thumbnail. Leonard turns his head to the side and vomits.

"Party foul, man!" Griffin scolds.

"Now we have to clean that up," Knox complains.

Leonard coughs, spitting out the rest of the acid in his mouth. "What was that for? I'm cooperating."

Shrugging a shoulder, I wear an indifferent expression. "I felt like it."

"Psycho bitch!" Leonard hurls at me.

A wide smile splits my face. "Well, if you insist." I drop the pliers and snag the first thing my hand finds on the worktable.

Hedge clippers, it is.

With a grip in each hand, I raise them above my head, disregarding Leonard's cries. As I tighten my core, I thrust the sharp end into his stomach. Leonard grunts and begins coughing up blood.

Bending down, I place my mouth next to his ear so he can hear me. "I am the monster you helped create."

Stepping back, I find his eyes wide and his pupils dilated. Raising the clippers again, I stab him again.

And again.

And again.

Eventually, I can't lift my arms, and my hands drop the clippers of their own accord.

Hesitantly, I face Griffin and Knox. "It's okay that I killed him, right? We didn't need him for anything else?"

They look back at me with a fire in their eyes.

Relief swarms me, and I sag backward. Two sets of arms

catch me before I can fall. My favorite scents engulf me—sea salt and bergamot mixed with vetiver.

"So beautiful." Knox kisses my cheek.

"So perfect." Griffin kisses the other.

Basking in the moment, I close my eyes and sigh.

Griffin leads me over to the worktable and clears a spot for me to sit down. "Let's get you cleaned up." He wets a rag with a bottle of water I didn't notice earlier.

As he wipes my face, I peek over his shoulder to Knox, who has a plastic tarp laid out. He carries what's leftover of Leonard and drops the pieces onto the plastic.

I wince. "Sorry, I made a mess."

"No apologies needed, Sunshine," Griffin replies for them both.

Knox shakes his head. "That was so damn hot."

Oh my word. We're all fucked up, aren't we?

I let Griffin finish cleaning me up as Knox ties up the tarp and places it in the back of Griffin's truck.

Together, they hose down the dirt, erasing any trace of Leonard and what I did to him.

Erasing the pain he caused me. Erasing the scars he gave me.

CHAPTER FIFTY-ONE

RAVEN

"Sorry, I didn't help clean up. My arms are basically dead." I emphasize my point by trying to lift my arms, but I can't raise them higher than my shoulders. I've never done an arm workout, and now I don't think I ever will.

Griffin winks at me. "We were happy to do it, Sunshine."

"We could help you relax," Knox suggests. His tone is a little too wicked.

I eye him suspiciously, but I'm curious to see where he's going with this.

"What do you think, Griff?"

Griffin takes on the same tone as Knox. "I think we could help her with some stress relief."

The way he says "stress relief" has me thinking they mean to make me exert more energy, but if it has a happy ending, I'm all for it.

Knox holds his hand out to me. "What do you say, Darlin'?"

The corner of my mouth twitches as I place my hand in his. "Let's try."

Knox guides me from the table over to the freshly cleaned chair and has me sit.

The cool metal sends a shiver up my spine. Every nerve in my body is hyperaware as Griffin and Knox circle around me. One at a time, they remove their belts from their waists. My breaths become closer together as a drop of fear mixes with my anticipation.

Knox kneels in front of me. "Do you trust us?"

My answer is easy. I don't have to give it a second thought.

"Yes."

"Good girl."

Knox leans forward, dominating my mouth with his. He nips at my lips, spurring me on. His tongue thrusts in my mouth, mimicking the motion his cock would make with my core. The force behind the kiss is passionate and devoted.

I lose myself in the heat.

It's not until he ends the kiss, rising to his feet, that I realize they've used their belts to secure my wrists to the arms of the chair.

That single drop of fear taints my pool of anticipation, and my rapid breathing gets faster for a whole new reason. I yank and pull at the leather restraints, my mind taking me to a different time and place.

White walls. Padded rooms. Sterile beds.

"Raven. Sunshine."

Blinking, Griffin's amber eyes swim into my view, and his sea salt and bergamot fills my senses.

"You're not there. Never again. We won't allow it."

Gulping, I allow myself to drown in his firm truth. He'd never let them take me away.

I motion my head up and down to let him know that I believe him.

His tone drips with allure as he brings his lips to mine, but never actually touching. "Good. Now relax and let us take care of you."

My mouth tries to follow him as he pulls away, but he moves out of reach.

Knox walks over to a duffle bag stored under the table that I didn't notice before. He digs around and stands when he finds what he's looking for.

My breath lodges in my throat and my cheeks heat when I see what he's holding in his hand.

"Where did you get that?"

Knox wears a knowing smile. "Where do you think? I got to say, I was shocked to find this in your nightstand."

He whirls around the massive dragon dildo Dahlia bought for me in his hand. It's huge. And I really do mean huge. The silicone is an ombre of gray and green, making it look more like an alien dick. Ridges and bumps cover the whole curve of the toy. Knox runs a finger over them, raising his brows in surprise.

"Kinky," Griffin comments.

I rush to explain myself. "It was a gag gift from a friend. I haven't even used it."

Knox's grin doesn't fade. "Then why was it stored in your bedroom?"

Biting my lip, I fail to come up with another explanation.

Griffin and Knox approach me, and I squirm in the chair. Griffin produces a knife, making me jump.

"Trust us," Griffin reminds me.

A glimmer shines off the sharp blade, but I still nod my head, letting him know that I do. With expert skill, Griffin cuts my shirt and shorts down the middle. Then he tugs on the center of my bra and slices it in two, causing my breasts to fall. He and Knox groan together as they gaze upon my pink nipples.

Griffin tugs at my thong right over my mound and cuts

that as well. He bends down and licks the arousal glistening on my pussy, but he doesn't do more than that.

A whimper builds in my throat from being teased.

Griffin tugs on one side of my ruined bra and shirt, sliding it over my shoulder, exposing me further. "Give me another, Sunshine."

My mind is too clouded with need to understand him. "What?"

"Tell me a secret. What do the crowns mean?" he clarifies.

My body locks up again, threatening to take my mind back to a place full of loss and emptiness.

"You're here with us, Raven," Griffin reminds me. "Stay here."

I mentally shove away the ugly memories. "They're for my brother and my son. When my brother was alive, I called him 'little king.' And with my son, it felt natural to do the same."

Griffin tucks some of my hair behind my ear in a praising gesture. "So proud of you, Sunshine." He bends down and gently kisses each crown.

A tightness in my chest builds at the tenderness he's showing me.

Griffin's soft eyes turn predatory as he unbuttons his pants, dipping his boxers down and letting his thick cock free. "Scoot your ass to the edge and spread those pretty thighs. It's been too long since I ate your delicious pussy."

My cheeks flush. "You just ate me out this morning. I woke up with your head between my legs."

"Like I said. Too long." Griffin wraps his hand around his shaft and squeezes, moving his hand up and down.

My insides heat as I do as he says. When I open my legs for him, he groans, dropping to his knees. He dips his nose between my center and inhales deeply, moaning on his exhale and vibrating my sex.

I drop my head back and buck my hips, offering him unfettered access to my core, but he moves back, delaying my pleasure. I shoot him a glare, communicating my frustration.

Griffin smirks again and, without warning, dives in. I cry out from his first slow lick. His chest rumbles, staring at the apex of my thighs. He hooks his hands behind my knees and yanks me forward even further. I yelp as half of my ass hangs off the seat, but Griffin's ravenous side is satisfied.

Griffin descends again, circling his tongue around my bundle of nerves. Then he swipes down over my opening and all the way to my rear entrance. He spends time back there, licking and tasting. My hips move with Griffin's motions, pressing him deeper into my crease.

Hands push the remnants of my top and bra open, trapping my upper arms. Knox leans into my ear, and his breath ghosts over my neck. "Such perfect tits." His fingers drum my tight peaks, sending jolts to my center.

My inner muscles contract, but I'm so empty that it's not satisfying. It just leaves me needing more, wanting more.

Knox stands, yanking down his pants, lowering his boxers with them. His rush reveals his smooth length and the liquid dripping from the tip. I want to reach for it, encircle my fingers around his girth, but the two belts hold me back.

Knox tsks. "You were told to relax. So just lie back and take it, Darlin'."

He shifts forward and paints my lips with his precum. My tongue peeks out, licking his essence from the source. His tip follows the retreat of my tongue, needing more.

"Open, Raven. I need to fuck your mouth. I need you to choke on my dick."

A mewl slips out, eager to get him inside me.

I relax my jaw and stick out my tongue as Knox slides in,

inch by inch. The saltiness of his cum explodes on my mouth, making me crave more. I suck him down until his tip reaches the back of my throat.

My gag gets stuck inside because just as Knox's cock slips down my throat, Griffin shoves a finger inside my ass and vehemently laves at my clit.

The explosion of ecstasy vibrates up my throat and my body shakes with my climax, making Knox groan louder. "Fuck, Raven," he swears, then rams his hips back and forth, causing his dick to glide in and out of my mouth with ease.

Right when I think he's about to finish in my mouth, he pulls free and grins down at me, drunk on pleasure. "Not yet."

Griffin doesn't stop his ministrations as I jerk with after-shocks. I moan, attempting to snap my knees closed, but Griffin's shoulders prevent me. "I can't anymore. Please," I beg.

"Not a chance," Griffin growls into my pussy. He uses one hand to part my slit, giving him better access.

Naturally, my hips move with him, humping his face.

Knox's finger trails down the line of my jaw. "Give us another one, Raven."

"I can't." I squeeze my eyes closed and thrash my head from side to side.

"Look at me," Griffin demands, and I comply. "I'm not stopping until you come again. Let us watch you fall apart, Sunshine."

I whine, half in protest and half in need. The sound of a bottle cap popping and the squirt of liquid have me moving my attention to my side. Knox grabs my monster dildo from where he stashed it and covers it in lube. He clicks a button, and it whirrs.

"Oh God," I curse in trepidation and shimmy my hips back. But Griffin wraps his arm around my lower back and slides me forward again into his face. He hits all the right spots of my pussy, sending flutters through me.

Knox hands the toy to Griffin, and Griffin finally gives my core a break to snag the vibrator.

Griffin holds it up for me. "Let's see how well your cunt takes this monster dick." Then he positions the tip at my entrance.

"Shit," I shout. My channel tremors just from the vibrations. I'm so tired, but my needy pussy wants more.

Griffin pushes in the first inch, and I cry out. "Good girl. Your cunt looks so pretty stretched wide."

The slapping of skin draws my attention, and I find Knox stroking himself as he stares in fascination at my center. "So pretty," he whispers in awe.

Griffin's free hand disappears from my view, then his arm starts moving back and forth. He pushes the dildo in another inch and swears. "So fucking sexy."

The eroticism of it all is too much.

Griffin gives me another inch and sweat spreads over my skin.

My hips turn slowly in a repetitive circular motion, pushing the vibrator to hit that spot inside.

My mewls flow freely from me as I chant, "Yes. Yes. Yes." When I bring my pelvis around again, the tip of the toy sets me on fire. I scream as euphoria wraps me in its embrace. My muscles convulse as my orgasm drags on.

When I come down, my ass drops back to the chair, and I struggle for air. "Okay. I'm done."

The hungry look in both of their eyes worries me.

Griffin grits his teeth. "Another one." He resumes his stroking as does Knox, like they stopped and held off their own release while I was lost in the depths of mine.

"I can't. I really can't," I whine.

"Yes, you can," Griffin argues.

"And you will," Knox commands.

I shake my head earnestly.

Griffin's eyes flare. "Yes."

Knox steps to the table and comes back with another item. He smiles proudly. "I bought this online and overnighted it when I found your vibrator."

I watch with interest, my core fluttering, as Knox dribbles more lube on a butt plug.

Knox hands the new toy to Griffin. He pulls out the vibrator and now holds a toy in each hand.

"I-I don't know about this," I stutter. My words say one thing, but my sex is saying another.

"I asked you to trust us, and you said yes. You can't take that back now." Griffin looks at me like I'm denying him water, and he's dehydrated.

Griffin doesn't wait for me to confirm and swirls the tip of the plug around my asshole. He nods to Knox, giving him an instruction I discover quickly. Knox grabs my legs and rests them on Griffin's shoulders. Even kneeling, he's taller than the chair, so the movement tilts my pelvis even more, exposing all of me to them.

My spine curves uncomfortably against the back of the chair, but the ache soon dissipates as Griffin begins to penetrate both of my holes with the toys.

Another button clicks, and the plug in my ass starts to vibrate in time with the dildo.

The cry that barrels out of my mouth comes from somewhere deep inside. Just when I think I can't handle any more, these two men prove me wrong.

The need in my belly swells, growing with each passing second, ravenous for another release.

"You're doing so good, Darlin'. They're almost all the way in."

"What! You mean they're not all the way in already?" I screech.

Griffin chuckles. "Only halfway. But you take them so well." He pushes them in more, and the muscles in my neck strain. "Your holes look perfect filled up like this." A little further. "Your cunt is so greedy, wanting more and more."

The toys slide the rest of the way inside, and I feel full. So full.

"There. It's perfect." Knox resumes beating his dick.

Griffin does the same. "Now, I need you to come again, Raven. Just one more."

I whimper and close my eyes, trying to concentrate.

A hand grips my cheeks, and my eyes fly back open. "No, Darlin'. You need to watch. I need you to see what you do to us." He pumps himself in my face and I become transfixed with the show he's giving me.

Then Griffin moves the vibrator in and out of my channel, and I cry. He syncs the thrusts of the toy with the stroking of his dick, and Knox does the same.

The whole scene is too much.

The coiling storm inside me is too much.

But it's not long before I'm right there again, staring out into the abyss of immense pleasure. I let myself fall into the fog, and my climax takes all of me. It takes everything I have, everything I am, and then more.

Warm ropes of cum paint my torso as Griffin and Knox stand over me, finding their own orgasms with me.

I don't even realize I'm crying until Knox licks them from my face.

"You did so good, Raven. You're perfect," he whispers.

Griffin unbuckles the belts and kisses the red marks around my wrists. "We're never letting you go. You're everything we need."

I hum, my throat too dry to form words.

They work together to put everything away and clean my center. Griffin removes the tatters of clothing hanging from my body as Knox produces a blanket from the truck. They don't wipe away the cum on my chest, leaving it to dry.

My eyes close, exhaustion trying to pull me away. Every time I open my eyes, we're somewhere else.

One blink and I'm being carried in Knox's arms.

Another and we're exiting the truck. I'm in Knox's arms again as Noah sleeps against Griffin's chest.

Another and I'm in the shower with Griffin and Knox as they wash me, massaging my scalp and muscles.

One last blink and I'm snuggled in bed, the warmth finally lulling me into a deep sleep.

CHAPTER FIFTY-TWO

RAVEN

Kat throws her hands up in the air when the bell chimes as I walk in the door. "Bitch, where the hell have you been?"

Her greeting brings an instant smile to my face. I open my arms as she rounds the counter and runs to me. We crash in a crushing hug.

"I've been so worried about you."

"I'm so sorry," I mutter.

Kat snickers as she pulls back but keeps her arms around me. "And I see you brought your guard dogs."

My head turns, finding Griffin and Knox right behind me with Noah between them. Griffin winks at us and barks. "Woof!"

After the other night, Griffin and Knox basically quarantined Noah and me in their house. The fights we had over leaving the house were more violent than WWE. Griffin and Knox finally acquiesced when Noah started to climb the walls. But I'm only allowed at pre-approved locations of their choosing. Their protection was adorable at first, but if they smother me anymore, I just might murder them.

My suppressed smile threatens to take over at their antics. Noah darts forward, and Kat and I break apart. "Miss Kat!"

"Noah!" Kat bends down, embracing him.

Sending Griffin and Knox a pointed look, I remind them, "You said you wouldn't hover."

"We'll be at the table over here," Knox promises, taking Noah and Griffin with him.

Kat turns back to me, pointing her finger. "I'll make the coffee. You pick a table and sit. And get comfortable too because you've got some explaining to do."

I give her a salute and sit down in our usual spot. The familiarity of the situation soothes the part of me that has been on edge for days.

Kat plops down in the chair across from me, setting down a hot coffee and a fresh chocolate croissant. My stomach growls, craving the pastry on the table, and I'm not even hungry right now. I ate before we left the house.

"Raven, what's been going on? The library was blown up, and then someone broke into your house?"

"Yeah…" I trail off. I talked with Griffin and Knox many times about what to tell Kat. The answer was simple—the truth.

So, I give it to her.

I tell her about my brother, my parents, my time in Mystic River Psychiatric Hospital, my kidnapping, and New York. The entire time, Kat doesn't say a word, but her face gives away every emotion. Anger, sympathy, frustration, sadness, pain.

When I'm done speaking my truth, Kat reaches for my hands. She holds both of mine in hers. Her chin quivers. "I am so sorry."

"It's not your fault, Kat."

"I know, but…" Kat trails off, blinking. "Are you serious about shutting down the hospital?"

"Absolutely," I affirm.

Kat nods, staring down at the table. "I have an idea."

Less than an hour later, Kat has sent her employees home and closed the curtains over the windows.

Griffin folds his arms. "Why does this feel like we're about to meet with the mob?"

Knox backhands Griffin's arm. "We'd have to be in an Italian restaurant or something for that. Not a café."

I glance over at Noah, who is occupied with my phone and a pair of headphones. When Kat started to shoo Annabelle away, I set him up with a movie.

"Mom? I'm hungry!"

Knox and Griffin snort at Noah's louder-than-normal volume, always a side effect when wearing headphones.

"I got it," Kat claims. She grabs a paper plate and loads it with one of everything from the bakery display case.

Noah wiggles with a huge smile as Kat adds each item to the plate. "Thank you! Thank you!"

Kat gives him the food and turns back to us. I hop up on the counter next to the cash register, Knox leans back against the display case, and Griffin stands sentry by the door.

Holding my hands out with my palms up in question, I try to get the ball rolling. "Sooo…What's your big idea?"

"He should be here any minute," Kat replies.

Knox squints. "He?"

We all hear the door from the back of the shop in the kitchen open and close. Knox stands, and his hand goes to the small of his back under his leather jacket as he turns to face the sound. The shuffle reveals the grip of a handgun sticking out of his jeans.

"You're not gonna need that," Kat comments bitingly.

"Knox, where did you get that?" I chastise him.

Griffin scoffs. "This is Texas, Sunshine. Everyone has a gun. You should know that."

My attention switches to Griffin, who also has a hand at his back. I hop off the counter and run over to Noah, standing in front of him. The less he sees the better.

How did I not know they had guns? I might've suggested more sleepovers if I'd known sooner.

"Kat?" A voice calls out from the kitchen.

Is that…

"Out here," Kat answers. The door creaks open as my skin prickles with alarm. The man who steps through is not who any of us expected.

"Camden?" My eyes scrunch.

Knox and Griffin relax, releasing their guns and leaving them in their place.

Camden looks ready to bolt out the way he came. "What's going on, Kat?"

"Hear her out, Cam." Kat gestures to me.

"You said you wouldn't tell anyone." Camden's voice grows thick.

Kat puts her hands out to calm him down. "I didn't tell them anything. Just talk to Raven and listen to what she has to say."

My lips tighten. "About the hospital?"

Camden freezes. "What do you know about the hospital?"

I rub my hands on my shorts. "A lot."

Camden's hands slip into his pockets as he eyes Griffin and Knox, who look back at Camden with worry. Knox rubs his chin while Griffin worries his lip.

"You can tell us, Cam," Knox reassures him.

I glance back at Noah and find that he's still blissfully unaware. With measured steps, I approach Camden. "He hurt me too," I tell him sincerely.

Camden pinches his lips and looks down at his feet. "It was a little different for me."

Linking my arm with his, I lead him over to a table and we sit together. Griffin and Knox stay in their respective spots they took up earlier, and Kat joins Camden and me at the table.

"My father sent me to Mystic River Psychiatric when I was sixteen," Camden confesses.

I cock my head to the side. "Why?"

"Please tell me that's a joke. Tell me he didn't." Griffin's tone is threatening, but we all know it's not Camden who's in danger.

"I'm missing something here," I comment.

Camden clears his throat nervously. "I'm…bisexual."

My forehead furrows as I look to everyone else to clue me in, but no one clarifies for me. "Okay…? I don't see the problem. What does it matter who you're attracted to? Love is love. What does that have to do with…" It all finally dawns on me mid-sentence, and my chest constricts. My hands fly to my mouth as I gasp. "There's no way that's legal."

Camden nods. "Gay conversion therapy is very much so legal and still is."

"Part of me can't believe the sheriff sent you there for that, but I'm also not surprised. He's a close-minded dick," Knox adds.

"Sheriff Jackson is your father?" My eyes just about fly out of my face.

"He wishes he weren't. I haven't spoken to him in years."

Blinking, I ask, "But doesn't he come to the bar for lunch? Does he know you work there?"

"Out of sight, out of mind. It works both ways," Camden comments sardonically.

I always thought Sheriff Jackson was annoying, and I knew he was ridiculously prejudiced. But I figured he was incompetent and ultimately harmless. Like a gnat that won't go away. But knowing what I know now, I've never wanted to wring someone's neck more.

"I'll kill him," Griffin promises.

"Hell yeah, we will," Knox joins.

Camden waves his hands, denying their offer. "He's not worth it."

I slap my palms on the table in frustration. "How do we put a stop to it all? How are we going to shut down the hospital?"

"I have a way, but…" Camden trails off.

"But what?" Knox asks, prompting Camden to continue.

"They could help," Kat encourages him.

Camden interlocks his fingers, resting his hands on the table. "My father has videos."

Griffin flexes his fists, trying to keep it together. "Videos of what?"

"Dr. Whitlock would bring in..." Camden struggles to finish his sentence. "Women. He said it would make me like them and only them."

I think I'm going to be sick.

"How old were these women?" I inquire as I will my stomach to keep its contents.

"I don't know for sure, but they were older than me."

"I know for a fact that's not legal," I remark. Texas doesn't have a statute of limitations on statutory rape. "Wait, Dr. Whitlock took videos of you with those women? And sent them to your dad?" My voice gets louder and higher with outrage the more I talk.

Camden bites the inside of his cheek, so Kat speaks up for him, "Yes. And we're pretty sure his father still has them."

"What!" I jump from my chair and begin to pace. "So, not only is your dad aware of what Dr. Whitlock did to you, he also has the proof and *kept* it." Each step I take does absolutely nothing to slow the rapid increase of my heartbeat. Pausing my angry steps, I look to Griffin and Knox. "I want in on the 'end the sheriff' plan."

Griffin smirks, and Knox gives me a swift nod.

I flip back to Camden. "Are you willing to give the videos to the police? That would mean multiple people have to watch them. If you're not okay with that, we'll find another way."

Camden sits up straight. "I've thought about it a lot over the years. I'm okay with it. I didn't do anything wrong."

Striding for Camden, I pull him up so he's standing and wrap him in a big hug. He's older than me and way taller, but I still pour every ounce of pride and admiration into the embrace. He's being incredibly brave.

He wipes his eyes when my arms fall away from his torso. "There's a problem, though. I'm pretty sure he keeps them in a locked drawer of his desk at the police station."

"That's definitely a problem," Griffin agrees.

"We'll figure it out. Between the five of us, we'll come up with something," I reply.

One at a time, Griffin and Knox hug Camden, whispering words into his ear that the rest of us can't hear.

Camden's nervous energy finally dissipates. I can understand his hesitance. We live in a town where acceptance isn't common. I can only imagine the ridicule and persecution he's had to endure his whole life here. It's not right. If people focused on their similarities with others rather than their differences, this world would be a much happier place.

And I've had enough. I've had enough of the torment and the cruelty.

Resting my hands on my hips, I look each person here in the eye. "Let's go get this son of a bitch."

CHAPTER FIFTY-THREE

RAVEN

Mystic Beans was closed for the rest of the day. Noah thought it was fun being there when no one else was. I've probably earned a bad mom badge for feeding him baked goods and letting him have a screen all day. But some of them had fruit and cheese, so he was able to get a few of the food groups. And he watched a few educational shows.

It's all about balance, right?

The rest of us were coming up with a game plan. It was like one of those Ocean's movies, except I had two overprotective men who think I'm made of glass and a best friend who is all about feminism.

The sun had disappeared from the sky before we settled on what to do. Griffin and Knox weren't happy with the result, Kat was ready for battle, and Camden was still a nervous wreck.

Griffin and Knox slept fitfully, but I slept like a baby, nestled between my two guard dogs.

In the morning, the general mood was grave. But I was ready to go. We took Noah to school, his first day back after he was drugged. We debated taking him to Kat's parents. She insisted they're desperate to be grandparents, but we decided on sending him to school. We recruited Benny to sit in the school parking lot to make sure no one tries to go after Noah again.

For the last twenty minutes, Griffin, Knox, and I have been sitting in the truck, idling outside the police station. Griffin sits in the driver seat with Knox in the passenger, and me nestled between them. Griffin lifted the center console earlier, turning it into another seat.

Griffin's stare doesn't leave the entrance. "Are you sure about this?"

"You asked me that a million times already."

Griffin shakes his head at my teasing. "It wasn't a million."

"Close enough," I mutter.

"Don't be a brat," Griffin returns.

I place my hand on his thigh, getting his attention. "I'm going to be fine. You'll be right there with me."

Knox bounces his leg in his seat. "Maybe we should go with plan B."

"We don't have a plan B," I remind him. My phone buzzes in my lap.

Kat: In position.

Showing the screen to Griffin and Knox, I nod to the door. "Let's do this."

Begrudgingly, Griffin and Knox slide out. I follow Griffin out of the driver's side. He places his hands on my hips, keeping me from crossing the street.

"You better come out of this in one piece."

"I will." Lifting up on my toes, I press my lips to his. With his hand in mine, Griffin shuts his door, and we cross the street with Knox, who grabs my other hand.

I've never been inside a police station before, and it looks nothing like I thought it would. Although my expectations are based on Hollywood movies.

The front desk is obnoxiously labeled with big bold letters and sits behind a window. There's a small hole at the bottom of the window that allows for documents and other things to be passed back and forth. Thin hard carpet covers the floor of the lobby, and a single bench is situated along the left wall. On the opposite wall is a huge bulletin board with fliers, wanted posters, and town information. Other than that, this front area is bare.

"Can I help you?" A woman with bright orange lipstick and bold dangling earrings blinks at us impatiently. The silhouette of her walnut hair is massive and looks to be intentional. A gossip magazine sits on her desk, open to an article about some sex scandal between celebrities.

"Hi." I step forward. "I'm here to see Sheriff Jackson."

Her tongue runs along her teeth behind her lips. "Is he expecting you?"

"No, I don't think so. I was hoping to get an update on the break-in at my house."

She blinks at me like she's inconvenienced that I'm even here. "Name?"

"Raven Henry."

She types a few things into her computer and dismisses me. "Have a seat."

Griffin and Knox join me on the bench. Folding my arms and crossing my legs, I lean back in a huff. "She's quite the charmer."

Knox sits back with me and places his arm across my shoulders. "That's Wanda for you."

"It's because we're here." Griffin places his hand on my knee.

I'm mentally compiling a list of all the people who are going to receive a burning bag of shit on their porch.

Pulling out my phone, I send a quick text.

Me: Waiting.

Kat responds with a thumbs up emoji, and I slide my phone back into my pocket.

A booming voice grabs my attention. "Raven Henry." Sheriff Jackson stands on the threshold between the lobby and the rest of the station. "Come with me."

The three of us stand together.

"Not them. Just you." The sheriff scowls at Griffin and Knox.

This wasn't part of the plan.

Griffin glowers back. "No way. I'm not leaving her with you."

"I'll be fine." I don't wait for them to get comfortable with the idea and stalk toward the sheriff. Griffin and Knox's protests are cut off when the door shuts behind me.

Hopefully they still follow through with their part of the plan. I'm counting on them. Sitting in their seats where they can be recorded, giving them a rock-solid alibi.

Sheriff Jackson leads me to his office through the other half of the station. Exactly three desks are arranged in what I believe they call the bullpen on TV. An open door to my right shows me a small kitchen, and right out in the open are two cells on the left.

The walls are decorated with various posters. A particular set catches my eye. They display the tattoos associated with different gangs and bikers. Ferrymen, Iron Coyotes, and Bandidos. A few more have MS-13, Aryan Brotherhood, and Latin Kings.

Wow. I think this is the entire station. Nothing like small town America.

"In here." Sheriff Jackson waves to another open door.

The room is bleak with a plain desk, two hard chairs, a

computer chair, and a computer. A huge bookshelf covering the far wall is the only thing that could be considered welcoming in this space. There's a window that looks out across the bullpen and another that gives a view of the back parking lot.

Sheriff Jackson enters behind me and falls into his chair. He sets his elbows on the desk and steeples his hands under his chin. "Have a seat."

Doing as he instructs, I occupy the chair closest to the door. "Thank you."

"What can I do for you today?"

"I was wondering if you had any updates on the break-in."

He sighs. "Miss Henry, this is still an active investigation. I'm not at liberty to disclose any details."

I figured he'd sing this tune.

Leaning forward, I drop my voice slightly like I'm telling him a secret. "Between you and me, I don't trust that Officer Langston. Isn't it weird how he showed up before you at the library *and* at my house?"

The sheriff raises his brows and uses his hands to hide his grin.

Got him.

"If you ask me, that's suspicious behavior. I know he claimed jurisdiction, but as far as I'm concerned, you're the sheriff of Mystic River. Not him."

Sheriff Jackson looks downright gleeful, and he's doing a poor job of hiding his satisfaction. He wipes his mouth with his hand, making his boastful smile disappear, and clears his throat. "Let me see what I can find out about the progression of the case."

He reaches for the corded phone on his desk, but he stops before he touches the handset. "What in the damned tarnation?" His gaze is focused on the back parking lot.

Forcing concern into my tone, I play dumb. "Sheriff? Are you okay?"

"Aw, hell!" He jumps from his chair, then glances at me. "Wait here, Miss Henry. I'll be right back."

Sheriff Jackson unholsters his gun as he grabs the radio at his hip and darts out of the room. "10-75! 10-75! Someone is stealing my truck from the station!"

Tilting my chair back and balancing on the back legs, I watch the sheriff freak out while holding in my laugh.

"Wanda! Try to get my deputies on the radio! Mine isn't working!"

Sheriff Jackson dashes out the back door, and I rush to the window. The sheriff chases his truck as someone drives it out of the lot, throwing dust in the sheriff's face. He doesn't stop running and follows his vehicle out onto Main Street.

Surging into action, I start pulling open the drawers of Sheriff Jackson's desk. My heart pounds in my chest as I rifle through drawer after drawer.

Camden should be able to keep the sheriff and his deputies busy with a missing truck long enough for me to find the evidence. But I still don't want to dally.

Yanking another handle, I sift through its contents.

Papers. Papers. Spare gun. More papers.

Finally finding one that won't open on the bottom left, I pull as hard as I can, hoping it's a crappy lock and the drawer will just come free. I huff when I can't get it to budge even the slightest.

This was supposed to be Griffin's job. But since he had to stay back, I'm improvising.

Digging through the wide, skinny drawer in the middle, I search for a key. Instead, I find a pair of scissors.

Images flash through my consciousness as my past threatens to take over and blind me.

But I'm not that girl anymore.

I'm stronger. I'm smarter. I've survived.

Opening the scissors, I stick one of the blades into the lock and jimmy it around until the blade can't go any further. I twist the handle, and the lock gives way. Inside, I find flash drives. So many flash drives. There has to be at least a hundred or more here.

Which one is it?

I begin picking them up one at a time, reading the labels, but each label ties my stomach in knots. CJ Session 65, CJ Session 13, CJ Session 72.

My throat squeezes shut as nausea rolls through me. Eyeing the open doorway, I make sure no one is coming.

I've seen some ugly things in my time, but I could never imagine allowing something like this to happen to my son. Let alone watching it afterward.

They're not getting away with this. I won't let them.

Grabbing a couple of pocket folders from a drawer I had already searched, I remove the papers and load them up with the flash drives. I refuse to leave a single one behind for this sick asshole's pleasure.

My hands shake as I take each flash drive and place it in a folder.

When I'm done, I close and lock the drawer and shove the loose papers into another. I replace the scissors and make sure everything is in its place.

I straighten my clothes, tuck both pocket folders under my arm, and march out of the office and back through the station.

My heart stops when Wanda speaks to me as I open the door to the lobby. "Sheriff Jackson will be back soon."

I force a smile at her. "It's fine. I know he's busy. I'll just come back later."

Wanda shrugs and goes back to flipping through the magazine in front of her.

Entering the lobby, I find Griffin and Knox still there, dutifully waiting for my return. They jump to their feet and follow me out.

When we're all outside, we take off in a sprint to Griffin's truck and hop in. Griffin briskly starts the engine and zooms away.

Knox looks at the pocket folders in my lap. "What's that?"

My hands squeeze the folders reflectively, as if they'll disappear into thin air at any moment.

"Whitlock's and Jackson's demise."

CHAPTER FIFTY-FOUR

GRIFFIN

I will never ever ever never ever never never let Raven do something like that again. The sound of Wanda turning pages of her magazine was about to set me off. Knox and I were on the verge of staging a hostile takeover of the police station.

Now I know what the start of a heart attack feels like.

When Raven finally showed her face again, we still weren't able to relax. The edge will only subside when Whitlock and Jackson are behind bars.

Camden and Kat played their part perfectly without any hiccups. After he hijacked the sheriff's truck, Camden drove a few miles outside of town, ditched the truck where Kat was waiting for him, and they drove back into town. Annabelle agreed to say that Camden and Kat were with her in the kitchen of Mystic Beans if anyone asked.

Thankfully, Langston was still in the area, so we were able to meet up with him and give him the flash drives. If he had left and gone back to Lubbock, we would've driven the couple hours to get him the evidence.

Once the flash drives were delivered, there was nothing left to do but wait. We've been holed up at mine and Knox's house for the last couple of days.

And this morning, Langston called to say he wanted to come by and update us. Noah is upstairs in what is slowly morphing into his room, playing with the newest toy Knox and I were excited to spoil him with.

Raven sits on the couch, chewing on her nails. Knox and I have tried everything to help her relax, but she's too wound up. And now her nervous energy has contaminated me and Knox. I've been unable to sit, and Knox hasn't stopped pacing.

A knock on the front door has Raven close to jumping out of her skin. Knox halts in his tracks, and I dart for the door.

The peephole reveals Langston and his cowboy hat, which he seems to never leave home without.

Opening the door, I wave him inside.

He nods in greeting. "Thanks for seeing me."

"Thanks for coming."

We join Raven and Knox in the living room. Knox stands behind Raven, his hands gripping the back of the couch. Langston sits in the unoccupied armchair, and I, still unable to sit, stand at the end of the couch with my arms crossed and my stance wide.

"I want to start off by saying thank you for handing over the evidence that you did. Camden confirmed that he couldn't bring himself to give it to me and asked you three to do it for him."

A lie we told him the other day, so we didn't incriminate ourselves.

"I'm choosing to believe the surfacing of the flash drives has nothing to do with the theft and return of Clayton Jackson's police vehicle."

None of us utter a word. Knox and I keep blank expressions while Raven bites her lip.

Langston continues, ignoring Raven's obvious tell, "The flash drives were more than enough to get a warrant to search the psychiatric hospital and arrest Lewis Whitlock. He had fled right before we got there, but rangers were able to catch up with him. We had to lay spikes on the road to get him to stop."

My body locks up. "So, he's been arrested?"

"Yes," Langston replies.

Tears line Raven's eyes, and her chin wobbles. Knox and I take a seat on either side of Raven. My arm wraps around her shoulders, and Knox holds her hand.

Langston watches us intently before continuing, "Upon searching Lewis's office, we found bags of pills. We know they weren't purchased through his pharmaceutical distributor. The pills are being tested for their contents at the lab now, but they'll most likely match some others we've found around the state."

Knox rubs his chin. "What was Lewis doing with the pills?" We already know the answer to that, but we can't let that slip to Langston.

Langston leans forward in his seat, resting his elbows on his knees. "We were able to get a few patients who we now know are his dealers to flip. They admitted to selling in exchange for living a cushy life and getting paid."

"Wow." I give zero enthusiasm behind that single word.

Langston narrows his eyes at the three of us. "The dealers gave us some names, and we were able to get another warrant for Frank LeBlanc. He had enough pills in his vehicle to be charged with intent to sell."

Knox and I look at each other. I can visibly see the weight that has been weighing him down for years lift from his shoulders. And I'm positive he can see the same with me.

Raven shifts in her seat. "What about the sheriff?"

"He's been arrested as well. Camden's testimony was enough to convince a judge and the DA. We were able to prove that Clayton Jackson asked for the videos to be made, so he's been charged with over one hundred counts of the production of child pornography. The videos were time stamped, so we were able to prove that Camden was underage."

The rush of air that leaves Raven's lungs is one of relief. "Thank you."

"No thanks necessary, ma'am." Turns out Langston has that southern charm.

"What about Seth and Alice?" I ask.

"We believe that Lewis Whitlock was behind their actions. Alice Tillman and Seth Beauregard were Whitlock's patients. Their blood tests showed that at the time of their deaths, they both had scopolamine in their systems, which we also found in Lewis's office. He hasn't admitted to it yet, but the DA believes we have enough circumstantial evidence to try him for two counts of murder and two counts of attempted murder. A man with Whitlock's skill set could easily use scopolamine to get people to do what he wants."

I knew it. I fucking knew it. This means he must've recognized Raven from the beginning. If he tries taking her down with him, we have connections. People die in holding cells and prison all the time.

Langston turns his hands in question. "Do y'all have any other questions?"

"I don't think so," Knox answers for the three of us.

"Well, if that's all, I'll leave y'all to it." Langston stands, tipping his hat.

We stand with him, and Raven darts to Langston, surprising him with a hug. Langston's eyes bulge, and his arms are held awkwardly at his sides. He looks at me and

Knox, searching for an answer on what to do. Knox motions with his arms to show Langston how to hug Raven back. I pinch my lips to keep my laughter locked inside. Langston blinks rapidly, hesitating, but eventually mimics Knox. Raven hugs Langston even tighter then steps away.

Langston dismisses himself before Raven can thank him again. "I'll see myself out." He tips his hat then makes his exit.

Raven turns to us, blinking. "What now?"

I give her a small encouraging smile. "Now, we live."

She runs to me, jumping into my arms and wrapping herself around me like a koala.

"Mom!" Noah appears at the top of the stairs.

Raven keeps her face buried in my neck. "What's up, little king?"

"Can we get a cookie from Miss Kat?"

Raven pulls back, smiling at Knox and me. She may get flustered with how easily we sense and read her emotions, but she has quickly developed the skill to do the same to us.

"Yeah, but you need to clean up your toys first."

Raven looks back at us, excitement in her eyes.

"Time to live, Darlin'."

ENTERING MYSTIC BEANS, NOAH RUNS AHEAD OF US AND goes right around the counter. "Miss Kat! Miss Kat!"

"Noah, wait." Raven moves to grab her son, but he's too fast. I snag her hand before she can take off after him.

"Hey, there!" Kat picks up Noah, holding him on her hip.

"May I have a cookie, please?"

"Absolutely!" Kat looks up at us. "Do y'all want anything?"

"I'm good," Raven responds, and Knox and I shake our heads.

The three of us sit at a table by the front window. Knox and Raven sit next to each other on one side, while I take the seat across from Raven. Knox places his arm on the back of Raven's chair. She glances back and forth between Knox and me and gets a mischievous grin on her face.

I'm not sure if that smile means we're going to have a fun time when we get back home or I should sleep with one eye open. I like that I can't predict what she'll do.

Jolting in my chair, I clear my throat. Raven chuckles as her foot continues its path up my inner thigh.

"Hey, Griffin! Hey, Knox! How's it going?"

This time, it's Raven who's caught by surprise. The tip of her shoe grazes along the seam of my jeans, narrowly missing the family jewels.

Knox and I wear puzzled faces as we all turn toward the friendly voice.

Standing next to our table is Old Man Hicks with a cup of coffee in his hand.

"Hi?" My reply comes out as a question.

He takes a step closer. "How's the bar doin'?"

"Good. How's the hardware store?" Knox rubs the back of his neck.

Hicks's smile is genuine. "Great! Thanks for askin'!"

"Sure thing." I tip my head.

"Well, see y'all later!" Hicks waves and exits the coffee shop, heading in the direction of his store.

Knox bends toward me. "What the hell was that?"

I shrug because that's all I can do. I have no clue what possessed Hicks to talk to us. We've known him our whole lives, and he's never been friendly like that.

Raven is still turned toward the path Hicks took. "I wonder…" she trails off.

Pam walks by our table. "Hey, Montgomerys! Good to see y'all!"

I give my head a slight shake, Raven's mouth hangs open, and Knox rubs his forehead.

Raven frowns. "Are we in the Twilight Zone?"

"We must be." Knox's expression goes slack.

"Maybe we should grab Noah and go home," Raven suggests.

Feeling my pulse in my throat, Knox and I smile at Raven.

Her brows wrinkle. "What?"

"You said 'home.'" I emphasize my statement with a wink.

Raven draws her head back. "So?"

"You called our house 'home,'" Knox explains further.

Raven's mouth forms a perfect circle in her shock.

We don't give her a chance to correct her statement. Knox and I grab her and Noah and pile in the truck. The entire drive *home*, Knox and I keep a hand on Raven's thighs in a possessive gesture.

I don't care if she tries to recant what she said. It won't matter. She already said it.

We're her home.

CHAPTER FIFTY-FIVE

RAVEN

"Goodnight, Benny!" I wave.

"Night, Raven!" he calls back and exits.

I resume sweeping the floor in The Wandering Raven, eager to finish up so I can get home and sleep. Brushing the last of my pile in the dustpan, my shoulders droop.

Tonight seemed busier than normal, and I felt like all eyes were on me. Is Mystic River so starved for entertainment that they have to ogle the woman who was attacked, not once, but twice? No one asked me about it, but I know it was on their minds. Everyone was careful with their words as I tried to make small talk with customers while I made their drinks.

Whatever.

I empty the dirt into the trash can and tie it off. When I enter the kitchen to place the bag by the back door, I find Knox and Griffin whispering.

Camden already cleaned up the kitchen and headed out earlier.

Dropping the bag, announcing my presence, I place my

weight on one leg and set my hand on my hip. "More secrets?"

Griffin and Knox quiet themselves and turn to me.

"Nope," Knox says with a grin.

I narrow my eyes. "Why do I not believe that?"

They take measured steps toward me, and I force myself to hold my ground. Although the way they're walking is intimidating. But it's the gleam in their eyes that has me staying put.

Knox moves the bag of trash out of the way and skims the tip of his finger down my arm, causing me to shiver. "You worked so hard tonight, Raven."

The bass notes in his voice make me clench my thighs, and I feel a puddle form in my panties.

Griffin pushes my hair behind my shoulder. "I think you've earned a bonus."

My suspicion reflects in my expression. "I haven't been working here *that* long. Besides, I think soliciting sexual favors isn't legal."

Knox smirks. "Oh, this won't be a favor. It's just as much for you as it is for us."

My pussy throbs, ready to see what they have in mind.

They don't wait for me to give a verbal or nonverbal confirmation. Knox picks me up by my thighs, and my legs automatically wrap around him. His lips crash with mine, swallowing me in a fiery kiss.

The air around us passes over my skin as Knox walks out of the kitchen and into the bar. My hyperawareness falters as Knox commands my mouth with his tongue. I roll my hips, trailing my clothed pussy over Knox's stomach.

Hands slip into the back of my shorts, grabbing two handfuls of my ass and squeezing, and Griffin's unique aroma surrounds me. Then the hands slide up and around my stomach to the top of my dark wash shorts, undoing the button and zipper.

I moan into Knox's mouth as Griffin's hands dive into the front of my shorts. Griffin uses his fingers to part my slit and gather my leaking cream. Then one of his hands leaves and dives down my back to my asshole. I jolt as he uses my arousal to enter my pussy and ass simultaneously.

"Fuck, Raven. You're squeezing my fingers like a vice," Griffin pants in my ear.

I keep my lips sealed with Knox's as Griffin pumps his digits in and out of me. My pelvis moves with him, humping his hand. Each penetration has me reaching more and more for release. Pretty soon, squelching sounds radiate from my holes as Griffin and I move together.

Knox shifts his hands from the back of my thighs to the bottom of my ass, spreading my cheeks wider, making more room for Griffin's movements. Then he starts moving me up and down, causing Griffin's fingers to impale me deeper.

My heart races, and my muscles begin to cramp with exertion, but I don't stop.

"Can you handle another one, Sunshine?"

My whimper gets trapped in Knox's mouth, but it's still audible. Griffin takes my sound as consent, which it absolutely is.

The next time Knox drops me down, Griffin adds another digit to my pussy and asshole, filling me up more.

I add a twist to my hips every time I accept Griffin's fingers inside my heat, causing me to sigh and moan.

"That's it, Raven. Feel it. Feel my fingers fucking you."

His dirty words set off fireworks behind my eyes, and my inner muscles squeeze Griffin. He groans in my ear and keeps up with his strokes and pets, causing ripples of ecstasy to keep rolling through me.

I slump forward into Knox, my forehead resting in the

crook of his neck. "I'm even more tired than I was a bit ago. I'm going to fall asleep on the way home."

Knox chuckles, shaking his chest. "Oh, we're not done yet, Darlin'."

My eyes snap open, and I sit up. "More?"

"Oh, yes." Knox smiles. He lowers my legs to the floor but keeps a grip on me, so I don't fall over. A good thing because my legs are jelly.

Then he spins me to face the bar. My mouth opens, and I'm immediately mesmerized by the sight in front of me.

Griffin sits on top of the bar, gloriously naked. Every muscle in his legs, abs, and arms is on display for my viewing pleasure. His veiny cock is hard and fully erect, pointing upward.

Knox steps up behind me and runs his hands over my sides. "You have too many clothes on for what's next."

In a hurry, I remove each article of clothing and scramble up to Griffin. He helps me straddle him, and our mouths slam together, desperate and eager for each other.

His shaft slips between my drenched slit, but he doesn't try to push inside me. I whine and whimper into his mouth, squirming in his lap.

Griffin twists, moving his legs up on top of the bar and letting one fall off the side to rest on a stool. He guides my knees, so they hug his hips. His hands easily find my ass, and he lifts. Then, in one motion, he drops me and thrusts upward, impaling me on his steel length.

The feel of his dick inside me feels so right.

A groan sounds from behind me, and I temporarily end the kiss to peek over my shoulder. I find that Knox has removed his clothes and he's kneeling behind me between Griffin's legs. His focus is fixed on my backside.

Wanting to give him a show, I arch my back and move my hips up and down so he can watch as Griffin's dick slides in and out, slick with my cream. He sits back on his heels and bends down, parting my ass to give him a better view.

Knox moans loudly. "Fuck me, Raven. Your cunt takes dick so well." Then he repositions himself and buries his face in my ass.

I cry out, and Griffin guides my lips back to his, silencing me.

The slip of Knox's tongue and the way he groans against my puckered hole have me moving my hips faster, searching for a second orgasm. Knox swipes back and forth, then he envelopes my tight hole with his mouth and sucks, sending me to a higher plane.

Griffin swallows down my scream and doesn't stop pistoning his hips.

I come down from my high with Griffin's girth still hard as a rock inside me, and Knox positioning his own at my ass. Knox produces a bottle of lube and squirts a good amount on his dick.

Griffin stills as Knox slowly drives his hips forward, pushing past my tight ring. I relax my muscles, making his efforts easier, and I let my head fall on Griffin's chest.

When Knox is fully seated inside my ass, we're all panting, overwhelmed with sensations.

"Just hold still, Raven. Let us take over."

I nod. I wouldn't be able to move even if I wanted to. The two orgasms have wiped me out.

Griffin's hands grip my rear globes, and Knox's hands grip my hips. Then, together, they move me back and forth, creating a rhythm where they exit and enter me at the same time.

My muscles tense from the barrage of pleasure taking over my mind and my body. Griffin and Knox's movements stimulate my holes in the best way.

My climax abruptly crashes into me, causing my muscles

to tighten around Griffin and Knox. The intensity of my orgasm pulls them into the depths of euphoria with me. They groan and pick up speed, emptying their seed inside me.

We collapse all together, crushing Griffin, but he doesn't seem to mind.

Their hands wander and caress every inch of my skin, soothing me into a relaxed state.

I can't help but to memorize this feeling. This feeling that everything is right with the world. That I'm where I'm supposed to be. That I was meant to find them.

CHAPTER FIFTY-SIX

RAVEN

"Is everyone ready to go?" I shout from Knox's bathroom as I put the finishing touches on my face paint.

I ended up letting Griffin and Knox pick my costume. They handed it to me yesterday but wouldn't show me theirs. They wouldn't even tell me what Noah is dressing as either.

Tilting my head, I check my outfit again to make sure everything is in place. The black bodysuit that covers me from the base of my neck to my wrists and ankles makes me feel exposed. The bare feeling has little to do with the white bones screen printed everywhere. It's more about the fact that it's so tight it's like a second skin.

At least it's not a bra and thong.

Noah stands in the doorway like he's a starfish, showing me his costume. "Mom, look it! I have bones!"

The beating in my chest shifts to a warm rhythm as I realize that we're matching. He even has a skull painted on his face.

Once again. They know what I need.

Running my hand through his hair, I smile down at him. "I love it, little king."

"Come see! Come see!" Noah snags my hand, tugging me downstairs and into the entryway, where Griffin and Knox wait.

They turn to face me wearing skeleton costumes of their own, but they have long-sleeved shirts and sweats instead of bodysuits. Their faces match Noah's and my own. Sniffling, I hold my tears at bay.

We look like a family.

Griffin's eyes wander up and down my body, making me feel even more bare than I already do. Knox does the same thing, biting his lip. My core pulses in desperate need of some Montgomery attention.

Knox whistles as Griffin comments, "Looks even better than I imagined."

The paint on my face masks the flush in my cheeks, but not the way my nipples pebble, turning into hard peaks.

"Can we go? Can we go?" Noah yanks on my hand, jumping up and down impatiently.

"Of course." I grin at him.

Noah is ahead of us and out the door, sprinting for Griffin's truck. We file out after him and head to the fairgrounds.

We still have some time before the carnival starts, but I have to be there early to make sure everything is where I put it this morning. All four of us were there bright and early to help get everything ready. We got the dunk tank set up, then aided Nicole Harlow with decorations.

Griffin and Knox continued to be weirded out by all the polite greetings and small talk. I think they were waiting for pigs to fly.

We pull into an unmarked parking spot and make our way into the carnival. Carved pumpkins lit with tea lights line the path to the entrance and ticket booth. Strings of lights connect from booth to booth, creating a beautiful starry night. Plastic bats hang from the lights every few feet.

Kaitlyn LeSnob went all out and rented attractions like a Ferris wheel, a carousel, and a fun house. They were set up toward the back and tower over the rest of the activities. Booths such as bobbing for apples, potion bottle baseball toss, pumpkin skee ball, fortune telling, and witch's hat ring toss are manned by other PTO volunteers and scattered about. There's a section near the front with all the food options.

The Halloween vibe is in full force. Even Mother Nature blessed us with a cool, breezy evening.

Kat and Camden catch up to us dressed in their own costumes. Kat chose a witch, and Camden wears his apron. When we all share the same confused expression, he huffs and admits, "I didn't know I was coming until ten minutes ago, and this is all I had on hand."

"Your work apron?" Griffin asks jokingly.

Camden rolls his eyes, but Noah isn't deterred. He hops, unable to contain his excitement. "Is Benny coming too?"

Knox nods his head. "Yes, Benny will be here. He volunteered to be the unfortunate soul who drops into the water."

I raise a brow in disbelief. "Benny volunteered?"

"When have you ever known Benny to do something he doesn't want to do?" Knox ends his rhetorical question with a wink.

Griffin storms ahead of us as the dunk tank comes into view. "What the hell?"

"Wait back here." Knox reaches for mine and Noah's hands to stop us. But I dodge him and scurry after Griffin.

The water in the dunk tank is covered with a layer of something that has a deep amethyst hue. Griffin already stands there, cursing up a storm. When I reach his side, my breath gets caught in my throat as my stomach knots.

Belladonna flowers float in the water tank.

I rub my eyes, shaking my head in an attempt to rid myself of the hallucination. But when I look again, the belladonna is still there.

Knox's expression turns venomous. "Who would do this?"

"My money's on Amos." Griffin's mouth twists wryly.

I stare incomprehensibly at the flowers. "Amos? What does he have to do with this?"

The muscles in Griffin's jaw flick angrily. "Amos knows just as much about Scarlett as we do. Belladonna is her favorite flower. And Amos has the resources to arrange something like this."

"Griffin's right," Knox agrees. "Amos hates that we never stood by him through the trial. He probably had a friend bring the flowers after we all left earlier."

My heart still races despite Griffin and Knox's logic.

Each time I saw my brother, he had belladonna in his hands. I thought seeing him confirmed that I'm insane. But was his ghost trying to tell me something?

"Do you think he'll try anything else?" I wring my hands behind my back.

Griffin sounds confident in his answer. "No. He had his fun with this stunt. We're in the clear."

Blowing out a breath, I will my pulse to slow. But my mom instincts flare, and I turn, looking for Noah.

Knox grabs my shoulder. "Kat and Camden took Noah to get a treat."

My shoulders slump. "Thanks."

Knox wraps me in his embrace. "Let's get this cleaned up, and then we can find Noah and ride the Ferris wheel. He told me earlier he really wants to ride it with all of us."

Griffin steps up behind me. "I say we focus on having fun and making memories tonight."

My heart flutters, and my body softens. Lifting on my

toes, I give Knox a quick peck, then turn and do the same with Griffin. "Sounds perfect."

After we've tossed all the flowers, families swarm the fairgrounds to enjoy the festivities, and Benny arrives wearing swim trunks and a black shirt that says, "This is My Halloween Costume." Though I'm trying to hide it, the corners of my mouth curl upward.

Benny glares. "Don't say it."

Ignoring his warning, I hug him. "I love it. Thanks for coming to help."

Benny's eyes turn soft. "Anytime." He takes his position on the little seat above the water and takes his shirt off, tossing it aside.

Oh. My.

My mouth waters at the muscles and tattoos that cover Benny's torso. Who knew the grump was hiding all this yumminess all this time?

Griffin glances between Benny and me, then shouts, "Put your shirt back on!"

Knox glowers at Benny as he says to me, "You're drooling."

Unabashedly, I wipe the corners of my mouth with my gaze still fixed on Benny's ink and sculpted muscles.

Benny smirks. "Worried I might steal your woman?"

Griffin slaps the target with his hand, causing Benny to fall in. Griffin and Knox laugh when Benny whips back up out of the water, but all Griffin did was turn a nice-looking snack into a delectable dessert.

Knox realizes it first and covers my eyes. "Text Kat to come take over the booth. We need to take Raven somewhere else."

I'm shuffled away in a rush. Knox doesn't give me my sight back until we're in a whole other section of the carnival.

Knox and Griffin give me a reprimanding look, but I

don't feel the least bit guilty. A belly laugh erupts from me, and that only annoys them further. They each take a turn spanking my ass.

"Hey!"

Griffin gets in my face. "Don't be a brat."

Quirking a brow, I throw sass back at him. "Don't be so sensitive."

He grabs my face and plants his lips on mine. His tongue demands entry. The kiss is punishing yet thrilling.

Right when I'm ready to jump his bones, he pulls back.

"You and Raven get in line for the Ferris wheel. I'll grab Noah, and we'll meet you over there."

Knox nods his head and leads me away.

My mind swirls with ideas, brainstorming ways I can get them to act like neanderthals again.

CHAPTER FIFTY-SEVEN

RAVEN

Noah dragged us through the Ferris wheel line a lot. He loved being able to look out across the town and saying everyone looked like little ants. He had even more fun pointing at random people and shouting what their costumes were.

After the fifth ride on the Ferris wheel, Griffin convinced Noah to try bobbing for apples. From there, we circulated the carnival. We played pumpkin skee ball, which Knox won. Then a water gun race, which Griffin won. Then the witch's hat ring toss, which Noah won. When Noah got hungry, we made our way over to the food stands where Noah had his first funnel cake. He was immediately addicted.

Kat texted and offered to watch Noah for a bit so the guys and I could enjoy some adult time together. When we dropped him off at the dunk tank, Griffin covered my eyes, shielding me from Benny again. I wasn't allowed to see until we were walking away.

Now we're waiting in line for the potion bottle baseball toss. My arm is looped through Griffin's as my head rests on his shoulder. Knox holds my other hand in his, rubbing the back of my hand with his thumb.

Releasing a large yawn, my eyes close as my back arches.

Knox nudges me. "Tired?"

"Getting there," I answer, blinking my eyes. I catch glimpses of a man frantically scanning the people passing him. Standing up straight, I let go of Griffin and Knox, taking a few steps away from them.

"Sunshine?"

"Darlin'?"

I disregard their concern and continue forward. The man wears an oversized unzipped sweatshirt, and his ash blond hair sticks up in every direction, like he's been uncontrollably pulling at it. When I'm a few feet away, my stomach contracts into a tight ball. "Waylon?"

"Raven, don't!" Griffin warns from behind me.

Waylon's caramel eyes fix on me, and I flinch at the ferocity lying within them. He stomps right for me and my instincts have me backing up slowly. Waylon opens his mouth and lets out a chilling rhyme.

This can't be happening. Lewis is in jail.

"Half a pound of needles and nails.

Half a pound of explosives.

That's the way the madman creates.

Pop! Goes the weasel."

Explosives?

My eyes dart around, searching for the implication in the rhyme.

"Keep walking backward toward me," Knox instructs.

My face pales as a gust of wind opens Waylon's sweatshirt, revealing what he's wearing underneath. I find the switch in his hand. "Waylon, this isn't you. You've been drugged. Whatever Dr. Whitlock told you to do, you don't have to do it." But just like Seth and Alice, Waylon doesn't hear me.

"Up and down the streets in town.
In and out the locked door.
That's the way I get out my cell.
Pop! Goes the weasel."

A father with his two kids stops in his tracks, eyeing Waylon. Another breeze blows Waylon's sweatshirt open, and the father catches sight of Waylon's vest.

The father cries in warning to the rest of the people in the carnival, "He has a bomb!"

Shrieks of fear break out all over the immediate vicinity. Parents grab their children and run as fast as they can.

"Every night as you slumber,
The madman's out your window.
Take the gun and pop him off.
Pop! Goes the weasel."

Out my window…Has Lewis been watching me sleep?

"Raven, run! Now!" Griffin demands.

My pulse echoes in my ears as I raise my trembling hands, indicating I mean no harm, but that seems to set Waylon off. His face darkens with a sinister grin.

"A penny for your thoughts he said.
A penny for your children.
That's the way of the madman.
Pop! Goes the weasel."

Children…He doesn't mean to just hurt me.

Turning on my heel, I push my legs in the opposite direction from the frightened people. I can't lead Waylon to them when he's wearing a vest strapped with C-4.

Griffin and Knox flank my sides as we weave in and out of vacated booths and carnival games, adrenaline increasing our speed. Waylon's steps pound through the grass behind us.

My gasped breaths make my lungs burn. "What about Noah?" I shout.

"Benny and Kat will get him out," Griffin replies. Satisfied with his answer, we head in the direction of the Ferris wheel.

A glance over my shoulder shows me that Waylon is gaining on us. A prickling sensation trickles up my spine, causing me to stumble a step, bringing Waylon closer.

"Raven!" Griffin and Knox shout together; the fear in their voices is evident.

We're a half a football field away from the back of the carnival when Waylon's next verse makes the hair on the back of my neck stand on end.

"All around the empty streets,
Griffin chased the madman.
Knox thought you were out of harm's way,
Pop! Goes the weasel."

As soon as the echo of his last word reaches my ears, I'm thrown forward and off my feet a few yards. Landing flat on my stomach knocks the air out of my lungs. Dirt, pieces of wood, grass, and other debris rain down on the backside of my body.

My ears ring from the blast, and my head spins. But my worry for Knox and Griffin pushes me to lift my gaze to find them. They're face down in the grass, covered in rubble and groaning from the pain.

Pushing myself up to all fours, I open my mouth to call to them, but a hand covers my lips, and I'm hauled up to my feet.

"You ruined everything," a masculine voice growls in my ear. A voice I would know anywhere.

CHAPTER FIFTY-EIGHT

KNOX

Aches and pains stiffen every muscle in my body. My head pounds like it has its own pulse. Pushing up to my feet, the world spins, threatening to knock me right off my feet again. I bend in half, resting my hands on my knees until the dizziness subsides.

What the hell is going on? Whitlock is supposed to be in jail, so how did he send this man after Raven? I believe Raven called him Waylon.

A terrified shout screeches over the annoying ring in my ears, but the shout is muted as if I'm hearing it underwater.

Slowly opening my eyes, I glance around and find Griffin stumbling to his feet. But instinctively, I know the cry wasn't from him.

That's when I notice Raven isn't between us. Spinning in a circle, I find a man with salt and pepper hair dragging Raven away. Her shouts don't travel far because his hand is over her mouth.

Wiping the dirt from my eyes, I get a clear picture of a battered Lewis Whitlock, hauling Raven away. She has a streak of blood on the side of her face from her hairline to her chin, and her face paint is half gone. She flails about wildly, scratching any part of Lewis she can reach.

My nostrils flare as my breathing becomes labored. "Griff! He's got her!"

Griffin snaps to and barrels with me after them. We catch up in a few seconds. When Lewis spots us, he whips out a knife, holding the blade to the base of Raven's throat. He removes his hand from Raven's mouth and wraps his arm around her stomach, continuing to drag her with him.

"Back off!" Lewis warns us, digging the sharp edge further into Raven's skin.

Griffin holds up his hands, showing Lewis they're empty. "You don't need to do this. You've escaped jail. You can go on the run and get far away from here. I'll even give you the keys to my truck. You can take it."

"Shut up! I don't want to hear anything from you! You two ruined everything!"

I make my own attempt. "Lewis—"

"I said, shut up!" he cuts me off, jolting as he yells. He inadvertently cuts into Raven's skin, causing a drop of blood to roll down her throat.

Griffin keeps his hands up, inching toward them. "Just tell us what you want."

"I want my life back!"

Raven scoffs, seemingly unafraid. "*Your* life? What about my life? What about Seth, Alice, and Waylon's lives? I'm sure they want their lives back!"

Lewis's crazed eyes fix on Raven. "That wasn't me. You know that wasn't me. I thought you, of all people, my Blackbird, would know that."

I grind my teeth while Griffin's shoulders pull back. Raven's expression becomes tight with strain, causing a mad smirk to turn up Lewis's lips.

"What? Thought I didn't know who you were? Your hair, your skin, your eyes—I would recognize them anywhere. My Raven. My Blackbird." He turns his head, breathing in her scent and exhaling with a blissful sigh.

My icy stare bores into Lewis as my body shakes from a surge of fire that rushes through me.

Raven's eyes fill with a scorching heat. "You're disgusting."

Maybe it's a good thing Lewis escaped jail. Now I can kill him myself.

Lewis takes another step back. "You two can turn around and leave. I'm taking Raven with me. Payment for the daughter you took from me."

"Daughter they took..." Raven's eyes grow impossibly wide. "You're Scarlett's father?"

"Scarlett was my everything." Lewis's lips curl with disgust. "And they killed her."

Raven laughs manically, and lines of stress crease my forehead.

"You've deemed other people medically insane, but you're the one who's crazy. You really are a dumbass." Raven clutches her stomach, doubling over as she continues laughing. "The irony is just too funny." She doesn't flinch when Lewis's knife makes a cut in her neck. She just keeps laughing and laughing.

"Shut up!" Lewis flips Raven around so she's facing him. "I said, shut up!"

Raven stops and thrusts her head forward, her skull connecting with Lewis's nose. A loud crunch precedes Lewis's screams. He releases Raven as he howls, covering the middle of his face. Blood flows through the cracks in his fingers, running down his arms.

She's a genius.

Raven escapes Lewis's reach and runs right for us. I open

my arms for her, ready to whisk her away as soon as she reaches me.

A figure with flowing bright yellow hair steps out from between two of the booths. With her arm raised in Lewis's direction, she stalks toward him.

I'm seeing things because there's no way that's her.

Lewis, completely unaware of the woman's approach, curses Raven. He spots her darting away and shouts for her to come back.

The woman interrupts Lewis's fit, "Hey, Daddy!"

Lewis's eyes blink dubiously. "Scarlett?"

"Your little girl's home." Her mouth quirks into a wicked sneer.

"You're here." Lewis's expression shifts to pure happiness. "I've missed you." He steps toward her, ignorant of the gun pointed at his chest.

Scarlett's eyes blaze murderously. "I missed you, too."

Raven slams into me as the barrel behind her flashes, a deafening bang sounding in the air. Smoke drifts from the barrel of Scarlett's gun.

Lewis sinks to his knees, his hands covering the hole in his chest.

"Bye, Daddy," Scarlett says with a satisfied smile when Lewis slumps the rest of the way to the ground. When Lewis's last breath leaves his body, Scarlett's glee changes into rage as she aims the gun at us. "Raven, dear, step away from my men."

CHAPTER FIFTY-NINE

GRIFFIN

Amos was right, and I hate that.

But she's here. Scarlett is here.

Time has done more than just age Scarlett. It seems to have also brought about the same delusional traits her father possesses.

Scarlett's dressed in expensive-looking tight jeans and a low-cut tank. Her appearance is put together and composed. She doesn't look like she's been living on the streets, suffering, but more like she's been living it up in Malibu.

Her painted makeup and styled blonde hair try to hide her raving hysteria, but they're not fooling anyone. Her eyes are cold and proud, and the gun in her hands doesn't waiver for even a moment.

But if she faked her death all those years ago, why is she here now?

Raven's mouth hangs open. "Ruby?"

The wild laugh that comes out of Scarlett's mouth is enough to give the boogeyman chills. "Aww, honey. I knew you weren't the brightest tool in the shed when I met you, but I didn't think you'd be that dumb."

"Excuse me?" Raven spits back.

Knox shoves Raven behind him. "That's enough, Scarlett."

Scarlett's eyes soften on him. "Knoxy, baby. Didn't you miss me?"

"You're not serious, are you?" Knox's ridicule isn't received well.

She nods her head, confusing the three of us. But that dissipates when Raven is grabbed from behind.

Raven shouts and kicks as a man grunts, taking the brunt of her thrashing. "Stop your fussin', Raven."

Knox and I step in their direction to help Raven, but the man has a gun of his own and points it at Raven.

I'm getting sick and tired of people pointing guns, knives, and bombs at my woman.

"Let me go, you creepy sack of shit!"

He cocks his gun, causing Raven to freeze. "You should've taken what I offered in the first place." He drags her the rest of the way to Scarlett's side.

"Not even if I was blind, Jed," Raven grits out.

The guy Raven went on a date with?

Focusing closer, I note his eyes are the same amber shade as my own. Wait, how…"Trey?"

Trey sneers at Knox and me. "Hello, little brothers."

Knox stares in horror. "What the hell is going on here?"

"Isn't it obvious?" Scarlett gibes with deceptive eyes. "I'm here for you."

Bile rises in my throat as my lips pull into a repulsed frown.

Trey's mouth opens, affronted. "But you said—"

Scarlett cuts him off, "Shut up, Trey! You're so damn gullible. I flash you my boobs, and you do anything I want, just like every other man who ever existed. Always thinking with your dick."

She has lost her mind. This bitch is insane.

My brows tip up. "Scarlett, honestly. Why are you here?"

Scarlett crosses the short distance between us, invading my personal space. The barrel of her gun juts into my ribs as she reaches for Knox and brings him to my side. She softens her voice to a seductive timbre. "I told you. I'm here for you. Don't you believe me?" Her fingertips trace my jaw and over my lips. "I haven't stopped thinking about you both."

A ripple of unease travels through me.

It's as if she's a minefield. One wrong step will set her off, and I don't want Raven in the blast radius when that happens. I have to tread lightly.

As I try to choose my words carefully, Scarlett becomes impatient. "This girl is just a passing ship. A piece of ass that kept you satisfied while I was away. I waited for you. I did all of this for you." Her words are directed at both of us.

Trying to decipher her implication, my eyes narrow. "What is 'all of this'?"

She looks at me like I should already know the answer. "My friends. They were supposed to get rid of her for us."

"The man with the grenades at the library. The woman who almost threw Noah out the window. The man with the bomb who almost blew us all up. That was you?" My voice resonates louder with each word from my mouth.

"Of course it was me, silly. Who else would it be?" She chuckles.

Another thought pops into my mind. "Did you visit Amos in prison?"

She nods. "That was fun. You should've seen the look on his face when he realized it was me." She sighs to herself as if it's a fond memory. "Priceless."

I can't hide the horror on my face, but she doesn't take notice.

"And Daddy had to pay for everything he's done. He would hurt me all the time. And then I found out he had terminal cancer, and I couldn't just let him die like that. It had to be me. Don't you understand? I was protecting us."

I'm not sure I believe her. She's twisted reality so much and convinced herself of her own lies. She talks as if we wanted her to kill Raven.

I stare intently into her eyes, searching for a semblance of truth. "If he was hurting you back then, why not tell us?"

Scarlett pouts. "I couldn't. He wouldn't let me."

Lie.

My nails dig into the palm of my hands as I tighten them into fists and lean to look directly at Trey. "And you helped?"

Trey's voice is ruthlessly hard. "You two were always the favorites. I joined the military, I worked my way up to be a demolitions expert, I even made lieutenant colonel. But not once did either of you, Amos, or Jed ever give me the recognition I deserved."

I will not take the blame for something that isn't my fault.

"We haven't heard from you since you left! How were we supposed to know?"

The vein in Knox's forehead beats faster. "And what about our dad, Amos? Why did you have to frame him? He's been innocent this whole time."

Scarlett's words are cold and exact. "Amos Montgomery is a pervert. He was always trying to touch me when you weren't looking. And I know what he did to you. Always hitting you with a belt."

There's no way she could've known that. We never told her, and Amos was smart about where he hit us.

"I did it for you," she repeats again.

Keeping her gun on me, Scarlett leans into Knox. "I'm so

sorry they ruined your pretty face. I know a good plastic surgeon in LA that can fix you up."

Knox winces. It's imperceptible to everyone else, but I see it. I know him. And no one treats my brother like that.

"What about Noah? He's just a kid, and you almost had him killed." My words are ground out in a strangled tone.

My shoulders pull back as a menacing heat pulses through me. Knox is the one with a short fuse, but it's me who loses it. Bitter resentment spews from my mouth. "Fuck. You."

Scarlett rears back as if I slapped her.

"I know you haven't been waiting for us in the sense that you implied. You weren't even faithful to us when we were all sixteen. You use your body to manipulate and get what you want. It's not going to work here." I look her up and down with a scowl. "Been there, done that. I'll pass."

Scarlett's face turns an ugly shade of red as her breaths become strained.

"We don't want you." I slow the delivery of my words so they're unmistakable.

Scarlett screams with fury and slams the butt of her gun in the side of my head. Her blow, hitting the perfect spot, causes me to fall to my knees. My hand covers the injury, and I feel something wet and slippery.

Raven releases an outraged cry and thrusts her head backward into Trey's face. Her attempt glances off his jaw, but Trey still lashes out. He spins Raven around and throws a punch right into her gut. Raven bends over, groaning and clutching her stomach. But Trey isn't satisfied with the punishment he's dished out. He cocks his fist back and sends it flying into the side of Raven's head.

I don't hear my own roar as I watch Raven's eyes close and her body fall to the ground. Shoving Scarlett aside, Knox and I bolt.

The whites of Trey's eyes become visible all the way around as he sees us coming for him. He points his gun at us and fires off a few shots as he runs in the opposite direction, but all his bullets go wide.

I lift the hem of my shirt, reaching for my gun where it's holstered at my back as Knox does the same. I squeeze the trigger of my gun three times, but none of my bullets hit him. Knox and I push our bodies hard as we chase Trey through the maze of booths. When Trey is out of bullets, he tosses his gun to the side.

Tired of the cat and mouse game, I stop and aim. Knox does the same with me. With both eyes open, I line up Trey in my sights.

Knox calls his shot. "Arm."

"Calf."

We pull the trigger at the same time, and Trey's body jolts in each spot. He falls like a sack of potatoes.

Knox and I approach with our guns still drawn. He goes right, and I go left.

Trey's body shakes with the force of his breathing. One hand is trapped under his body, and the other is balled in a fist. He glowers up at us, shooting us with a different kind of bullet. But they have no effect.

"Fuck you guys!"

Knox shakes his head. "It didn't have to be this way."

Trey's hidden hand swings out. The hanging lights glint off the side of the sharp blade. Trey slashes out at Knox.

Our reaction is pure reflex. We unload the rest of the bullets in our magazines into Trey's back. He's riddled with bullet holes, and his eyes remain open, unseeing.

I should feel something after just killing my brother, but I can't muster up even a drop of guilt or sorrow. Trey ceased being our brother when he abandoned us. He didn't want to be the family we needed, and that's fine. But he couldn't let it go. He chose to come back with a chip on his shoulder and a loaded gun. Trey threw down the gauntlet, and he lost.

"Isn't the saying 'don't bring a knife to a gun fight?'" Knox scratches the back of his head.

I grunt my affirmation.

Knox sighs. "What an idiot."

CHAPTER SIXTY

RAVEN

My head feels like a drumline has taken up residence inside. I struggle to open my eyes as bits of light make my skull feel like it's being crushed.

"God, you're a fat bitch."

Something rough and cold scrapes against my cheek in intervals. With each scrape, someone grunts. Then I feel the tug on my wrists.

My eyes finally open all the way to find Scarlett dragging me across the grass of the fairgrounds. I have no idea where she's trying to take me, but it's not going to happen.

She almost had my son killed. She ridiculed Knox's scars. She threatened Griffin.

Scarlett played dead for years.

I think it's time I make that true.

Twisting my hands, I grasp Scarlett's wrists and pull. She screeches in surprise as I use her weight to help me stand. Spinning my arms, I break Scarlett's hold, then grab a handful of her hair, yanking her closer. As I shove her head down, I swing my fist into her face.

Scarlett cries out and tries pulling away despite my grip on her hair. "You broke my goddamn nose!"

She twists her position to glare up at me. With one hand, she reaches for her gun secured at her hip. When she swings the barrel to aim at me, I spin, positioning myself behind her with my hold on her hair. My new stance causes Scarlett to stand with her head tilted backward toward me. I keep my hand in her blonde locks as we grapple for the gun.

Scarlett flips it to aim over her shoulder toward me, so I grip the barrel and dip my head to the side while pulling the gun in my direction. Pivoting, I place Scarlett behind me and swing my elbow back, nailing her right in the stomach. She grunts, but her grip doesn't let up, so I elbow again and again until she releases her hold.

Never firing a gun before, I hold it awkwardly in my hands.

Scarlett notices my lack of skill and cackles. "Oh, God. All the work to get the gun, and you don't even know how to use it." She fans her face as tears pour out of her eyes. I'm not sure if it's from pain or from hysteria.

Flipping the gun over in my hands, I seize the barrel and hold it above my head. "I know it's heavy."

Scarlett's pupils dilate in fear, and her hands rise to shield her face. She tries to push me away, but her efforts are weak. I barely feel it when she rakes her nails down my arms. My consciousness takes a back seat as a frenzy of savagery takes over. I ram the gun into her head until she collapses. Following her descent, I fall to my knees and continue.

I don't stop.

Not when I can see her skull.

Not when that skull fractures inward.

Not when the tissue of her brain becomes visible.

The muscles in my arms scream for a break, but I can't

stop—I can't. This woman almost killed everyone in my life who means something to me. I can't stop until I know that even her ghost won't be able to come back.

"Raven, Darlin'."

"Sunshine."

Arms encompass my upper arms and chest, prying me away from Scarlett's bloody corpse. Another person wrestles with me to wrench the gun from my hands.

"Get off me!" I kick my legs.

"Raven, calm down. It's us!"

"Let me go!"

"RAVEN!" Large, rough hands grasp my face, forcing my gaze to connect with theirs.

Beautiful amber eyes swim into view, and everything in my mind stills.

"Come back to me, Sunshine."

A warm glow softens the ache in my chest as the need to fight leaves me.

"That's it, Darlin'."

Blinking, a friendly face emerges. "Griffin?"

"Hey," he whispers softly. "It's over. We're safe."

"We are?"

This is a dream. I've never been safe. It's never over. It's always one thing after another. I'm always fighting, always surviving.

The one holding me still answers my question. "Yes, we are."

Turning my head so I can look up, Knox's sweet smile meets my eyes.

"Hey, there." The corners of my mouth curve up.

Knox's grip loosens. "How about we clean you up?"

I nod, and struggle to keep myself standing upright as exhaustion swamps me.

"Whoa." Griffin catches me. "I'll carry you." He sweeps me up into his arms, and I let him.

"If you insist," I mutter, snuggling into his warmth.

"Always."

CHAPTER SIXTY-ONE

RAVEN

The radiating heat from the small bonfire Griffin and Knox built in the backyard warms my body despite the chilly night. It's the first cool night of fall, and Noah said s'mores sound yummy, so obviously Griffin and Knox made it happen. They're going to spoil him rotten. But if anyone deserves some spoiling, it's Noah.

"Can I have another one?" Noah's face is covered with marshmallow and chocolate. He wiggles excitedly in his camping chair.

At my side with his arm around me, Knox grins at Noah's eagerness. "Are you sure you can handle it?"

Noah nods his head with a certain zest only a six-year-old can summon.

I use my mom voice to sound firm. "Last one, okay?"

"Uh-huh," Noah says as he adds another marshmallow to his skewer.

Griffin sits on my other side, tracing his fingers up and down the scars decorating my arms. The scratches from Scarlett have left a permanent mark on my skin.

After Griffin and Knox pulled me away from her, they washed all the blood away. With the lack of a sheriff, the Mystic River police officers took longer than usual to get to the fairgrounds, giving us ample time to formulate and execute a plan of action. Griffin hid Scarlett's body in the back of his truck, so we could dump it later. While Knox and I planted Scarlett's gun on Trey, making it look like Trey shot and killed Lewis. Thankfully, we were interviewed by Officer Langston when he arrived, and he seemed to buy our story.

And once again, Knox wouldn't let the EMT touch me and used their supplies to bandage me. I made him stop when I started to resemble a mummy. Then we called Benny, who did indeed get Noah and Kat out of the carnival when the screaming started.

When we were reunited, we ended up with Griffin and Knox at their house. Noah admitted he didn't want to go back to our house, and with Griffin and Knox wrapped around his little finger, they moved us in with them.

The library has reopened, but I no longer work there. I'm strictly a bartender, but I still visit the library to check out smutty books.

A large-scale investigation was launched into Mystic River Psychiatric Hospital. Law enforcement found multiple cases of medical abuse, and the charges just keep piling up. The hospital has been shut down.

Since then, it's been nothing but peace and quiet.

Griffin puts together two graham cracker squares with extra chocolate on a plate. "Alright, little man. I think your marshmallow might be done."

Noah takes the offered plate and assembles his treat. I watch him, locking this memory of a happy Noah in my mind. Noah starts nodding off before he can finish his s'more.

Knox chuckles as Noah leans back in his chair and passes out.

Resting my head on Knox's shoulder, I watch the fire sway. Through the flames, I catch a glimpse of my brother. But this time, his face is bright, and his mouth is stretched into a smile. He stretches his hand forward, offering me a white chrysanthemum. My eyes fill with tears as he drops the flower into the flames and fades into the night.

Griffin's hands cup my face. "Everything okay?"

I lean into his touch. "Everything's perfect."

Knox draws me closer. "Then why are you crying?"

"Because I'm so happy." My smile is faint but sincere.

"Then cry away, Sunshine, because the rest of our lives are going to be filled with many more moments like this."

EPILOGUE

RAVEN

"Mooooom! I can't find my blue train!"

Massaging my temples, I rein in my frustration. We've been living in Griffin and Knox's house for months now. They convinced me that I didn't need our house anymore, and it's not like Noah and I were spending much time there anyway. So, I put my house on the market, and it sold almost right away.

But that means that we've been piled on top of each other in this two-bedroom house.

Three adults in one room? I'm going to lose my mind.

"Mooooom!"

Be patient. Be patient.

I find Noah in his room, which is Knox's old room, digging through his pile of toys. It's a legitimate mountain.

I need to organize that.

"Noah, your train is probably in there somewhere." I gesture to the heap.

He plops down on the ground, slapping his hands on the carpet.

Noah finished first grade last week, and I'm already eager for the next school year. My patience is wearing thin, and I'm sure Noah's is as well.

Downstairs, the front door bursts open, and Knox's voice shouts, "It's adventure time!"

Noah hops up, darting past me and down the stairs. "I want to come!"

The thought of getting out of the house even makes me a little giddy, so I follow Noah to Griffin and Knox. They're standing in the entry, smelly and sweaty as they laugh with Noah.

The sight of Noah smiling and happy with them makes my heart ache, but in a good way.

"Where are we going?" I ask.

Griffin smiles. "It's a surprise."

Noah beams. "I can't wait! Can we go now?"

"That's the plan," Knox confirms. "Let's load up in the truck and get going."

Noah slips on his shoes and runs out the door with Knox on his tail.

Griffin approaches me, but I hold up a hand. "Don't you dare. You stink."

He brushes aside my hand and wraps me in his arms.

I try to push him away, but he's much stronger than I am. "Ew! Stop. You're so sweaty!" My squeals and yelps echo in the entry. I let my body go limp, hoping my dead weight will make him drop me, but it doesn't work.

"This would all stop if you'd just give me a kiss, Sunshine," he teases.

Reluctantly, I press my lips to his, getting a taste of his salty musk. The kiss becomes intense as he coaxes my mouth open, and I get lost in the movement.

Griffin breaks our kiss. "We need to get going."

I smile up at him. "Okay, but first, why are you and Knox all sweaty?"

"You'll see," he promises. Griffin grabs my hand and leads me to my sandals by the door. He kneels down and slides each shoe onto my feet. Then he guides me outside and into the truck.

When I realize the direction we're headed, I ask, "Did you guys do work on the bar?"

"Nope," Knox responds.

Skepticism colors my face. "Then why are we going there?"

Griffin grins. "You'll see."

I'm getting tired of that answer.

We turn down the dirt road and drive past the bar. Before we come across the barn, there's a fork in the road that wasn't there before.

"Where—"

"You'll see," Noah cuts me off.

I peep to Noah in the back seat. "Do *you* know where we're going?"

"No."

My face wrinkles. "Then—"

"We're here," Griffin announces.

I turn back around, facing forward and peer out the windshield. My breath freezes in my lungs as my jaw drops.

In front of us is a house. An honest-to-goodness house.

Windows make up most of the front on the first and second story, and a wide porch wraps around the sides. The wood and stone accents are a dream. On either side of the steps leading to the porch are white chrysanthemum bushes.

Noah unbuckles and leans over the seat so he can see as well. "Wow! That's a big house!"

My eyes water, spilling over with tears. "What is this?"

"It's our home."

"*Our* home? As in…" My throat chokes up with emotion.

Griffin leans in. "As in, welcome home, Sunshine." His lips brush my cheek, kissing the tears on my face.

Noah's brows just about disappear in his hairline. "We get to live here? All four of us?"

"Yeah, bud."

"Can we go inside?" Noah asks, bouncing in his seat.

"Of course." Griffin slides out of the truck, taking Noah with him. They walk hand in hand up the steps to the porch and disappear inside the house.

"When…How…" I'm in such a state of shock that I can't finish my thoughts.

Knox shrugs. "We've been working on it for a while. This is where our childhood home used to be, but we tore that down years ago."

My eyes pop in surprise. "You and Griffin built this?"

"We had a contractor, but we put in a lot of work ourselves as well."

Blinking, I process his statement. "How did I not notice any trucks and all that driving by the bar?"

"This road goes to the other side of our property. We have the construction crew use that road to get here."

I have a difficult time smiling because I can't stop crying. "Thank you for this," I whisper.

"Let's go inside, Darlin'." Knox grabs my hand and escorts me through the front door.

My jaw drops as I walk into an open area with a kitchen, dining room, and living room. It's even furnished with a beautiful wood table, cozy couches, a TV, and everything we'll need.

"Mom! This place is huge!" Noah exclaims from the banister above.

Griffin finds us, and Knox jogs away to find Noah.

Griffin surrounds me in his embrace, and I rest my head in the middle of his chest.

These men didn't "fix" me. I don't know if that's even a possibility after everything I've been through. But they've patched up the holes that I never thought would heal.

They've given me hope where I didn't have any before. They've shown me what it means to be taken care of and to be loved.

Griffin whispers in my ear, "Tell me a secret, Raven."

More tears roll down my cheeks as I peer up at him.

"I'm happy."

AUTHOR'S NOTE

Dear Readers,

Thank you for taking a chance on Dark Whispers. I hope you found love, excitement, and/or solace. If nothing else, I hope you were entertained. Raven's story is not just one of revenge; it's a healing journey. Learning to trust again, opening her heart to two men who make her feel safe, and navigating motherhood. I hope you felt seen in some aspect. Whether it was through Raven, Knox, or Griffin…I hope you know that your experience is valid, your emotions are valid, and your truth is valid.

Sincerely,
Ivy King

ACKNOWLEDGMENTS

My Other Half—I love you more than anything. Thank you for your genuine words and your unconditional love. I wouldn't be where I am without you.

My Sister in Motherhood—Thank you for…well, everything. You have given me the courage to feel my emotions and not be ashamed. You never get to joke about quitting work because then who would I eat lunch with?

My Favourite Canadian—The way you take care of all the little things, so I don't have to is a blessing. You're my rock.

My Plant Bestie—Literally would not be who I am or where I am without you. Thank you for being my right hand woman and showing up for me.

My Ride-or-Die—Thank you for being by my side when I was so lost, I couldn't find my way. Thank you for being my pillar when I didn't know how to navigate through the complex ugly bits of life.

Siblings—I know one of you told.

Kelli—I hope you punch your own Lewis in the face one day. Please let me be there to witness it.

Mara—You're an essential part of this book. Thank you for working with me and my messy timeline and wild life events.

Aurelia—Your brain is a beautiful place. The way you take my book descriptions and turn them into an absolute masterpiece book cover is phenomenal.

Eliza, Lilian, Melissa, Breanna—Thank you for not getting

annoyed with my plethora of questions. Your encouragement and your support have been crucial to my process.

Beta & ARC readers—Thank you, thank you, thank you! Your reviews and kind words are what give me life. My books would not be what they are without you taking the time to read them.

The Woman Who Took My Power—I didn't even realize I wrote you in here until the end. I struggled to write your role in this story because I was so young when you came into my life and played me like a puppet. That trauma has cemented itself to my soul, and breaking free feels like a pointless task, but this is my first step. This book is my way of saying you can't control me, and fuck you for manipulating a helpless two-year-old and molding her into your idea of the perfect little girl. I'm not your child and never will be.

RAVEN'S BOOK RECS

Ice Planet Barbarians by Ruby Dixon
Gifts by Brynne Asher
Find Me by Ashley N. Rostek
Cuervo's Carnival by NJ Weeks
The Diavolos by Nouha Jullienne
Letting Go by Liz Colbert
Chasing Goldie by Holly Roberds

ABOUT THE AUTHOR

Ivy King is a why choose dark romance author who lives in the mountains of Idaho with her book husband, four wild kids, and cuddly pitbull. When Ivy isn't writing smut, you can find her tending to her emotional support houseplants, wrapped in a fluffy blanket reading romance novels, doom scrolling on her phone, or watching true crime.

OTHER BOOKS BY IVY KING

The Devils of New York

Fractured Fear

Tainted Truth

Veiled Vengeance

UPCOMING RELEASES BY IVY KING

Standalones

Silence in the Snow - December 2025

Wild Embers - 2026

Broken by the Covenant - 2026

The Ferrymen MC

All Their Wrath - Book 1 - 2026